all but elevate it to supper club status)
with a masterpiece as a bar piece.

From here on out this big, enormously appealing romantic novel is in
the can't-put-it-down class. In its
wealth of detail, its living portraiture
of minor characters, it is a book full of
the kind of richness and depth that
Rembrandt himself created on canvas.
Enriched by the kind of golden wit
and benign irony that warmed *The
Mudlark,* Theodore Bonnet's DUTCH
is a delight.

ABOUT THE AUTHOR

San Francisco is both the birthplace
and hobby of Theodore Bonnet. As he
no longer lives in that city, however,
he is able to regard its many attractions with the clearheaded objectivity
and realistic perspective that distance
affords, and is thus able to say, quite
simply, "The Golden Gate Bridge is
possibly man's noblest structure."

Mr. Bonnet, a former newspaperman, lives in Los Angeles, a coastal
city far south of San Francisco.

JK
ns
"T}
unlike
was a
of Llag
San Fr.
ran the
the face
thing s
uine Rem
Immed
much m
newspa
the less
Little 1
pride c
wife, f
ture in
Then
have his bar
motif and re m
Dutchman." It wo
area tavern (inde

DUTCH

BY THEODORE BONNET

DUTCH

THE MUDLARK

THEODORE BONNET

DUTCH

DOUBLEDAY & COMPANY, INC.

GARDEN CITY, N.Y., 1955

To Helen Merrill and Theodore F. Bonnet

EXODUS:

I have been a stranger in an alien country.

CONTENTS

CONTENTS

DUTCH

WINDFALL

The chimney smoke of Llagas rises in a comfortable valley, and the surrounding hills are fat, yellow all summer with wild oats from the Spanish days, and dappled with great spreading live-oak trees. There are fine barns and brooder houses and old rail fences in the valley, and homely farmhouses, and long processions of eucalyptus trees, and down the middle winds a stream that a stranger might take for a river, and there are good wide highways filled with cars and trucks and fronted upon by advertising signboards, gas stations, and eating places, and on the slopes of the hills chewing cattle gaze down with indifference on the busy valley.

Llagas is a town of packing plants and creameries and hatcheries and warehouses. It has a fine modern hotel of brick and steel, called the Morera Inn, and a small stone classic-revival City Hall which has lately replaced a quaint white clapboard one, and on Main Street there are drugstores, dress shops, and hardware stores, cocktail parlors and coffee shops, and narrow doorways where you climb old wooden stairs to lawyers' offices opening off deserted corridors dimly lit from skylights; and on warm evenings before television people in Llagas would sit on their front porches, as in other market towns from Middlebury to Big Spring. A stranger might say that Llagas is like any market town in the country. But Llagas would not take very keenly to the stranger if he did.

For Llagas, to begin with, is in California, the northern half of California, with the additional distinction of having been born and bred on a thin but navigable slough of San Francisco Bay, and Llagas is the chief market town for thousands of chicken farms, called ranches hereabout, with millions of laying hens, and the hens are hatched, raised, and encouraged by the most scientific methods so that the Llagas Valley has a pre-eminence of which any stranger would be expected to have heard: more hens' eggs are laid in it than in any other nest on earth.

Llagas is older than anyone knows. Once, it was an Indian village.

Its folk were weavers of fine watertight baskets and tellers of wonderful legends about the creation of the world, but on the whole a poor lot, strangers to agriculture, stock raising, pottery, and the wheel, eaters of acorns, insects, rodents, and vension, and strict abstainers from grizzly bear, and they lived in hovels of sticks and mud, and spoke the poorest of tongues, and what their neighbors said was Greek to them. When in 1579 Francis Drake came up the trade route of the Manila galleon and put in near by to career and repair the *Golden Hind*, he found the Stone Age. And when, nearly two centuries and a half later, the new Californios pushed up from across the bay, the old ones were still much as they had been in Drake's time.

Then Llagas became a Christian village, baptized Las Llagas de Nuestro Padre San Francisco, The Wounds of Our Father St. Francis, and attached to Mission San Francisco Javier del Norte. The neophytes learned farming, spinning, weaving, tanning, masonry, and the like, and learned to speak a little Spanish and to sing the Bendito, and a few to saw on stringed instruments in the choir; and the lands and herds of the mission estate belonged, in trust, to them. But the paisano government seized and sold San Javier, lands, herds, and the church that they had raised out of the earth with their hands, and they found themselves peons on the hacienda of the great lord Roque Morěra. Then the Americans, in the name of Manifest Destiny, seized California; and in a little while the Llagas Indians became extinct. In the year 1947 Llagas was as civilized as Kansas. It had a population of ten thousand. It had several churches and several schools, a hospital, a public library, a daily newspaper and a weekly one, two movie houses, two banks, a chamber of commerce, a ladies' service club, and a uniformed municipal band.

That June there was discovered in Llagas a buried treasure.

No Spanish silver or gold was this; it was a far less likely trove for these diggings. It caused even more surprise than the famous strike of '33—the discovery, in a small bay of the Pacific just over the hills from here, of an antique brass plate with an inscription which Drake, if the thing was authentic, had cut into it with the point of his dagger, jumping the Spanish claim to California:

> WHOSE KING AND PEOPLE FREELY RESIGNE THEIR RIGHT AND TITLE IN THE WHOLE LAND VNTO HERR MAIESTIES KEEPEING NOW NAMED BY ME AN TO BEE KNOWNE VNTO ALL MEN AS NOVA ALBION.

For it was recorded history that the *Golden Hind* had passed this way, but this new treasure's presence could be reasoned back to nothing but the silly winds of chance. And yet for years before this treasure was discovered it had been more or less clearly seen by certain citizens every day, barring only election days. It had often been pointed out by them one to another, been admired by some, jeered at by others, and once even publicly insulted by an old man named Doughty; but no one had guessed that it *was* a treasure. And then, through the dirt that obscured its excellence, it had been vaguely recognized by a passing stranger, then by another stranger who had heard about it from the first one, then taken to San Francisco, cleaned, scientifically examined, and given its certificate. It had been certified not only an Old Dutch Master, as suspected by the strangers, but a signed painting by Rembrandt himself.

This Rembrandt painting was a portrait, apparently of some Dutch cavalier: it was that certain portrait now known to the art world by a name borrowed from the legendary lost gold mine of the Superstition Mountains: *The Lost Dutchman.* For no such Rembrandt painting as this had ever been catalogued or heard of before. And at first the art world was skeptical. Drake's plate, yes, perhaps, but already dozens of paintings attributed to Rembrandt, many of them in famous museums, were in dispute as to whether they were really his, and how might a genuine Rembrandt have turned up for the first time at this late date in the California chicken country, hanging, of all places, behind the bar of a cheap tavern called—quaintly, it was true—the Traveler's Rest, and situated back of a railroad yard?

The proprietor of the Traveler's Rest was a man named McClatchy, and not even he could say.

"But the way I figure," he stated on being interviewed across his bar by young Hubert Ritter of the *Sentinel*, who served also as Morera County representative for the San Francisco *Chronicle*, "it could have been one of them railroad auctions. You know—man ships his stuff by the railroad, then before he can claim it he kicks the bucket or something. Happens all the time, don't it? Sure it does. Then one day the road auctions off all the unclaimed freight; and this picture's most likely in a trunk, aint it? But the N.W.P. don't know what's in the trunk—they got to auction it off without opening it up; that's the law, you know. So maybe some joker gets it for a fin. With him it's just a flyer, see? a gamble, a hunch, like. Maybe it's his last five, too. Sure, they's plenty of men like that—that's what makes horse races, aint it, am I right? Sure. But when he gets this trunk outside and opens it up, what does he find? Nothing but this old picture. He thinks he's drawed a blank, don't he? Sure he does; what does this guy know about art? 'Snake eyes,' he says. No, but he sees the old Traveler's across the street.

'What the hell,' he says, 'might as well get something for the blame thing.' So he lugs it in here and trades it for a bottle, maybe. Sounds logical, don't it?"

"They don't have railroad auctions in Llagas," Hubert Ritter said. "They have them in San Francisco."

"Oh! Then maybe *that's* where he got it. Or maybe they used to have 'em in Llagas." But McClatchy saw that Hubert Ritter was not of the breed to appreciate this fascinating explanation. "Anyways," he said, wiping the battered red mahogany bar with his towel, "all I know is the picture was here when we bought the place, and that's fifteen years ago. We didn't think nothing about it neither; not till that fellow come in—*you* know, the little stained-glass drunk from the church; and so help me, I thought it was the load he was carrying."

Mr. McClatchy did not sound like the owner of an Old Master. Nor like a Llagan. He belonged, as Hubert Ritter knew, to the city, would always belong to it, and this voice which said "pitcheh" for picture, "heeh" for here, and sometimes "they" for there, and yet spoke with a decided and puzzling suggestion of the brogue, was as out of place in Llagas as a street organ would have been. And it was precisely because of his mislocation, Hubert Ritter thought irritably, that this ignorant saloonkeeper had come into possession of a Rembrandt.

"Who owned the place before you did?" Hubert asked.

"Oh, they're dead, the both of 'em. German fellow and his wife; Mr. and Mrs. Herman Brausch their name was. When they left they bought a little ranch up here, and the way I heard he was gathering the eggs one day when a hen pecked him. Zingo," with a snap of the fingers: "blood poison. Then here a couple of years ago I seen in the *Sentinel* where his widow died in the old folks' home. Poor woman didn't have nobody." McClatchy shook his head sadly. "Funny, aint it. Funny the way things work out sometimes."

"Yeah," Hubert Ritter said dryly, thinking not of the German couple but of McClatchy, for as he looked at the little barman, at the coarse but guileless red face, the faded blue eyes groping for a moment in the inscrutable, he was aware of the utter preposterousness of this windfall, and he resented it. Why to him? he was thinking—to *him*?

And in that moment behind Dan McClatchy's eyes there passed the dingy odyssey that by devious trials and hazards had mysteriously brought him into his inheritance. "Yeah," he said slowly, "it sure is. Now who'd have thought that picture was anything. Anything big, I mean. But you know, 'Ubert, I always kind of liked that picture. Why, I don't know. But you go into most saloons and what do you see? *Custer's Last Stand*—am I right? Sure; they all got it, or used to have. But this here picture was different. This wasn't no beer ad. This was the McCoy, a real oil painting. Yes, sir! You could tell that just by looking at it."

Last year's new-fledged bachelor of arts inwardly winced.

The painting, on this day still in the San Francisco art shop to which McClatchy had permitted it to be taken for cleaning and study, portrayed a dissipated man with a disdainful expression, the eyes looking down at you haughtily under lifted brows, the half-smile really a sneer: a noticeable kind of face which, when present in a barroom in the flesh, is apt to bring on a quarrel. And Hubert Ritter, who had sipped his beer beneath that face several times, could remember having noticed it. It was therefore plain to him that he had recognized in the portrait a first-rate character study, but that seeing it in such a hole as the Traveler's Rest he had naturally mistaken it for a copy.

"Going to sell it, I suppose," he said.

"*Sell* it?" The man grinned; his grin was cocky, yet it had an element of cheerful self-disparagement, and when he grinned his little red face had a scrubbed and shining look and seemed to glow like neon gas. "Sure I'll sell it." (He said "Ah'll," Hubert noticed curiously.) "That picture must be worth a fortune. Me and the family can use that kind of money. Oh I tellya."

And Hubert Ritter felt an even sharper resentment than he had felt before, a moment of quiet fury at the uncouth ways of chance.

Beside him, in overalls, sat the third and only other occupant of the barroom, old Bob Doughty, both in years and custom the oldest patron of the establishment, bleak as an uncalifornian oak in winter, upon his usual bar stool, gripping an empty whisky glass. He peered through half-closed lids at the greenish rectangle on the wallpaper behind the bar where, as long as he could remember the Traveler's Rest, had hung the damnable portrait now revealed a work of art, then he painfully squeezed his lids together as if to shut out the ghost of it. He heaved up from his moldering lungs a gob of phlegm, turned, and without opening his eyes to take aim, dropped it accurately into the spittoon beside his stool. Still blinded, he turned back again, a creaking automaton, wiping his lips with the sleeve of his hickory shirt (the last hickory shirt in California), and growled:

"All *I* got to say is it's a damn poor wind blows *no*body good."

And McClatchy, reminded that this aged barbarian had one night committed vandalism on the masterpiece by hurling his whisky into the cavalier's face, scowled at him. "Aw, go on. You drink too much. You got so you was thinking the old billygoat in that picture was a real man."

2

GIVE YOUTH A LITTLE TIME

From the east side of Main Street, Llagas, the ground slopes down to the Morera Slough, which here resembles a canal, and then continues its descent some fifteen feet to the flat industrial district, which lies, therefore, below sea level. At the foot of the hill is the railroad yard, scarcely used at all these days, and across Hill Street from the yard in 1947 stood the Traveler's Rest.

Traveler's Rest is a name reminiscent of the English countryside in coaching times, which in this case must have been the intention. The place had begun with the coming of the railroad to Llagas, and its main purpose had originally been the feeding of passengers. Old photographs show it to have been an attractive little place then, neat and white, standing in a grove of trees, behind a comfortable porch; and in the public library you may still see the gaily illuminated wine list of a banquet held there in honor of Governor Bartlett in 1887. But the decline of the Traveler's Rest is a lost detail of larger histories celebrating the improvement of train service and the rise of Llagas. Dining cars, the great chicken rush, and the thundering convergence of eggs on the freight platform destroyed its world around it. Down came business even as Business boomed, down came the grove of trees, and the pleasant porch came down to make way for a street; up went warehouses, incubator factories, blacksmith shops, and finally garages; and the Traveler's Rest changed hands five times.

It stood now, one of the oldest institutions in town, and possibly the sorriest, in the midst of a solid front of industrial buildings, a cramped one-story relic made of brick and painted the color of mud, with a door in the center and a sash-weight window at either side, the left-hand window showing behind its pane a small neon Acme Beer sign, the other labeled cryptically: Eats. It was shouldered on the right by Jack's Auto Repair, kneed on the left by the tall warehouse of the Poultrymen's Cooperative, and threatened in front by a procession of snorting monsters laden with coops of chickens, crates of eggs, sacks of grain, bales of hay. There was no longer anything but the whistle of the train to remind it of the world it had been born to serve—that and the faded souvenir over its door, the sign in Old English characters, almost unreadable now: *Traveler's Rest.*

And beneath this legend, in smaller, newer letters which had been fading away now for fifteen years, was the title of another story: Under New Management.

"When I grow up," Daniel Joseph McClatchy had announced at the age of reason, "I'm going to be on the Force."

He did not say this out of mere romance. He, a boy of the poor district south of Market Street in San Francisco, a boy with a Scottish name who firmly believed himself to be pure Irish, was the only child of a longshoreman who squandered his pay on East Street about as often as he brought it home, and of a harassed woman who scrubbed floors, and he said it because being on the Force appeared to him a position of decent security reasonably within his reach. It combined the desirable with the possible, and it commanded respect; the pay was not only good but steady; and then there was the pension. Once you were a cop you were "fixed for life," Danny said, and almost any kid could be a cop. That was why he said that he was going to be one. And he believed that he really was.

In time he undergrew this ambition. He stopped growing at five feet four, which was not tall enough for a policeman. So again he surveyed the field of human endeavor, bringing to bear now the wider experience and better judgment of twenty-one, chose, and became, instead, a bartender.

It was 1913. Both his parents were dead. For three years he had been supporting himself, as for years before that he had helped to support his widowed mother, by selling papers. And the shanties south of Market Street had vanished, destroyed by the Great Earthquake and Fire of 1906; their sites had been taken by industrial buildings; and the clan that had lived in them lived in the Mission district now. That was where Danny lived, in a rooming house on Fifteenth Street just above Valencia. And by this time he had an understanding with Elizabeth Moyles, daughter of a timekeeper in the carbarns: a pretty black-haired blue-eyed girl. But Bessie dreamt of a house with a lawn, on the other side of the city, a house that to him seemed treasonably situated, and of having an automobile and possibly even a maid, and when one evening he told her what he had decided to become she looked at him distressfully.

He asked: "What's the matter? Don't you like the idea?"

"Oh, but Danny—a bartender! That's no career. Anybody can be a bartender."

This point had seemed to Danny one of the calling's principal attractions, and to hear it cited as a drawback nonplused him. Bessie pointed out: "Look at Mr. Sullivan—there's a bartender for you."

"Mr. *Sullivan?*" he said. "What kind of a bartender is he? He can't even hold a job. And you know why—he's a boozer, that's why. Bartenders aint supposed to touch the stuff. Aw, but you don't get it. Wait. Listen, Bessie. You got to figure. You're a woman, see? a good woman, and naturally you can't be expected to know about bartenders, but the thing about bartenders is they *meet* people—im*por*tant people. Are you beginning to see the light? Wait. Look at Supervisor John P. Donovan. What would you say if I told you *he* used to be a bartender? And A. J. Rountree of the Board of Public Works—take *him. He* used to be a bartender. And how did they get where they are today? By meeting the right people, that's how. Because fellows standing at a bar just naturally start gassing with the bartender, see? so the first thing they know they're good friends with him. That's logical, aint it? And if I play my cards right, why I might get to be a supervisor myself or something. But in the meantime I got to be a good provider, don't I? And this way I'll have something to keep me going. I'll have a trade. They's always jobs for good bartenders, Bessie, and the pay's good, and besides that, the tips!"

He believed it all, and he looked so earnest about it and so much in need of her faith and encouragement that Bessie temporarily gave in. She put her arms around his neck. "All right, Danny. I guess you know what's best for us. But remember: it's just a stepping stone."

So Dan McClatchy became a bartender; and in June they were married.

What he had said about the opportunities of the bartender was not unreasonable. In those days not only the political chieftains but also the financial lords of San Francisco commonly fled the office to do business with their feet on the rail. Here in the hardwood-paneled sanctum where gods could be gods (goddesses being not yet admitted) great affairs went forward, careers were made and elections won, to the drum roll of the dice in the leather cup and the soft, beguiling bell sound in the crested glasses, and the more convivial business became the greater grew the esteem of all parties for the obliging white-aproned genie on the other side of the counter. He was in a fair way to receive a tip on the stock market from the financiers, should he care to risk a little something, and if he was a personable and popular and sharp-minded young bartender with a taste for the public trough he might receive even better of the politicians.

Many of the most prominent politicians of San Francisco, whom only a good ear could distinguish from Tammany men, had sprung from the same environment that had mothered many of the best bartenders. They came, as they frequently and quite needlessly announced, from "south of the Slot," a reference to the cablecar tracks that had once run up Market Street, and to yesterday's shantytown, which, in the memories of its former denizens, was already taking on the rosy tint of Tirnan-Og; they were all, it seemed, of Irish extraction, and predominantly Catholic, and the clan instinct was strong in them. They were well disposed to recruit a personable young man from the Mission who was of their own race (and both McClatchy's parents indeed had come from Ireland) and persuasion, particularly if he was an "old" South of Market boy and happened to be a prominent young bartender with a following.

But prominent bartenders were not made overnight, and jobs behind the choice bars were not to be had by novices. McClatchy began at the Potrero Saloon, a workingmen's resort far, far south of the mystic and immortal Slot.

He quickly picked up what lore of the trade the Potrero could teach him and never took a drink during working hours. Not that he went in for drinking on his own time. The curse of his father's life had made too strong an impression on him. When he drank at all it was an enormous foaming glass of steam beer. He was a quick willing conversational young apprentice with a slight strut, only comical in such a small man, and with a cocky yet self-disparaging grin which seemed to wreathe his ruddy little face in Christmas cheer, and which was somehow rather touching. The patrons of the Potrero liked him. He had a stock of Irish stories and an imitation brogue that warmed their hearts, and a high tremulous singing voice which he believed might have been the equal of McCormack's, with the training. He and Bessie had heard McCormack from the balcony of the Scottish Rite Auditorium in a crowd of housemaids and policemen; and on Sundays they used to go to the Empress, the Pantages, or the Orpheum to see a vaudeville show. They saw Valeska Suratt and Mrs. Bob Fitzsimmons and Carter the Great and Eddie Foy and moving pictures of Harry K. Thaw in his cell and a special moving picture presentation of themselves entering the Empress Theater, and John F. Conroy, the world's greatest lifesaver, assisted by his swimming and diving girls; and because Dan worked nights he could go to ball games on weekdays when he chose. He was a promising if not yet a prominent young bartender, and within a year had left the Potrero for Kelly's place on Pacific Street, which he assured Bessie was a shrewd move and a long step upward. But Bessie was scandalized, and she was frightened.

"Oh, Danny, the Barbary Coast! That's a terrible place. All of them sailors down there and the fights they get into—with knives, Danny. Think I want my husband to get killed?"

"Naw, naw, Bessie, the Coast aint like that no more, that's just the way it *used* to be. It's tame down there now, honest it is, 'specially since the City revoked the dancing permits. I wouldn't have took the job if it wasn't; I wouldn't want to worry you that way, honest— 'specially now."

"Yes, that's what you say, but I'd be worried all the same. The Barbary Coast! Gee, Danny, what if they shanghaied you or something?"

"Aw, now, wait awhile; they don't shanghai you down there no more," he said; and in fact the Coast had fallen on virtuous days, by comparison at least with the old ones, though old Coasters clung to the hope that it would revive. "It's tame down there now," he told her truthfully—relatively truthfully.

But she said: "*Tame?* What about those—those—*women?*"

"Women? Aw, what kind of a place do you think this is, anyhow? It's just a saloon now. What kind of a man do you take me for? But Kelly's place is famous, Bess; all over the world it is—you heard of it, aint you? And that's why I want to go down there, see?—you *meet* people. And I promise you I'll be careful. And anyways, gee, I already *took* the job."

"We'll have more than just ourselves to think of now, Danny."

But he answered: "I know, I know—that's just it. I got to be a better provider now, don't I? I got to get somewheres."

They had a real quarrel over Kelly's place, and Bessie cried. But Danny went to work there all the same.

In March their daughter was born. She was to be called Arline, a name then coming into fashion in the Mission, to the disgust of old Father Flynn, to the best of whose knowledge there was no such saint as yet. Told the name at the baptismal font, he snorted and arbitrarily christened the child Eileen. But Arline was the name Bessie fastened to her daughter; and she dedicated her direct to the Sacred Heart. Arline was a healthy child with the large sturdy bones of her mother.

The next year, the year of the Panama-Pacific Exposition, Bessie's father died, and in September their son was born. He was called Thomas Moyles after Bessie's father, but he promised to be Dan McClatchy all over again, small and wiry, with the same blue eyes and carroty hair, the same set of the head, even the grin. You could see that he was going to be his mother's favorite. But Bessie, without knowing it, had paid more for Tommy. It was discovered that she had two great cysts in her. A surgeon removed them successfully. But she was told that she could not again have a child.

To Bessie it was a shattering blow. She felt shamed before all nature and before her husband. She rejected the sentence in horror and called on her Church to uphold her in defying it though it kill her; so much of a woman was Bessie, and so little did she understand. But Father Flynn explained that it was not a question of sin, it was simply that the bearing of children was not possible to her now, God's will be done. But he asked how it could be said that she was sterile. Was she not full of the power of love, and was that nothing? He said that God had blessed her with two children in His image and that she must live for them now, and for her husband. Good counsel to a woman like Bessie, for in such circumstances it was only to God and her family that she could turn; and finding comfort in both, she grew to accept it.

But there was one affliction that Bessie could not accept: her husband's job at Kelly's place. Now for the children's sake she returned to the attack against it. But the double fatherhood of Dan McClatchy made him all the more stubborn with this old bone. He had to "get somewheres," he insisted; he was meeting some influential men in Kelly's now, he said, and he seemed to imagine that one of them was going to make his fortune at any minute. But in this Bessie had allies for whom neither McClatchy nor Kelly himself was a match. In 1917 the Barbary Coast was blockaded by the police, a thousand women were driven from the brothels, and the saloons had to close for lack of business. McClatchy was thrown out of work along with dozens of the most prominent bartenders in the city.

But the nation was at war now. San Francisco, while ringing with patriotism, also jingled with prosperity. For those not marching off with the heroes there were extraordinary opportunities everywhere. McClatchy had told himself that he wanted to march with the heroes —he was only twenty-five; but he had a family to support now, and varicose veins: he marched instead to the bar of the Techau Tavern, a cabaret of some pretentions catering to the family trade; and seeing him thus risen in the world due to circumstances beyond his control, Bessie was proud of him. She reflected that he now moved nightly among some of the best people in the city. And the pay being a little better at the Techau, too, she suggested removing their residence north of Market Street. But her husband would not hear of it.

"What's the matter with the Mission? Aint the climate better over here? Listen: statistics prove they get more fog over there and we get more sunshine over here, and we got to think of things like that on account of the kids. Besides, this is our kind of people over here; this is where we belong." None of which convinced Bessie, but she saw that she would have to bide her time.

It would have been useless for Dan to tell her that he was not satisfied with his job at the Techau. Yes, the pay was better, but, surprisingly, the tips were not, and the place did not lend itself to the male camaraderie that he felt was so conducive to "meeting people." He said nothing but kept his eye open for a better job. And the times being what they were, he found a paragon of a job behind the bar of the Palace Hotel.

"Can you imagine?—the chance I always been dreaming of!" he exulted to Bessie. "Why, in ordinary times it takes years to get jobs like this. Gee, it don't seem right, I know, but as long as I got to stay and keep the home fires burning I might as well do it at the Palace. Sa-ay, the biggest men in Sampm Cisco go in there. Regular customers. You know who was in there today? Tiv Kreling—sergeant at arms of the Board of Supervisors! And a lot of other big men I don't know their names yet. Boy, wait'll I make their acquaintance. I may be on the road to something."

But suddenly the ancient trade of bartending became as illegal as witchcraft. It was the age of Prohibition. "Wartime Prohibition" they called it, but a constitutional amendment was marching through the legislatures of the states and few men thought it could be stopped. McClatchy bayed the moon with the rest of the disinherited pack at the headquarters of the new and already disbanding union, and moped at home. Bessie, with two children to think of, was as worried as he, but she told herself it was for the best. Hadn't they decided that bartending would be only a stepping stone?

"Don't worry, Danny," she would say. "You'll get something." To which he would answer: "Yeah—what? They took my trade away from me, didn't they? I don't know nothing else. What kind of a country is it where they do that to a man? What'd we fight the war for, anyhow?"

Gently then she began to challenge him. "You're young, Danny, and you can learn; you got ability, aint you? Look how far you went as a bartender in just a few years—right to the top of the profession!"

This was a line of argument to which he could not be impervious. "Uh huh," without much conviction at first; then: "Yeah, I guess so. It aint like I was Mr. Sullivan; he's too old to learn. But I'll get something somewheres. It's just that I got to figure, that's all. I got to figure."

So he surveyed for the third time the field of opportunity, and one day came home from the union hall brimming with an idea.

"No!" Bessie said flatly when he told her what he had decided to become. "I won't let you. Think I want my husband to wind up in McNeil Island? Besides, we got the children to think of. Why, you must be out of your mind!"

"Now wait awhile, wait awhile," he begged her. "How do you figure, NcNeil Island? They aint no chance of being arrested. Listen——"

But it was not until the next evening that he could persuade her even to listen. Then he explained:

"In the first place, this aint like being a criminal. Why, up to a couple of months ago this was a respectable business, you know that yourself, and just because a bunch of bluenoses slipped a law through while the boys was away, how does that change it? Listen, Bessie. People been drinking since Adam made applejack and they aint going to stop now or feel any different about it neither, aint that logical? Why, right now they's bars running in some of the biggest clubs in Sampm Cisco just like nothing happened. Sure; the Bohemian Club and the Olympic Club I know for a fact. And this here Prohibition can't last, Bessie. The workingman won't stand for it. And how about the big liquor interests? And the big wine industry right here in California? All of them farmers. Why, the cops aint even going to enforce this here law. And they's dough to be made in this business; a fortune! So what do you want me to do, carry a hod? Give me a few years and we'll be fixed for life. And look, Bess, we'll be moving to the other side of town!"

Bessie was not the only woman in America who gave in to such reasoning and such promises in that historic year. She did so with many misgivings, clutching a dream of affluence north of Market Street which she felt might be the last chance for her children.

McClatchy bought whisky and alcohol from a "syndicate." He made his own gin in the bathtub, bottled it, and labeled it "Gordon's," as all bootleggers did in those days, deceiving nobody; and Bessie, with wrinkling nose, scrubbed the tub after each batch, that her young might not be overcome by leftover fumes while bathing. At first he made the deliveries a bottle or two at a time on the streetcar; later he bought a secondhand Ford and on Saturday nights employed an assistant. The first year his income reached only twenty-six hundred dollars, but the second year thirty-five hundred, and the third almost five thousand. That was the year the McClatchys took a flat in the Hayes Valley district, which, though barely on the other side of Market Street, was as far as Dan dared to go as yet from his Mission trade. The busi-

ness grew. Their income approached eight thousand dollars, and Bessie
began a campaign for their removal to the Marina, which, geographi-
cally at least, was about as far north of the Slot as they might go without moving into a boat.

The country was midway into the booming decade that was to end
with the stock market crash. But when the market fell it would not fall
on McClatchy. He left the market to others, saying he was not a gam-
bler. A risky business, stocks, he thought. It appeared to him that he
was in a much safer and steadier business and stood to amass a small
fortune at it, too.

But one day McClatchy came home to find his wife under a doctor's
sedative and his daughter whimpering in the arms of Mrs. Freel from
downstairs. His son Tommy, aged twelve, lay on a slab at the City
Morgue.

"Bessie! Bessie!" he screamed when Mrs. Freel told him, but they
would not let him into the bedroom. There was a strange man who
put a beefy arm around him restrainingly and patted him and urged
him to keep his head and leave his wife alone. The man got him into a
chair. The man meant well but his powerful domination only emphasized for McClatchy his helplessness in this calamity. He began to sob.

Tommy had been playing in front of the house and, darting into the
street, had fallen under the wheels of a police car. His mother had
heard the screeching brakes and tires and the cries of alarm, run to the
window, seen the excited witnesses converging, and rushed out to find
him lying there in the midst of them, his neck grotesquely twisted,
blood at his mouth, and the life already gone from his body.

When the undertakers brought his image home to lie in the parlor
the blood had been wiped away and the neck straightened expertly.
They had removed his torn sweater and his corduroy knickers with the
leg hanging down and had dressed the image in his new suit. The face
was clean, the cheeks had a rosy tint, and the carroty hair was as neatly
combed as a new doll's, and on the closed eyelids the lashes curled upward like a doll's or even like a child's, and the small hands were
clasped upon his beads. All who came for the Rosary that night said
how sweet and natural the image looked.

Bessie had a grip on herself now; at the foot of the coffin she sat in
her rocker with hands folded, tightly folded. Mrs. Freel prepared food
and coffee for the guests, and Arline, red-eyed and white-faced, helped
with the serving. Mrs. Freel was a chaotic housekeeper: the kitchen
was a litter of greasy pans and dishes, and the sink strainer was heaped
with soggy coffee grounds, and Bessie did not even know. Those who
excused themselves and felt their way to the end of the dark corridor

noticed that the bathtub was filled, and the only one who pretended not to know what it was filled with was the policeman who had run Tommy down.

The blue of McClatchy's eyes looked bleached by the tears that continually welled up in them, and he wailed: "If we'd moved to the Marina like Bessie wanted, he'd still be alive, he'd still be alive, he'd still be alive. . . ."

Bessie saw a more terrible explanation in the fact that the car had been a police car. But she said nothing of this, not to her husband nor to anyone. The rain beat against the panes of the pinched bay window, and outside the tires of passing cars made a sticky hum on the pavement, and in the parlor the rockers of her chair groaned and the two candles burning at the head of the small coffin shone on a face that was like a boxed doll's in a shop window, and the air was sweet with flowers.

Next morning the funeral was held at the Church of the Nativity on Fell Street. The corpse in its appalling bandbox with the white satin cushion was buried in Holy Cross Cemetery. And afterward, when McClatchy had brought his wife and daughter back to their flat, it began to rain again and Bessie had another spasm of weeping because she knew that it was raining on the grave.

It no longer mattered to her that she could not have another child; only that she could not have Tommy; and the words that the priest spoke to Bessie this time did not comfort her. Locked in her heart was the thing that she could not bring herself to tell even the priest as yet, the awful judgment of the police car. She felt that tacitly she had been a party to her husband's outlawry and blamed him for Tommy's death no more than she blamed herself, but she prayed to the Blessed Virgin to help her reform him.

One evening after Arline had gone to bed, as they sat in the kitchen, Bessie with her darning, he pretending to read the paper, the unlisted telephone rang. "Aint you going to answer it?" she asked when he did not move.

He gave his head an annoyed shake. "Not tonight."

They sat letting it ring and ring, and when it stopped he put his paper down. "Listen, Bessie. I figure we ought to get out of here. All this traffic and everything—this aint no place to raise a kid. Listen to all the cars out there." And from the street came the muffled roar and grind and honk of the thing that had killed Tommy. "It's getting worse all the time," he said. "The city aint no place to raise a kid no more."

"City?" she repeated dully, uncomprehending.

"I figure we ought to go to the country, Bessie. That's the place to raise a kid. I got about ten thousand bucks saved up, and with the money your mother left you that makes about eighteen-five; we're pretty well off—you realize? We could get a little joint in the country. A little farm, see?"

"A farm? *Us?*"

"Sure."

Had he, too, thought about the police car? Poor Danny, she thought.

"And a farm's a good business," he was saying. "Why, farmers are the most independent people in the country." He talked on, but she scarcely heard him until he asked: "How's it sound to you, Bessie?"

It did not inspire her. But she did not oppose the suggestion. This might be the answer to her prayer.

So when, two years later, the stock market crashed, the McClatchys were established on a ten-acre chicken ranch ten miles from Llagas, where the temblors from that great Babel broke not a single egg.

What undid McClatchy was his own matchless ineptitude as a poultry farmer: that and the Depression. The wonder was only that it took five years and that he salvaged as much as he did; for it was 1932 now, and at the age of forty he had got out with thirty-five hundred dollars.

"Bessie," he said one night, a week before they were to vacate the now desolate ranch, "I got an idea."

"Yes?" she said warily.

"First let me tell you something. Maybe we did get into this business at a bad time; but that aint all, Bessie. We wasn't cut out for this business."

Bessie held her peace.

"The next business I get into," he went on, "first, I'm going to know something about it; because the way I look at it, no matter what business a man is in today he aint going to succeed unless he *knows* it; because look at all the competition he's got today. Am I right?"

"I won't have no more bootlegging, Danny."

"Bootlegging? With Roozafelt in, they aint going to be no more bootlegging. No, but the old days are coming back again, Bessie; they're coming back with a boom. . . ."

"Danny, you don't want to be a bartender again?"

"A bartender? Not if I can help it, no. But will you wait'll you hear? They'll be bars springing up like mushrooms; and listen: the big liquor interests are going to help 'em get started. *You* know—like the Standard Oil does with gas stations. It'll be the chance of a lifetime, and I figure if we put up, say, a thousand bucks—— Hold on, now. Wait. I figure—— No, will you wait'll I tell you? Listen. I figure if we put up a thousand bucks, why, a man of my experience in the trade can get the rest from some big liquor company, see? And we'll be in business for ourselves, owners and operators of our own business. We won't be able to get a very big place, not at first we won't, but we can get a good *little* joint that'll bring us in a good income, and if we get in *before* the boom we'll be able to pick one up for a song; then when the boom comes all we got to do is open the doors! Well?" He sat back and grinned at her. "What do you think of the idea?"

His wife bent over her darning with a sigh. She, like all her compatriots that year, had read the broadsheets announcing the triumphal return of Barleycorn from the wilderness. Barleycorn and her husband were after all old associates, and what other business did her husband know except the one that was coming back with a boom? Should Bessie's daughter's father therefore become a bartender again, or should he take advantage of an opportunity to set up for himself with the assistance of the liquor interests? Bessie wagged her head and entered objections, but the objections were chiefly for the purpose of drawing him out to convince her, though partly for the record. . . .

And they came to the Traveler's Rest.

Not a very big place, sure enough; not a prepossessing one, either; not in the city, as Bessie had hoped it would be; and the view of the railroad yard was not bon ton. But this was the best they had been able to do with the faint little song they had been able to sing, the liquor interests having let McClatchy down. Credit had been arranged on all the liquor they should undertake to dispense when liquor became legal again, and, beer being already "back," the brewing company had installed new tap fixtures free; but in order to take over the Traveler's Rest they had been obliged to part with two thousand dollars cash and assume the payments on the fifty-five-hundred-dollar balance of a mortgage held by the bank.

"But we got a restrunt and apartment thrown in," McClatchy said, "and the land alone is worth more than we put up, and for five thousand five hundred more we own the joint lock, stock, and barrel. With Repeal coming in, that's a pretty good investment, aint it? Look at *us* —in on the ground floor!"

But Bessie knew that until Repeal came their income would depend principally on her own department, the little counter restaurant behind the window that said "Eats." Bessie had never thought to be in the restaurant business, but she was an efficient if plain cook and had a talent for marketing and could learn. And Arline was eighteen now and just out of high school and could wait on the customers. They were freight handlers, warehousemen, truck drivers, and farmers come to town on business, and they were principally a lunch trade; they ate without complaint the thick bean soup or chowder and the "blue plate specials" of heavy stew, scallops, or chicken-fried steak, hash-brown potatoes, lettuce and tomato salad, shoveled up their apple pie, drank their coffee, paid, lumbered into the street again, picking their teeth, and paused, full-bellied, gazing about.

And in the adjoining barroom, through the window with the red neon Acme Beer sign, McClatchy could be seen serving up the 3.2 per cent brew to a thin line of fugitives from the heat of the day or the dark loneliness of the night, polishing his bar glasses, and discussing the times. It would be along any day now. At last it came, a gusher from the dry rock touched by Mr. Roosevelt, a New Deal for tipplers and old bartenders and the Internal Revenue Department. And that evening the old upright piano of the Traveler's Rest, tuned for the occasion, came alive; the barroom was filled with songs of the "old days" sung to its tinny accompaniment; and McClatchy, a man in his element, leaping to the bells of his cash register, sang in his imitation brogue a favorite ballad of the "old" Potrero Saloon: "Ohhh——

> *"With the beer and the whisky the whole blessed night,*
> *"We couldn't stand up on our pins.*
> *"What an elegant time at the christening we had,*
> *"Of McSorley's two beautiful twins."*

"A little gin, please," called a hoarse bass voice toward midnight. At the bar sat a red-headed man, very tall, heavily set, in a baggy top-coat.

"Shot?" McClatchy asked.

"Double shot and water." It was a voice that seemed to pull itself over ragged tissue, up from bottomless lungs. Its owner was regarding the bartender in drunken derision.

"Yes, sir!" Reaching for the gin bottle with one hand and for a glass with the other, "Did I ever tell you," prattled McClatchy the merchant, "about the woman was crossing the border from the South of Ireland to the North? A bit of a bottle she had with her, and the customs guard says to her, says he: 'What have you there, missus?' 'Holy water,' says she. 'Let's see,' says he, and he uncorks the bottle and takes a whiff. 'Holy water me eye—'tis gin,' says he. 'Gin?' says the woman. 'Mother of God, a miracle!'"

The red-headed man ignored the story. "What are *you* doing in Llagas?"

"Me?" McClatchy thought that he must have known this belligerent customer somewhere before and ought to be able to place him.

"Not exactly a native, are you?" the customer rasped.

"Oh, a native is it? Of Llagas? Faith, that's like the hotel clerk asking the man did he have a reservation. 'A reservation!' the man says. 'What do you take me for, an Indian?' No, but I'm a native son, all right: born in the old South of the Slot in the City by the Golden Gate, and raised in the good old Mission."

The red-headed man barked out a single triumphant laugh: "Hah!" and quoted: " 'Not in entire forgetfulness, And not in utter nakedness, But trailing clouds of glory do we come.' " He raised the glass that McClatchy had set before him, and in that great frog voice of his declaimed: " 'You and I are but a pair of infinite isolations, with some fellow-islands a little more or less near to us.' . . . *Eh?*" he demanded. "You *know* it, don't you? You *know* it. *Eh?*"—with the drunkard's air of mysterious wisdom, as if all the secrets of the human heart were bare to him, a seer. Grinning amiably, McClatchy said "Yes, sir!" as he wiped the bar; and the customer appeared content. "Damn right," the customer said. "Damn right." And he drank his gin.

But if the red-headed man had guessed McClatchy's native heath, McClatchy, without being told, knew something about him also—had known him well on the Barbary Coast, even at the Palace Hotel. They were two strangers meeting across a bar on Repeal Night, each instantly recognizing to a degree the other, yet knowing themselves to be poles apart, supposing that their lives could cross nowhere except at a bar; and by closing time McClatchy had forgotten the red-headed man. It had been a busy night.

"What did I tell you?" he said to Bessie when it was over. "All we had to do was open the doors!"

But for the Traveler's Rest that night's business had been a delusion. It soon became plain that the "old days" were not coming back after all. There quickly sprang up throughout the town an institution with which they were unable to compete, a rival modeled not upon the saloon but upon the speakeasy, and not designed for the gods but for the goddesses: a dim-lighted place of chrome and leatherette, with bars where no dice rolled, booths, and nests of neo-tearoom tables, and no spittoon: the cocktail parlor.

Yet the bar of the Traveler's Rest had the most faithful following in town: veteran drinkers like the red-headed man and old Bob Doughty, nippers like Mr. Horsfall, the depot telegrapher, and George Duncan, the printer, and men who clung to beer glasses in that state of inner perception which is akin to what the opium smoker seeks, like Ed Primrose, the housepainter. To these the saloon of the Traveler's Rest seemed built to order, as to so many travelers does its match in dark streets across the continent: a sanctuary devoid of frills but accordingly cheap, where one can be in company that does not hold itself too high and be ministered to by a man in white vestments whose face somehow is always the same. It is always a quiet twilit place, smelling as if its timbers have been steeped in sweet liquors, and over it a spirit broods, old and wise, foolish, sad, ugly, and ineffably tender. But it is a doomed institution. Churchmen and the League of Women Voters have never approved of it, the churchmen sensing perhaps that it is too much like a church, and the women that it is too much like a home.

The trouble was McClatchy's flock was small. The main revenue came from Bessie's customers, without whom they would not have been able to keep their doors open at all. And so by day and early evening the Traveler's Rest partook of the life of the community, but night seemed to cover it with leaves.

The world fared on, and through the little box radio that he kept behind his bar, McClatchy had word of it. John Dillinger had been shot dead, San Francisco was in the grip of a general strike, Mussolini had invaded Ethiopia; and he was listening when the St. Louis Cardinals won the Series. The Supreme Court had rejected the NRA, and the President had signed the Social Security bill. That year the Series went to the Tigers. Edward VIII divorced Britannia to marry Mrs. Simpson. There was civil war in Spain and some trouble about the Jews in Germany. The Yankees won it. Joe Louis knocked out Jim Braddock and became Champion of the World, the Japanese were in Shanghai, and Amelia Earhart was reported lost at sea. The Yankees again. Hitler had annexed Austria, but Louis knocked out Schmeling. England and Germany had signed a treaty at Munich. Hitler was in Czechoslovakia. The Yankees, four games straight.

"Well," McClatchy greeted the red-headed man one evening, "I see where the governor finally pardoned Tom Mooney."

San Francisco got two great bridges, and an International Exposition opened on a new island in the bay. George VI and his Queen were visiting the Roosevelts. Louis knocked out Tony Galento——

Suddenly McClatchy's radio was full of war correspondents shouting news of Poland, Denmark, Norway, Belgium—Dunkirk. Of "analysts" predicting even worse. Of announcers exhorting him to the defense of baseball, hot dogs, and apple pie. Then, while he sat intently facing Europe, behind his back the Japanese bombed Pearl Harbor; and the next evening the frightened fugitives of the Traveler's Rest stared at a radio gone abruptly dead: there were rumored to be five hundred enemy planes over San Francisco.

The Traveler's Rest retired behind blackout curtains into the queerest period of its history. But events in the world were shaping their effect upon it, while through the grime of his disguise on the wall behind the bar a Dutch cavalier dead three hundred years looked down with his supercilious sneer. And so, on the twelfth of June, Arline McClatchy married William Lucas.

The healthy large-boned child Arline McClatchy had thriven in the country. She was two inches taller than her father and in high heels she dwarfed him. She was wide in the hips like her mother, but broader of shoulder, with the big breasts and limbs of a farm girl. Her eyes were like Bessie's, deep blue and expressive, though not so soft as yet, but her hair was an indecisive reddish brown and the freckles obscured behind a film of powder gave her face an odd, faintly auburn tinge. People sometimes complimented her on her willingness or the warmth of her nature, never on her beauty. She was twenty-eight and had been educated through high school by nuns.

She had never "gone" with anyone but Bill Lucas. It had been a vague courtship of five years, memorable chiefly for long talks, many motion pictures, a few dances, and some pawing at times, usually when Bill had taken too much to drink, but memorable for nothing to make Arline feel that she was really engaged. Did she love him? Soon she would be thirty.

Bill Lucas was a tall thin earnest youth with a large elliptical skull, a scrawny neck, and lank black hair, and he dreamt of becoming a research chemist. He had not gone beyond high school but had been taking correspondence courses in chemistry, and in the meantime, wishing to be as close as possible to the calling of his desire, he worked at the Right Prescription Pharmacy, behind the soda fountain. He was a young man with no family, raised at St. Vincent's Orphanage; but "a nice boy," Bessie said, "and so ambitious." Somehow he had saved eight hundred dollars.

There was a war, and, like many girls in those days, Arline suspected when her boy suddenly proposed to her that the war had forced his decision. "Do you love me, Bill?" she had to ask, coloring.

"What do you think?" was the earnest answer. "Would I be asking you if I didn't?"

There was a war and girls were marrying and their young men were going off to it, and Arline knew that Bill was 1-A on the draft list and had no one but her, and she guessed that he was afraid. "All right, Bill. Whenever you say."

They were married in St. Peter's Church. Arline wore a white suit which her mother had bought for her with the practical advice that afterward she should have it dyed, and they had a wedding breakfast in the counter restaurant, closed to the public that morning. Then they left for San Francisco. They said it was for their honeymoon, but it was also to begin their life together, Bill having left his job at the drugstore; and her father had tied a pair of old shoes behind Bill's 1933 Ford coupe for luck, and as they drove away he stood in the doorway of the Traveler's Rest with his arm around her mother, waving —parents immemorial. Bill got a job in a shipyard, and Arline found one in a lunchroom on Geary Street, and in all her letters she said that she was happy. Then she wrote that Bill had been drafted after all.

She came home then, to her parents' two-room apartment off the kitchen of the Traveler's Rest, and her parents gave notice to the waitress they had engaged to take her place, and Arline went back to waiting on truckers and railroad men and roustabouts at the counter where she had eaten her wedding breakfast. There was a war, and William Lucas the chemistry student, conscript Lucas of the Field Artillery, went into training at Fort Ord, Monterey County, and one day stumbled upon a loaded Bouncing Betty.

They said afterward that you could tell he knew what had happened the moment his foot hit the trip wire, that he saw the mine leap into the air in front of him, and that if he had remembered to throw himself flat on his face he might not have been hit. But none of the witnesses called out to him. They stood transfixed by the spectacle of a man who suddenly knew what William Lucas knew; and he was all alone, terrified, unable to move, waiting, in that long split second before he was killed.

Arline claimed his body. He was buried in Llagas from St. Peter's Church, and the women noticed that the black suit his widow wore was dyed. His widow also claimed his army insurance, which was to be paid to her in monthly installments. There was a war that he had never seen and it had killed him and six weeks later his death helped to pay for the birth of his son.

But there was a boom in Llagas now, another boom. Eggs were coming high because there was a war. Farmers came to town and exchanged their money for other things that were selling high also. And there were many soldiers in town, not with much money to spend, but not with much inclination to save what they had, either. Liquor too was coming high, and so were taxes, but the Traveler's Rest had its share of the boom, because at the ends of the earth there was a war, there was still a war. The Army invaded Italy, and across the world the Marines landed on Tarawa, and in Llagas people were scrambling for nicotine, scheming to get more gasoline coupons, and quarreling in shops over rolls of toilet paper; and there were more marriages and births, more crimes of passion, more men drinking too much and women sorrowing, in Llagas, where there was a boom.

But Llagans remembered the other world war, when there had also been a boom. That had not been anything like this, in Llagas. Something was different. Was this war closer, or did the radio make it seem so? There had not been any radio last time, they remembered. Was it just that radio, then, tearing at their nerves?

But who in Llagas did not listen? Llagas heard it all, to the sundering of atoms at Hiroshima. Some Llagans thought they knew what it was then. And they feared that this time there would be no rainbow.

The saloonkeeper Dan McClatchy saw that there was peace without calm, and that there was still a boom, but only a paper boom after all. "I tell you we wouldn't be in this fix if Roozafelt was alive," he declared to Ed Primrose, the housepainter, across his bar. "Old F.D.R. never took nothing off Staleen. He never took nothing off the Limeys, neither, or off of Congress. Look at what happened to price control soon as Roozafelt died. Look at housing. Look at the way rents are today. And all of them vets without roofs over their head. What'd we fight the war for, anyhow?"

No one bothered to answer. It was now a question of fighting the peace, the radio said. But the world had changed. The great nations of Germany and Italy had collapsed. France was enfeebled. England was a socialist; her Empire was crumbling. Russia, once but a far name to McClatchy, now challenged him at close quarters. The world was smaller, it was said, and he could see this clearly, and yet he felt that his world had grown larger because he now had to worry about distant things that had never before been part of it.

At home he perceived more cheerfully the new paternalism of the state and the union and the benevolent bird's-eye view they took of the populace. Yet he scarcely realized how much his country had changed. Baseball, hot dogs, and apple pie, they had said, trying in their gentle kindness to simplify for him the ideal of it; but it was also a country where nearly every man had a number now and most had their fingerprints in Washington. It was a prosperous country of suspicious employees and frightened employers, icy new social doctrines and unappeasable preachers of a loveless brotherhood, imperative radio announcers, public opinion polls, and a browbeaten bewildered public, with an inexpressible feeling in the air that something awful and final was going to happen, a country of appallingly widespread alcoholism, narcotic addiction, and insanity—"the most prosperous country in the world," and famous, the radio said, for its "know how." Industry offered a man substitutes for butter, leather, and silk, served him up milk in the cream, whiskies it described as "blended," and wines unscrupulously mixed, and had evolved palates that did not know the difference. Business harassed a man with time-clocks and efficiency experts. Government did it with tax forms, license fees, and parking tags. Medicine bucked him up with vitamins and knocked him out with sleeping pills. And it was a country whose elected leaders neither composed their own speeches nor did their constituents the courtesy of memorizing them nor rose to the effort of being audible, even in a school auditorium, without a microphone, and yet were listened to. A country where even the noble sport of wrestling had been reduced to a farce.

But never mind; when the radio was off it was possible to stand in the saloon of the Traveler's Rest, itself a victim of change, and imagine that nothing had changed at all. At the great rosy bar running the length of the room you might lean in the twilight of the century before and smell the same sweet dampness that came from the wood and see the same faces your father saw in San Francisco, New York, or St. Louis when Harrison and Cleveland were running and John L. Sullivan could still lick any man in the house, barring Billy Muldoon, who was home in bed anyhow. And this was the state of the McClatchy fortunes up to the moment when the art world turned a shocked face upon the tavern where it was said that someone had surprised the old god Rembrandt lurking.

A good deal of McClatchy's gin had flowed under the red-headed man's belt, but it was not only the gin that had turned the color of his hair. And George Duncan, the printer, was dead of a burned-out liver. And old Bob Doughty, his teeth gone and his shriveled face the color of marinated pork, could not touch a bite of breakfast till he had swallowed three fingers of rye and circumnavigated the block, yet afterward he ate three of Bessie's hotcakes every morning and drank two cups of coffee, as if, like Antaeus, he had drawn new strength from the earth, so that it seemed Death's only hope of Bob Doughty was to waylay him on that morning walk and strangle him as Hercules had strangled Antaeus—in the air.

Arline McClatchy, as they still called her in Llagas, no longer lived with her parents, because Bill Lucas, Junior, was four now and there was not room. She had taken an apartment on the other side of town, having her government insurance and compensation checks every month to bolster the thirty dollars a week that she received as waitress in the restaurant. She was thirty-three, a strapping young woman who ate too much and was often tired and complained of her feet, and who betrayed deep veins of unhappiness which shocked her mother. Bessie told her that she ought to marry again, but she rejected the suggestion with a hard laugh, and blamed her son. "Give Billy a stepfather? He'd thank me for that, wouldn't he? But who wants a husband? I've got Billy, haven't I?"

Billy was a weedy child, with his mother's thin skin and reddish-brown hair and with his father's large elliptical skull, as yet so large for his body as to look grotesque on him. She brought him to work with her in the early mornings, later took him to a day nursery, brought him back to the tavern in the afternoons, and in the evenings carried him home.

And Bessie at fifty-five was a little stout woman with a great dead weight of bosom, round red arms which she habitually folded while standing to talk, as if to rest them, short heavy steps, and a waddling gait. Her black hair had great sweeps of gray in it, but the texture and coloring of her face were young, her blue eyes in repose were marvelously soft, and she had a way of laying her head over on one shoulder and smiling a soft smile at you while you were talking. Gentleness and kindness and patience were the qualities you got from Bessie.

There was as yet little gray in McClatchy's carroty crop, but it had thinned out considerably. His head sat as cockily as ever on his shoulders, and he told the same stories in his imitation brogue, and the same grin still switched his face on like a neon sign. He never spoke of new enterprises any more, but that was nothing. He had his own business, such as it was, had paid off the mortgage, and felt that he was "independent." Only sometimes, as when on a dreary afternoon he stood gazing past the Acme Beer sign in the window at the trucks laden with chickens and eggs, when irritated by the clamorous voice of Billy Lucas in the rear, burdened with the slow weight of time on his hands, and troubled by a vague discontent, there would come over him a sense of the barren comedy of his life and a revulsion before the inane collaboration of fate and free will that had brought him to this dismal scene in it. He would recall the red-headed man's question that had so startled him on Repeal Night, and say to himself in disgust: "Llagas! What *am* I doing in Llagas, anyhow?"

There was a small battered wild goose of Ireland with the nose smashed flat on his face, a bald head, a snigger, a foul tongue, and many ribald stories. He could paint and etch and sculpt, and he worked beautifully in stained glass, and he found himself in Llagas with a commission to make a window for the Gospel side of the sanctuary of St. Peter's Church. It would depict the Blessed Virgin mourning over the body of her Son at the foot of the Cross and be inscribed at the bottom: *Pray for Anthony Ruffo, Jr.* But on the evening of the day he received this commission he got drunk, and somehow he found himself in the darker part of town across the slough, in a haven that he had never seen before in his life and yet recognized at once—not a cocktail parlor but a saloon, authentic to the very smell, and kept by a little stranger in white vestments whose face was as the face of an old friend.

The painting behind the bar caught his professional if hazy eye. Being of a cynical turn of mind, he saw it not as a copy but as an imitation, the work of some crafty rogue, and he sniggered at it, mocked it, and cursed the painter like a brother. It was as if he felt that they might have made a fine night of it, that rascal and he. But turning up next evening in somewhat better condition, he looked at the painting with more curiosity, then walked round the bar to examine it. And this was the passing stranger who by telephone on the next day called it to the attention of Alfred Markham, of the Markham Galleries, San Francisco.

Markham could not abide this man but, grudgingly respecting his eye for a work of art, drove up to Llagas. Yes, he agreed, the painting did appear old, and of the Dutch school; if Mr. McClatchy wished he would take it back to his shop for cleaning and study. McClatchy said: "Sure, take it; maybe it's worth something, huh?"

But in fact Markham had no very high hopes for the painting then. It was only when it had been cleaned that he began to regret not having bought it on the spot for perhaps ten or fifteen dollars. And then, when he had received the metallurgist's report on the nails with which the canvas was fastened to the sticks, when he had examined the X rays, the pigment analysis, and the rest, had consulted with two experts, and was convinced that this was indeed that prodigy of finds, a Rembrandt, he was tempted to keep the secret till he had bought the picture for, say, twenty-five dollars now. But Alfred Markham thought of himself as an honest merchant and knew the man of the stained-glass window to be a blackguard and feared a suit. He could only take as much credit for the discovery as possible. But the credit for having discovered a lost Rembrandt of which perhaps no record could be found was a thing of no small moment to a man like him, and after he had made his decision he was able to plume himself upon his honesty as well, so that he had regained the sense of triumph on the morning when he telephoned the saloonkeeper and told him the truth.

"Yeah?" McClatchy said. "It's really worth something? Sa-ay, that's pretty good, huh?"

"Yes! . . . *Good?*" Markham realized that the man had no conception what a Rembrandt painting was. "A Rembrandt?" he said. "Lord, man, surely you know, you must have heard—why, that's, that's——Good Lord!"

At the other end of the wire McClatchy's happy face had clouded. "What's the matter?" he asked.

Markham sighed. "Mr. McClatchy, this picture is a museum piece." McClatchy smiled again. "Yeah?"

But Markham insisted: "A treasure!"

"Huh?"

"Yes!"

"No! That picture?"

One minute later McClatchy burst into his wife's kitchen. It was breakfast time; Bessie had a skillet in her hand when he came trumpeting the news:

"Bess! We struck it, we struck it! It's worth a fortune!"

"What? What is?"

"The picture! Mr. Markham just phoned." And he told her.

"Wonderful! Well!" Bessie said. "Aint that grand." But although she smiled fondly upon his jubilation as she listened, Bessie went right on cooking. She recognized the story as the very type of that wonder of which men were forever dreaming and talking and which never happened in her world; but it was a long time since Danny had looked and talked like this. If she credited the story at all it was only to the extent that the painting might bring them a hundred dollars or so, which would be marvelous enough for her. It was only as the day wore on, as she saw the effect of the story on others, and then when Hubert Ritter of the *Sentinel* came round to interview her husband, that Bessie began to be suitably impressed by their windfall.

3

SUMMER NIGHT

Walsh Reardon, once a red-headed man, yes and once the college athlete of that name, strode erect up Main Street at eight o'clock that evening, six feet five in his brogues and heroically proportioned, power in his shoulders, authority in his paunch, and, though he was only forty-seven, the hair which bulged at his neck a mane of silver now. By night he made indeed a lordly figure. But as he stopped to buy a newspaper at the corner the streetlamp betrayed the blotchy red bloat of his face, the shabbiness of his tan tweeds, and the battered condition of his brown felt hat, shaped and worn in such a way that it looked as if it must once have had a plume. He turned down Hill Street into the darkness, into a sharp odor of salt and fish, and crossed the bridge over the thin lost arm of the distant bay. Before and below him lay the Northwestern Pacific yard like a deserted battlefield, backed by a ragged silhouette of industrial buildings, as of ruined towers, against the sky, and low on the left the red quarter moon hung, knocked askew.

It was the route he traveled three, four, or five evenings a week after dining on his own cooking and a bottle of wine in his rooms over the O.K. Machine Shop. And reaching once more the bottom of the hill, the only living thing upon the landscape, he turned in at the Traveler's Rest just as on any ordinary evening of the year.

His old haunt presented no sign that it was not an ordinary evening. He entered the same dusky saloon of long red bar, gleaming bottles, and gleaming brass rail, presided over by the same small red-faced man in white, and tenanted by only one other customer, the same Bob Doughty, seated on the same stool and apparently asleep as usual, an empty whisky glass on the bar in front of him. It was a scene that to another eye might have appeared without reality in the modern world, a picture reached out of the American past and held for a moment by some photographic time machine. But at sight of Reardon's huge body in the doorway the bartender broke out in a grin and sprang to action.

"*Wie geht's?*" he called, and was pouring a double gin and water by the time the newcomer reached the bar.

"Well!" Reardon's hoarse profundo grated in the narrow room like a scraped bullfiddle; it made the old customer at the bar start, hunch his shoulders, and shut his eyes the tighter. "In your previous incarnation, Mac," the giant rasped, straddling a stool, "you must have been a St. Bernard."

Little Dan McClatchy's face was aglow with hospitality. "On me tonight," he said.

"On you? What, all of them?"

"*All* of them? Faith, you'd drink us dry."

"You must be trying out a new brand of poison. Wake up Bob there and I'll buy him one."

"Him? Oh," with a wink, "*he* don't want nothing."

"You 'tend to business," Doughty said, and rapped on the bar with his glass.

"Yes, sir!" McClatchy grinned, leaping for the rye.

His glass refilled, the old man raised it to his benefactor, smirking, and swallowed the drink whole.

Beaming, McClatchy said "Yes, sir!" again, and turned eagerly to Reardon. "Did you hear about the picture, Mr. Reardon?"

"The painting? No. Have they reached a verdict?"

"*Have* they? You know who painted that painting?" McClatchy touched the big man on the arm impressively. "Rembrandt."

"What!"

"That's a fact! Mr. Markham rung up from Sampm Cisco this morning—Rembrandt, he says. What do you think of that?"

Reardon lowered his heavy reddish brows and glowered at McClatchy. "Rembrandt van Rijn——"

"Ryan?" McClatchy said.

"Van Rijn; his last name. . . ."

"Holy Moses, I thought Rembrandt was his last name."

"You mean to tell me——?"

"Maybe it aint the same man."

"Certainly it's the same man. There's only one Rembrandt. Do you mean to tell me he painted that black daub of yours?"

"Well, Rembrandt's what the man said."

"No! Is he sure?"

"Sure he's sure; it's going to be in the papers! Damned if the *Chronicle* didn't call up 'Ubert Ritter from Sampm Cisco! I give 'Ubert all the dope. Oh I tellya. The McClatchys'll be famous yet."

Reardon pulled the late edition of the San Francisco *News* from his pocket, growling: "Let's see if there's anything in here about it," and he spread the paper on the bar. The story was on page one:

FACE ON BARROOM WALL
CREDITED TO REMBRANDT

Reardon burst out laughing with a sound like a blast from an alpen-horn; he threw his head back and hurled his deep rasp at the ceiling while through slit eyelids old man Doughty, who had folded his arms on the bar again and to all appearances gone back to sleep, glared at him as old clubmen everywhere glare at disrupters of their peace.

McClatchy was trying to turn the paper halfway round on the bar. "Lea' me see."

Reardon choked, coughed, took a swallow of gin, and twisting his head round beside McClatchy's over the newspaper on the bar, read on, chuckling horribly. "I'll be damned!" he said when he had finished. Three more blasts of laughter, and he looked at the little bar-keeper. "The owner of a Rembrandt!"

"Yep!" McClatchy said.

"You and the plutocrats! The Traveler's Rest and the Louvre!"

"Yes, sir!" McClatchy said. "Oh I tellya."

"A Rembrandt! I'll be damned!"

"Oh it's the luck of the Irish."

"Well!" Suddenly half rising from his stool, Reardon reached across the bar with both arms, seized the little barman by the shoulders, and shook him. "You son of a bitch!"

"Yep. Oh I tellya."

"Now I'll buy *you* a drink."

"Yes, sir!"

Reardon drank the last of his highball, and taking the glass from him, McClatchy refilled it before attending to his own drink. "How much would you say a Rembrandt's worth, now?"

"Worth! A king's ransom!"

"Yeah?"

"What are you going to do with the money?"

"Well . . ." McClatchy had not yet decided that; he only wagged his head, still grinning. "We'll be getting out of this damned little Llagas, anyhow."

He had a glass of beer while he reviewed for his own fascination as much as for Reardon's the story of how the painting had come to light and his wonderful theory of the railroad auction. "So here I am," he said cheerfully, "with a Rembrandt painting; a guy that wouldn't know art from your uncle Ned. Oh, and wait'll I tell you; you'll get a kick out of this." He touched Reardon on the arm again to emphasize that this was going to be good. "I didn't even know Rembrandt was a man's name; now what do you think of that? When they said a Rembrandt I just used to think they meant a classy picture."

"Well, photographers use the name that way; it's a figure of speech."

"Yeah, but I didn't know there was any such party; how do you like that? But now that I got a Rembrandt myself I guess I ought to be better informed. Holy smoke, people are going to be asking about it. Now you're an educated old buzzard, maybe you could tell me—what about this guy Rembrandt, anyhow? Where did *he* tend bar?"

"In Holland."

"Holland? No, is that a fact."

"Amsterdam. Back in the seventeenth century."

"Seventeenth century, you don't say! Wait, I'm going to write that down." McClatchy punched open the cash register, took out a small pad and a pencil, put on a pair of silver-rimmed spectacles, and in a surprisingly fancy hand wrote: *17 cent. Andsterdam, Holland.* "How do you spell Rembrandt?"

Reardon spelled Rembrandt, and then, at McClatchy's request, the last name. "Rembrandt," he said, "was one of the greatest painters that ever lived, and one of the most popular of his time. But he turned the rich people against him because he painted the truth as he saw it, and he died broke."

"Broke! You don't say."

The alcohol and McClatchy's interest warmed Reardon to the subject. In that cheap den, where only a slummer would have been surprised to hear a lecture on an Old Master, the customer obliged by hauling further information about Rembrandt from a mental cargo uncommonly large and motley; his admiration for the artist increased as he talked, and his judgment of the burghers grew bitter. His gnarled bass, produced upon vocal cords thickened as if by some malady, ravaged, and toughened, a voice worthy of Davy Jones himself, achieved a forbidding eloquence; and McClatchy listened, leaning on the bar, enjoying it. "A great talker, Mr. Reardon," he often told Bessie, adding with a grin: "Especially when he's oiled." And a great talker he was, of a breed of great talkers to be heard by night in the drowned world of old saloons. His faded banner was flung across a window above the O.K. Machine Shop's yawning doorway:

WALSH REARDON
ATTORNEY AT LAW

He had not had a real client in years. Yet it was said and believed in Llagas that he knew enough law to argue a case before the Supreme

Court of the United States; and stories of promise shown long ago still trailed him. There was one from which Llagas still got a malicious chuckle, the story of his defense of Henry Jancke's will in a contest brought by Lloyd Jancke, an estranged son cut off with virtually nothing. With Lloyd on the witness stand, Reardon had asked:

"How old was your father?"

"Seventy-three."

"You read that on the tombstone."

"No I didn't."

"You're under oath, Lloyd. You did read it on the tombstone."

"No! I've never seen the tombstone."

"Never seen the tombstone?" Reardon turned to the small-town jury. "He never laid a posy on his father's grave."

But Reardon was best remembered as the Stanford football hero— "the greatest passer in Pacific Coast history"—a picturesque young giant with hands that went halfway round the ball, but a giant given to drinking sprees too spectacular to be overlooked by the university. There had been a brawl one Big Game Night in San Francisco, after which he had been expelled. Then, it was remembered, he had managed to get into some small night law school in San Francisco and to pass the State Bar, and had come home to Llagas and opened an office; and it was remembered with a smile that a brilliant future had been predicted for him. It had been said that he was going into politics and would someday be the governor of the state.

Reardon never *had* gone into politics, though. And, as women no longer remarked, he had not married. Imperceptibly he had grown physically larger, his face had turned redder, and his voice had become hoarse, deeper, hoarser, and crippled. Sometimes at San Javier, the county seat, indulgent judges who admired his abilities had postponed court hearings when he could not appear—sometimes he could not be found. The judges had lost patience with him. His thirst had increased with his practice, and he had found himself on debauches of increasing length and damage, sometimes waking up in jail. Neither the town nor the county was large enough to support both the pleasure and practice of such a man; the practice had fallen away. Nowadays other lawyers gave him bookwork to do and speeches to write, and sometimes in secret they consulted him. He earned enough to keep himself in the two rooms over the machine shop, working in one, sleeping in the other, and to maintain himself as star patron of the Traveler's Rest.

McClatchy, though he was sorry for Mr. Reardon, greatly admired him. The little man looked on the big one as a gentleman born and an oracle of learning, and was proud of his size and kingly bearing, fascinated by his great-ogre voice, and flattered by his patronage. And tonight, full of curiosity about the Rembrandt, he had eagerly awaited the gentleman-oracle's arrival.

In the sitting room off the kitchen, meanwhile, the women were talking.

"Did I tell you?" Arline was saying to her mother, "—Mrs. Silvestro came up to me on the street today to ask if it was true."

"She phoned me," Bessie said.

"Trust her, she hears everything," Arline said. "She had on her new beaver coat; just gorgeous. My, her husband's good to her, isn't he."

"Yes," Bessie said, gently rocking in her wicker chair, "there's nothing stingy about Mr. Silvestro. And he can afford it. During the war he did wonderful."

"Well, there's nothing stingy about Dad, either, and I guess he can afford it now too. God knows it's about time you had some clothes yourself."

"Now," Bessie said, "let's not go counting our chickens before they're hatched."

"Oh, Ma! You'll get plenty for that painting. Don't you realize? Why, I'll bet there isn't anybody in Llagas could afford to buy it."

"Oh, now, there's plenty of rich people in Llagas."

"But nobody has a Rembrandt painting but millionaires and museums! You ought to get yourself a *mink* coat."

"Me?" Bessie laughed.

"Sure; if you want to. One thing's certain, you're going to sell *this* place"—Bessie's daughter swept a scornful hand at their surroundings—"and retire. You can get yourself a nice comfortable house, or a nice apartment, and a car."

"Let me tell you something," Bessie said, stopping her rocking and holding up a forefinger. "If there's any money coming to us from that painting, we're going to put it in the bank."

"Not all of it; I guess Dad'll have something to say about that. He's going to see you enjoy life for a change, if I know anything about it. And gee, Ma"—Arline turned earnest, pleading—"you certainly deserve it. You worked hard all of your life, and what have you got to show for it? What would you have to show for it if it wasn't for this painting?" She looked at her mother's face as if seeing it for the first time in years, seeing the marks of suffering and the humility, patience, and kindness there; and the sad truth of what she was saying overcame her. "Oh, Ma! I'm *so* happy for you." Jumping up, she enfolded Bessie in her big freckled arms and kissed her.

"Oh—you!" Bessie protested roughly. "Go 'way, now." But at this spontaneous display of affection, of joy in her good fortune, Bessie's eyes, like Arline's, overflowed, and for an instant she held her daughter; then she pushed her away. "There, now," fumbling for her handkerchief. "Nonsense."

Arline laughed, happy and a little embarrassed. Her cheeks were flushed. "Just the same," she said, throwing herself back into her chair, "I think it's wonderful."

"Ohhh, dear," Bessie sighed, having wiped her eyes and blown her small red nose, "when I think of your dad. *He's* the one. You'd think he was Floodobrienmackayandfair, to hear him." She chuckled. "Well, Providence works in strange ways. He used to think he'd make it in politics, and then during Prohibition he thought he was going to make it in the liquor, and then he thought he'd make it with the chicken ranch, and when the liquor come back he was going to make it with this place; and he never did. Then all of a sudden the pot of gold hits him on the head. Land's sakes!" she laughed. "Poor Dad!" And her bosom, still full of emotion, shook with the humor and gladness of it.

"I know," Arline said. "And that chicken ranch! Remember how he used to swear at the chickens? In all my life I don't think I ever heard Dad swear, really swear, except at those chickens. Not much, anyhow. You know, I think he was afraid of chickens."

"Why, sure he was," Bessie said, still chuckling. "I remember one day at the start there I walked in on him while he was gathering the eggs and found him trying to pry an old hen off of the nest with a shovel."

Arline screamed with laughter. "I know, I know! I've seen him. Don't you remember the day that old hen chased him clear out of the chicken house?"

"Yes—that one. She had him buffaloed. Oh, she used to peck him. She knew he was scared of her."

"Poor Dad," echoed Arline. "He was some farmer."

"Well, but Dad was a city boy," Bessie reminded her, defensively. "You know what they say about country boys—you can take the boy out of the country but you can't take the country out of the boy; and it's the same with city boys like your father, you can't change 'em. My, he did get so lonesome out there. I used to feel sorry for him. And then when he failed, I think he was kind of glad—relieved to have it over with, you know."

"But for heaven's sake, Ma, what did he ever buy a chicken ranch for, anyhow?"

"Oh, I do' know." Bessie rocked pensively. "I suppose lots of city men get a notion they'd like to have a little place in the country, one time or 'nother. And that was right after Tommy died; I guess he didn't rightly know what he was doing—or me neither. But there, you see, there's another thing—Providence works in strange ways. If we hadn't bought that chicken ranch we probably wouldn't have bought this place after, and now it'd be somebody else'd have this painting everybody's so excited about. And I was thinking today—— Here's something else, now, but don't you ever let on to him I said it. I was thinking today we certainly wouldn't have bought this place if your father hadn't gone and been a bartender to begin with. And I didn't want him to be a bartender, you know; he talked me into it. And if he hadn't, we wouldn't have this painting. And then during Prohibition if he hadn't gone and been a bootlegger—— Oh, I made an awful fuss when he wanted to do that, but if he hadn't been a bootlegger maybe we wouldn't have bought the ranch, and then we wouldn't have bought this place, and now we wouldn't have this painting."

"What do you mean, if he hadn't been a bootlegger? What did that have to do with it?" Arline frowned. She had always resented that her father had been a bootlegger, and to be reminded now that he had been annoyed her. Somehow she did not want the fact associated with the painting.

But Bessie said mysteriously: "Oh, that had plenty to do with it."

"What do you mean? How did it?" It seemed to Arline that her mother's reasoning took fantastic flights at times; it was as if Bessie thought herself endowed with some mystic insight and leaped to conclusions beyond the grasp of ordinary mortals.

"Oh," Bessie said evasively, rocking the least bit faster, "I do' know. But one thing leads to another. You can't pick up a pin in this life but it don't make a difference some way. And you never know—you never know *what'll* happen."

The story of Tommy and the police car, as Bessie understood it, would never be told. There were several reasons, and underlying them all perhaps was the feeling that if given breath it would come alive like a curse.

"Oh, Ma!"

"Well, it's the truth. You'll find out. Someday you'll look back and know what I mean. You see if you don't."

This somewhat unsettling suggestion dwelt for a moment on Arline's face. But she let it go. She was depressed by the recollection that her father was a saloonkeeper, a bartender still. Just now it spoiled things a little. In the daughter there stirred some of the regret, the frustrated ambition, that so long ago had troubled the mother. She said petulantly: "What did Dad want to go and be a bartender for in the first place?"

"Well, he wanted to have a trade. That was the first thing. And he thought he could get into politics that way; he thought he'd *meet* people, as he used to say. And if Prohibition hadn't come along he might have made it. Oh, he was full of schemes when he was a young man. My," Bessie smiled, "how he used to talk."

Arline murmured: "Politics." She tried to visualize her father as he had been then. "Poor Dad," she said again, with a smile, her affection coming to his defense. "Well, he could have done worse. He might have been a longshoreman like his father."

"Oh," Bessie said, looking shocked. "He didn't want to be like that old devil. His father was a dirty old bum."

"Ma!"

"Well, what else would you call him? A man that never made a decent living for his family? He threw it all away on booze, that's what he done, and led your father's mother a dog's life. Oh, he was a terrible man. Used to come home raving-drunk and scare the daylights out of 'em calling the devil out of the fireplace. It's a wonder Dad turned out to be the good man he is, with such a father."

Arline looked at her mother curiously. "What did you say?—'calling the devil out of the fireplace'?"

"Why, yes, that's what he'd do. He'd come home and get the old cat up and then he'd call the devil out of the fireplace. 'Come out!' he'd holler. 'Come out, I dare you.' And the poor cat'd get its back up and start to spit at the fire, and tongues of flame'd come shooting out at the poor old cat. Oh, it must have been dreadful!"

"Ma! That's cra-zy. 'Calling the devil out of the fireplace'! Dad was kidding you when he told you that."

"Oh no he wasn't!" said Bessie.

Arline laughed with delight. "Why, I'm surprised at you. A smart up-to-date woman like you believing a story like that!"

"Oh! I suppose *you* don't *believe* in the devil."

"Oh, but Ma!"

"H'm," said Bessie, rocking grimly. "There's lots of things *you* don't know."

"Now, Ma! Honestly! Did you ever see anything like that yourself?"

"Not in *my* family, no! But I've heard of it, and a grea' deal worse. You'd be surprised some of the things I could tell you."

"What, for instance?" Arline was fascinated.

"Never you mind; it's ten o'clock, time you got that child home.

No, no, go on, now; do you want to raise him up to be a nervous wreck? He should have been home in his own bed long ago. Wait, now, and I'll give you some of that jelly to take home for 'im."

The moon of that summer night was sitting on the Golden West Milling Company's roof as Arline McClatchy, as she was still called in Llagas, went round the Northwestern Pacific yard with the sleep-sodden Billy Lucas in her arms, and up Hill Street toward the slough, which Llagas calls a river. How much was the picture worth? she wondered. It must be worth a lot. Nobody had them but millionaires and museums, and there wasn't another in Llagas, maybe not in San Francisco, even. All the excitement—the man from the art gallery, the reporter from the *Sentinel*, and the look on the face of Mrs. Silvestro! It must be all over town by now, she reflected pleasantly; all over town.

She was distracted by the growl of a car climbing the hill behind her; the car caught up with her as she was crossing the iron bridge, and gave her a fright by stopping beside her. Then she saw the policeman at the wheel. He leaned out, perceived that the woman had a child in her arms, and changed his mind about her. "You okay, lady?"

"Oh—sure. For a minute I couldn't see who you were. I'm okay, thanks."

"Kind of a lonesome part of town to be in so late at night."

"Oh, I'm used to it. I work back there. I walk home every night; only not usually this late."

"Yeah?"

"I'm usually home by eight, anyhow."

"Yeah?" The policeman did not approve of such recklessness. A lone woman, and with a kid. "Where do you live?"

"Just three blocks. On Union Street."

"Okay, get in; I'll take you."

"Oh!" Arline said. "Thanks!" She went round to the other side of the car, he opened the door for her, and she got in beside him. Her son, half waking, whimpered a protest, wriggled, and sought his dream again. "This is service," Arline said.

"What number on Union?" he asked as he let out the clutch.

She told him. "The big white apartment house on the corner."

"Yeah, I know the place." His eyes were on the street ahead. He was a man of perhaps thirty-five, a tall rawboned man with lean brown cheeks. "Where'd you say you work?"

"Down at the Traveler's Rest. Dad owns it."

"Oh, the old Traveler's—yeah?" He turned his head for a moment to look at her with interest. "That's where they found the painting, isn't it?"

Arline was surprised. She laughed joyously. All over town. "*Honestly!* Where did you hear about it?"

"Fellow was telling me. Is it on the level?"

"Oh, sure. *He was?*"

"Yeah. He read it in the paper. Sa-ay——"

"In the *paper?* Oh, no! Really? Which one?"

"I don't know. But it's on the level, huh? That's a pretty valuable painting, isn't it?"

"I guess so," she admitted modestly. "It's a Rembrandt."

"Yeah, that's what he was telling me. Boy! Where'd it come from? How'd you happen to find it?"

"Oh, it was hanging on the wall all the time. Nobody knows how it got there. It was there before we had the place."

"No kidding!"

"Dad thinks maybe somebody picked it up at a railroad auction and sold it to the people that had the place before we did. They sold it to us with the property. And they're dead now, anyhow."

"Yeah? Then it's all yours, huh?"

"Um *hm!*"

"How do you like that! This the house here?"

"Yes, this is it."

He swung round the corner and stopped the car in front of the steps.

She said: "It was awful nice of you to bring me home."

"That's all right. Kind of dangerous for a woman the other side of town this time of night."

"Thanks. I usually leave earlier," she said, getting out. "I'm home by eight, mostly."

"Guess you'll be living on Easy Street from now on, huh?"

She laughed. "Hope so. Well—g'night."

" 'Night." And he touched his cap to her.

The car pulled away from the curb as she let herself into the house. She climbed the flight of stairs to her single apartment, undressed Billy, and put him to bed on the couch. She kissed him lightly, pushed back a lock of his hair, and stood looking down at him a moment. *He* wouldn't be a bartender. In the bathroom she changed slowly into her pajamas, looked in the mirror of the medicine cabinet, looked appraisingly, critically, and began to cleanse and cream her face, a thing she seldom did any more. She was not a bit sleepy. She returned to the living room and knelt beside the pulldown bed mechanically.

But tonight a feeling of well-being and hope rushed up in her, and she was speaking to Heaven in warm thanksgiving. She got up, switched out the light, and crawled, greasy-faced, into bed. She lay pillowed on her hands, her eyes wide open, her lips faintly smiling. All over town . . .

Down in the little apartment at the rear of the Traveler's Rest, Bessie in her nightgown knelt beside the bed that she shared with her husband. It was his practice to close the tavern at eleven o'clock, there being no point in keeping it open any later in this part of town, though in fact there was hardly any point in keeping it open that late. Bessie usually finished in the kitchen before nine, and then worked at her darning and listened to the radio till the Richfield News signed off with trumpets at ten-fifteen, and then got ready for bed, and got down on her knees, and said the Rosary. Tonight she was saying it in thanksgiving for the Rembrandt painting, but not with joy, rather with a vague inner anxiety, and yet with trust. Bessie's thanks were more properly a due acknowledgment to God, tied to a little memorandum asking the Blessed Virgin to see that all went well. She got to her feet heavily, and into bed, sighed, and lay there with the light on, waiting for her husband.

"You're going to sell *this* place," Arline had said. Maybe—if the painting brought as much as everybody expected. But then what? Retire? Bessie had never thought about retiring; she supposed that she had expected to work till the day she died. Move back to San Francisco, as Danny had always wanted? Into an apartment? That would be nice. But then they hardly knew anyone in San Francisco any more. And what in the world would Danny *do*? But this was no life for Arline. Nor for Billy. For Billy's sake she hoped the painting did bring a lot of money. And for Arline's—poor girl. Arline hadn't had much of a chance, her husband being killed in the war, and all. Yes, and for Danny's sake. He had so wanted all his life to be successful. But wasn't it strange! Like finding money in the street. Money they hadn't earned, money they had no right to. Still, they had bought the painting with the place; it was legally theirs, everyone said, and all because they had unknowingly bought it with the place, because they had bought it with this particular place after the chicken ranch. Goodness! So queer! But painting or no painting, there would still be the breakfast to get in the morning. What was keeping Danny? She never could sleep till he had come. Getting up, she put on her flannel robe and her slippers and went padding into the saloon in search of him. "Danny . . ."

"Oh! I was just coming." He rose from the stool of the old piano, on which, having said goodnight to his last two patrons and closed the

door behind them, he had sat down to read again the story of his
good fortune in the newspaper, which Reardon had left with him.
"Look at this; it's in the paper! Here—see?"

"What? It is? Already?" Bessie said, taking the paper. She held it
away from her and peered at it, making out the heading but none of
the small print. "Well! So it is! Well!"

"Oh, the McClatchys'll be famous yet," he said for the second time
this evening. "Say, did you know that picture's three hundred years
old? Mr. Reardon was telling me Rembrandt was an old Dutchman
lived over in Holland, Europe, in the seventeenth century—only that
don't mean the seventeen hundreds, that means the sixteen hundreds,
he says: they call the sixteen hundreds the seventeenth century. I don't
get it, but anyhow this picture's three hundred years old. But it's worth
as much as it ever was; more, begorry; like an old antique. Rembrandt
painted it in the sixteen hundreds, and died broke, and we come along
in the nineteens and can get more for it than he could. That's what I
call beating the Dutch. Ouch!" Recoiling comically after this sally, he
held up his hands as if to ward off a blow.

Bessie said affectionately: "Happy, aint you?"

The rosy bar gleamed in the light of the weak bulb in the middle
of the ceiling, and the brass rail gleamed, and the spittoon, and outside the moon was shining down on Llagas.

"Sure, Mike! Aint we struck it at last? All of a sudden? After all
these years? By golly, though, it was a long pull, wasn't it? All the way
from the old flat on G'rrera Street; huh, Bess? Who'd of thought then
the McClatchys'd wind up with a Rembrandt painting in the little
town of Llagas! Ah, Bessie—

"Down by the o-ld m-ill sta-ream-m . . .

"Wait, now." He flung himself down at the piano and with a the-
atrical flourish struck a chord of the meager accompaniment that he
had picked up as an apprentice bartender at the Potrero Saloon.

"Where I firrrst me-et t-chu . . ."

His coarse little red face as he looked up at her was aglow with
amusement at his own foolishness, and his eyes, though suddenly a
little moist, twinkled merrily; but the muscles of his red neck stood out
in earnest, for his humor did not extend to the voice that he thought
could have been the equal of McCormack's with the training.

"You were six-teeen-n,
    [chord]
My vil-lage k-weeen-n . . ."

And Bessie, with her head laid over on one shoulder in the way she had, was regarding him with a soft smile. She thought that she had not seen him look so happy since the day he had got the job behind the bar of the Palace Hotel.

4

THE MASTERPIECE

It remained for next morning's paper to bring news of the treasure to the man of the stained-glass window. He had made a fine Pietà to wring tears from the sunlight for Mrs. Anthony Ruffo's youngest boy, Tony, killed in New Guinea at nineteen years of age, and he had brought it to Llagas in pieces to install it in the church himself, when he read that Alfred Markham had pronounced McClatchy's painting a Rembrandt. He snorted. The picture wasn't that good. Or was it? He decided to knock off work for the rest of the day, and went to San Francisco to find out.

Markham assembled the evidence to convince him. "Here, look at this." He offered, first, the pigment analysis.

But the man was standing before the cleaned portrait, his lips twisted in a cruel grin. A snigger escaped him, and he commented: "By God but *he*'d seen better days. Look at his coat."

"Yes."

"Old! And he was old himself, this hustler. Sure, I couldn't see him before; all I could see was his eyes. This was no gold-plated bucko that paid for his portrait; he got paid for it himself, I'll go bail! The painter must have picked him up in some gin mill." And the little man sniggered again, but with a kind of malicious affection, as if the discovery of so much frailty in a fellow mortal delighted him.

Markham let him examine all the evidence. Then the man asked: "What's my cut, Markham?"

"Your cut? Why, I expect you'll get your reward from the owner when it's sold."

"How much, exactly?"

"That will be up to Mr. McClatchy. I'd say fifty dollars would be fair."

"Fifty dollars! Be damned to that; I'd say ten per cent from him and the half of your commission."

"Would you, though! That's ridiculous."

"In God's name, man, I could have gone to another dealer; you're not forgetting that, I hope."

"Not at all. And if the other dealer had troubled to go to Llagas on the strength of your vague supposition, as I did, what do you suppose he'd be telling you now?"

"Not Pharis."

"Indeed! Then why didn't you go to Pharis?"

The man cursed and said: "I won't haggle, it's against my nature. I'll make you a simple cut-rate proposition. Give me a blasted C and we'll call it quits. Then you get it from our friend."

"Sorry. Mr. McClatchy hasn't authorized me to enter into any such transaction."

"Have you lost your mind? You'll be saving him money. The only reason I'm making the offer at all is it so happens I'm needing it now."

"Yes, it happens so often in your case, doesn't it? What's the matter? You're working. Don't the good fathers pay you?"

"Ah, Christ. The old woman with the dough paid half in advance and half when I finished the window, but my wife got most of it, she found out where I was. So I'm putting the window in myself, just to eke out a bit more. I'm on my uppers, man."

"I'm sorry to hear it."

"Boloney. Listen, Markham. How would you like to be the man that discovered this Rembrandt?"

"Why, what do you mean! You had no suspicion it was a Rembrandt."

A sly smile. "That's your story. A hundred on the barrelhead and you make it stick."

Markham suppressed his anger. "So!" was all he said, bitterly.

"Put it in writing and I'll sign it. Date it back three weeks: 'Paid in full' for conning you on to a picture I think is by some little woodenshoe bum. Then you show the receipt and collect. And listen to this, Markham: I'll sign a receipt for a hundred and fifty."

"Is that the way Pharis does business?"

The man persisted. This old campaigner with the bald head and the smashed nose, a man in his sixtieth year, became like a nagging child. He demanded, argued, sulked, and began to whine. Markham was repelled. But Markham, for all his stubbornness, was bargaining now, and the man knew it. Markham came to an agreement with him, and he left, not with a hundred dollars but with seventy-five.

And the man disappeared for a week.

In St. Peter's Church, Llagas, one corner of the canvas that he had left stretched across the gaping hole where the last panel of the great window was to fit came loose in the night, and the wind huffed in and put out the sanctuary lamp. The sacristan secured the canvas and relighted the lamp in time for early Mass, but the altar candles kept guttering in the draft. And the next day, with a frightful litter in the sacristy, the pastor gave instructions that he was to be informed when the man returned.

It was just past the Friday noon hour when the man appeared in the sacristy, his face pale, dark rings under his eyes. The sacristan was putting some flowers into a vase. "Well!" he said. "We've missed you." The man grunted and said: "The job'll be finished today," avoiding the sacristan's eyes. The sacristan said nothing, but after a moment went out, leaving the flowers.

The man put on his overalls, found his tool kit, and took it out to the foot of the scaffolding by the left wall of the sanctuary. The breath that he exhaled in the presence of the Lord stank of whisky; sweat lightly beaded his upper lip and the cleft of his chin, and the hand with which he smeared it away trembled. He climbed the scaffolding to remove the canvas. He was on his toes at mid-wall, reaching up, when Father Cobb's hail from below frightened him. He turned too quickly, lurched, clutching at the canvas for support, and the cassocked old priest shouted a warning and thrust both hands upward as if to steady him from fifteen feet below. He fell, the dome above the altar muted the bonebreaking thud he made, and the canvas came down like a let-go jib on top of him. The priest rushed to him, asking: "Are you hurt, are you hurt?" and stooped and fumbled with the canvas, threw it off, and saw the man lying on his back, his eyes partly open but only the lower whites visible, and the sacristan came hurrying from behind the altar.

"Get a doctor! an ambulance! quickly!" the pastor said. "The man has fallen!"

"Fallen! Oh! I will! . . ."

As the sacristan hurried off, Father Cobb got down stiffly on one knee. "Can you speak, man? Can you speak?"

The man's face contorted and he spoke in an agonized guttural between clenched teeth. "Aaah—Christ!" There was no reverence in it.

"Don't talk like that, now—don't; bear the pain as best you can till the ambulance comes; it was my fault, I shouldn't have called to you like that; does it hurt bad?—There, I can see it does; but let—let me——"

Father Cobb broke off, startled, and looked up.

It was one o'clock of a bright summer day. Like an effect in an old-fashioned melodrama, a cue for a sinner to repent huskily and movingly, steep shafts of sunlight were streaming down through the stained glass of the window and falling directly upon the injured man. The priest had become conscious of it all at once; he was looking up at the Pietà. Father Cobb feared superstition as he did the devil and abominated the practice of reading heavenly messages into natural manifestations, particularly into obvious ones, but this one piercingly reminded him of a phrase in the liturgy for the dead—*Let perpetual light shine upon him*—which was so much at odds with his impression of the old stager lying here in the Presence that it seemed to him God would never have been so careless as to allow such a thing to happen by accident. He turned and looked in perplexity at the tabernacle; then, whether in submission or for the benefit of the doubt, he lowered the other knee. He looked down at the man again, folding nervous hands and trying to compose himself, all priest now. "This—this could be the hour of your death," he said. But the man gutturally profaned again in his agony, and lost consciousness. He died in the church, in front of the altar, his last breath reeking of stale alcohol, in the colored sunshine of his Pietà, at the feet of the crucified Redeemer and the Sorrowful Mother.

At all Masses on Sunday the priests of St. Peter's asked prayers for his soul. He had not been a Catholic, nor anything else, as he had told Father Cobb, and it was easy to tell that he had led a profligate life; but seeing that he had been brought to the altar to die, it was believed that he might have been given grace at the last moment—for what reason, for what good deed, for whose prayers, only Heaven knew; and if he had, of course, whether he had accepted it was a question that earth could not answer. The McClatchys were shocked when they heard of his death, and they did pray for him, the passing stranger. But whether Heaven took his soul, no one claimed the body that bore so many scars of devotion to the world. That the County burned.

Alfred Markham too was shocked when he heard of the accident. But then, he saw, it had cleanly eliminated the danger that his professional triumph as discoverer of an unknown Rembrandt painting might someday be clouded by the claim of a double-dealing blackguard.

The only trouble was other dealers, artists, and critics everywhere, reading of a previously unknown Rembrandt's coming to light on the farthest shore of America, in a cheap saloon, in a town called Llagas, were sure to be skeptical. Markham took steps to convince the world.

To certify this Rembrandt he brought to San Francisco, with Mc-Clatchy's consent, the eminent Sir Patrick Locklear, who was then exploring America for the first time, and who happened to be no farther away than Beverly Hills.

Markham could not have chosen a sterner judge; but if he had sent all the way to Europe neither could he have engaged for ten times the sum a more considerable authority, nor found a better advertisement for McClatchy's painting and the Markham Galleries.

"No, no, I never grant interviews, never grant interviews," the famous old man told the reporters who met him at the railroad station, but the twinkle in his sharp blue eyes took the unfriendliness out of his words, though he meant what he said. "Can't afford to grant interviews. What I say they pay me for, and I need the money. What? Rembrandt? There, there. All's not gold that glisters, is it, eh? Lots of fakes in the world, you know; world's full of fakes, what? Scoundrels. Blasted imposters. Ah. But that's enough. Talk's not cheap with me. Scat, the lot of you."

"And then," the *Chronicle* reported, "he disappeared into a long black limousine and was whisked away."

Was whisked clear across the Golden Gate to Markham's house in Mill Valley.

In their swift recording of events the newspaper city rooms had already lost interest in the little story of the Llagas Rembrandt, but with the coming of Sir Patrick Locklear their interest revived. The painting had brought to San Francisco one of the great news figures of the day. And there began a curious enlargement of the story, bound up with the character of a city.

Out of a history dominated by scenes of violence—shootings and brawls, riots, lynchings, earthquakes, and fires—has grown a San Francisco still obstreperous at times, hard-drinking, highly romantic, supremely snobbish, and incorrigibly sentimental. Here, Boston is the wrong side of the tracks; and history aside, San Francisco nods mistily at George Sterling's description of it: "The cool, grey city of love." But if it began in violence, in exuberance, in a tearing scramble for money, it began also with a depressing consciousness of isolation borne in upon it by the physical facts. Under the tutelage of early boosters who dreamt of it as so gay, so rakehelly, and so artistic that it would be known everywhere as the Paris of the West, it learned to enjoy and cultivate this feeling, and although many a year has passed since San Francisco was isolated in the physical sense, the feeling lingers in its soul. It seems to remember itself bestriding, once, its spit of land at the edge of the earth in solitary grandeur. The traveler has only to glance round the walls of its hotels, restaurants, and barrooms, at the tables of current reading in its bookshops, or at a copy of any of its newspapers, to see that this beautiful city at the water's edge has one of the worst cases of narcissism going. But what no traveler suspects is that the love her people bear San Francisco is of such a nature that they will not share her with one another.

The amount and variety of local cultural material to be found here are surprising in a city so close to the Stone Age: friars, rancheros, wagons across the plains and ships round the Horn, sealing and whaling ships, tea clippers and fishermen, gambling hells and joss houses, the Shakespearean history of William Ralston and the epic of the Great Earthquake and Fire and the Rising from the Flames, the sad love story of Concepción Argüello and the sorry ballad of the Rose of Sharon, a considerable literature, indeed, and a whole cycle of old wives' tales, and a thousand and one nights in the theater, and it is all the patrimony of each San Franciscan personally and exclusively, with his hills and his vistas, his fogs and his unforgettable foghorns, his cablecars, his vanishing ferryboats, his Chinatown, his Fisherman's Wharf, and his tiny antique Mission, a basilica now, to whose churchyard each Memorial Day still comes the Fire Department to decorate the graves of early volunteers, including the grave of James P. Casey, lynched by the Vigilance Committee of '56 for shooting to death an editor who presumed to style himself James King of William. To each, rich or poor, belong the tall buildings, the two mighty bridges, Bret Harte and Mark Twain, Ambrose Bierce and Jack London and Frank Norris and Jim Corbett and Lola Montez and Luisa Tetrazzini. It may come as a surprise in Scotland that San Francisco feels a proprietary interest in Robert Louis Stevenson as well. This is easily explained.

First, nowhere else in the world is *Treasure Island* so much beloved as it is in San Francisco, which is only natural; second, no sooner had it made its author famous than someone remembered that he himself had been here only a little while before. He had, in fact, married Fanny Osbourne here. After a bit of digging it was discovered that he had stopped also at Monterey, to the south, sojourned on Mount St. Helena, to the north, and while contemplating the view from the mountain been inspired to write something called *The Silverado Squatters*. Then it was noticed that Spyglass Hill on Treasure Island was not unlike a certain hill near Monterey, though some said it was more like a shoulder of St. Helena. San Francisco could not help but perceive that, though abandoned by Stevenson, itself and its environs had been adopted by him, and in recognition of this compliment it tacitly bestowed citizenship on him, built him a monument in Portsmouth Square, and raised him Treasure Island in the bay. It is a hospitable city in its way, and has made room in its legend for dozens of other famous beings, including Francis Drake and Sun Yat-sen. And now something of the kind was about to happen to Sir Patrick Locklear

Sir Patrick approached the McClatchys' painting with a suspicious eye. He studied spirit, style, composition, brushwork, and impasto, examined the signature, which had been indistinguishable until the painting had been cleaned, scrutinized X rays, pored over the pigment analysis, and the reports on canvas and nails, squinted through a microscope, and said:

"Yes, yes, Rembrandt, of course! Who else? Bol? Gerard Dou? Rubbish. They would not have forged his signature, in any case. Who, then? Some counterfeiter? Pfa! Rembrandt was inimitable. Rembrandt did it and Rembrandt signed it. Of course!"

At Markham's urging, moreover, he repeated his conviction at a press interview, because this time he *was* being paid for what he had to say; and to the Markham Galleries with the art critics came the news reporters because this was the first time Sir Patrick had received the press in America and it very well might be the last. They found him a garrulous old man once he had got started. He stood beside the painting like a lecturer, using as a pointer his eyeglasses; from the painting he veered into a critique of the painter, then he shot off into a satirical monologue on modernists; and when a woman reporter, the first to get a word in, asked for his impressions of America, his reply rather took their breath away.

"Oh, come, come, give me time to digest what so far I have not even been able to swallow. Ha! But there; you have something right here in San Francisco that has impressed me as much as anything. Really, had any intelligent report of it reached us in England I should have been willing to make this journey solely for the purpose of gazing at it. I refer, of course, to the New Apollo in the entrance to your harbor."

They looked at him blankly for a moment until it overtook them that he must mean—"The Golden Gate Bridge?" the woman asked.

"Precisely!"

And they smiled. New Apollo—*there* was a name for it.

Someone asked: "Have you seen the other one?"

"The other bridge? Tut! Surely you don't speak of that makeshift apparatus in the same breath with this bridge? But yes!" Sir Patrick said. "Some of you do not appreciate this bridge. I have been here only three days and I have seen that already. I have been informed with pride that it is 'the longest single-span suspension bridge in the world,' as if I cared a fig for that. It does not occur to you to call it the finest bridge in the world; but that is what I would call it. I'd not hesitate to speak of it in the same breath with any of the great works of architecture. And I have heard a woman complain that it spoils the view! An empty truth if ever I heard one. Her house is high on one of your hills and looks down upon it; the bridge is lost in the panorama. Spoils the view! To see that bridge properly you must be able to look up at those splendid towers; or better yet, you must take your place in its own dimension, in the dimension of the twentieth century, the dimension of speed; and you must see it in intimate relation to its setting and its purpose: you must see it while crossing it at forty or fifty miles an hour."

Sir Patrick raised his arms high to depict for them the reaching towers of the bridge, a structure that, he went so far as to say, was as articulate of modern America as Chartres Cathedral was of thirteenth-century France. Oh yes, he said, it was a mistake to suppose that the great art symbol of America was the skyscraper. The bridge, bespeaking so eloquently the restlessness of man, his enterprise, his will, his conquest of the bush, was a better; and how forcefully this struck one here in the West! To cross the continent in a railway carriage, cross the same land that had known the plodding boot of the bushranger, and find here at the end of the trail the perfect expression of his achievement—this great steel stride! Observe how purposely it went, its classic vigor, its integrity!

"But I gather," he said, "that there are some among you who disapprove of this work of art because of its color, this bright orange red with its assertive contrast to the blue of strait and ocean. You speak of the color as if it were a disfigurement, explaining apologetically that red lead alone will keep out the corroding salt that drives in on your Pacific wind—not realizing, mind you, that the color therefore does the work of caissons: *it holds up the bridge!* Ha! I submit that with the exception of Nature herself, no artist before has used color so well!"

Now the truth was that red lead was used as the basic coat of paint on both bridges. The Golden Gate Bridge, which earned less in tolls than the Bay Bridge to Alameda County, was given a top coat of an orange paint that was sturdy and relatively cheap. But the orange overlying the red lead did give a weathered red-lead effect, and most San Franciscans already believed that on the Golden Gate Bridge red lead was used exclusively. The romantic conception expressed by Sir Patrick Locklear made the error ineradicable and sent it down to posterity.

"And," he continued warmly, "some among you mutter that the New Apollo, as I insist upon calling it, is built upon your earth fault. Whether that is true I do not know. The Apollo of Rhodes must have been built upon an earth fault, for an earthquake destroyed it; yet it remains one of the seven wonders of its world. Whether the earth will destroy your bridge also, no one can say. But if this colossus stands here with its feet in the tides challenging the earth to do so, does it not speak to us all the more movingly of man? Is it not all the better symbol of the century of the cyclotron? And if *you*, of all beholders, are not moved by it, then what are you doing in this city whose flag it is—this city which the earth ever threatens to shake to its knees? No, *you* must not distrust this bridge; and you must never say again that it spoils the view."

San Francisco was divided into two camps where its two bridges were concerned. One camp had been insisting for years upon the superiority of "the longest single-span bridge in the world," although this choice had been based chiefly upon admiration of the Golden Gate Bridge as a feat of engineering. The other camp had been deprecating this bridge as a gaudy blemish on nature and acclaiming the Bay Bridge, with its six shorter spans and its color of a respectable business-suit gray, as "*the* longest *bridge* in the world." And now had come a foreigner, an Englishman, hailing the Golden Gate Bridge as a masterwork and a wonder and dismissing its rival as "that make-shift apparatus." But it was noticed that most of the complaints to the letter columns of the newspapers came from Alameda County.

Both San Francisco morning papers published full pages of camera studies of the Gate Bridge, one calling it: NEW APOLLO; the other: THE FLAG OF SAN FRANCISCO. Reporters had canvassed the city for comment: they quoted the mayor, members of the Art Commission and of the Bridge Authority, architects, painters, sculptors, clubwomen, and tollgate men. And that Sunday the bridge traffic meter recorded an increase of fifteen per cent over the traffic of the previous Sunday, an increase which, the day being overcast, could be attributed only to art lovers out to have another gaze at the bridge at forty or fifty miles an hour.

Thus old Sir Patrick Locklear became an item in San Francisco's collection of international figurines. At the moment he was a somewhat controversial one, though already prized by many of the collectors. But in time, as the rest got used to him, he might take his place with Stevenson, Drake, and Sun Yat-sen, or even beside José Francísco Ortéga, who had discovered the Golden Gate but left the bridge for him.

The Llagas Rembrandt came in for its share of the story. Photographs of the painting and its owners appeared in all the newspapers; and it was now that the *Chronicle* dubbed the mysterious Old Master by the name that was to stick to it: *The Lost Dutchman*. But by association with Sir Patrick Locklear and the Golden Gate Bridge, *The Lost Dutchman* was something more than an Old Master now. It was a lesser artifact of San Francisco.

The picture had been photographed in the city and the McClatchys in Llagas; it was suggested that the owners ought to be photographed *with* it. Bessie and Arline could not spare the time to go to San Francisco, but there was little doing in the bar of the Traveler's Rest in the daytime, and the barkeeper hankered to see his painting again, now that it was cleaned and famous. So one morning Dan McClatchy locked his saloon and set out for the city of his birth.

5

VOYAGE OF AN OLD SOUTH OF MARKET BOY

It was the tenth morning of July: still puffs of cloud in a field of summer blue; tawny hills with pools of shade under great live-oak trees for which already the cattle were making; the air was still, and it was going to be hot. But it won't be hot in Sampm Cisco, McClatchy assured himself as he waited for the bus at El Camino Real and Fremont Street: ocean breeze keeps it cool, all but two three days in the year: finest climate in the world for a white man, fog and all.

It was twenty years since he had lived in San Francisco, and his return visits had grown longer and longer between. For the first few years of their residence in Morera County, he and his wife and daughter had left the chicken ranch each Memorial Day and passed through the city on their way to Holy Cross Cemetery, but after they had taken over the Traveler's Rest they had been less faithful, and now it came to him that his last visit to San Francisco had been on the Sunday when he and his family had gone round that way on their trip to the Fair on Treasure Island—eight years ago! And the town had changed since the war, he'd heard. Bigger now. Houses all the way to the Ocean Beach in the Sunset district, where he could remember nothing but sand dunes. But the Richmond had been like that too when he'd been a boy, and look at it now. They'd call him an old-timer now, he supposed. Think of all the friends he hadn't seen for so long. He grinned to himself. By golly, they'll think I'm dead for years.

The Greyhound bus pulled in awkwardly. He climbed inside, a little man in a blue serge suit, and came to a vacant seat on the aisle. "This taken?"

A young soldier, only a boy with a single chevron, looked up at him. "Help yourself."

He sat down, hitching up his sharply creased trousers at the knees, and folded his arms.

The bus was nearly full. It was not a local but a big dusty Land Cruiser all the way from Oregon. Weary passengers in wrinkled clothes were looking out the windows curiously or idly at the town. The driver slammed the door, the bus hissed, lurched, and was off again, pounding out on the highway. McClatchy felt a little thrill, as when in boyhood he had ridden a few times on railroad trains.

Going home to Sampm Cisco; and in his mind its hills and towers rose before him. Be taking the family back for good, once the painting was sold. Once, if somebody had told him he'd ever leave it, he'd have told 'em they was crazy. But a man could never tell. Things happened you'd never expect. And sitting there with folded arms in the plunging bus, he marveled at the way they had happened to him. Once, he'd thought he was going to be a cop. Maybe if he'd grown a few inches taller he'd have been one, too. Inches! Think of that—how a few inches could change a man's life. . . .

"Nice country," the soldier said, turning to him from the window.

"Huh? Oh—yeah." Purely out of courtesy McClatchy glanced at it: the same yellow hills with broad green trees; a horse raising its head to look at the bus going by; suddenly a white barn, an old frame house. Hardly McClatchy's idea of scenery. His own taste ran to mountains covered with redwoods or tall yellow pines, where rivers ran down rocky gorges and cool lakes mirrored the clouds; landscapes vivid to him from photographs and movies of the high Sierra, where, he scarcely realized, he had never been.

The boy said: "Reminds me of Indiana, a little."

"Indiana!" McClatchy had never seen Indiana, but it shocked him to hear it compared to California. "That where you're from?"

"Yep."

"Ever see Yosemite?"

"No. Neat, uh?"

"*Oh-h*, yeah. Now there's something you ought to see while you got the chance. Or up on the Redwood Highway, where they got all them big redwood trees."

"We just come through there."

"What? Oh, down the Redwood Highway, sure." McClatchy had never been farther up the Redwood Highway than Healdsburg, but he said: "Well then you *seen* something. This here aint much."

The boy looked out more critically at "This here," and revised his opinion. "I guess Indiana aint as dry."

The native son was stung. "Dry year," he said lamely.

"Uh huh. Anyway it sure looks good after the Pacific."

"You been in the Pacific?"

"Yeah," wryly. "Just got back."

"You don't say. What part?"

"Over in the islands. Hawaya."

"Hawaya! Sa-ay, that must be all right, over in Hawaya. All of them palm trees and bathing beauties—huh? Always kind of wanted to see that."

"It's okay," the soldier said, "if you're not in the Army. I'll take Indiana."

"You mean you would for a fact? Aw, that's just 'cause your home's in Indiana. But someday you'll look back; wait, now, and see if you don't. Oh I tellya—it's a fine thing for a man to be able to see the world when he's as young as you are. And someday in Indiana, when it's snowing, you'll wish to God you was back in the land of the palm trees and the old hootchy-kootchy. Take a tip from an old buck, now, that's what you'll do."

"Not me," the boy said. "What's this place?" They were pulling in for another stop.

"This here? San Rafael. See that big bridge they got now—right over the town? That's new. That's what we want in Llagas. They're making lots of improvements like that now, all over the state."

From San Rafael the road arched over the railroad tracks, and for a moment suddenly, through the windows to the left across the aisle, a sweep of blue water was visible. Swiftly up a reaching grade, a plunge down, and again the water. The soldier was leaning forward to see it. "Oh," said his guide, "that's the bay. And see over there on the point? Gone now. Did you see that big gray building on the point? That was Sanna Quintin Prison."

"Yeah?"

"I was in it once. I seen a man hung. Had a friend that was a guard." McClatchy was shaking his head at the memory. "It give me the creeps to see that. They got us all in a little gray room behind the print shop, and here was this big platform, the gallas they call it, with the noose hanging down, and when they brought the man in he had a face on him like a man in a coffin. They had to hold him up. And when they dropped him through the trap half the people got sick. I seen even the warden was shaking, and it was old stuff to him—all in the day's work with those boys. I wouldn't trade with 'em."

"Who was the man that got hung?"

"Oh, nobody big. You never heard of him. Some poor stiff that killed a woman in L.A. Stanley C. Pike, his name was. But they don't hang you no more in California. They got the gas chamber now."

To the right Mount Tamalpais rose green against the sky, with the land rolling over to meet the broad base of it in a piedmont dark with trees through which the roofs of scattered houses could be seen. It was a view that quickened McClatchy's pride before the tourist. That was Larkspur over there, he announced, and Mill Valley, and *them* little places. And then the bus was crossing a broad bay meadow where meandered a little slough lined with the leaning arks of duck clubs, and where a few cattle grazed, their hoofs sinking deep in the soft earth, and the sky dappled the scene in varied lights, strangely, like a dream of summertime. Then they were crossing the low trestle over the end of Richardson's Bay—on the right the water lapped quiet as a lake at the foot of Tamalpais, a snowless Fujiyama; then skirting the mudflats, then ascending a long hill through a series of little cuts in vivid red and yellow rock, and to the left, very blue and close now in the intervals between the cuts, flashed the great Bay of St. Francis. Up the gracefully curving road roared the bus from Oregon, and inside there was a sense of imminence, of approaching something big and beautiful. At the crest of the hill the view opened wide into a blue panorama of water, islands, hills, and sky. Suddenly the bus was plunged into darkness pinpointed with yellow lights, and the tunnel walls hurled back at it the headlong clamor of its wheels. Daylight came up again in a burst. Ahead were the overwhelming red towers of the bridge, wheeling gulls, and San Francisco in the sun.

"Je-sus!" the soldier said.

And McClatchy answered, shining-faced: "Oh I tellya."

Then they were vaulting the Golden Gate at fifty miles an hour; to the right, the glancing ocean all the way to the sky; to the left, the bay, Alcatraz Island like an aircraft carrier, Goat Island (serving now as central caisson for that other bridge, the gray one, that reached across to Oakland), Treasure Island, ships, the slate-blue hills of Berkeley speckled with roofs; and dead ahead a tower of clean red steel that seemed to be slamming down on them like a giant blazing bolt from heaven. It is an exhilarating experience, this vault; it feels like a heroic deed; and the passengers, all but a few who presumably lived in this region and made the journey too often, lifted their heads and looked out the windows in excitement, or smiled at one another, companions for a few minutes upon a different plane.

"Yep," McClatchy said. "Quite a bridge they got here. People used to say it couldn't be built, you know, on account of the tide. Oh, they got a hell of a tide here. Look at the way the ocean rips in through the Gate there. That's Land's End over there. Point Lobos. And Mile Rock Lighthouse—see? And on this side . . ."

But the soldier's eye kept straying ahead to look at San Francisco; and no wonder. The perfect stranger approaching it on this bridge on a fine day might be inclined to accept San Francisco as advertised, a city of high romance: he comes upon it as upon one of those pinnacled medieval hilltop cities in a colored picture book. It waits upon its headland wreathing itself in a faint mist, through which its tall buildings rise like towers, rosy white and brown, the image of Carcassonne in the old story. The stranger might half expect to be greeted by troops of maidens with floral offerings and with eyes inquiring his pleasure.

"Nice!" the soldier said.

"Yep. Sampm Cisco; there she stands." And they looked at it together, the soldier with curiosity and appraisal, McClatchy with the fond pride of ownership. "First time you been here?"

"Uh huh."

"Is that a fact." McClatchy eyed the boy in happy vanity, and not without the pleasure of patronizing him. Like most San Franciscans who have never seen it, he conceived of the great mid-section of the country as a dreary stretch of betwixt and between denizened by yokels; and like many San Franciscans of his breed and generation, born on the brink of the beckoning ocean, he had never gone farther than a hundred miles in any direction—no, not twenty yards off the beach. When he had been a young man a Sunday picnic in Marin County had been deemed quite a sally. But looking at the soldier who had seen coconuts ripening in the sun, he thought: Poor kid; and was glad the boy's eyes were being opened to the wonder of the world. "Well," he said, "you've got a treat coming; it's quite a town. Yes, sir! I suppose you'll be taking one of them sightseeing busses—rubbernecks, we used to call 'em. Well, that's a good way to see the points of interest."

"Not me," the boy said. "I'm meeting a couple guys."

"Oh, now I see. Well, they's plenty to do; it's a pretty hot town, you know. Oh, I've had some hot times there in my day. I was born and raised there, you know. Born in the old South of Market and raised in the Mission. I seen the last of the old Barbary Coast. It was a hot one then, I can tell you. And I worked at the Palace Hotel."

"Where's a good place to eat?"

"Dinner, you mean? Oh, they's lots of places. City's famous for eating places, you know. The Haufbrau—the States, it is now. The Poodle Dog. Solari's. . . ."

"Expensive?"

"Some of 'em. You better try some place like Charles's Fashion Grill up on O'Farrell Street. That's a good place. But lea' me see, now. Well, now, it's a long time since I lived here. Twenty years. Maybe you better ask somebody if the old Fashion's still going. . . ."

Twenty years! The tourist looked at him dryly. "Yeah," he said, and as the bus pulled up at the tollgate he turned back to his window. Twenty years—*Jesus!*

McClatchy rode the bus to the terminal, which, to his surprise, was on Seventh Street now. He parted from the soldier with another recommendation that he look up Charles's Fashion Grill, shaking his hand and wishing him luck; and glancing about as he passed through the strange new terminal, he went friskily into the street, where the first slap of fresh air in his face was a satisfying reminder of his prediction that it would be cool in Sampm Cisco. People passing briskly, an old man in an old brown overcoat chomping his gums and inaudibly hawking newspapers on the alley, and across the street pigeons still fluttering in the cornices of the post office—the same as if he had never left.

But when he turned into Market Street, the thickness and bustle of the crowd that caught him up surprised him. Town must be humming, he thought: two years since the war and still humming. Growing. Before Pearl Harbor it was dead, to this. And dodging, weaving along, he looked into the passing faces as if searching for the face of a friend. Men with preoccupied faces striding by. Jouncing women downtown to market, with scarves over their heads—didn't used to see that in Sampm Cisco. Always wore hats. Children being dragged along by the hand, scolded; a little boy crying. Snatches of Midwest twang and Southern drawl. Negroes. Mexicans. A blind woman waddling up the street with an accordion: *Le-t me ca-all you sweet-heart,* and he smiled. He dug into his pocket and dropped a dime into her cup, not realizing that it was his homecoming offering, that he had given it to her because she was as much a part of home to him as the doddering newsboy and the pigeons.

Sampm Cisco!

The crowd was making him walk faster than he had been accustomed to walk in years, kept him dodging, weaving, but it all came back to him and he enjoyed it. He filled his little chest lustily and found the cool air poisoned with carbon monoxide. Busses, he thought, not noticing that the invaders were trolly busses: too many busses now. He cut across the broad street and observed that only two of the four sets of cartracks were still in use. Streetcars looking rickety too. City letting 'em go to pot. Finest transportation system in the world once. Putting in busses now. Big mistake. But they'd have subways soon. Talking about 'em now. Elevated freeways, even. Had to have 'em; bound to come. He could remember when Jim Rolph drove the last horsecar down Sutter to Market and down to the Ferry Building. . . .

He paused to gaze up the long rising reach of Powell Street to where a little marionette of a cablecar was just bending stiffly over the skyline for the descent. Powell Street. Man with a camera taking a snapshot of the car on the turntable at the bottom: tourist, probably; and McClatchy grinned at him, passing by. Bet the hotels are full of 'em. Usual gang in front of the bank, he saw. "Meet you in front of the Bank of America"—Bank of Italy, it used to be. Dingdong of a cablecar, clang of a traffic bell. Two pretty Chinese girls in sweaters, sports skirts, and bobby socks. Modren. And coming to the cigar store at the corner of O'Farrell, he enjoyed a knowing interior grin at the memory of whose parlor house had stood here once (which he had never entered in his life). He looked up O'Farrell Street for Charles's Fashion Grill. Yep: still there; kid'd find it (taking it for granted that the kid would try): get a good meal reasonable. Up to Geary Street to the St. Francis Hotel and across the street to peer down the ramp into the great concrete chamber under Union Square. Look at that! Make a good bomb shelter all right. Put the monument back up, too. Grass, trees. Even the pigeons. What'd they do next? He walked up to the corner and turned down Post Street as a red-faced young traffic officer in the intersection blew his whistle. He could remember when the cops wore helmets and long coats and had big mustaches and used to spit tobacco juice and you always used to hear 'em bang the lam'poles with their billies. . . .

But it was timidly that he entered one of the shops. A shop narrow, deep, serene, with walnut wainscoting halfway up like the great corridor of an English manorhouse, and hung with stately pictures in heavy old-golden frames—paintings of quiet landscapes, of women with piled hair and sweeping gowns, of men in ruffled collars or cuirrasses who looked as though they would have drawn and quartered such a villein in a minute. The dun-yellow carpet was silken, the walls above the woodwork were covered in burgundy cloth, and there was about the place an air of such intimidating gravity that McClatchy took off his hat. He saw four other mortals, two men and two women, grouped before a painting on the end wall; voices communicating in altar tones reached him indistinctly; then one of the four, a tall concave young man, began to speak in a tone so normal it was shocking. McClatchy approached uncertainly and saw with a thrill that the painting under discussion was his own. Then the tall young man noticed him, raised his brows, and said: "Ye-es? Something you wanted?"

"Me? Oh, I don't want nothing, only"—McClatchy dropped his voice to a whisper and raised his chin as if speaking across a barrier—"could you tell me is Mr. Markham in?"

"Mr. Markham?" the young man repeated, frowning, and said to the others: "Excuse me a moment." His mien, as he came round to McClatchy, was that of a man politely coping with a situation. "Perhaps I could help you."

"Oh no; no, thanks; I wouldn't want to butt in on the folks there; but if you'd just tell me where I could find Mr. Markham."

"I see. Well, what is it you wish to see Mr. Markham *about?*"

"It's about that painting there. He knows. McClatchy's the name."

"Oh—the owner!" From the clerk's expression the owner evidently looked worse to him than he had imagined. "Ye-es! Mr. Markham found the painting in your baah!"

"Yep," McClatchy grinned. "The old Traveler's."

"Ye-es. I must say you were very fortunate, weren't you? Well! Just wait a moment; I'll tell Mr. Markham you're here."

The alien in the art world was left standing hat in hand, fifteen feet from the painting and at an angle from it. He peered at it as he waited, unable to see it very well; and the temptation overcoming his shyness, he stepped up to it, saying as the others looked round at him: "Pardon *me;* I'm the owner, you see; first chance I had to look at it since they cleaned it off."

"Oh!" exclaimed the taller of the two women; she was a handsome gray-haired lively-looking matron in a Persian lamb jacket, who towered over McClatchy. "You're the man who keeps the tavern in Llagas!"

"Yes, ma'am."

The other woman, yoked in martens, was a little younger than the first, shorter, stouter, coarser of features, and of austere bearing. "Oh," she murmured a bit stiffly.

The two women were accompanied by a frail, pink-cheeked, and rather sweet-faced elderly man in a gray homburg. He smiled and nodded.

"And you really don't know where the painting came from?" the first woman asked.

"No, ma'am. All I can figure, maybe somebody got it at one of them railroad auctions that they have and peddled it to somebody had the place before we did. But nobody knows. But it sure looks different now they got it cleaned off. Yeah. Sa-ay, look at the man's face—don't that look like real skin? You'd think it was a human being looking at you."

"Yes indeed," the elderly man said.

McClatchy was looking at the painting, and the man and two women were looking at him. The tall woman was looking at him with amused curiosity, and the elderly man with an appearance of deep inward laughter, but the shorter woman with hard eyes which suddenly glinted, surprisingly enough, with rancor; and from the self-conscious half-smile on McClatchy's parted lips and the too frequent blinking of his lids it was plain that he knew their eyes were on him, but also that he thought they were looking at him in admiration. In fact he felt himself to be a romantic figure in those eyes. He was basking as modestly as possible in what he took to be gazes charmed by the luck and celebrity of the man whom fate had singled out to be the owner of the mysterious Rembrandt.

"Yes, sir!" he said; and then, partly because he was proud of the painting, partly because he felt that some further information was expected of him, he said: "And this picture's three hundred years old; would you believe that? Yes, ma'am, Rembrandt lived 'way back in the sixteen hundreds, over in Holland, now that's a fact."

At this the shorter woman's mouth tightened and she looked grimly at the other woman; but Persian Lamb only smiled rather tenderly and said: "Really?"

"Yes, ma'am."

There was another pause. McClatchy stood with hands on hips, blinking self-consciously at the painting. The cavalier sneered back at him across the centuries, out of another world. And suddenly McClatchy's face broke into a prankish grin, he raised one palm, flipped it sidewise from his temple in an urchin-like salute, and said antically: "Hi there, Dutch."

The tall woman threw back her head and laughed. McClatchy slid her a glance full of tomfoolery, saw Markham coming up with the clerk, and said: "Oh, hello, Mr. Markham; I was just saying if the old Dutchman don't look different cleaned up. I wouldn't hardly know him."

"Yes," Markham said, nodding pleasantly to the others, with whom he was not acquainted, "I think we did a pretty good job. There was one little spot on it, though, that we couldn't quite get off. There on the collar; see it? That's not dirt, it's a stain. Perhaps made by a chemical of some kind."

McClatchy put his face close to the Dutchman's and examined the spot. "Yeah, I see what you mean. By golly, I can tell you what done it, too—Four Roses! Holy Moses, it was that old Bob Doughty that done it, I should have wrung his neck."

"Whisky? Oh no, I hardly think——"

"*Sure* it was; I remember I wiped it off and that's just where the old s.o.b. threw it; excuse my language ladies but it burns me up; this old man that hangs around my place, regular old booze fighter he is, one night he gets sore at the picture—*I* don't know—*you* know how they get when they're all tanked up; and one night he gets to mumbling and grumbling, *talking* to the man in the picture, he was for a fact, and *I'm* not paying no attention to him, when all of a sudden bingo! if he don't throw his drink right across the bar at the man, what do you think of that, and now they can't get it off; can you blame me?"

"Oh, but," Markham smiled, "I don't think whisky would have made a stain like this. Anyway, there's not much damage done. You can hardly see it." He glanced at his wristwatch. "The photographer should be here any moment. Suppose you come up to my office while we're waiting. I have some news for you."

"Oh—sure. News, huh? Fine." McClatchy turned to the others. "Pleased to meet you."

Smiling, the tall woman looked after him as he left with Markham. "So that's the man."

"Yes," the clerk said. "Doesn't it just make you sick?"

"Ludicrous!" the other woman said. "Simply ludicrous! Whisky, indeed. Thank heaven it was rescued in time."

The pink-faced old man chuckled; his brows went up roguishly and he stood for a moment as if trying to bring some amusing story into exact mental focus; then giving his head a bird-like tilt to the right and throwing out his right knee, he flipped one hand off the top of his homburg and said: "He*llo*—Dutch."

Only the tall woman laughed. But then she made a compassionate face and said with an appeal: "Oh! the poor little man."

McClatchy was eagerly following Alfred Markham up the stairs to the office on the mezzanine.

The art dealer was a man of medium height and middle years, with blue eyes, sparse brown hair graying at the sides, and a cropped mustache; dressed in dark gray tweeds.

"News, huh?" McClatchy prompted as soon as they were seated.

"Yes," said Markham, leaning back in the swivel chair. "We had an offer this morning."

"An offer! For the painting?"

"We were offered a thousand dollars."

McClatchy looked shocked. "A thousand dollars! He-y, it's worth a lot more than that, aint it?"

The dealer chuckled. "Of course."

"We-ll, that's what I thought. What, were you kidding me?"

"Oh no; the offer was genuine."

"Well what's he take us for? *That* chiseler."

"He may have thought a thousand dollars would tempt you."

"Who, me? He'll have to do a lot better than a thousand bucks, I'll tell the world."

"Do you want to set a price on the picture now, or wait and see what the bidding is?"

"Well, but it's worth a fortune, aint it?"

"A fortune? Oh, my!" But then Markham considered that McClatchy kept a small country tavern. "Now that depends on what you mean by a fortune."

"Yeah, but that's what *you* said. I mean—I thought you said it was a—treasure."

"Oh, a treasure, certainly. But not exactly a commercial one. As I told you, too, this picture is a museum piece; but not all museum pieces are 'worth a fortune.' "

McClatchy looked at him in anxiety. He was remembering Walsh Reardon's appraisal, "A king's ransom," and wondering what the art dealer's idea of a fortune was. "Yeah, but—but how much?"

Tolerantly despising the tavernkeeper's purely commercial approach to a masterpiece, the man of art drew from his desk a badgered-looking copy of *Art Prices Present*. "The prices of Old Masters are governed by the market. This booklet is our guide. It tells us what is being paid these days in the leading galleries of the world. So let's just look up the quotations on Rembrandts," said Markham, who had in fact looked up the quotations on Rembrandts at the first suspicion that he had his hands on one. "Now here's something—Rembrandt's *Pilgrim at Prayer*. It sold at the Parke-Bernet Galleries in New York for seventy-five thousand dollars."

The tavernkeeper's face lit up with joy. "It did?" he said.

Markham glanced at him, smiling thinly, and looked up another "quotation." He found that at Sotheby's, London, Rembrandt's *Lady* had sold for the equivalent of only $188.

McClatchy looked thunderstruck.

But Markham next found that *Early Self-Portrait* had sold in London for the equivalent of $54,000. Next, *Saskia:* $2400. Then *Gentleman:* $464. *Portrait of the Artist's Father:* $900. Another *Father:* $750.

To the owner of *The Lost Dutchman* it was like hearing his fate toyed with by a lunatic stock market ticker.

There was a knock at the door; the clerk entered. "The photographers are here, Mr. Markham. They've brought lights and things."

"Oh. All right. See that they get set up, will you, Stanley. We'll only be another minute or two."

"Right." Raking contumelious eyes over McClatchy, Stanley withdrew.

McClatchy's eyes were back on Markham. "Go on," he urged, and swallowed; his mouth was dry.

Markham quoted on: *Zacharias in Temple:* $9,240. *Circumcision:* $240. Another *Father:* $11,500. *Portrait of the Artist's Mother:* $120. "You see?"

McClatchy was pale. "Uh-huh. Gee, only a hundred and twenty bucks for his own mother."

"Some are better than others."

"Yeah, but—but what would you say this painting of *mine* is worth, though?"

The stressed word pierced Markham. He hesitated, selecting the dullest sword. "Well, we have an appraisal from Sir Patrick Locklear, one of the best judges of Rembrandts in the world. Sir Patrick based his fee on it, so we may assume he didn't set it any lower than he thought reasonable." Smiling at his own gentle humor, Markham paused, looking at the man who hung with so much anxiety on his words. "He appraised the picture at five hundred pounds—two thousand dollars."

"Two thou——" McClatchy's breath failed. He looked at the floor.

Markham watched him with a quizzical expression, the avenger of his world, of the two concentric worlds of culture and money, upon the brash intruder. He resumed: "Fortunately, however, Sir Patrick's appraisal hasn't come out publicly. At the press interview I was afraid it would, but they got him off the subject. And we must remember that Sir Patrick is not a dealer; I doubt whether he understands salesmanship, at least as we practice it in America," went on the man of art. "He may not have realized that several unusual factors in this case can boost the price if we play our cards right. To begin with, this painting has no market history; no value has ever been set on it, so far as anyone knows; and a story goes with it, some mystery attaches to it, so aside from its merits as a work of art it becomes a sort of curio, at least for a while. And we've got this picture a good deal of publicity. Why, this picture is famous. Millions have heard of it who've never heard of *Night Watch* or *The Syndics* or *Christ at Emmaus*. Sir Patrick himself, you know, did that for us," Markham smiled cunningly, "and without extra charge. There are tricks in every trade, you see. Even in art we have to be a good salesman. And you may depend upon it, I'll get the very top price."

The tavernkeeper had been following this discourse closely, tense with revived hope and new uncertainty. "How—much do you think?"

"Oh, I don't want to commit myself to a definite figure yet. Let's wait and see how the bidding goes."

"Yeah, well, uh, I wouldn't want to pin you down and then hold you to it, but what would you say, just offhand, like, at a guess?"

"At a wild guess? We might get five thousand. Possibly six."

McClatchy's hopes were dashed for the second time. He said "Oh" almost inaudibly, and looked at his clasped hands. "Six thousand'd be tops, huh?"

"Oh, come, Mr. McClatchy, six thousand would be a magnificent price for your picture. And mind you, I'm not predicting we'll get it. We don't live in the fabulous twenties, you know. If I weren't a very optimistic man I'd have said four, and that would be going Sir Patrick double."

"Oh, oh sure, I know; I was just asking." He sat leaning forward with his elbows on his knees; he ducked his head and ran his thin hair through his fingers. "And you was saying about Sir Locklear—what did *he* soak us?"

"His charge? Two hundred dollars; and very cheap, I must say. Plus his expenses, of course, which only came to about a hundred more. I put him up in my own home, which saved something, and wouldn't think of charging you for it. I'll more than make it up in my commission, since the good Sir Patrick's name has increased the value of the picture."

"Commission—oh—yeah. And what will that come to, if you don't mind me asking?"

"Ten per cent—some dealers would charge more, but ten per cent is equitable, I think. But of course that doesn't include the charge for cleaning and so on—X rays, infra-red rays, pigment analysis, metallurgist's report, canvas report, expert opinions—I had to pay for those things myself. I really don't recall what they came to, but I think about four hundred dollars."

"Four hundred dollars! Well, let's see, now: with Sir Locklear's bill, that's seven hundred right there. Oh, and the commission. Say we get six thousand bucks, that'd be six hundred commission; plus seven hundred is thirteen hundred."

"If we sell the picture for six thousand, which I can't guarantee. And the man who found the picture, remember?"

"Oh-h, yeah. . . ."

"He undoubtedly was entitled to something. As a matter of fact, he demanded ten per cent, but I settled with him on your behalf for seventy-five dollars, which I think was a bargain."

"Uh huh. Yeah, *that* poor guy. If it hadn't been for him we wouldn't of had nothing. And here he's dead and gone. Yeah." McClatchy briefly mourned again the passing stranger; but his own troubles reclaimed his attention. "Well, that makes thirteen hundred seventy-five. . . . Oh!" he started. "And I suppose they'll be taxes, sure as shooting!"

Markham laughed. He had not thought of the taxes. "Yes, those we can always be sure of—death and taxes, as they say. And that brings up another interesting question. How will they compute the tax?"

"How do you mean?"

"Why, they'll have to charge you a capital gains tax on your profit. But how will they find the profit? Did you actually pay anything for the picture when you bought the tavern?"

"No. That was just part of the whole layout."

"Wasn't the picture itemized among the fixtures?"

"No."

"Then they'll have to set a percentage of what you paid for the fixtures—arbitrarily—and subtract that figure from whatever you realize from the sale of the painting; and charge you twenty-five per cent of that."

"Twenty-five per cent!"

The dealer solemnly nodded. And as a successful merchant he naturally enjoyed the pained surprise of the newcomer to the higher tax brackets. "Oh yes," he smiled, wagging his head, "that's the capital gains tax, you know. Twenty-five per cent of anything held more than six months. Fifty per cent if you've held it less than six months. Oh yes."

"But—wa-ait awhile. If they allow me, say, fifty bucks as a per cent of the fixtures—but, hell, I wouldn't bet they'd go that high. But even if they did, fifty from six thousand is fifty-nine hundred and fifty; and twenty-five per cent of that would be—what? Well, on six thousand it'd be fifteen hundred, so it'd be a little under that. Plus thirteen hundred seventy-five for the commission and all is—is—almost twenty-nine hundred! That'd only leave me about thirty-one hundred! And that's if we sell it for six thousand. But maybe we'll only get five, or four, or——"

"Tha-at's right." Markham said, moving his head up and down. He did not remind McClatchy that the capital gains tax would be computed on the net and not the gross profit, but smiled sympathetically and reminded him of the state income tax and the sales tax.

"Holy mackerel!"

"Yes, that's the way it is these days, you know. That's why we can't get as much for Old Masters as we used to. Why, a man with a hundred-thousand-dollar income has all he can do to live and pay his taxes. Oh yes, that's what the New Deal did for us," Markham said complacently. "Oh yes."

"Hell," McClatchy said dazedly, "it looks like when it's all done I won't have nothing to show for it but the green spot on the wall."

"Oh, now! it isn't that bad. Whatever you wind up with will be clear profit. The picture didn't cost you a cent, after all!"

"No . . . that's right . . . it didn't." But the tavernkeeper showed no enthusiasm for this view. He sighed. "I guess my hopes was too high, that's all. It looks like I was a damn fool."

"Well, the picture isn't going to make you rich, if that's what you thought. If you did think so you're better off being set straight about it at once. But, man!" Markham said encouragingly, "you're ahead of the game! ahead of the game!"

"Yeah . . . I guess so." But how could he explain that to Bessie and Arline?

Markham jovially chuckled. "Well, then." He gave McClatchy's shoulder a heartening shake, and rose. "We can't keep the photographer waiting any longer, you know. Shall we go down?"

"Oh! I forgot. Sure. Okay. After you."

Downstairs they found the painting arranged on an easel in the middle of the floor, a camera standing on a tripod in front of it, and three adjustable lamps on iron standards trained upon it from the sides. The photographer's assistant lighted the lamps. McClatchy took his place beside The Lost Dutchman. The photographer posed him, directed changes in the lighting, ducked under the black cloth of the camera, and reappeared.

"Now!" he said to the woeful man standing blind in the glare. "Smile!"

He came out of the gallery and went yawing down Post Street, staggered by disappointment and heavy with the news that he must take home.

For myself it don't matter so much, but it's going to be a blow to the folks. Women get their hopes up about a thing like this, and it's my fault, I shouldn't have let 'em get all worked up about it. But how did I know? Everybody was so blame excited—the newspapers, even.

Then a suspicion flashed into his mind. Had Markham deceived him? Oh, but hell, Markham had the book to prove a painting wasn't worth a fortune just because it was a Rembrandt. Hundred and twenty bucks for the man's own mother! And Markham was an honest man. Hell, look at the rent he must pay. He give it to me straight, and the only question is what am I going to tell the wife and daughter.

Out of Montgomery Street swarmed a multitude from the financial district, which informed him that it was lunch time. He rolled round the gore corner of Schwabacher & Company, walked up to Kearny Street, and into Geary, and entered a cafeteria.

At the table he deliberated. "Well, Bess," he might say, "Mr. Markham thinks maybe he can get us six thousand bucks for that painting; we can do a lot with six thousand bucks"—maybe he'd put it that way. But what was the use of getting her to expect six thousand when it might be only five or four or . . . And all of them expenses out of that—and the taxes! What was the government trying to do? Too many chiselers in Washington, that was the trouble. . . . But what was he going to tell Bessie and Arline?

He wandered into the street again and stood on the corner, aimless, watching the people. By golly but they was a lot of dinges in Sampm Cisco now—war must have brought 'em. And it struck him that there was something different about the other people, too. Didn't look like Sampm Ciscans; not many did, anyhow. Look at this guy, now. And that one. They aint Sampm Ciscans. And that woman; looks like she come from the hot country—Texas, maybe. War brought a lot of strangers. And maybe for all I know the new generation of pure dyed-in-the-wool Sampm Ciscans is different. Not like the old-timers at all. Anyhow, something's the matter. Different. The place has changed.

And he felt lonely.

So he went into a cigar store and looked up the address in the telephone book. It was at 1623½ Market Street now. He boarded a streetcar and rode up Market Street.

It had been his custom when riding a streetcar to stand on the back platform talking to the conductor, who, in his loose Union-blue or Confederate-gray uniform, had always been of the same breed as the policemen, firemen, bartenders, and politicians of the city, as sure as one found pigeons in Union Square. It gave him a shock to discover that the conductor of this car was a Negro. For the first time in his life he experienced the rancor of intolerance against the black race. He watched the conductor critically. It's all Muni now, he thought; must be them jokers up at the City Hall looking for the colored vote. I bet he don't even know the names of the streets. What are they trying to do, ruin the city?

But when he got off the car, his eyes brightened at the sight of Local 41, Bartenders' Union.

There she stands! And with an eye on the traffic he scuttled across the street to it.

Local 41 is entered like a lair of mountain banditti, through a dark cavernous corridor opening at the distance of twenty or thirty feet into the great hiring hall, and here it is as if a few men have gone into hiding with their toys and comforts from the essentially feminine culture of the times. No chrome here, nor mirrors, nor carpets, nor indirect lighting. Everything practical and forthright: a floor of bare boards, a high ceiling where the smoke can go, plain round tables covered in green felt, round wooden chairs with supports for the elbows, a pool table, a snooker table, and spittoons. The offices are out of sight behind wickets in one wall; and today there was a sign that said JOHN DEASY FOR SECRETARY. McClatchy guessed that Deasy was a new man come up fast, never having heard of him. The click of ivory balls took his attention to the pool table; but the players too were strangers. He sauntered over to the left, where the men at four card tables were playing the eternal pinochle and panguingui. Some looked up as he came among them grinning. Their faces were the old faces, large at the jowls, purple and red, and they sat as they had always sat, with their hats pushed back on their heads, some with cigarettes pasted to their lips, others munching the butts of cigars, or chewing, and he heard the same old voices. Bartenders, colleagues, his own kind. But he was not acquainted with any of them. They nodded impersonally and went on with their games, the same games. They laughed, cursed and joshed one another with the old camaraderie, and the cards were the same, and the smoke curled up as of old, but he stood among them a stranger.

After a few minutes of watching he wandered over to a wicket, and a man in a white shirt looked out at him questioningly. It was not Joe Henshaw.

"What can I do for you?"

"Joe around?"

"He's off sick."

Sick or not, Joe became for the moment McClatchy's link with this place, his card of reference. "He is? That's too bad. What seems to be the trouble?"

"Oh, the old trouble, I guess."

"Yeah? What trouble is that?"

"Diabetes."

"No! I didn't know Joe had diabetes."

"*Oh-h,* yeah. Had it for years. Has to give himself a shot with the needle every morning."

"You don't tell me. He always looked like such a healthy fellow."

"Joe?"

"What's the matter, is he failing?"

A shake of the head. "That shot in the leg is all that keeps him going. It's stoke up or goodbye with *those* fellows, you know."

"No, is that a fact. Poor Joe. He was the salt of the earth."

"Yeah, they don't make 'em like Joe no more. Something I can do for you?"

"Oh, no. Just thought I'd drop in and see some of the old gang. But I don't see none of 'em around."

"You a member?"

"*Me?* Well I got a traveling card over at the local in Llagas now; I got a little place of my own over there. But I was a member here for years. This used to be my old hangout, only it was at McCoppin and Valencia then—before Prohibition."

"Old-timer, huh?"

"*Oh-h,* yeah. I broke in at the old P'trera Saloon, back in 'thirteen. Then I was at the Techau Tavern, and on the Barbary Coast, and after that I was at the Palace Hotel. Ferguson was president then; God rest his soul, I seen in the paper where he died. And then Prohibition come in and we had to give up the charter."

"Uh huh. Who was you looking for?"

"Oh, nobody in particular. But I thought it'd be a cold day I wouldn't find Barney Doyle here."

"Doyle? Don't know him."

"Don't know Barney Doyle, the Butchertown delegate—old According-to Doyle we used to call him?"

"Just a minute." The man disappeared from the wicket for a moment, and returned. "Oh. Bernard J. Doyle, yeah. He's dead."

"Dead!"

"Yep. Nineteen forty-one."

"No! Is that so! Why, Barney Doyle was younger than me! God rest his soul, I'm sorry to hear it. I suppose you don't know how it happened, huh? No. Well. We all get it sometime."

"You ought to know Mike Bartelmy."

"Mike Bartelmy? Do I *know* him? Old Mike? Sure I know him."

"Mike's generally around, but he lost his wife the other day."

"Oh, that's too bad. His wife, you say? Did he have a wife?"

"Sure he had a wife. He's got two boys in high school. I thought you said you knew him."

"Mike? Sure I know him. I know him for years. Only I didn't know he was married."

"Well, all I know, he had her in the hospital for the last five years."

"No, is that a fact! I didn't even know he had a wife. Poor old Mike. I know him for years."

"Well, now, there's somebody you ought to know," the man said, pointing, and McClatchy turned to behold hobbling across the floor from the entrance an old man with a cane; he was badly bent over and his head shook as he walked.

"That old man? Now who's he?"

"That's old John Sullivan."

"Sullivan! Mr. Sullivan?" In amazement McClatchy recognized the horrible example of his youth, the man of whom he had said to Bessie before ever they were married: "He can't even hold a job. And you know why—he's a boozer, that's why. Bartenders aint supposed to touch the stuff." "Holy Moses, is *he* still going?"

"Sure. He was working for the Union League Club here till about four or five years ago; they retired him. He's over eighty."

"You don't say. Has he all his faculties?"

"Sa-ay, you'd be surprised. Mind's as keen as yours is. Yeah, he knows his way around. He's a wonder."

"You don't tell me. Well, I'll just pay my respects to him. Thanks for your trouble. I know him ever since I was a boy." And McClatchy went after the old man. "Mr. Sullivan, excuse *me* . . ."

"Huh?"

"Excuse me, Mr. Sullivan. I'm Dan McClatchy. Remember me? My wife's folks lived in the same flat you did on Fifteenth Street. Bessie Moyles, she was; Tom Moyles's daughter."

"Tom Moyles? He's dead."

"I married his daughter, Bessie Moyles. She's my wife now."

"Oh! Little Bessie? That so? Yes, I remember Bessie." The voice was a croak; the wasted neck looked scarcely strong enough to sustain the wobbling skull.

"I'm Dan McClatchy. Used to live on the same block, right across from Recreation Park there."

"You did? Well! You a bartender now?"

"Me? Sure. I got a little place of my own over in Llagas now."

"Llagas? Oh. That so?"

"How's Vince?"

"Vince? Oh! Fine. Fine. He's down at the Palace now."

"The Palace Hotel? Vince is? I used to work down there myself!"

"Ye-uh. Pied Piper Room. Good job. You know Vince?"

"Sure I do. I went to school with him."

"You did? Is that so. Well. Glad to of seen you."

"Thanks. You're looking fine, Mr. Sullivan."

"Yeah. Oh, I'm holding on, holding on."

"Good luck to you, Mr. Sullivan." McClatchy watched him hobble off, a man he would have supposed "dead for years," the boozer who had not been able to keep a job, who had broken all the rules, and lost all reputation, and who, thirty-some years later, was still "holding on" in the bosom of the union. But a ruin of a man for all that, a human hourglass confronting the ex-boy who had lived on the same block and telling him the time. McClatchy shook his head after him, chilled, but marveling, then, with a last look round, turned and went back into the street.

And poor Barney Doyle dead. And Joe Henshaw only cheating the undertaker by hopping himself up every morning with the needle. And Mike Bartelmy all at once married and in mourning, and him with two boys in high school. And a fellow named Deasy running for secretary. Sure enough, they's been changes made. I must be changed myself. Time marches on. Not a pinochle or pan game with a face in it I knew, but the king, queen, jack, and joker. Twenty years —there's the joker. . . . And he still had to tell Bessie and Arline about the painting.

He took a streetcar for downtown, half resigned to going home now, much as he dreaded it; and this time, though the conductor was a white man of the breed he knew, he did not stand on the platform, but went and found a window seat in the front compartment, preferring to be alone with what had happened to him today; and the two misfortunes chased each other round in his mind. He had come home to San Francisco and it had not known him, and he was going

back to Llagas, where he had never belonged, to live out the rest of his
able days, probably, in the Traveler's Rest. And in Llagas at this
minute Bessie and Arline were building castles in the air; especially,
he knew, Arline. In her mind Arline had the Traveler's Rest already
sold, and had them all living in San Francisco; and could he blame
her? I was thinking the same way myself, thinking this was going to
give us a new life; and didn't I tell Bessie the painting was worth a
fortune? I got the both of 'em thinking we struck it rich, and now I
got to tell 'em I made a little mistake and it's going to be the same
old stuff, Bessie cooking the grub and Arline dishing it out and Billy
hanging around the joint while the old man hustles the booze. And
what else have they got to look forward to from me? I'm fifty-five.
Where's all the years gone to? An old-timer is what the fellow called
me, and that's what I am. It's too late. A man don't realize till it's too
late. I used to have Bessie believing I was going to be a big shot in
politics. Politics! And then I told her if she'd stand for a little bootlegging we'd all be rich in no time. And Tommy got killed. And then
I told her we'd have a big ranch-o in the country, and we almost
went broke having it. And then I told her we'd be in on the ground
floor when the liquor come back and we'd make it yet. And there she
is today, cooking! Day in, day out, in that damned little Llagas. But
not a peep out of her. Thank God anyways for a good woman. But
what has she got to be thankful for? She should of married Pete Co-
halen. And Arline all of a sudden widowed, waiting on the counter.
And little Bill—what has he got to look forward to from me? In five
years I'll be sixty. Holy Moses! And he turned anxiously to look at his
face in the window.

But, swaying, jerking, and clanging, the streetcar had struck the
downtown traffic now, and after a moment his gaze pushed through
the window to the streets of San Francisco. Buildings, streetcars, automobiles, busses; pedestrians striding along; each unit of that orderly
chaos intent upon its own errand. Familiar, yet strange. He remembered the flat in Clara Street, his earliest memory of home; and the
Great Earthquake and Fire, and standing with his mother in the soup
line at the Potrero Camp, and the miserable downpour of Saturday
night, and the merciful sunshine of Sunday morning, Mass in the
open, and that evening someone's playing "Buffalo Gals" on a salvaged piano, with the city in ruins and the air choked with cinders
—*Buffalo gals, you coming out tonight? To dance by the light of the
moon!* And the house on Fifteenth Street, and the crowds swarming
up to the ball park, and the flat on Guerrero Street where he and
Bessie had lived after they were married, and the night of June 30,

1919, the wild, singing, staggering eve of Wartime Prohibition. Gone. And inexplicably as he gazed out the window he remembered the man with the enormously swollen back of the neck whom he had used to see so often on the streets, and whose name he had never known; then suddenly in his mind he was confronted by the face of Eddie Graney, and thought: He must be dead for years. And the familiar spectacle of Foghorn Murphy bawling out that there was going to be a ballgame today. Yesterday. And Kid Sullivan; the king of the pickpockets, they used to call him, he remembered; had a place on Ellis Street. And Johnny O'Brien that played the piano; whenever McCormack'd come to town, Johnny'd go up to the hotel and play for him, and they'd go to it all night. Men about town, the old town; gone. The scene from the window saddened, fascinated, repelled, and beckoned him. But the thought of Llagas made him sadder. Next was Seventh Street: should he get off there and take the bus to Llagas? He tried to think of somewhere else he might go in San Francisco first. And then he remembered Vince. . . .

He had not been inside the Palace Hotel since he had worked behind its bar, so he was able to fix exactly how long ago it had been: twenty-eight years! But he saw, entering the lobby from New Montgomery Street, that it did not look very different from the way he remembered it. It came back to him that to reach the bar in those days you had gone down a flight of white marble steps, and after a bit of exploration he located exactly such a flight. But at the bottom he stopped in astonishment—he was in the men's room.

He went up the steps, and in the main corridor found two barrooms side by side, the Pied Piper Buffet and the Happy Valley. He entered the Pied Piper. This was the men's bar, the old bar, restored after Repeal. There were many sturdy oak tables and chairs in this spacious sanctum, and down the left-hand wall, where by the vanishing monastic tradition it always used to be, ran the long mahogany altar of the old god of the place. And there came to serve him a priest of the temple, all in white, over his left forearm his maniple, a bar towel. He was tall, heavy of haunch, paunch, and purple jowl, and almost completely bald. On recognizing him, indeed, the pilgrim was shocked; but then the pilgrim's face went warmly aglow, and he said:

"Hello, Vince!"

Vincent Sullivan looked at him uncertainly, but nodded and like a good merchant said: "Hi."

"What the hell, don't you know me? I'm Dan McClatchy!"

"Oh!" A large welcome expanded the purple face. "Sure!" Vince swung across the bar a great soft paw, which McClatchy shook, and said: "Hello, Dan! Sa-ay, I been reading about you. Seen your picture in the paper."

"Yep. That was me."

"Yeah, I know. I says to the wife: That's old Dan McClatchy used to live at Fifteenth and Valencia, I went to school with that fellow. But just now you had me going for a minute. Long time since I seen you."

"Yeah, I wouldn't have recognized you neither, but I just seen your father, he told me you was working here now."

"Oh, you run into the old man, huh?"

"Yeah, up at the union. Say, he's a wonder for his age, aint he. I thought he'd be dead for years."

"Pop? Naw. He'll live to be a hundred. Goes down to the union every day and hangs around."

"Is that so!"

"Yeah—hangs around."

"Now is that a fact."

"*Oh-h*, yeah. He'll be eighty-three, you know."

"Eighty-three! Well, look at that."

"Yeup. He's a wonder, all right. What'll it be, Dan?"

"Oh, the bevo, I guess."

"Sure thing." Vince drew a glass of beer.

"I used to work here myself, you know," McClatchy said.

"Here at the Palace?"

"Sure. In the old days. Before Prohibition. Oh, this was a great place in them days."

"Yeah, I'll bet. It aint what it was," Vince said, setting the drink on the bar.

"It aint?"

"Oh, it's busy around noon, but not much after. A men's bar don't go so well no more, you know."

"No, I guess it don't at that. Aw, that's too bad. Why, at this time of day the place'd be jammed. Biggest men in Sampm Cisco used to come in here."

"Yeah?"

"*Oh-h*, yeah. Jim Coffroth, Tom Finn, K.C.B. . . ." McClatchy cocked his head, half closing his eyes, as if seeing the room thronged with bygone heroes. "Mr. Tom McCann—oh, he was a fashion plate; I remember he always wore a derby hat. Senator Nealon, Tod Sloan— remember him, the world-famous jockey? I seen him standing right here at the bar with Charles F. Hanlon, the big lawyer. Say, didn't this place used to be down where they got the men's room now?"

"Could be." Then Vince brought him up to date with a jolt. "I guess you're sitting on top of the world now, huh?"

"Me?"—bitterly. "Yeah, that's what I thought. They told me it was worth a fortune, but now it turns out it's only worth a few thousand, and when I get through paying the cost of the investigation and the cleaning and the commission and the taxes and I don't know what all, I'll be lucky if they don't throw me out in the street."

"No! Do you mean it?"

"Sure I mean it."

"How come?"

"Well"—and McClatchy told the story.

"Uh *uh!*" Vince grunted painfully, and he shook his head, not so much in sympathy with his old friend, perhaps, as because he, being a man also, was disappointed at the negation of anything magic and joyful in the world, dimly sensing that somehow it affected him. "And you never knew where the painting come from, huh?"

"Nope."

This was the wonderful thing. This was the thing that some invisible, intangible, ever hovering, iconoclastic force in their midst had deflated and cheapened, to sadden every mother's son who ever believed in rainbow ends or put two dollars on a horse. And again Vince shook his head. "I guess you can't believe everything you read in the papers, huh?"

"The papers!" McClatchy snorted. He sipped his beer.

"That's the way it goes," Vince said.

"Yeup."

And they were sad together, because that was the way it went.

"Anyways," McClatchy said, "how's it going with you?"

"Oh, can't complain."

"How's the family?"

"Growing. I'm a grandfather now."

"No!" McClatchy remembered Vincent Sullivan as a lean youth, and a few minutes ago had been grieved to discover the same person in the bald-headed purple-faced mass that had come forward to serve him; it had made him wonder how he himself had changed; and now the information that Vince was a grandfather made him think of himself again in terms of what had happened to Vince.

"Yep," Vince said. "Got a grandson almost four."

"So's mine!"

"Yeah?" Half covertly, Vince shot at McClatchy a sharp glance of observation, under which McClatchy's morale bent a little. But just then Vince was called to the service of another customer.

Fat, McClatchy thought; makes him look older; and he's bald. And look at his face. . . .

Toying with his glass, and lamenting, as he waited for Vince, he looked up at the well-remembered painting behind the bar: Maxfield Parrish's storybook illustration (somehow so appropriate to San Francisco, and of course to a barroom), after which the room is named: *The Pied Piper.* The huge rectangular canvas depicts the legendary vagabond piper of the Middle Ages charming the children of the village of Hamelin to their mysterious fate in the mountains—Bunting, the minstrel knave, piping some demoniac lullaby which the children cannot resist: they follow: their parents will never see them again. One tradition connects the legend with an incident of the Children's Crusade of 1212, another with some forgotten tragedy of 1284, the year from which Hamelin long dated its documents, in memory, it is said, of something that happened to its *Kinder.* And in the faces and postures of the children the artist has caught something that has touched hearts across the Palace bar for nearly half a century. It touched McClatchy's now, and as he sat there, an uncritical, easily touched little Celt, seeming to see in the painting the face of his dead son, low voices startled him. He turned his head; there stood a man and *two women!* They were looking at the picture. They left as Vince returned, but annoyed by this invasion of what was supposed to be exclusively a men's bar, McClatchy indicated their departing figures with a jerk of the head, and complained:

"I thought they kept the ladies out of here."

"They let 'em in after five o'clock now," Vince said.

"They do? Oh, that's a big mistake. They never done that in my day. But what the hell, it aint even two-thirty yet."

"Aw, those two just come in to see the painting. You can't keep 'em out anyhow. Their old men get a few shots under their belt and go out and tell 'em about it and then they want to come in and have a look at it."

"They do?"

"Sure. That painting's famous. Do you know they got it insured for thirty thousand dollars?"

"They have?"

"Betcha. That painting's known all over the world. It's a big asset to a place like this. People come in here just to look at it."

"Is that a fact!"

McClatchy, of course, had known this before, but now it appeared to thrill him. He gazed at the picture with an electrified expression. He was remembering Alfred Markham's words about *The Lost Dutch-*

man: "Why, this picture is famous." The black disappointment that he had carried here from the Markham Galleries fell away. It had come to him that he was the bearer of good news, after all. It had come to him that, properly exploited, his Rembrandt *was* a treasure. And in his mind he was already heralding to his wife the vision that had smote him in the painted hills of Germany:

"Bessie, I got an idea!"

6

A LEAF FROM THE PALACE HOTEL

Arline was so hopeful, so sure. Who wouldn't have been sure, after all that had happened? After all those pictures the family had been posing for, after seeing them appear with the story in newspapers and magazines, after those announcements to the world certified by the famous Sir Patrick Locklear? It was a Rembrandt painting, worthy of millionaires, and the news was all over town. She had been shown a vision of a new life. And the effect on Arline could be marked in her appearance.

She knew that she might never hope to become a beauty. When she looked in the glass she saw a broad face tinted faintly auburn by the sprinkling of freckles lightly overlain by powder, a broad and fleshy nose, hair neither red nor brown, brows and lashes a pallid auburn against fair skin, which made the blue eyes look darker. The eyes comforted her. But she despaired of her frame, her broad hips and shoulders, her farm-girl thighs and arms; and although she thought well of her "bust line," she had always dressed to minimize it, out of modesty.

Modesty was hers by training; by nature she was a lusty young woman with the Celtic imagination. Experience and her own kindness had humbled her, but when, after only a few months of marriage to a dim young man, she had found herself a widow and then a mother, trudging a dismal rut, joked with by the old regulars she served in the restaurant, taken for granted, she had begun to neglect what looks she had. Billy, she told herself, was the one that mattered now. But Billy was a burden. There had been times when she wished she might abandon him to his grandparents and go off somewhere.

There had been times of regretting her marriage and dreaming how it might be if Billy had not been born. The thought had horrified her. It had seemed a manifestation of some monstrous perversion in her nature. Then, lying awake, she would hear him murmuring fitfully in his sleep, and getting up, would go and kneel beside his bed and soothe him till he slept peacefully again, and would think how much a baby he was still, how innocent and helpless he looked, and how poor a childhood he was having, her fatherless boy, and her throat would ache with loving him. The truth was, perhaps, that she had been made for many children, but that, as yet, children could not have taken all she had to give. Discouraged, she had neglected herself, but not without blaming Billy.

So far as the change in her appearance was tangible, it dated from the night only a month ago when she had begun again to cleanse and cream her face before going to bed—the night of the day Mr. Markham had telephoned from San Francisco to say that the painting was a treasure. She did her face every night now, and had subscribed at Grace's Beauty Shop for six facials, of which Grace had already given her two; and after posing with her parents for the first newspaper pictures, she had gone on a diet. She had already lost six pounds. Grace was also rinsing her hair with henna, "just to bring out the bronze highlights." Her hair was never untidy now, and because she was giving it more attention it looked crisper. Her eyebrows, thanks to tweezers and pencil, were, if not in the best of taste, gracile and more sharply defined, and she darkened her lashes. Her lipstick was more often renewed and more carefully applied. Her eyes were brighter. And she had bought two new dresses—one, most optimistically, a dinner dress, just in case, the other, unfortunately, a spectacular print; and a new hat and——

"Now here's something," the salesgirl had said, "that would go well with your coloring."

"That? Oh, I don't wear them."

"You don't?"

"I'm too large."

"What? Heavens, I never heard of anything so silly. With that bust line you *should* wear them."

"Oh, no! I'd be so conspicuous!"

"Attractive, you mean. Why, the smartest women in the country wear them."

—And a kelly green sweater; though she had insisted on one that was a size too large for her, and planned to wear it only with a jacket.

She was still too heavy, of course, but she was trimmer and livelier. And it was all because she was so hopeful, so sure. What was more, others had remarked on the change in her—"What have you done to yourself, Arline?" . . . "Hey, I notice you're all fixed up these days, kid; what's cooking, got a new boyfriend?"

No, she had no boyfriend, but the possibility that one might come along seemed less remote to her. She did not think it so unlikely that she would marry again. Why shouldn't she? Billy needed a father; Billy had never known a father. And she was still young; why couldn't she find him one? Why not—in San Francisco!

This was her outlook as she went lightly down her rut toward the Traveler's Rest with her son by the hand on the afternoon of her father's visit to the Markham Galleries.

Passing the gas station, she noticed that the eyes of the policeman who stood beside his car talking to the attendant were following her with a speculative, unofficial gaze. It was the same policeman who had driven her home that night with Billy. Going by, she smiled at him and said hello silently, with her lips. She saw him start a little, like a man caught staring, and ask himself: Who's that? And then she saw it strike him. He called: "Sold that picture yet?"

"Not yet."

"Better hurry up."

"Want to buy it?"

"Sure wish I had the dough."

He was a tall rugged-looking man, and she judged him "kind of cute." She laughed, nodding goodbye, and passed on, towing Billy. And in a breathless whisper Billy asked: "Was he a *p'licemun?*"

"Mm hm."

"Has he got a gun, a really one?"

"Naturally."

"Did he ever kill anybody?"

"No!"

"Why didn't he?"

"Because policemen don't go around killing people unless they have to."

"But *then* they do, I bet," Billy said. "If they *have* to, they kill um—*don't* they?"

"Not unless somebody tries to kill them first. Because it's wrong to kill people."

"Why is ut?"

"Because God says so. He made us all and He wants us to love one another, that's why. You'll understand when you're a little bigger."

"But if somebody tries to kill them first, *then* they kill um."

"No! They only wound them."

"But they shoot um."

"Never mind!"

Dinner for the McClatchys was not what it was in most families. Bessie, Arline, and Billy dined at the restaurant counter at four-thirty, when business in the restaurant was slack, and Arline took a tray to her father in the bar at six. But today—Arline would not forget this day so long as she lived.

She found the door of the Traveler's Rest locked and a card stuck behind the glass: "Closed till 5 p.m."

"For heaven's sake, what's the matter?" she asked when her mother answered her knocking.

"Your father wants us to eat together. He's got something to tell us."

"He has?" Arline said eagerly. "Oh, what do you suppose it is?"

"I wouldn't go expecting much if I was you."

"What? Why not? What do you mean?"

"Well, it aint so good, from what he told me. But wait and let him tell us the whole thing."

Arline was chilled by her mother's words and by the grim look on her face. But when she saw her father she could have cried. He appeared to be plunged in gloom.

At dinner in the kitchen he reported what Mr. Markham had told him, and explained at length. "So you see," he finished, "by the time we get through paying Mr. Markham and the government we won't have beans left. It'll be just like it never happened, like we never had the painting at all. It's going to be the same old stuff."

And he looked at them, and they at him, and Billy was drumming on his plate with a spoon. Bessie put her hand on Billy's arm. "Don't do that, like a good boy; you'll break the dish."

McClatchy said: "We been living in a fool's paradise."

Bessie sighed and stole a glance at her daughter. "Well, it's too bad, but we're no worse off anyhow. It didn't cost us nothing. That's the way to look at it."

This irritated him. "Now that's a fine consolation, that is. Here we thought we was going to make a fortune, and the whole town was thinking the same thing. It's going to be a great comedown any way you take it."

Silence.

Then, judging the women to be sufficiently depressed by the outlook, he allowed a gleam to appear in his eye, he raised a significant forefinger, and he said: "Providing . . . Providing we don't *sell* that painting."

Arline said: "Don't sell it? What do you mean?"

"I mean if we keep it we can make some *real* dough."

Bessie sniffed. "How, pray?"

"Well, this painting aint just a painting, you know. It's a kind of a curiosity, Mr. Markham was saying today. And it's had a lot of free advertising, too. You realize? Why, this painting's famous, he says. Like *September Morn!* Like *Stella!* But if we let him sell it, why, even so, by the time we get through paying the bills and the taxes we won't have nothing. But wait, now. When I left Mr. Markham's place I went down to the Palace Hotel, down to the men's bar there, where I used to work; and you know that big painting they got—*The Pied Piper?* Well, that painting's famous too, you know. And Vince Sullivan was telling me—— That's old Mr. Sullivan's son, you remember, Bessie. I seen the old man today, too; he's still going. What do you think of that!"

"Mr. *Sullivan?*"

"Yep. I seen him up at the union. It's up on Market Street now. He'll be eighty-three."

"Eighty-three!" said Bessie.

"Yep. He's a wonder. Goes down to the union every day and hangs around."

"Dad, go on!"

"Yeah. Well, anyhow—"

"Think of that!" said Bessie.

"Yeah. And Vince was telling me—— He works down there now, down at the Palace bar. But you remember how skinny he used to be?" McClatchy shook his head. "Fat, with a face on him like a side of beef. *He'll* never live to be eighty-three."

"Dad!"

"All right, I'm only telling your mother how he's aged. But he was telling me people go in there just to see that painting. They got it insured for thirty thousand bucks, he says, on account of it's a big asset to the place. It brings in the customers. Even the ladies go in there now, just to look at it; you can't keep 'em out, he says; they all want to see that painting. See?" And he grinned at them. "Are you beginning to see the light?"

But Bessie said: "Well, my goodness, do you mean you want to put that old painting of ours back behind the bar where it was for God knows how many years? You think people'll come down to this old place to look at that?"

"Sure they will! It's famous now. But hold on, what do you mean, this old place? I mean fix the place up."

Bessie dropped her hands into her lap and looked at him with ironic pity. "Well, did you ever! And where do you think you're going to get the money?"

"Listen. We got the place all paid up, aint we? And we got a few thousand bucks saved, aint we? And we can get another little loan, can't we?"

"We most certainly'll do nothing of the kind!"

"Aw, wait awhile. Listen. If we get a loan, all we'll need is a few thousand bucks, and we can pay that off in no time. Because with this painting the old Traveler's'll be famous. Look at the free advertising it's had already."

"Dan McClatchy, that's a crazy idea."

"There you go; there's a woman for you! I tell you it's a good idea."

"Oh, it is, is it? Well, you can just forget it, Mr. Smarty. We're not going to saddle ourselves with another mortgage."

"What's the matter, you want to sell the painting and have nothing? You want to go on cooking till you die? You want your daughter to be a waitress all her life?"

"Let me tell you something, that's a great deal better than being out in the street."

"There you go! There you go!" McClatchy slammed down his napkin. "How can a man get anywheres with his own wife holding him back? Look at us today. What have we got? Nothing. Oh no, nothing but a Rembrandt painting that's a great curiosity and that's had a million dollars' worth of free advertising—a thing that could make us a fortune. And what does she want to do with it? Sell it, sell the damn thing, and go on cooking for the rest of her life!"

Billy was staring at him, spoon in midair.

"Never mind, now, Dan McClatchy. Taking on like that in front of the child! Don't pay no attention to him, Billy. Go on and eat that."

"I don't want ut," Billy said, dropping the spoon.

"Ah," McClatchy said, "Billy—there's the one I feel sorry for."

"Eat it," Arline ordered her son.

"Don't you, Arline?" McClatchy said. "Don't you think Bill's got some rights around here?"

"I want to go outside," Billy said, sliding off his chair.

"No!"—Arline pulled him back again. "Sit there and eat your dinner."

"Let him alone," McClatchy said moodily. "God knows he don't have nothing to look forward to outside or in."

"I don't want no more," Billy said petulantly.

"Well," sighed Bessie, "let him go if he wants."

"No! Eat your dinner. And for heaven's sake stop squirming!"

But the child in making a restless movement brushed his glass of milk; it upset on the cloth, rolled from the table, and shattered on the floor.

"Oh!" Arline seized his arm. "What's the matter with you!"

Billy tried to jerk away and slide from the chair, beginning to whine.

"Stop that! Stop it!" Arline seized him by both arms roughly and set him back in his place.

Billy screamed.

Arline's face suddenly twisted, a sob broke from her, and she covered her face with her hands.

Bessie had got up. She and her husband looked at each other.

Arline ran into the bedroom and slammed the door.

Billy was wailing. Bessie bent over him, enfolding him in her arms, and glared at McClatchy, saying: "*Now* see what you done."

That was a painful evening. McClatchy retired, grumbling, into his saloon. Two railroad men came into the counter restaurant and noticed when Bessie instead of Arline appeared to serve them that she came out red-eyed and blowing her nose.

"Where's Arline tonight, Miz McClatchy?" one asked, wondering if tragedy had struck the place.

"She'll be out in a minute. What'll it be?"

Ten minutes later Arline came out of the bedroom in her uniform; she passed her mother at the kitchen sink without looking at her, said "Sorry, Ma," and walked out behind the counter—back into her rut.

Washing the dishes, Bessie thought: Counting her chickens before they were hatched, that's what she was doing. I told her but she wouldn't listen. And Dan McClatchy giving it to her right out the way he done, like the crack of doom—— Same old stuff, he says, rubbing it in, and all the time him with that crazy idea up his sleeve. Get a little loan, he says. Dear me, but it was a hard pill for him to swallow too, I guess, and no fun for him to bring it home with him. Poor Danny. But land!—him and the Palace Hotel!

He was still sulking when after closing the tavern at eleven o'clock he came into the bedroom and without a word to her began to undress. Bad as Billy, she thought. He knelt down in his nightshirt and said his prayers, got into bed, and switched off the lamp.

"Dan McClatchy, we'd be out of our mind to do a thing like that."

"All right, all right, we'll go on like this to the end of our days, then, and let a fortune slip through our fingers. Only leave me in peace."

"Don't worry. I'd rather not hear any more about it." She stared into the darkness. "How much of a loan do you think it'd take?" she inquired.

Bessie had no faith in the power of their disappointing masterpiece to attract trade, but, knowing how much her husband and her daughter had been counting on a new life, she had not the heart to deny them the consolation of a brighter tavern. She began by conceding that it might do no harm to inquire into the possibilities of making a few improvements, at least.

But Arline showed little enthusiasm for the proposal. Against her dream of San Francisco it appeared to her a dull project and a dubious one. Why should anyone who could afford to go to the Blue Moon or any of those places patronize a tavern in this part of town, painting or no painting?

The bank too was doubtful. Taverns, Mr. Nickerson said, were always a risk, the bank was more cautious about investing in them than it had been when the Traveler's Rest was mortgaged by Mr. and Mrs. Brausch, and the Traveler's Rest was poorly situated. On the other hand, he said, the McClatchys had a good record with the bank, and the land must be worth more than it had been, but land was not a good risk either. McClatchy offered to throw in *The Lost Dutchman* as part of his security. Mr. Nickerson told him to submit an appraisal of the painting along with the plans and an application for a loan. Then, he said, the bank would see.

Only at the office of Seifert & Johansen, building contractors, did Dan McClatchy's idea meet with any encouragement. Frank Johansen, the short graying junior partner of the firm, who received him, was a licensed architect, and the opportunity of designing a setting for a Rembrandt painting appealed to him. How much did McClatchy want to spend?

"Oh, four, five thousand bucks."

Some of the enthusiasm went out of Mr. Johansen. But he put on his hat and went with McClatchy to look at the Traveler's Rest.

"Man," he said, after a short inspection, "do you realize the City will make you put a firewall between the kitchen and the restaurant?

You're lucky it hasn't made you do that already—you're breaking the law! And your wiring's illegal. And you're lucky that water heater didn't blow up long ago. Why, it's going to cost you a few thousand dollars just to keep the City from closing you up! You're the worst fire hazard in town."

But Johansen yearned to have a try at this job. Finally he proposed what he thought would be the most practical solution of the problem. He proposed to convert these decrepit premises into "an authentic old Dutch tavern." No fancy fixtures, mind you. It would have to be "completely simple." But it could be "one of the most attractive little taverns in the county." And he thought he might accomplish this feat for "around twelve or thirteen thousand dollars."

McClatchy recoiled.

Bessie smote her forehead. "Gracious! There you are, Dan Mc-Clatchy. I hope you're satisfied."

But McClatchy hesitated. He pointed out that everything was "up" now: the value of their property was up, food and drink were up, food and drink were their stock in trade, and if it would cost them more than they had expected to improve their tavern so that the place would attract more trade, why, it stood to reason that more trade would boost their income in proportion. And hadn't Mr. Johansen told them that they would have to spend a few thousand dollars anyway, just so the City wouldn't close the tavern as a firetrap? Then why not spend a little more and capitalize on the famous painting? Sure, twelve or thirteen thousand bucks was a lot to spend, but that was just a guess the man had made. Maybe he could cut it down. . . .

While they argued, Johansen was busy. A few days later he submitted, unbidden, three pictures and a new floor plan. Preliminary sketches he called the pictures, but really they were finished watercolors, and they transformed the Traveler's Rest beyond recognition.

In the pictures the muddy paint had been removed from the front, the brick was bright red again, and the mortar joints were lines of warm gray. The front door was delft blue, with a leaded and mullioned window on either side of it, and from an iron bracket just above the door hung a small brown-stained board with a sign burned into it in medieval characters:

The Lost Dutchman

McClatchy said the name aloud, and commented: "Now that aint a bad idea."

He had suggested that a larger kitchen would be needed in which to cook for the many diners he expected, so the new floor plan showed the kitchen extended to include the space of the present sitting room; and the bedroom was a storage room now, for he dreamt that he and Bessie would take an apartment with their daughter and grandson uptown. And the partition between restaurant and bar had been taken out, leaving a room of fifty by thirty-seven feet. And in the pictures the walls were of rough plaster tinted pastel green. The floor was a red-and-white checkerboard inspired by Jan Steen's *Feast of St. Nicholas*. And gone was Bessie's counter. Instead there were plain wooden tables and chairs and, along the right-hand wall and part of the back one, little booths upholstered in red leather. To the left, the long mahogany bar had been refinished as walnut. Back of it was a false chimney piece with glass shelves set into the brick-lined opening to hold the bottles. And above the mantel was the painting. The painting had been removed from its old gilt frame and was now framed by walnut paneling, and it was dramatically illuminated by a small spotlight set into the ceiling.

McClatchy gazed, fascinated, at the pictures.

And to Bessie they cruelly emphasized the meanness of the present tavern. It was like a glimpse of the house she had set her heart on as a bride, the neat white house with a patch of lawn, north of Market Street. Bessie, as she looked at the pictures, hid her rough red hands under her apron. And thinking of Arline and Billy, she grew wistful. In so short a time even Bessie was too deep in this project to be able to turn back without a pang. She conceded that they might be able to afford a set of plans and a definite bid, anyhow.

So the plans went forward, and Bessie began to fuss over them. First, she objected to cutting the front windows larger. Johansen assured her that this was necessary and would cost little, and she gave in with a puzzling reluctance, saying it wasn't the money. But Bessie had her way about retaining the back apartment. Yes, she did want a larger kitchen, but why go to all that expense until they were sure they really needed and could afford one, or pay rent for an apartment if they could go on living right here? McClatchy was not hard to win over to this plan: he had begun to worry that if they left the place unguarded at night burglars would steal the painting. And on Bessie's insistence, Johansen made other changes in order to keep the cost down.

Johansen finished the plans, but with them he submitted no bid. Prices since the war were so unstable, he explained, that no contractor could afford to take a job except on a guarantee of "cost plus ten per cent." But he did submit an estimate: "About fifteen thousand dollars."

Bessie threw up her hands. "Whoops! That ends it. Merciful heavens, that's the finish."

But McClatchy kept looking at the pictures. He spoke of inflation and the necessity of meeting competition. "With the old Traveler's the way it is, we aint got a Chinaman's chance," he said, "but look at how much more we could make with a place like he's got here"—pointing to the pictures.

"Sure," Bessie said, "and we'd make more out of the Palace Hotel! Why not buy that and be done with it? We might as well talk about it anyhow as talk about spending fifteen thousand dollars. Where in the world would we get that much money?"

"We got six thousand saved up, aint we? and if it's a good investment the bank'll loan us the rest, won't it?" He knew that Bessie had great respect for the judgment of banks. "If a bank'll go for it, it's a good investment, aint it?"

Not for them it wasn't, Bessie said. And besides, what about the new kitchen range she would need, and the charcoal broiler, and the big new icebox—where would *that* money come from?

Why, he said, they'd get the bank to tack that onto the loan. Those things wouldn't cost much; they'd get those secondhand. Would she wait and see what the bank said?

He got from the Markham Galleries a new appraisal of his Rembrandt. Markham, after a struggle with himself, appraised it at four thousand dollars, which he said was as high as he would go on paper. Meanwhile Johansen, by trimming the plans and specifications still further, cut his estimate by three hundred dollars. Bessie was not won over. But she did not stand in the way when McClatchy submitted to the bank an application for a loan. She was amazed when the bank offered only a thousand dollars less than he had applied for. And Bessie did respect the judgment of banks.

She signed her name under her husband's on a mortgage for nineteen thousand dollars.

As they walked home that day, McClatchy was silent. Bessie saw that he was worried. It was as if the accomplished deed had shaken his faith, as if for the first time he understood the gravity of what they were doing. She put her arm through his. "You got more from the bank than I thought you could."

"Yeah?"

"I guess the bank figures it's a good investment, like you said."

"Sure."

"With our savings, that gives us a working capital of twenty-five thousand dollars. My! That's a good start, Danny."

"Uh huh."

"If we're careful, maybe we'll make it yet."

He looked at her. "Oh, we'll make it."

She pressed his arm. "I know we will," she said.

Hubert Ritter, hearing what was in the wind, came to interview Mc-Clatchy again. The *Sentinel* carried the story that the Llagas Rembrandt was to remain in Llagas. The news appeared in the San Francisco papers as well. And McClatchy's confidence returned. "Look at all the free advertising we're getting. What'd I tell you? I wouldn't be surprised if this painting was to bring people all the way from the city!"

It was true, the painting *was* famous, and Arline began to be excited. What if her father was right! He talked of fine foods to be served, and of hiring help. What if people did come all the way from the city! She spoke to her friend Phyllis Plover about it, and Phyllis said: "Why not? They go over to Trader Vic's in Oakland, don't they?" Trader Vic's was a place that Arline had only read about, a haunt of the rich and famous. Well, it wouldn't be like Trader Vic's, of course. But how different from the Traveler's Rest! She began to picture herself as "hostess" in a dinner dress.

Alfred Markham was furious. He felt, he told himself, as if he were being made a party to a crime; for a crime was what the civilized world would call this cheap exploitation of a work of art. But in fact it was the outraged sense of possession that maddened Alfred Markham. It was the helplessness of not being able to prove or even to mention that the painting really belonged to *him*. And it was the conviction that no work of art could possibly belong to McClatchy.

There were other protests. These came not from the art world but from certain persons who were loudly indignant in the name of art without having the slightest recognizable authority to speak for it. They were a familiar crew, veteran campaigners of the letter columns in the San Francisco newspapers. But in the same columns, McClatchy had his champions too; and from this side came something like an authoritative note, for numbered here were painters who felt strongly about bringing art to the people, their paintings being exhibited for sale only in the cafés and barrooms of upper Montgomery Street.

McClatchy was amazed and hurt. He thought of writing a letter himself, but the arguments for his side were being ably presented by his defenders and he feared to stir up more trouble.

"It beats me what all the hullaballoo's about, anyhow," he said across his bar one night to Walsh Reardon. "Anybody that wants to see this painting can come in and see it; so what's wrong with it being in a tavern? Look at the Palace Hotel. It's like you said, Mr. Reardon, a beautiful thing is good any time, any place."

"That depends," Reardon said, being on his third double gin and water.

"What? No, that's what *you* said. Don't you remember? Sure—I wrote it down. Wait." McClatchy punched open the drawer of the cash register and took out his notebook. He hooked on his spectacles and found the place. "Here." And he read: " 'A thing of beauty is a joy for ever.' "

"Oh, Keats!"

"What?"

"I was quoting a poem by John Keats."

"Oh, poetry!" with a grin. "And what was the thing of beauty, a painting?"

"No; the story."

"What story?"

"The story of the poem. It was an old Grecian myth. Keats came along and told it all over again because he thought it was beautiful, and that line was his apology: 'A thing of beauty is a joy for ever.' "

"Oh." McClatchy leaned on the bar. "And what was the story?"

"Well," Reardon said, "it was about a fellow named Endymion; a shepherd of ancient Greece. One night, Mac, while Endymion was tending his flock on Mount Latmos, the Moon fell in love with the poor devil and cast her spell on him and appeared to him in her best dress."

"What, the moon?"

"Certainly."

"Now you don't say. So what happened?"

"So Endymion fell in love with her. In the end he moved in with her, right up there in the sky. He used to call her Cynthia."

"The moon?"

"Who else?"

"By golly, he must have been bughouse. And so that's supposed to be how the man got in the moon! Well, some jokers can make up a story about anything. I remember when I was a young fellow working at Kelly's on the old Barbary Coast, Kelly used to tell about Jack London. Oh, you know, he could put the booze away, *that* fellow, and there he'd be, hanging on the bar in Kelly's place, and Kelly'd come along. 'Come on, Jack,' he'd say, 'you've had enough for a while; come on and sit down till you cool off.' And he'd take Jack London over to one of the tables and sit him down; and there the man'd be. And you know what he'd do?" McClatchy touched Reardon on the arm. "He'd write a book."

"What!"

"Sure he would. Kelly says the man'd be sitting there dead-drunk and pretty soon he'd pull out a pencil and paper and he'd write a book. Now what do you think of that?"

Reardon threw back his head and shook the room with his grating bass laughter.

"Sure," McClatchy said. "Kelly told me he could write better drunk than sober. They say it's that way with a lot of those fellows, some of 'em can't write at all till they get oiled up. I wouldn't be surprised if that was the way it was with the fellow wrote that story about the Greek sheepherder, he must have had a load on, *that* fellow. The booze speeds up a man's imagination, like. Sure. You're pretty good yourself when you're oiled.

"Yes, sir!" McClatchy turned back to the cash register and replaced the notebook in the drawer. "Anyhow it's no use anybody talking about that painting. It's going right up there on the wall soon's the place is ready for it."

And a week later, objections or no objections, the Traveler's Rest closed its doors, a board wall went up in front of it, and on the wall appeared a sign:

FUTURE HOME

FAMOUS

LOST DUTCHMAN TAVERN

FINE FOOD   DRINKS

FAMOUS REMBRANDT PAINTING

WATCH FOR

GRAND OPENING

7

THE WORLD OF GOING-TO-BE

One morning Arline kept Billy home from nursery school and took him shopping: he too must be outfitted for the New life. Afterward she took him to the park, where there were swings and slides. She sat on a bench and watched him playing with the other children. Then, arms extended on either side of her along the top of the bench, she leaned her head back and turned her face up to catch the warmth of the sun and closed her eyes. Under her open jacket she was wearing the kelly-green sweater. She heard feet approaching on the gravel path. They stopped and a friendly baritone said:

"Pretty soft."

She blinked up into a rugged brown face, familiar even without the policeman's uniform that went with it. "Oh! Hel*lo!*"

"Hear you're not going to sell that painting after all."

"No, we're going to keep it. Dad thinks it'll draw trade now. He's remodeling the place."

"Yeah—I see." He was wearing a tan blazer, the open collar of his shirt revealing a strong brown neck and a few chest hairs which caught the sun. He had a brown felt hat on and was smoking a long cigar.

"Day off?" she asked, and he nodded. "Pretty soft," she gave it back to him.

"Yeah." He removed the cigar, smiling. "Your name's Arline—right?"

"That's right. How did *you* know?"

"Cop's business."

"Oh, now, really!"

"Mine's Harry Fahs."

She inclined her head in a mock bow. "Well, hello."

They looked at each other. His eyes traveled lightly over her face, touched her hair, fell for just a moment boldly on the sweater, came back to meet her own, and he lifted his brows to her and said: "Hi."

She was amused, but her face had turned pink. His archly specula-tive manner was full of male vanity. But it was a long time since any male had looked at her like that, and not many ever had. "*Well!*" she said.

"Hear you're going to have a grand opening."

"That's right."

"I might be working that night."

"That's too bad." There was a twinkle in her eyes. She was waiting. Now, honestly! is he going to ask me for a date?

But at that moment her son came running toward them, crying. His underlip was thrust out and he was digging his fists into his eyes and half stumbling along the path to his mother.

"Billy!" She swept him into her arms. "What happened?"

"Eddie *hit* me."

Harry Fahs guffawed.

"He did? Well!" She set the boy back on his feet again. He would have to learn to fight his own battles was her policy. "You go right back there and hit him! Go on."

But Billy only stood there knuckling his eyes and snuffling. "He *aint* a him—he's a *girl*."

"Haw! Haw! Haw!" roared Harry Fahs.

"What! Oh, gosh!" Arline said. "Eddie's a girl? Well, I mean! Don't you know better than to fight with girls? I'm ashamed of you. Come on, now." She took her handkerchief and wiped his face. "Blow!" He blew. "There!"

Harry Fahs said: "Don't let the women faze you, fellow. I'd show her who's boss."

"Oh, you would!" Arline said.

The boy looked up under his brows at the man with the cigar, and blurted his defense: "She's *bigger*'n me."

"Haw! Haw! Haw!"

His mother was laughing too. He felt abandoned. But Arline's laughter was forced. It had struck her that she herself had suffered under Eddie's blow, that it must have spoiled her in the eyes of Harry Fahs. And wouldn't it be the same with other men? Her son had spoiled it. Wouldn't he always? Then the boy began to cry again, and in a rush of repentence she took him back into her arms. She rocked and soothed him; her face was crimson, but she was telling herself: I don't care, I *don't* care, and he better not laugh. But Harry Fahs just stood there with his cigar in his teeth and his lips drawn away from it in a twisted smile.

She wiped Billy's eyes and cheeks and nose. "There, now. Run along and be a good boy." But he shook his head and put his lips to her ear and whispered. She flushed again. "Oh, all right, come on, then." And to Harry Fahs: "Honestly, did you ever see anything like them?"

And guessing what the matter was, Harry Fahs guffawed again.

She got up, drolly sighing and shaking her head, but it was spoiled.

Then Harry Fahs astonished her. He indicated Billy with a nod, asking: "You got a sitter?"

"A sitter? For Billy?"

Did he mean it? Was he still interested, hinting at a date? Not that she was interested in Harry Fahs; but it seemed important to her just then that Harry Fahs should still be interested in her. "Oh, sure," she said. "I leave him with his grandparents." As if it were a common thing in her gay life.

"I'll call you sometime," he said.

And she turned away with no answer but a smile that could be taken as an invitation.

What have you done to yourself, Arline? . . . Hey, I notice you're all fixed up these days, kid; what's cooking, got a new boyfriend?

Lying in bed that night, she wondered if he would call.

Temporarily, Dan and Bessie McClatchy had moved out of the living quarters behind the tavern, into an apartment just across Union Street from their daughter's.

The tavern echoed all day long to the racket of men at work, and every morning McClatchy went down to inspect progress. He set the grand opening for the Saturday night of December 6.

This was to be a gala event. He was going to have an orchestra that night, he said. "Not an orchestra, Dad—you mean a band," Arline corrected him; and when she made it clear that a band, to her, was not the kind of musical organization that John Philip Sousa had led, but the kind that played popular dance music, he agreed that this was what he meant. But to Arline's disappointment he said that there would be no dancing. To clear enough space for dancing they would have to move out a dozen or so tables, which would cut down the returns of the party, he pointed out practically. But then he decided that just to start the festivities they would have a cleared space after all, filling it with tables immediately after a grand march.

"Grand *march?*" Arline said. "Oh, Dad, no!"

"Why not?"

"For heaven's sake, Dad, nobody has grand marches any more. They're out of date."

"What do you mean, out of date? They have 'em all the time. Not at plain little shindigs, no, but on special occasions. Look at the President's Ball—they have a grand march there, don't they? Out of date nothing! We're going to have a grand opening here that'll make Llagas sit up and take notice. We'll start off with the grand march and then we'll have the grand unveiling. We'll unveil the painting, see?"

"Oh," Bessie said, "that'll be nice."

"But, Dad, a grand march!"

Bessie laughed. "Oh, let him have one if he wants; the folks'll enjoy it. My land, I haven't been in a grand march for years. Remember, Danny?"

"Sure—at the South of Market Boys'."

"Mayor Rolph led it," Bessie recalled, "with Mrs. Gaffey on his arm; and her all in white, with a big tiara."

"Say!" her husband said. "I think I'll invite Mayor Schuman."

"Oh!" Arline said. "Do you think he'd come?"

"Sa-ay—tickled to death. Those jokers eat that stuff up. And Bess, Mayor Schuman can lead the grand march with you on his arm."

Arline whooped, but Bessie, laughing, threw up her hands and said: "Oh, mercy, leave me out of it."

"No!" Arline said. "Now, Ma, that's your place; you're the hostess. If there's going to be a grand march you have to lead it with the mayor."

"Oh, sure," Bessie said, "I'd be a fine one to lead a grand march. Good gracious, I'd probably step all over the poor man's feet; and me without a decent dress to my name."

"No, now, you can get a new dress; can't she, Dad."

"Sure. We'll have her all dressed up, and she'll make Mrs. Gaffey look like two bits. She'll be the queen of the joint."

"Never mind!" Bessie said. "You better not go counting your chickens, anyhow, till you see what the mayor says. As if he'd do it!"

"*Sure* he'll do it. Just wait'll I ask him. . . ."

But the grand opening was two months off. The McClatchys went twice to San Francisco, bought a new kitchen range, a charcoal broiler, a refrigerator, and a coffee urn, and traded in their two old cash registers for new ones. McClatchy insured his painting for four thousand dollars. And his plans grew.

The food at the Lost Dutchman, he boasted, would be as good as any in miles, which was saying more than he knew; and when he computed the number of employees warranted by the trade that he expected, Bessie became frightened again. But he cited the Blue Moon, the Hacienda, and the 101 Club, and argued that if the locality would support those places it would certainly support the Lost Dutchman Tavern, which was going to be superior to them all and have a famous painting to boot. "You got to get it through your head, Bess, we aint in the penny ante no more; we're going to be pretty big operators now," he said.

He reckoned that to begin with they would need at least six waitresses, two cooks, two bartenders, and two dishwashers. Bessie would surpervise the kitchen, he the bar; Bessie would be cashier, Arline the "hostess," and the three of them would oversee the restaurant.

Bessie was frightened, all right, but it did appear that if they were to realize an adequate return on their investment it must be so. They needed a large trade and would have to engage the help that it required. It was this or nothing now.

And Danny encouraged her: "Sure; it's like old According-to Doyle used to say: 'A dead fish can swim downstream but it takes a live one to swim up.'" Then he remembered. "He's dead himself! Yeah, I guess I told you. Passed away in 'forty-one, God rest him. I would have been forty-nine then, and he was younger than me. Think of that. And here Mr. Sullivan'll be eighty-three. Now there's something I wouldn't have believed. But you never know." He added piously: 'You know not the day nor the hour.'"

"No," Bessie sighed, "you never know."

But they went to San Francisco again and bought dining tables and chairs, plates and dishes of heavy white pottery decorated with pictures of Dutch boys and girls and windmills done in blue, glasses, flatware, kitchen knives, ladles, cooking forks, great pots and pans, napkins, and tablecloths.

Another day they went down the Peninsula to Tommy's grave and to the graves of their parents, each couple side by side, the carbarn timekeeper with his wife, the scrubwoman with the terrible longshoreman who had baited the devil. And on the way home they went into the neighborhood where they had grown up together and been married and where their children had been born.

But they felt sadness in Valencia Street now, a damp ineffable sadness as of defeat and heartbreak and loneliness and decay. It was in the pinched faces of the houses, the narrow bay-windowed "carpenter's gothic" houses, which seemed to have shrunk and to be huddled together; in the peeling paint of gray or brown, in the weathered wood itself that lay exposed and rotting in patches, in the rusty curtains wafted wearily in the breeze like handkerchiefs still waving to ships long sailed and out of sight and done for; and it was in the darkness behind the panes of shops, in the faded gilt signs, in the aged worn and broken sidewalks from which all traces of hopscotch had disappeared and through which were sifting, here and there, the sands trodden by the Indians. And where Recreation Park had been stood a modern concrete apartment building with lawns and much glass, obviously a housing project. In that setting it bulked enormous, making the other buildings in Valencia Street look all the sadder. Yet how small it seemed when you tried to fit into the space it occupied the baseball diamond and the outfields and Home-run Fence and the crowds in the grandstand and bleachers on those gone afternoons.

They walked up Fifteenth Street, and stopped before the house where the Moyles family had lived. The paint was peeling and all the blinds were down. How little it looked to Bessie, how old, how squalid. It was the same with the house where the McClatchys had lived; and a window of the very flat was broken, and the battered little basement door, half below the level of the street, was off its hinges. They walked to Guerrero Street and looked at the flat that had been their first home after their marriage, where both Arline and Tommy had been born. It looked nearly as old and defeated, and just as small.

Then they walked to the church in Dolores Street where they had been married and where both their children had been baptized—the "new" Mission Dolores next to the little white adobe built by the Spaniards. The exterior had a freshened look, but inside it was the same, so far as they could tell, and it felt the same. It was a solemn but comforting end to the tour that had begun at the graves of their dead, their parents and their son. They knelt. The sanctuary lamp still burned. The powerful tranquility of the place enfolded them. They felt that He had been waiting here all the time, unchanged, kind, and forever, Who alone knew the day and the hour.

Arline's excitement was mounting. The tavern where the McClatchys were to command so many retainers, and to which people were coming "all the way from the city" to see the masterpiece, was taking shape before her eyes, and the grand opening for which there were so many plans was only six weeks in the future, and Mayor Schuman had agreed to attend.

"And guess what else!" Arline reported to her friend Phyllis Plover. "He's going to have one of those big searchlights like they have in front of movie theaters."

"He isn't!"

"He is—can you imagine?"

"Gee, honey, and the mayor!" Phyllis was the waitress at the lunch counter of the Right Prescription Pharmacy, where Bill Lucas had worked (so long ago). "Know something?" she said thoughtfully.

"What?"

"I'd like to ask your dad for a job."

"Oh, do you mean it? Would you really like to work there?"

"Well, sure, I think so. I guess your dad'd pay scale, wouldn't he? That's all I get here, you know, and the tips are awful. In a place like you're going to have, they ought to mean something. Besides," Phyllis said in almost the same words that Arline's father had used as a young man, tilting her chin and smiling her mischievous smile, "down there maybe I'd have a chance to *meet* somebody."

Which caused Arline to laugh gaily.

The two friends appeared to have little in common, but it could be said that they complemented each other. Phyllis, the younger, was also the prettier, and needed to be. She was small, had yellow hair, gilded, a bright red petulant mouth, soft white skin, and a fine delicate figure. At twenty-nine she had been married and divorced twice, and she spoke with a pretty leer of current adventures. She was so frankly on the prowl, and struck so roguish a pose of lechery, that Arline was charmed by her, without for a moment believing that Phyllis was the devastating siren she let on to be. Arline thought of her as "a little devil," and half envied Phyllis her heathenism, extenuating her sins on the ground of her benightedness, but at the same time was sorry for her. She knew that Phyllis had no real talent for romance, had no judgment in men, always came off the loser. And to Phyllis, Arline was a number of things: her best audience, barring a man, her foil, her sympathetic and admiring friend, never her rival. In fact Phyllis plainly looked on Arline as an ugly duckling and an innocent, which Arline resented. Through Phyllis, perhaps, she savored forbidden fruits, and in excusing Phyllis really excused herself, but the young widow felt herself to be possessed of powers that Phyllis did not suspect.

Phyllis asked: "Do you think your dad'd give me a job?"

"Why, sure, Phyl. You're experienced, aren't you? I'll ask him tonight. I know he will. Oh, Phyl, this is wonderful!"

And when Arline asked her father, he consented. But Bessie, when she heard about it, frowned. "I don't know, now, Arline," she said. "You're too thick with Phyllis as it is, if you ask me."

"Oh, Ma! Good heavens, of course I'm thick with her—Phyllis is my best friend. What do you mean? What's the matter with her?"

"Never mind. I wouldn't be the one to say a word against the girl, but I don't like her coming to work for us, that's all, and you know well enough what's the matter with her."

"I don't either! Oh, sure, I know what some old cats say—just because she's pretty and has been divorced a couple of times. It wasn't her fault she was divorced, and believe me I know! Phyllis Plover is just the victim of a lot of malicious gossip, so there!"

Bessie sniffed. "If she is or not, we don't want her giving the place a bad name, neither; that's another thing."

"A bad name? Oh, my God, what do you think Phyllis is, a street-walker?"

Her father interposed: "Here! what kind of language is that to be using in front of your mother?"

"Well, good heavens, that's what it sounded like she meant. Ma, you're condemning Phyllis before she starts, and just on account of——"

"I am *not* condemning her. I only said——"

"But gosh, Ma, I already told Phyllis I'd ask Dad, I said I knew he'd give her the job. And now what do you want me to do, tell her she's not good enough for us?"

"I never said——"

"But, Ma!"

"Well, we'll see. But you tell Phyllis Plover if she comes to work for us she'll have to behave herself."

So it was settled that Phyllis would be a waitress at the Lost Dutchman.

Suddenly the enterprise received a setback.

It was discovered that the wooden flooring of the old tavern was all but eaten away by termites. The floor had to be ripped out and replaced. More money. More time.

And the grand opening was advanced to New Year's Eve.

8

DANCING

Harry Fahs did call.

"What you doing tonight?" he asked.

"Tonight? Nothing much. Why?" She made herself sound disinterested. But she was thrilled. She could wear the dinner dress that she had bought out of sheer optimism a month before: black form-fitting bodice, scarlet sash, flaring taffeta skirt, sequins.

But all he offered was: "How about taking in a show?" When she hesitated he threw in: "And maybe we can drop in somewhere after."

"After? Where do you mean?" It wouldn't do to let him think he could take her just anywhere.

But all he had in mind was the Willow Tree.

"Oh," she began regretfully—but maybe it was all he could afford; and she did need practice. "All right, then."

"Okay, kid. Pick you up about seven."

And she had done it. The Willow Tree was a little roadside tavern with a dance floor and only a juke box for music, yet when she hung up her eyes were sparkling. She felt that this was the beginning. It was the opening of the door into the New life. I can wear my new print anyhow, I guess, and . . . Gosh! I wonder if Grace can take me. She telephoned the beauty shop and found that Grace could. Then she telephoned her mother. "Can I leave Billy with you tonight, Ma? I got a date."

"A date!" Her mother sounded astonished, but quickly made amends. "Now aint that nice." Then ruined it: "Or aint it with a fellow?"

"Oh, Ma! Who do you think it's with?"

"Phyllis?"

"Phyllis? Now wouldn't I look fine dancing with Phyllis!"

"Dancing? Oh! that sounds grand. Dancing. Who is it, do I know him?"

"No!"

"What's his name?"

"What difference does that make if you don't know him?"

"What, is it a secret?"

"Of course not—his name's Harry Fahs."

"Harry Fahs? No, I don't think I know him. What does he do?"

"Oh, Ma! He's a policeman. Satisfied?"

"A policeman?"

"Look, Ma, I'm in a hurry. See you at dinner. . . ."

So to the beauty shop; and afterward she could not resist dropping in at the drugstore to tell Phyllis Plover. But when, slipping off her stool at the counter, she said "Well, got to go now—got a date tonight," Phyllis looked only mildly interested—because, Arline saw, it had not even occurred to Phyllis that the date might be with a fellow.

Phyllis asked: "Where you going?"

"Dancing."

Phyllis's eyes lighted up. "Dancing! Yeah? Hey, that's swell. Who with?"

"Oh, just—a cop."

"A cop? No kidding! Cute?"

"Kind of."

"He-y, it wouldn't be Harry Fahs, would it?"

The triumph curdled. "Yes; why?"

"It isn't! Oh, baby, watch out for that guy; he's a wolf!"

"What? How do you know?"

"Don't worry, I been out with him—once."

"Oh, you have!"

A woman had sat down at the counter but Phyllis ignored her. She asked: "Where's he taking you?"

"Oh, I don't know," Arline lied. "Why?"

The woman called: "Miss . . ."

Phyllis, paying no attention to the woman, laughed. She asked: "How'd you happen to meet him?"

"—Miss."

"Huh? Okay." Phyllis leaned across the counter and patted Arline's arm. "I want to hear all about it after."

"Maybe. 'Bye now."

"Remember what I to-ld you," Phyllis sang after her.

Arline would remember. What Phyllis had said of Harry Fahs disturbed her. And yet, as she walked to the nursery school to pick up her son, it pleased her. But Phyllis had been out with him. Once, she had said. What did that mean? And Phyllis's laugh had hurt.

At dinner in her parents' apartment, her father said: "Well! So we're stepping out tonight."

Her mother said: "Never mind, now, Dan McClatchy, it's none of your business."

"Oh, I wouldn't say a word! Nothing like a little *romance* in the family. And I hear he's quite a fellow, this Harry Hines."

"*Honestly*, Dad," she protested. "And I don't know any Harry Hines."

"You don't?" He looked at her mother. "I thought you told me——"

"*Fahs*, I told you; and it don't make no difference to you what his name is."

"Well, he's a cop, aint he?"

"So what?" said Arline.

"Well, aint that the big war hero?"

"*War* hero?"

"Sure. He got the Croy de guerre or something, didn't he?"

"*I* don't know. Did he?"

"Oh," Bessie said, "maybe it's not the same man."

He insisted: "Sure it's the same man."

Arline asked: "Do you know him?"

"Sure I know him—by sight, anyhow: a big fellow. There was quite an article in the paper about him when he come back. Don't you remember?"

"No."

"Well, how do you like that?—She's going out with a man and she don't even know who he is."

Bessie said: "Maybe you're the one don't know who he is, Mr. Smarty. You're probably thinking of the wrong man entirely. The table's no place to be discussing it anyhow," with a tilt of her head to draw their attention to Billy, "so we'll say no more about it."

But it was true, she was going out with a man she didn't know, and later, in her own apartment, waiting for his ring, she thought about that. She didn't even know if he was married. Oh, but he couldn't be; Phyllis would have known, would have told her. *Oh, baby, watch out for that guy; he's a wolf!* He probably was, all right. . . .

The front doorbell rang. She stood at the glass for a last look at herself, switched off the light, and went down. The streetlamp burning behind him as he waited on the porch threw his shadow on the curtain of the front door.

Who *was* he?

They went to see Betty Grable and Dan Dailey in *Mother Wore Tights*.

"Isn't she a doll?" she whispered, of the pretty dancing blonde who looked so well in tights. "Imagine having a couple of babies and keeping her figure like that."

He clucked his tongue and said: "Some dancer, too."

Yes—with bright gold hair and bright red lips, radiantly dancing in Technicolor: slim-waisted, small-boned, and shapely; and twice a mother. How did they do it? Exercise and diet and expensive beauty treatments, that was the way. Could Arline do it? With a stricter diet? With exercise and with the facials that Grace was giving her now? Why not? If only she hadn't been born so big; and in the dark she felt her wrist, regretting her skeleton which no amount of diet or exercise could shrink, regretting her broad hips and shoulders, the thickness of her legs and arms, and her age—thirty-three; feeling gross and awkward; touched with envy of the dancing doll.

Mr. and Mrs. Linnegar, friends of her family, were in the foyer as they came out, and Mrs. Linnegar said: "Wasn't that a good picture?"

"Just darling!" Arline agreed.

She had no intention of introducing Harry Fahs, though she saw Mrs. Linnegar looking at him curiously; but Mr. Linnegar said: "Evening, Harry," and her escort answered: "'Lo, Pat." Pat Linnegar kept a news and tobacco shop, and undoubtedly knew every policeman in town.

Then they were in the car, the headlights reaching out for the highway, Harry Fahs driving fast, as she supposed he always did, a policeman geared to it, and he was saying:

"I see you're going to have that grand opening on New Year's Eve."

"Uh huh. Going to come?"

Ruefully: "On New Year's Eve?"—reminding her that New Year's Eve was no night of joy for a policeman. "Might look in, though, if I get the chance. Sa-ay, that looks like it's going to be quite a spot. I hear a lot of people talking about it, too."

"You do?" She was pleased.

"Sure. I guess your dad made a smart move, at that, not selling that painting."

"Hope so."

"How much do you suppose he could have got for it?"

"For the painting? Oh, I don't know." Because why tell him that it was not worth a fortune after all? Because it was a Rembrandt, and famous, and people were coming to see it, and what difference did it make what you could get if you sold it? Because it was not for sale. "But he thinks he can get more for it this way."

"Yeah?" There was wonder in his tone. "Boy!" he said. "It's like finding an oil well in your back yard."

She laughed with pleasure.

The beginning!

Then they were turning off at the Willow Tree, and misgivings seized her.

Until now it had not occurred to Arline to wonder how good a dancer Harry Fahs was, but suddenly she was sure he was a good one, because of what Phyllis had said of him, because he had many dates and must dance often. And what if he should want to rhumba? Arline could not dance the rhumba. It was years since she had danced at all; and she had never been a good dancer. Once, at Catherine Apostoli's wedding reception, Phyllis, the little devil, had turned on the radio and said to her: "Come on, let's dance." Arline had said: "Oh, Phyl, no!" because she knew that Phyllis was only trying to attract attention to herself and get some man to cut in, and because it was rude to take charge like that at someone else's party. But Phyllis had said: "Oh, what's the matter with you? Come on," and seized her and begun to dance with her anyway, and Arline had yielded for fear of making the spectacle worse; but suddenly Phyllis had said: "Hey, you're hard to lead, you know it?" and everyone had heard. Now she reminded herself that this was just for practice anyway, that she was not really interested in Harry Fahs, and that this was just the Willow Tree, but as they entered she was remembering that Harry Fahs had been out with Phyllis Plover and was sure that all the other girls had been good dancers too.

They sat in a booth and had a drink. He lifted his glass, looking at her with the archly speculative and self-assured smile of that day in the park—*was* he?—and said: "To us."

"Us." In spite of her reservations, the words thrilled Arline a little, and the drink, so cold on her lips, warmed her throat and slightly shocked her whole system, so that it seemed the thrill itself was physical and voluptuous.

But the Willow Tree depressed her: a bleak room with stained wooden booths round a rough dance floor which, like all the booths but theirs, was vacant.

The only other patrons were seated at the bar at the far end of the room with their backs turned, and only two of them were women. One of the women was a great-rumped gray-bobbed creature in blue jeans and a leather jacket who was laughing raucously above the din of the juke box. One of the men had his hat on. The bartender was in his shirtsleeves, and she had noticed that the waiter's nails were dirty. Her escort had called the waiter Sid, and she wondered if Harry Fahs came here often. Maybe he likes it here, she thought hopefully, willing to forgive such taste in him if only in order to escape inferring in the Willow Tree the measure of his regard for her. The juke box shuffled itself and began to play "Glocca Morra."

"Dance?" he invited her.

"Mm *hm!*"—as if she couldn't wait.

Harry Fahs danced evenly and confidently. He had control and authority and was easy to follow, and his tallness and breadth and strength diminished her. She took heart and even felt that they must look well on the dance floor together, she and Harry Fahs. But then he was holding her too close. She drew back from the waist and looked up at him in half-coquettish reproof. He laughed softly. "Relax." Then she felt his arm tighten to pull her closer, resisted before she realized that it was because he was beginning a whirl, and suddenly was off balance: she lurched against his chest.

"Oh!" with the breath going out of her. "I'm sorry!" They had come to a dead stop.

He grinned. "My fault."

"No, but I guess I wasn't expecting you to swing me like that, so suddenly."

They began again. It *was* his fault, she thought, but her face was crimson. *Hard to lead.* Then he was holding her too close again, and she was letting him.

When they sat down he reached for his glass, said "Us" again, and finished the highball at a draught. His evident relish alarmed her a little. She hoped he wasn't going to drink too much tonight.

"Want another?" he asked.

She shook her head.

"All right. Let's eat!"

Harry Fahs ate in the same way he drank—with gusto. He opened his mouth wide to welcome great dripping forkfuls of food, and buttered his toast thickly with the motions of a man stropping a razor, chewed vigorously, and seemed to roll the coffee on his tongue. His eating had that quality of honest enjoyment which transcends table manners and universally evokes only a humorous admiration. He took out a cigar, lighted it evenly, drew on it, and removing it from his mouth, blew into the air a thin blue stream.

She said mischievously: "I heard something about you today."

"About me? What?"

"I heard you were a war hero."

"Me?" And he laughed. "I guess you mean Heinie Vance. He's with the State Highway Patrol."

"Oh!" she said, disappointed.

"Somebody got me mixed up because they call me Major, I guess. I come out a major."

"A major! You did?" To the widow of an enlisted trainee whom corporals had overawed, a man who had been a major was almost as impressive as one who had been a hero. But her feeling about officers was still confused. Bill Lucas and she had been bitter about them. When Bill would tell her how he had to stand rigid for inspection while not being permitted to look the officer in the eyes, when she would see him smartly salute an officer on the street and receive a limply condescending response, even when she would contrast the cloth and cut of his by-the-million uniform with those of the uniforms the officers wore, resentment would burn her. "What is this," she had flared once, "the United States or Germany?"

As if reading her mind he said: "Funny, isn't it."

"What is?"

"Oh, this—after that."

Yes, she thought, I'll bet it is, and for a moment enjoyed her revenge for the humiliation, anger, and revenge of that far time. There must be thousands of former officers who felt as he did, she knew: men whom the war had taken from humble stations and given tastes of aristocracy, and who were now back in the plodding mob. Justice. But she could not gloat over him, he looked so wry about it all. "Were you overseas?"

He said that he had been in England, Italy, France, and Germany.

"Did you get to Paris?"

"Once—for three days, was all."

"Oh, I'll bet you had a time there!"

"Some," he admitted with a grin. "But New York, that was where I had the time."

"Did you?"

"Mmm!" Elbows on the table, he tapped the ash of his cigar against the side of the ash tray. "I hit there with a fellow in my outfit that came from the same town as Fay Cody. Ever hear of Fay Cody?"

"The actress? Yes! Did you meet *her*? Oh, what's she like?"

He gave his head a wag and said: "What a gal! She said she'd show us the town, and boy, *did* she." He gazed off, his eyes bright with the recollection—of what?—and repeated: "Boy!" It was one of those moments when the face of a man with a great power of zest is lighted with a magnetic afterglow of pleasure. Looking at him, she pictured the fabled Manhattan with its towers, as in the movies, nightblooming; bright lights and silken gowns, uniforms, dancing, and champagne.

She asked: "What did you do?"

"Everything!"

A wave of depression swept over her. She sighed. "Some war!"

The only other customers in the Willow Tree now were the woman in the leather jacket and the man with his hat on.

Harry Fahs said: "Your husband was killed, wasn't he?"

She regretted having spoiled it. She nodded.

"Where?"

"Fort Ord. In training. It was an accident."

"I see." He looked at the glow on his cigar, respectfully silent.

"We were only married a few months," she reassured him, and felt like a traitor when he glanced up at her searchingly and then again dropped his eyes to the cigar.

He murmured: "Too bad." Then looking up again with a smile: "Dance?"

She was resentful of his blind perception and his bluntness, and wanted to decline but could give no reason.

He went to put a nickel in the juke box, and, waiting for him on the floor, she was glad when he chose another waltz: "Moon" something, a "South Seas" tune. He took her in his arms with easy confidence and again held her too close, and they danced slowly. Dancing like this was easy: they glided and swayed and hardly moved; and the poor Tin Pan Alley nocturne beguiled and wooed her under the palms of its lyrical Never Never beach. She thought that if this were wartime she would be dancing with a major, and closed her eyes. Dancing. A new life now. The beginning. She felt his cheek against her hair, and heard his rapturous whisper:

"*Stacked!*"

She drew back instantly. "Wha-at?"

He laughed and would have pulled her close again, but she held back and gave him, amiably, a knowing look. He laughed again, and bending his cheek close to hers whispered: "What do you say we get out of here?"

"Already?" she said. (He *was,* all right.) And the music stopped. She glanced at her wristwatch. "Gosh, I have to. Look at the time."

"So what?" he said. It was only ten forty-five.

"Be with you in a minute," she promised, smiling, and was on her way to the women's room.

She was frightened—not of Harry Fahs, but of the moment that she now fully expected to be the climax of the evening, and the reason was that she lacked confidence in her ability to put him off with poise and cleverness. She wanted to collect herself for it. She was also disappointed. She hungered after life, but this was not the way she wanted it. And she was offended that he should presume so much on short acquaintance—but only a little offended, for on the other hand the fact that he desired her was encouraging. Applying her lipstick at the glass of the women's room, she recalled *Stacked!* with pleasure. It meant—meant that a girl had a good figure, didn't it? But oh, she lamented, looking at her full figure, I'm so big! She thought of Phyllis, who had been so much surprised to hear that she had a date, who had always seemed to suppose that she could attract no man. But she thought that if Phyllis heard of the circumstance in which she found herself now with Harry Fahs, Phyllis would laugh, would howl. And then, with that regret which she conceived to be unnatural, she remembered the little boy who at this hour would be sound asleep on the couch in her parents' apartment.

No, but how strange, after these years of widowhood and motherhood, to find herself suddenly at such a point with a man whom she had barely met until this evening, with the man who had come out of the dark on the Hill Street bridge that night and offered to give her a safe lift home with her son. She had got into the car thinking he was the law, and he was not the law but a man and what Phyllis had said he was, and during the war had been a major and seen Paris and probably London and Venice and Rome and been shown New York by Fay Cody, and he was out there waiting for her now—waiting for her!

When she came out, she was the image of worldly aplomb. She was freshly groomed and walked with a genteel mince on her high heels and wore that expression of indifference which is seen so commonly on the faces of women leaving that room that there can be no doubt it is the proper one. Harry Fahs put out his cigar at her approach and stood up with a ribald grin. "Atta girl," he said, and held her coat for her. In a minute they would be in his car and driving into the dark.

She was slipping her arms into the coat when she saw the door of the Willow Tree open and a man come in, a white handkerchief masking his face, Western style, and a pistol in his hand.

9

THE KID

The gunman shouted something and she turned—"Harry!"—afraid not of the gunman but of Harry Fahs now after all because he *was* the law. She saw him looking at the gunman in surprise, and his face harden.

"Reach, I said," came the taut voice from the doorway.

He slowly raised his hands.

"Now walk! Up here with the rest."

Still looking at the gunman, Harry Fahs nodded to her, and they moved toward the bar.

The slim tense figure of the holdup man, with that blank dead-white triangle of a face, the hat pulled down to the eyes, and the small black revolver clenched and menacing in one black-gloved fist, appeared unhuman, unearthly. The shirtsleeved bartender, a fat bald sloppy man, wide-eyed behind the bar, with his palms turned outward beside his ears, looked astonished. The waiter, Sid, stood near the far end of the bar and in front of it, his hands high and his little eyes fearfully watching Harry Fahs. The gray-bobbed woman in the leather jacket and the man with his hat on, seated next to each other on bar stools, also with their hands raised, had turned parallel to the bar to face the gunman standing just inside the doorway.

"Watch out, sonny," the woman said. "Somebody might get hurt."

"Yeah, they might!" With his free hand the gunman closed the Willow Tree's inner door and shot the bolt. Then he noticed the door in the opposite wall, a swinging door. "Who's in there?"

"Just the cook, that's all," the bartender said; "the cook."

"Oh, yeah?" The gunman said. Sonny, the woman had called him, and to Arline it was now plain that he was little more than a boy. His voice was the voice of a tough kid and it was nervous. Now for an instant he seemed uncertain what to do about the cook. He said to the bartender: "You! C'mere!"

"Me?" The fat bartender came from behind the bar and stood before the gunman, hands in air.

"Turn around."

"Don't shoot!" The bartender turned his back and flinched as the point of the gun was thrust into it. "Please!"

"Shut up! Now the rest of you—get over by the wall," the kid said. "And turn around. Not you," he told Sid. "You stay where you are."

The four patrons of the Willow Tree stood against the far wall, facing it. The kitchen door was to their left.

"And keep them hands up! All but this guy—and you over there," to Sid. "You two put 'em down; and don't try to get smart. All right. Now you," to Sid again, "when I tell you, you go push that door open just a crack and call the cook, see? Don't try to go inside, just call him. Because if anybody tries anything, including him, this guy gets it, understand?"

"Yes, sir," the waiter said.

"All right.—Now!"

The waiter went to the door, pushed it in a little, and called: "Gus!"

A heavy guttural: "Yuh?"

"Come out here, will you?"

"Me?"

"Yeah."

"Om bissy."

"Yeah, but will you come out here a minute? Somebody wants you."

"Bissy."

"Gus, I'm telling you to come out here. Mel wants you. It's important."

"Bissy! Bissy!"

"Listen, he needs you. Will you do him a big favor and come out here?"

A growl: "Wassa trouble?"

"Gus—please. Come on out, will you?"

"Aw"—something banged in the kitchen. "Chri'sake!"

The waiter stepped back from the door, letting it swing to. After a moment it was kicked wide and there lumbered out a large unshaven man in full-length white apron, wiping his fingers and palms across his cumbersome belly. The kid barked: "Put up your hands—quick!" The cook stopped, looking stunned, then with a tremendous gathering of energy bolted back into the kitchen: the gun exploded. Arline thought: He's killed the bartender, and looked around, but the bartender stood there stiff and straight and deathly pale. The kid had fired at the cook; he fired again as the door swung back. They could hear the cook scrambling across the kitchen; then out behind in the darkness among the garbage cans he was yelling for the police.

The kid cursed. "Listen, if anybody sticks his head through this door while I'm still around I'll put a bullet through it, I'm warning you, see?"

They heard the bolt shot back, the inner door yanked open, and the screen door slam. Harry Fahs turned and sprang. Arline took two steps after him, begging: "Harry, don't!"—knowing that he had to, that it was his job. He was drawing his gun from under his coat as he plunged across the room. She heard a motor roar as he went out, saw a flash and heard the loud report of his gun, and the screen door slammed again, there was another shot, and the car was roaring away, then another shot, another, and another. "Get down!" someone shouted at her, and someone else said: "She's with *him*—the cop!"

Sid, the woman in the leather jacket, and the man with his hat on were huddled behind the far end of the bar, and the bartender was crouching by the front wall. Arline was the only one in the room who was still standing up. She was in no fear for herself but in growing dread because now there were no more shots. The bartender crawled to the door and looked through the screen, and Arline watched him.

She was silently tensely distractedly praying. The bartender said: "Here he comes," and got up and opened the door. "Did he get away?"

"Yeah," Harry Fahs said, coming in. "But I hit him, I think." He went round behind the bar to the telephone on the back counter. Then she saw the dust on the back of his coat. She went to the bar behind him.

"Are you hurt?"

He had put the receiver on the counter and was dialing with his left hand. He half turned and glanced at her. His face was taut and white. "Now don't get scared——"

"You're wounded!"

"He just winged me." Then he turned away and bent over to talk into the phone. "Officer Fahs speaking; Llagas Police. I want to report an attempted robbery and shooting—your territory. . . ."

Arline stared at his hanging arm. Behind her the man with his hat on was saying to the woman in the leather jacket: "I knew he was hit the minute I saw him."

"The Willow Tree," Harry Fahs was saying into the phone. "Out on——" . . . "What?" . . . "Oh. Must've been the cook." . . . "Yeah —me. Got me in the shoulder. But I think maybe I got him too. . . ."

Far down the road a siren screeched. "Here they come already!" the bartender said.

"No," Harry Fahs was saying into the phone, "two of 'em. A girl was driving the car. . . ."

She marveled: A girl!

"Yeah; driving a tan open job. Mercury, I think." He swayed.

"Harry!"

He slumped to the floor.

She started to run around behind the bar to him but the woman in the leather jacket blocked and caught her.

"Honey!"

"Don't!"

The woman clung. "The doc'll take care of him till the ambulance gets here."

"Doc?" Arline saw the man with his hat on, a wiry man with a seamed and weatherbeaten face who looked to be in his sixties, hurrying behind the bar. "Is he a doctor?"

"Vet," the woman said, and Arline thought: Oh, my God, he's probably a chicken doctor! But the woman assured her: "Don't worry, he knows what to do till the ambulance comes." And the siren was closer.

The veterinarian had disappeared behind the bar. The bartender had followed him behind it; he seized the telephone. "Hello? . . ."

The woman turned to Sid. "Get her a drink."

"No!" Arline said, angered by the woman's interference.

"Take it easy," the woman said. "We don't want the doc to have two of you on his hands." And to Sid again: "Make it a cup of java."

"Never mind!" Arline said. "I'm not going to faint."

"All right; so far so good; so why risk going back there? There's nothing you can do, is there?"

"There might be."

"Use your head, honey. You'd only be in the way."

The bartender hung up. "It was the sheriff's office," he announced to the floor, and stood there gazing down, a look of horrible fascination on his face. "Is it bad, Doc?"

"Couple of small bone fractures, maybe. Bullet's still in him, I think. But it don't look real serious to me, no," Doc drawled in a dry voice.

"There," the woman said to Arline. "You hear that?"

A chicken doctor! God!

The siren was subsiding in front of the building. Arline watched the screen door. It opened and two men came in. They were big men in civilian clothes and they moved with purpose and authority. She said: "It *wasn't* the ambulance." That cook, she thought, he hadn't known that anyone was shot, hadn't even called for an ambulance. But the woman said:

"It's coming. The hospital's just up the road."

The officers went behind the bar, saw, asked a few questions, and then for a moment were silent, only looking down, and Arline anxiously watched their faces for a bulletin on Harry Fahs.

The woman asked: "Your husband?"

"What? No."

Then one of the officers took out a notebook and a pencil, and the two of them began to elicit the story of what had happened and as much of a description of the enemy as the bartender and the waiter could supply.

The woman asked: "Engaged or anything?"

"No," Arline said, and remembered that she barely knew Harry Fahs. Then she realized that their slight relationship had curiously changed now; and all at once that official-looking scene behind the bar appeared to shut her out. He was a policeman wounded in the line of duty, he was in the hands of brother officers, and suddenly again he was a man in whose life she had no place, a stranger. A faint blush appeared on her face.

"Come on, honey," the woman said. "Let's wait over here."

Arline went with her to a booth; and the woman introduced herself as the veterinarian's wife, Mrs. Beamer.

Standing in front of the bar and looking over it at Harry Fahs, the waiter became conscious of a great whiteness at his side. It was the cook. Gus had ventured cautiously back through the kitchen door and now he too stood craning at the spectacle on the duckboards behind the bar. In an awed guttural he observed: "Somebody get shot, uh?"

"Yeah," the waiter said disgustedly, "and I wish it was you. You were a big help, you were."

"Me? I call police!"

"Yeah, and it's lucky Mel here aint dead. The punk had the gun right in his back. He said he was going to plug him if anybody tried anything, and then you——"

"He plug Mel?" the cook said, looking dumfounded at the bartender.

"Naw——"

Then they heard the second siren.

"There's the ambulance now," Mrs. Beamer said.

"About time!" Arline said unreasonably.

At the bar the officers were listening to the cook's tale:

"I was in kitchen getting ready stuff for morning. Sid—*him*—come to door, call to me: 'Gus!' I say: 'What you want?' He say I should come *out* of kitchen, say: 'Somebody want to see you.' I say: 'Who?' He say: 'Mel'—bartender. I say: 'No time.' He say: 'Important. Mel *need* you.' I come out. Then I see this *guy*. He's got white clot' on face like bondit. Say to me: 'Stick 'em up!' and I see gun! He don't *say* he plug Mel; I think he plug me! So I run! And he shoot—*not* at Mel—at *Gus!* Son of a gun, I hear bullet jus' miss! Twice he shoot, that guy—at me! I run out back, go quick gas station, hear again shooting, tell man: 'Call police—quick! Holdup!'" The cook raised his palms and let them fall. "That's all!" Then he turned on Sid. "You say 'Come out,' you son of bitch—you don't *say* it's holdup. Almost end of *Gus!*"

She wondered if Harry Fahs had been right about having hit the kid, and if somewhere in the dark night the kid's girl was bending over him and trying to think what to do.

Outside several persons were crowded in front of the screen door, looking in. One of the officers went and shooed them off and closed the inner door.

Then someone at the bar said: "He's coming to."

Arline stood up. "Oh, thank God!"

"Wait," urged Mrs. Beamer.

The siren reached the top of its scream and fell into a dying snarl outside.

The doctor came in first, a stocky blond young man with a crew haircut, no hat, and an open brown topcoat over his white hospital tunic, carrying a black case. He had already disappeared behind the bar before the two attendants entered with the stretcher. The officer, the bartender, and the veterinarian came out from behind the bar to make room for them. She went to the bar and looked over. "Harry?"

His voice sounded tired. "Arline? That you?"

"Yes." She could not see his face.

One of the officers took her elbow. "Hold it, miss."

Sid explained: "She's *with* him."

"Lee?" Harry Fahs called. "Braden?"

"Yeah, Harry?" The officer was a thick-chested powerful-looking man.

"See that she gets home, will you?"

"I'll take care of her."

"All right, boys," the young doctor said, and they began to carry the wounded man out.

"Wait," he said, but they did not wait. "Arline?"

"Yes, Harry?" She followed out the door and through the little crowd of the curious to the rear of the ambulance. "Harry?" she said as they were lifting him in. "How—how is it?"

"Arline? Aw, he just winged me."

The doctor climbed in. "He'll be all right," he said cheerfully.

"They'll get you home," Harry Fahs said. "You hear?"

"That's all right. Harry, I—I'm sorry."

"Me too. Kind of spoiled things, didn't it? We'll try it again, huh?" She stood back to let one of the attendants climb out.

"Give me a month," Harry Fahs said, and she could sense that he was grinning. "Baby!"

The attendant closed the doors and went round to the front. The motor started. The siren began to snarl again as the ambulance pulled away. The whole experience suddenly seemed unreal to her, and in the darkness the fleet white automobile was disappearing like an apparition, trailing its terrible scream.

She had to give the officers her name, age, address, and occupation, tell her story of the holdup, and describe the gunman as best she could. She said that he had been about two inches shorter than the bartender, and assented to the estimate of five feet six, and said that he had been slim and "just a kid, a tough kid." His eyes, she said, had been black or dark brown, and she thought that he might have been "Italian or Spanish," she couldn't say why, except for his eyes. . . .

It was characteristic of her that, though he had put a bullet into Harry Fahs, she did not say "I hope you catch him." He was a tough kid who had tried to hold up the Willow Tree with his girl for an accomplice and had walked into a trap, lost his head, and done what probably he had never meant to do; so it appeared to Arline. She might have taken another view if he had not been a frightened kid, hunted, perhaps wounded, and with his girl. She wondered what his girl was like (tough, too, probably, and loose), and whether she was pretty, and how old they were. She despised his imitation toughness and his bullying, and supposed he was the stuff gangsters were made of, but she could not help feeling sorry for the kid and his girl.

Deputy Sheriff Lee Braden drove her home in Harry Fahs's car. She entered her apartment at ten minutes to twelve.

And in bed she lay bemused by the strangeness and wildness of the evening.

A passing truck woke her: it was half past eight in the morning. She had just finished dressing when her telephone rang. It was her mother.

"Arline! Are you all right?"

"Yes, Ma, I'm all right."

"Thank goodness! I just heard about it."

"How did *you* hear about it?"

"Don't leave till I come. Your father'll stay with Billy and I'll be right over."

And in five minutes Bessie was there. "You're sure you're all right?"

"Of course, Ma. I'm fine. See?"

"My goodness, it must have been dreadful!"

"Did you hear if they caught the robber yet?"

"No, I didn't, but I hope they do! That murderer!" Seeing the shock on Arline's face, Bessie quickly gathered her big daughter into her arms.

"Ma!"

"He died in the hospital this morning," Bessie told her quietly.

"*Died?*" Arline drew back and looked at her mother. "He was only wounded in the shoulder! . . . He was! That's what he said! I talked to him in the ambulance. Even the doctor said he was going to be all right. . . . Ma!"

"It's true," Bessie said.

"But—with a wound like that?"

"Maybe it happened on the table, then."

"How could it?"

"Well," Bessie said, "sometimes it's just the ether. I heard of a healthy eight-year-old boy dying of the ether while he was having his tonsils out. They say there's maybe one case in a million that ether's poison to, and you never know if it's you till you've tried it."

"Ether?"

"Or sometimes it's a weak heart."

"But he——" Arline stopped, a dead certainty appearing in her eyes. They narrowed and her mouth set. "That chicken doctor!" she said.

10

THE FRIENDS OF THE DECEASED

It was neither chicken doctor nor ether nor a weak heart that had finished Harry Fahs. But after the bullet had been taken from his shoulder and the patient had been put to bed, a little clot of blood had moved from the wound into his pulmonary artery, choking off the flow of blood to his heart. It was a thing that happened sometimes in spite of the best of medical care, and it happened in the best of bodies.

But as the McClatchy women sat in Arline's apartment that morning, a few minutes after Bessie's arrival, the cause of death was still unknown to them. Arline briefly told her mother about the holdup and shooting, and Bessie told how she had heard the news—by telephone from Mrs. Linnegar, who had heard it in the same way from her husband, who had heard it at his newsstand from Hubert Ritter of the *Sentinel*; and Arline said:

"Dead! I can't believe it."

On the streets, on the highways, in every newspaper, sudden death was a platitude, but when it struck like this, struck a man who had been a girl's dancing partner the night before, who a doctor had said would be "all right," whose last word to her had been "Baby!"—and a man like Harry Fahs!—it was weird.

Bessie, her eyes on her daughter's appalled face, asked quietly: "Did you like him?"

"Oh, it isn't that. I only went out with him once. I hardly knew him."

"Well," Bessie said, "maybe that's a good thing. Poor man, we'll pray for him. Was he a Catholic?"

"I don't know."

"You don't? Now, dear, you ought to think of things like that. You'll be meeting other men and you can't tell, you might want to marry again, and mixed marriages——"

"Oh, Ma! What did you want me to do, ask him if he was a Catholic as soon as he invited me?"

"Well, it's a good thing to keep in mind just the same. Prudence can save us a good deal sometimes. My, don't it make you think, though. Nobody knows when their time'll come; and what are we here for anyhow but to work out our salvation." This was the philosophy that had been drummed into Arline in school, and she heard it often from her mother. They would be discussing the tribulations of a neighbor and her mother would say with a sigh: "We-ll, we're here to work out our salvation." It was like a sampler hung on the family wall. Expressed now, out of a reference to the suddenly dead man of rakish reputation who on his last night had hoped, she was sure, to add her to his conquests, it had a dire sound even in her mother's almost sing-song tone. But Bessie followed it with a statement outrageously inconsistent with her religion. "Land, I knew something like this'd happen the minute they cut the windows bigger down at the place. 'Cut a window and you cut a grave.'"

"What! Oh, for heaven's sake, Ma, that's ridiculous."

"Well, it's what they say," maintained Bessie.

It was a superstition that Arline had never heard before; sometimes she wondered where her mother got them. "Honestly," she said. "What could *windows* have to do with it? What did Harry Fahs have to do with *our* windows. What did *he* ever do to them?"

But her mother changed the subject with: "Gracious, you haven't even had your breakfast, have you?" and got to her feet.

Arline gave up. "I'll get it."

"No, now, as long as I'm here. And we'll have a nice little visit till your father comes."

"Is Dad coming?"

"Sure—he was worried about you. But I made him take Billy to school first. And I had a nice little lunch for Billy to take with him."

"Thanks, Ma." Arline followed her mother into the kitchen. "Does Billy know what happened?"

"Not a word. I told your father to say nothing about it to him. I didn't want him excited."

"Good. I don't want him to know."

"I think you're wise. He's just coming to that age now—shooting people." Bessie looked into the refrigerator. "Now where are the eggs?"

"Just one egg, Ma," Arline said, and was struck by the seeming callousness of this. Goodbye Harry Fahs but breakfast for Arline, and she still watching her figure.

While she was eating, her father arrived, excited, with a copy of the San Francisco *Examiner*, and pointed out:

POLICEMAN SHOT
IN MORERA DUEL

"*Shot?*" Arline said.

"They say he only died about six A.M. The *Sentinel*'ll have it, but that aint out yet."

The story was in two succinct paragraphs on the front page. Arline was not mentioned.

She had to tell her father the whole story.

He asked: "Was it the war hero?"

"No! You had him mixed up with somebody else. He was in the war, though. He was a major."

"A major!" her father said.

"Uh huh. He said they called him that: Major."

"You don't say! Well," her father said, wagging his head, "I hope they get the dirty bum that done it. The time I got held up I told 'em they could take the joint, but with him it was different. Off duty or not, he was still a cop. I was almost a cop myself, you know. If I'd grown a few inches taller maybe I'd be one today."

"Yes," her mother said, "maybe a dead one like him."

"Well, when you come to think of it, I *might* be," he said. "Inches— that's a narrow escape."

The *Sentinel* published Arline's name and address and identified her as the daughter of D. J. McClatchy, in whose tavern the Rembrandt painting had been found. It said that the kid and his girl were "objects of an intensive state-wide hunt." And it published a photograph of Harry Fahs in his uniform, his face as expressionless as if he had been standing at attention when it was taken; the Police Department photograph, Arline guessed. The paper told that he had been a major in the Army and served in Europe during the recent war, and that he had been born in Cairo, Illinois, and it said that whether any relatives survived him was unknown.

Lee Braden drove Arline to the sheriff's office at San Javier and she spent an hour looking at photographs of suspects—uselessly, of course. The kid's face had been covered with a handkerchief. But she said that she thought she might recognize him anyway if she saw him again and heard him talk.

Phyllis Plover, who had said that she wanted to "hear all about it after," had read the newspaper stories when Arline dropped in at the drugstore that afternoon, but greeted her in solemn wonder with: "Hey, what happened?" and listened aghast to the story. "Gee," she said, and "No kidding!" and "Were you scared?" and "Harry killed—I can't believe it," and "Harry, gee," confronting empty space across her soda counter, "I can see him sitting right there with a malted milk." Then she asked: "Did he make any passes at you?"

It seemed a crime to tell on the dead, but Arline nodded, looking grave.

Phyllis looked almost incredulous. "*Yeah?*" Then she looked disgusted. "Yeah, that was him, all right." Suddenly she gave a contemptuous laugh and said: "The Willow Tree! What'd you let him take you there for?" and scornfully slapped the air, saying: "It's a dump."

Arline never felt quite the same toward Phyllis after that.

She testified at the inquest. There she heard for the first time what the immediate cause of death had been, and the great fee-faw-fum name of it: pulmonary embolism. How frightful it seemed to her that such a little thing could kill a man in a hospital bed; especially a man like Harry Fahs. A clot had formed, had moved—how? Why? And he was dead.

And not the kid at all, then, but the clot. The kid, trying to escape, had only wounded him in the shoulder, after which Harry Fahs had stood up, walked, telephoned, fainted, come to, asked for another date, said "Baby!" And the doctor had assured her: "He'll be all right." It hadn't been murder *then*, had it? Even now he shouldn't be dead. And the kid hadn't intended anybody to be dead. He had run. He had shot in fear, in a wild act of self-preservation, and only wounded his pursuer in the shoulder. Then the clot had formed, and hours later, when the kid was God knew where, had moved, stealing a march on the doctor, and it was murder. They would hunt him down and probably kill him in the gas chamber now. And his girl, who had not fired a shot, who had not even taken part in the holdup really, but had only helped him get away—she might be sent to prison till she died. So three lives would be destroyed because a little clot had, from some mysterious and unlooked-for cause, moved into the pulmonary artery of a man only wounded in the shoulder. To Arline the facts of the matter seemed almost as weird as her mother's nonsense blaming windows.

But the jury found that Harry Fahs was dead of a gunshot wound inflicted by an unknown assailant attempting armed robbery, and recommended that the assailant and his accomplice be brought to trial for his death—for murder!

The house of Milton Groom, Fine Funerals, bore on its neat white Georgian front its best visible advertisement: a clock. Somewhere on the roof was an even better *in*visible one: a solemn bell which tolled every half hour to remind all waking citizens that the clock was ticking and that Groom was biding their time. To certain citizens, in fact, as the clock ticked off the years, the bell began to sound more and more *like* Groom. At night it could be heard at the Llagas Hospital near the edge of town, and now and then a querulous dying man complained of it. But Dr. Groom's political influence sustained him: he was also, as it happened, the coroner. His bell continued to *Groom* people into the grave, and more often than not it was Groom who buried them.

Harry Fahs had been an atheist and opposed to funerals on other grounds also. His views were well known in the department. The trouble was that he had died a hero and had to be buried like one. But when Arline heard that his funeral would be conducted at Groom's by the mayor, she was shocked. They were going to lay him like a cornerstone.

When she arrived, the police honor guard was gathering in the street in white gloves, and she saw Ferd Gilman, the plumber, getting out of his car in his Municipal Band uniform and hauling out his bass drum. She had come early in order to say the Rosary before the ceremonies should begin. But when she entered the chamber where they were to be held, it gave her another shock to find that she was the first to arrive and was alone with his body.

The coffin stood on a stage-like platform at the end of the room, and near it was an oak lectern. There was an American flag over the foot of the coffin, and a flattering array of floral pieces at the back of the platform. She could not distinguish her lilies. The piece that caught her eye was a garlanded three-quarter wreath inverted on a wire stand. It looked distressingly like the kind of thing that is placed over the horse's neck in the Winner's Circle.

She knelt in a back pew and began to pray for the dead man's soul. But it was hard to concentrate on the Sorrowful Mysteries alone like this with his body. It comforted her to hear someone else coming in.

Bead by bead she followed the Passion of Christ, and when she finished and sat back she saw that the pews were filling up. On one side
of her was Alec Frick holding his American Legion cap; on the other,
a woman she did not know. Chief of Police Lally was sitting in the
front pew; next to him was Fire Chief Hackett. And a few pews ahead
of her, stiffly shoulder to shoulder in dark suits, were Mel and Sid and
Gus. Then to her horror she saw Josie Cantrell. But Josie, she supposed, was inevitable at this funeral.

Josie Cantrell was a short burly grim-looking old woman left over
from a banished era. Once, she had kept a bawdyhouse; today there
were no bawdyhouses in Llagas. Today Josie lived in ostensible re-
spectability in a red-brick house on Morera Street, and there she
maintained a telephone service, dispatching her girls from their own
addresses to wherever her clients wished them to go. She was never
arrested nowadays; not for lack of evidence, nor because she paid for
immunity—her money was not accepted any more—but because, it was
said, of her threat that if ever arrested again she would "blow the lid
off" the town; and the story was that she made it a practice to attend
the funerals of public officials and of all influential citizens who had
been her clients, no matter how long ago, in order to remind the living
that she was a walking skeleton closet and better let alone. It was her
last stand. "Was Josie there?" it was asked after the funeral of every
man of authority or influence who died in Llagas, and the answer,
more likely than not, would be: "Josie was there." It had become a
town joke.

And just across the aisle was Orpha Baines. Orpha Baines did house-
work and lived in Mudtown, a litter of shacks along the slough. She
was a buxom woman of about thirty, with a tawny skin and a pretty
face lighted by warm black eyes, who was believed to have Negro
blood, and her poverty, ignorance, humility, cheerfulness, and willingness led the wives of Llagas to pity rather than condemn her because
she went on having children out of wedlock. Women said that men
took advantage of Orpha Baines. But the County never could find a
man who would admit that he had, and Orpha never told. Poor Orpha,
Arline thought—but what was *she* doing here? It might look as if . . .
People might think—— Arline banished the thought. He had been a
policeman—probably he had just befriended her. But there sat
Josie Cantrell. *"Oh, baby, watch out for that guy; he's a——"*

And suddenly she realized that this impressive gathering at Milton
Groom's was composed chiefly of women. Women, pretty and plain,
ranging in age, most of them, from mid-twenty to mid-forty, women
of lady-like aspect and women not, women of various shades of blond

and brunette, women short, of middle height, tall, robust, medium, and slim. And just then, from somewhere, softly, as if to itself, an organ began humming "The End of a Perfect Day."

She reasoned that what she was thinking was absurd. She stole a glance at the woman beside her: thin and straight, not pretty, wearing a plain black wool dress; a woman apparently of refinement. What could Harry Fahs have been to her? (A policeman who had been a major and had seen New York with Fay Cody and had been a——) Anyway, he couldn't have been back from the war very long; he wouldn't have had time for so many. And Orpha Baines wouldn't have come here if—— But it struck Arline that come here was exactly what simple Orpha Baines would do. Then, while the organ hummed its mad choice, the woman beside her raised a handkerchief and began to weep.

Was it possible? Arline was carried away by her staggering suspicion. Purgatory seemed a dim hope for Harry Fahs. Then the organ changed to "Just a song at twilight" and she thought: Not even a hymn—nothing. Then she saw a girl looking at her, and it dawned on Arline that what she was thinking about the others, the others must be thinking about her. It had been in the newspapers that she had been out with him the night he was killed! She reddened. She reminded herself defensively that she had been going to repulse him; but she found herself wondering how that night might have ended if it had not been for the holdup. Or if she had spent just a few minutes' less time in the women's room and they had left before the robber entered. Minutes —she had not got that off the treetops; a bullet; a clot; and where was he now? Then she realized that the title of the piece the organ was playing was not "Just a Song at Twilight" but "Love's Old Sweet Song," and then, in a muffled way, from the roof, the bell chimed in: *Groom, Groom, Groom, Groom, Groom.* . . .

On the platform, a man appeared. He was portly and solid-looking and grave; his suit was blue and double-breasted. He established himself behind the lectern, gripping the top edges with both hands, and waited. The organ stopped and with his knuckles he gave the lectern three measured raps for order. He was Sam Schuman, mayor of Llagas and owner of the Empire Hatchery. In a tone befitting the occasion, and in phrases spaced and laid like milestones, he spoke into the hush:

"As mayor. Of Llagas. It becomes. My sad duty. And my sad privilege. To say a few words. (Here today.) Over the body. Of a brave man. . . . I knew. Police Officer Fahs. In life. You too. Knew him. And we knew a man. Whose code. Was courage. Fidelity. And honor.

By these principles. He lived. And for these principles. He died. And so we have come. To pay him tribute. Here today."

The mayor recalled that during the late war Officer Fahs had gone to the defense of his country and the free world. It had been a time, he said, that tested what men were made of, and in recognition of his capacity for leadership his country had commissioned him a major. After the war he had continued to serve society. As a peace officer he had been dedicated to the preservation of the principles of law and order; and it was thanks to men like him, the mayor said, that Llagas had the fourth lowest crime rate in the nation. The mayor told how Harry Fahs had shot it out with a gunman and had fallen. He had died, the mayor said, to preserve the ideals for which he had lived, and he had died for his fellow men. Greater love had no man, the old saying went, than he who laid down his life for his friends. But Officer Fahs had gone further. He had sacrificed himself on the altar of public service.

Gripping again the top edges of the lectern with both hands and leaning backward as if to lift it from the floor, the mayor continued: "I am not. A clergyman. I have no formal. Religion. But I believe I know the difference. Between right. And wrong. And I try to do. What's right. And I believe. In a Higher Power. A Power that appreciates. The difference. Between good. And evil. A Power that will not let a good man down. A Power that I believe will echo. What I. As mayor of the community this man served. Say. On behalf of our people. Here today." The mayor turned to the coffin and said: "Well done. Good and faithful servant." He turned back again. "And I believe we should not mourn such a man. We ought to get down on our knees and give thanks for him. And I say we should not mourn him because. He is not dead. For although he lies there in his casket. His spirit lives on. In the spirit of courage. Fidelity. Law and order. And public service." The mayor then brought out a paper and said that he would close with a few verses by the beloved American poet James Whitcomb Riley, and he began to read:

"'I cannot say. And I will not say. That he is dead.—He is just away! With a cheery smile. And a wave of the hand. He has wandered into. An unknown land. . . .'"

Half a dozen of the women were crying. Others were gazing soft-eyed or critically at the speaker, or sorrowfully or dully or meditatively at the coffin. It was a scene multifariously repeated that morning in towns and cities and jungles to the ends of the earth, the living confronted by the tremendous first and final questions.

Sam Schuman did believe in a Higher Power, and he hoped that there might be something to this talk of a Higher Plane. He did not wish to die forever when he died. But it appeared to him that all a man might do in order to get to heaven, if you could call it that, was live the best life he could, according to his lights and conscience; and if the character that he had given Harry Fahs, which was the same character that he prized in himself, would not get a man into heaven, if there was a heaven, he did not know what would. He refrained from asking himself where a man might go if there was a heaven and a man did not get in. But he considered that as mayor of Llagas he was giving Harry Fahs an excellent sendoff. He had even edited out of the poem, as unbecoming the manly subject of his eulogy, references to violets and the little brown thrush and the mockingbird and a honeybee wet with rain. He finished:

" 'Think of him still as the same, I say: He is not dead, he is just away.' "

To Arline, Harry Fahs was dead all right. Dead, to her, meant gone to render the final accounting to the God who had created you and placed you on earth to choose, and the business of a funeral was to evoke the mercy of God upon the dead and to remind the living that they had better set their own accounts in order. To use a funeral for denying or glossing the immortal truth was to betray the living and cheat the dead. She was silently putting in another word for the dead hero: Eternal rest grant unto his soul, O Lord. . . .

The mayor made his exit into the wings. Women wiped their eyes and noses and turned to one another to comment on the funeral oration. The organ began to play "Rock of Ages"—a hymn at last. Then a man in black stepped out on the platform and said that those who wished to pay their respects would please pass by the casket and out the side door, which he indicated. Chief of Police Lally led off awkwardly. And the only rebel to leave by the front door was Josie Cantrell.

Soon the queue was made up entirely of women. Arline hardly looked at the body. Her face was crimson.

Outside the police honor guard had formed in two ranks at the foot of the front steps, making a corridor through which the hero was to be carried to the hearse. The Municipal Band was drawn up in the middle of the street. Then down the steps between the ranks of the honor guard marched three men with floral pieces to be loaded aboard the hearse, and in the lead was the horseshoe wreath.

Women were all around her, some of them red-eyed from crying. She felt that she could be part of this no longer. She began to walk home. But her conscience rebuked her; and before she had gone a block the band was playing "My Buddy." She groaned and changed her course for St. Peter's.

When she came out, the sunshine of the morning lifted her spirits. Death might awe her with its presence, alert her inner ear to waves of silence from the infinite land, drive her back upon her faith, and quicken her piety, but in a brighter atmosphere she recovered quickly. Orpha Baines—could Harry Fahs really have been the father of any of those children? And there had been that awful Josie Cantrell and all those others; but some had looked so nice. If it had meant what she had thought it meant, Harry Fahs had been a man who could attract and win women of all kinds. But he had not won Arline; and persuading herself that her conscience was clear, she was able to feel superior to those others, and raised her chin, remembering that comforting fable of the proper female education: Men may amuse themselves with one kind of woman but they always marry the other kind. And she had attracted him! When she got home her mind was back where it had been weeks ago: the New life; people coming all the way from the city; the beginning. . . .

The radio in the next apartment was turned on loud, and Arline began to hum its tune with it as she took her hat off. Suddenly she stopped humming and stood still, recognizing the very tune to which she had danced that first time with Harry Fahs:

How are thinnngs in Glocca Morraaa?

In the cemetery just then the hearse was coming to a halt. A dozen cars and the bus carrying the musicians were pulling up behind it. The dead man was about to be borne to the grave by the chief of police and brother officers, piped over the side by the Municipal Band, saluted with pistols by the honor guard, and having been certified by the mayor of Llagas, California, officially sealed in eternity with a horseshoe on his chest.

GOOD LUCK, HARRY FAHS!

But after the first shock of recognizing the tune that was coming from Mrs. Wagner's radio, Arline was no longer thinking of him dead. The music had reminded her that while dancing with him that first time she had stumbled. It had not been her fault; it hadn't! She listened attentively to catch the rhythm of the music. First her head, then her shoulders moved with it, and then she raised her arms, closed her eyes, and turned. . . .

DEEPEST SYMPATHY

She was dancing.

11

THREE TO GET READY

Her father opened the door to her ring. He was in his shirtsleeves, his vest unbuttoned, his spectacles on his nose, and he had the look of a man interrupted.

"Oh it's you," he said. "Your mother's at the market." He went to the apartment's living room table, which held papers and an open ledger, and sat down at it busily. "I was just doing the books."

She dropped into an armchair and looked at his bent back. "Dad?"

"Huh?"

"I don't see why you're going to have the opening on New Year's Eve if there won't be any dancing."

"No dancing, no," he murmured, preoccupied.

"But if you're going to have a band——?"

"No band."

"No *band*?"

"Huh?" He looked round.

"You're going to have a band, aren't you?"

He came round in his chair, and sighed. "Well, I was thinking what's the good of talking. This aint a ballroom we're opening. The band'd be nothing but a big expense."

"Whaaat? But the grand opening!"

"I know, but we got to cut our coat according to our cloth, as your mother says. And I was thinking we could do without the big searchlight, too."

"Dad! What's the matter with you?"

"Who, me? I'm only trying to be sensible."

But she knew her father. And she knew that he had set his heart on that grand opening. And she knew that the searchlight was his darling. Alarmed, she demanded: "Tell me the truth!"

"What do you mean tell you the truth, it's a plain and simple business proposition."

She stamped her foot. "Dad!"

"Holy mackerel, I suppose you think I'm trying to put something over on you—my own daughter. Do you think I'm stealing money out of the family till? All right, then, I'll give you the figures, I'll give you the cold facts. But not a word of this to your mother—they's no sense worrying *her* with this."

"All right. What?"

"O-kay. Well"—he paused and sighed again. "Between you and me it's Mr. Johansen's latest. Now he says he estimates the job'll come to about seventeen thousand five hundred. How do you like that?"

"Seventeen thousand five hundred?"

"Yep. And that aint all. Wait'll you hear the rest of it." He pulled toward him a sheet of paper covered with sums. "According to my calculations we laid out exactly four thousand eight hundred and forty-eight dollars and twenty-eight cents for equipment as of this day inst. And we paid Mr. Johansen seven thousand three hundred on account. And I owe the Markham Galleries around eight hundred, as close as I know yet. And since we been waiting for the new place to be finished, we spent another six hundred just for living expenses. On top of that, now, I'm getting in a big new stock of booze. We got to get in food besides. And to run the place it's going to cost us close to seven hundred a week for the help alone. Over and above which they's the payments and the taxes and the insurance and the utilities and the laundry and the God knows what. And as of this day inst., we got exactly twelve thousand three hundred fifty-two bucks and oh-five cents in the bank. Which *means*," he finished, "that when we get through paying the debts we got now, and not counting the new booze and the grub and the running expenses that'd knock your eye out, we'll be down to something like sixteen hundred bucks."

"Sixteen *hundred?*"

"Oh, it's these cockeyed prices they got nowadays, this blame inflation everybody's talking about, what we used to call the high cost of living. And then they was the new floor to put in on account of the termites et up the old one on me. But by golly all I know is when we started out we had over twenty-five thousand bucks and now we're down to peanuts." He wagged his head defeatedly. "I don't get it."

Neither did Arline. By comparison with their former estate it had seemed that they were rich. "But how——?"

"How? I just told you, didn't I?" her father flared. But seeing her distress, he relented. "But wait, now. You don't understand. It aint as bad as it sounds. No. You got to remember we got all this dough tied up in a pretty good investment. I'm only trying to keep the expenses down till we get going. That's what you got to do in business, see?—keep the income high and the outgo low. That's the secret. Especially when you aint even open yet. But just wait'll we get going," and he grinned cheerfully. "Wait'll the old spondulics come rolling in. Don't worry. Leave it to the old man—I'm an old hand at this game. And don't go worrying your mother."

"Don't *worry* her? We'll all be out in the street!"

But just then there was a key in the lock, and he silenced her. "Shh! It's her! Don't say a word or I'll brain you," and turning back to the table he pretended to be lost in his calculations.

Arline was frightened. The Lost Dutchman Tavern was in danger of failure before it ever opened. And if it did open, where would her father get the money to keep it open during the crucial first few months? Sixteen hundred dollars! And nineteen thousand owed to the bank! The New life seemed a lost hope unless something was done, and done quickly. "Leave it to the old man"! They'd be bankrupt. And her parents weren't young any more. And what would become of Billy?

She, with a child to bring up, had been frugal. Her government in-surance check came to thirty-nine dollars a month, and her "compen-sation" for her husband's death, to a hundred twenty-one, and she continued to receive her wage of thirty a week from her father. Food still cost her nothing, for she and Billy ate with her parents, but she paid sixty a month rent, and the nursery school cost forty-five a month, yet in about four years and a half she had saved almost five thousand dollars, and this, with what her husband had left, brought her bank account to just under six thousand.

She went to the bank and drew out three thousand.

In the living room of her parents' apartment that night, while her mother was in the kitchen preparing dinner, she bent over her father as he sat reading the *Sentinel,* and tucked the folded cashier's check in an upper pocket of his vest, whispering sternly: "Now take this, and not a word to Ma."

"What? What are you doing?" He fished the check out, unfolded it, drew back his head and peered at it through his spectacles, gave a start, and said: "What's this? Where did you get this?"

"Never mind; it's a loan—and *keep quiet.*"

"What?" His red face blazed redder. "Take it back! You must be crazy. I wouldn't touch it, I don't need it, take the damn thing. . . ."

She was holding his arm away. "No! Keep *quiet.*"

"What the devil! No! Take it, I'm telling you; I wouldn't—— No!"

His eyes were wet as he indignantly tried to force the check on his daughter, she thrusting his arm away by the wrist, and Billy, sitting with a picture puzzle on the floor, watching in astonishment. From the kitchen Bessie called: "What's the trouble out there?"

Father and daughter broke off the struggle at once, and Arline called back: "Nothing, Ma."

"Well, you better finish setting the table. I'm just taking the roast out. And you can put the potatoes on."

Later that night, in her own apartment, Arline had just put Billy to bed when her downstairs doorbell rang. She pressed the button to release the catch, opened her apartment door, and waited. Up the stairs came her father. He walked in and slammed the check down on the table. "Here, I'm giving it back," he said, "and that settles it. Of all the crazy—— What're you doing?"

She had shut the door and put her back against it. "Not here!" she warned, with a meaningful glance at the boy on the couch; and she led her father into the dinette, turning off the light in the outer room before she closed the door.

Immediately the boy sat up, and he could hear his grandfather's low indignant voice but could distinguish none of the words:

"This is what I get for trying to explain business to a woman! Not that I don't appreciate—— Wait! Listen! Did you think I'd take money from widows and orphans? What kind of a mother are you, taking it from your own son? Taking the bread out of his mouth! That money——"

"What do you mean!" Arline was infuriated by this attack on her motherhood. "It's for his sake I'm doing it—for his sake and Ma's just as much as for yours—all right, and for my own sake. Sure, the new place means a lot to me; or didn't you know that? And it means a lot to my son. You're not the only one that'll be out if it flops, you know. That little kid your grandson will be out too, and so will Ma and me; or did you think it was all yours?"

He tried to cut her off, taken aback by her violence. "Oh, oh, wait, now——"

But she rushed on: "You and Ma have got your whole life savings in that place; and your future! What if it flops? What if it doesn't even open? And the mortgage! Don't you think Ma cares? Don't you think Billy and I care?"

"Why, sure, I——"

"You can't even afford the band and the searchlight. You told me you were down to sixteen hundred dollars. A couple of months ago you had twenty-five thousand! Then you tried to tell me it was all right because we had a good investment. What do you mean a good investment? Why, you don't even know if the place'll open. You're scared to death. My God, it's got to open. You owe it to Ma and Billy and me."

The boy could hear his mother's fierce tongue plainly. He was sitting up tense and still, frightened, listening. It was one of the times he would remember all his life—the night his grandfather came to the apartment after he was in bed, and went into the other room with his mother, and she turned off the light and shut the door, and he heard her railing at his grandfather:

"Accusing me of robbing my own son! Investing for him, that's what I'm doing. Trying to see he gets a little security. And what about Ma? Do you think I want to see my mother thrown out in the street? Talking about 'wait till the old spondulics come rolling in'—when all the time you knew we might go broke. Think I'm going to sit by and let this flop like the chicken ranch? No! I'm going to *do* something. It's our last chance!"

Her father sank down on a chair, crying.

"Oh, Dad!" Instantly her arms were around him. "Dad!"

He was blubbering: "The chicken ranch—it was hard times then—the Depression. . . ."

"I didn't *mean* that."

"And I wasn't cut out for it, I wasn't cut out for it."

"Oh, Dad, *that* wasn't what I meant. . . ."

"And the termites and, and we——"

"I know. Oh, Dad, Dad, forgive me."

"And I didn't want to tell you. I thought if we could just, just get going. . . ."

"I knowww." She was holding the side of his face against her breast, rocking him. "And I didn't mean that about the chicken ranch. Dad, don't, don't cry. It wasn't your fault. And anyway this is different. This is what you *were* cut out for. It's your trade."

"Sure; and, and once we——"

"But don't you see? All I was trying to do was help you get started. Because it *is* a wonderful investment just like you said. People'll come all the way from the city. And all you need is a little bit to tide you over, and it'll be such a big success, and you do deserve it so."

"I—I didn't mean you were stealing the money."

"Of course you didn't. And it's only a loan. . . ."

"I can't," he said, "I can't."

But his back was to the wall. At last he gave in. He wiped his eyes

and blew his nose and said that he would give her a note. It seemed
to Arline that what had passed between her father and herself in the
dinette this evening was sordid enough as it was—a note would only
make it worse. But her father explained that she did not understand
business. What if he died, he explained, and the estate went into
probate? There ought to be a paper, he said, that could be filed in
court against the will; which reminded him that he ought to make a
will; and he said that she must remember never to lend money to anybody without a note, the way they did it in business. And it hurt and
shamed her even more because she understood that her father was
trying to regain his dignity. He called for a sheet of white paper, and
she brought him a tablet of letter stationery. He put on his silver spectacles and unscrewed his fountain pen. He rested the ball of his arm
on the table, rotated the pen above the paper, and wrote:

> Nov. 21, 1947, Inst.
> Llagas, Cal., U.S.A.
> To my daughter Arline Lucas nee McClatchy that was.
> Whereas and in consideration thereof to be paid back in
> full plus 5% interest to same or heirs to wit William Lucas Jr.
> by name.
>
> I.O.U. $3000.00
(Signed) D. J. McClatchy

His was a flowery hand; it looked like a piece of writing belonging
to another age. Tears sprang to her eyes again as she read it.

The newspapers said that in an abandoned boathouse on Tomales
Bay, which was not far from Llagas, two children had found the body
of an unidentified girl of about twenty years of age. She, like Harry
Fahs, had been shot through the shoulder, but from behind, and the
bullet had been fired from Harry Fahs's gun. She had been dead six
days. Under the trees outside a tan convertible Mercury automobile
had been found, and on the car, fingerprints. But the kid was gone.

So not the kid at all, then, but the girl—she had been the one shot
by Harry Fahs that night in the darkness; and the kid carrying her
into that lonely refuge instead of taking her to a doctor; and then the
children finding her—dead six days! Which meant that she must have
lain there four days before she died. And because no trace of food had
been found in the boathouse the sheriff's office thought that the kid
might have abandoned her on the night of the holdup. Abandoned
her? Murdered her—he *was* a murderer, Arline thought. And the girl's

handbag was missing. Robbed her and left her to die! Now Arline hoped they would catch him.

A few days later the girl had been identified, and the authorities had the name of a boy who they thought might be the kid.

The girl had been identified as Nancy Croan, daughter of Mr. and Mrs. Emmett Croan, small Nebraska farmers. She had not been twenty years of age, but only nineteen. She had left home three weeks before —with, it was believed, someone named Raymond Dirigo. And Arline was horrified to read that the father had said that he did not care what was done with her body. "She run off, didn't she?" Emmett Croan had said, according to the newspapers. "Never even wrote to her mother. I guess she was ashamed. We always been people that worked for what we got. But not her. She was a wild one. Well, she made her bed. . . ." And it was only a month till Christmas. The newspapers published a snapshot of her standing beside a drab wooden porch, in blue jeans and a gingham shirt, her thumbs hooked in her belt, elbows forward, head thrown back, blond hair blowing, mouth laughing. She did look a wild one, but so young, Arline thought, and pretty—"so cute." Poor little Nancy Croan.

About Raymond Dirigo the newspapers told only that he was a war veteran and twenty-two years old, so tall and so heavy, with black hair and eyes and an olive complexion. But the description seemed to fit. So did the name. And this tentative identification of the fugitive, which focused the hunt and gave reality and imminence to the possibility that the law was going to take a life, raised apprehensions in Arline—she would have to testify at the trial. To her mind now the kid was a treacherous and brutal murderer, though not exactly the murderer of Harry Fahs, and she wanted to see him brought to justice, but at the thought that she might help to send him to his death she shuddered. Suddenly it amazed and sickened her that she was involved in this newspaper story of blood and retribution. Minutes, a tough kid and his foolish girl, shooting, a clot. . . .

It was crazy.

Like "Cut a window and you cut a grave."

McClatchy had some signs printed to advertise the grand opening, and had them posted in town and along the highway. But the first result was a new burst of antagonism against the tavern: The Ladies' Service Club adopted a resolution denouncing his plans for the Rembrandt painting as a crime against art. The *Sentinel* reported this action and published the following editorial:

Recently a lost painting by the great Dutch master Rembrandt was found in a Llagas tavern.

Art lovers the world over rejoiced.

Llagas rejoiced, both for culture's sake and for the local merchant into whose possession this priceless picture had fallen by sheer chance.

But what is now being done with this masterpiece?

It is to be kept permanently behind the tavern bar—used as an attraction to drum up trade in liquor!

This is a prostitution of art and an insult to the artist.

It is culture made the harlot of Bacchus.

Great art belongs to the world.

Many art lovers will be deprived of viewing this masterpiece simply because they would scruple to set foot in a barroom.

School children should see it. But are children to be led through the sawdust and up to the brass rail on the pretext that it is good for their education?

Hardened tipplers are not the people who will appreciate this painting.

"Art," says Ben Jonson, "hath an enemy called Ignorance."

This painting belongs in a public museum.

"There they go again!" McClatchy exploded. "What's eating them a museum? And what kind of a place do they think we're going to have here in the first place? 'Through the sawdust,' he says—you can tell that old party aint had his foot on a rail since the days of the free lunch. And you'd think I was going to make hardened tipplers out of all the little shavers in town, me that wouldn't sell a drink to a minor if he was shaking with the d.t.'s!"

Arline said: "It's just those old hens at the Service Club," and Bessie commented grimly: "They have little to do."

McClatchy would not let the Llagas protests go unanswered like the ones in the letter columns of the San Francisco papers. But it was easy to guess that the editorial had been written by old A. B. Satterfy, proprietor of the *Sentinel*, himself, a prohibitionist—"known," McClatchy said, "as the worst old hellroarer that ever come down the line." So the tavernkeeper tried to be tactful. He wrote to the Ladies' Service Club and sent a copy of the letter to the *Sentinel* with a request that it be published. It said:

> Dear Ladies
> In regards to you ladies resolution about the famous painting by Rembrandt Van Rijn that we are going to have in the new Lost Dutchman Tavern formerly known as the old Travelers Rest I can see you ladies have got the wrong idea what kind of a place we are going to have here. In the first place the old Travelers is being remodeled at great expense into a first class place with a new floor that never had sawdust on it in my time anyhow. A-1 food will be served by courteous uniformed waitresses and you can see the painting free of charge you dont have to buy a drink for that at all. Take the Palace Hotel where they have another famous painting behind the mens bar there the ladies go in and look at it all the time. The same with this painting here it will soon be installed as a free service to the customers ladies welcome and if you want to bring the children I guarantee no drinks will be served to them as I am a family man myself and I know I would not serve a drop to my own grandson age four. Grand Opening New Years Eve and you ladies are cordially invited to come and give us the once over. No hardened tiplers allowed.
> Yours truly.

But from the ladies there was cold silence, and the *Sentinel* published a second editorial, this time accusing the tavernkeeper of having dared to invite children into his barroom.

"Holy smoke!" he said. "He's got it all wrong! It was the ladies that wanted the kids to see the painting. I only stated if they brought the kids along I wouldn't even give 'em a smell of the cork. I'm going to write him a letter and ask him who does he think I am, Jerry Bassity?"

But Bessie advised: "No, Danny, don't do it again."

"What do you mean don't do it? Do you think I'm going to stand for a roasting like this?"

"Now, we've done nothing wrong and there's nothing he can do to us; but if you write another letter you'll only get another article right back at you."

"You mean anything I say could be used against me."

"Why, sure. Look at what he's done here. But he's only talking—there's nothing he can do and he knows it; or the Ladies' Service Club, neither. So just don't give 'em another chance."

He thought that over. "The only thing," he said, "a man ought to be allowed to tell his side of the story. But maybe you're right at that. We're in the clear and I don't want to incriminate myself. Maybe the thing to do is keep mum and let it all blow over like it did the last time."

But before it blew over, it blew harder. Hubert Ritter of the *Sentinel* and Alice Fritz of the weekly *Leader* telephoned him as Morera County correspondents for the *Chronicle* and the *Examiner* of San Francisco. He gave them his side of the story. Next morning the *Examiner* had:

'DUTCHMAN'
IN LLAGAS
CIVIL WAR

And the *Chronicle*:

ART VS. RUM:
DEBATE OVER
MASTERPIECE

And the controversy in the letter columns of the San Francisco papers was resumed. But A. B. Satterfy wrote no more editorials, the Ladies' Service Club adopted no more resolutions, and he found that all his friends were treating the affair as a joke. It was only the "long-hairs" and "the temperance crowd" that were "after" him, Walsh Reardon said, and laughed. He saw that Reardon was right; and when he began to receive reservations for New Year's Eve his confidence returned. "It was just a lot of free advertising all over again," he said. "You wait, now—on New Year's Eve all roads'll lead to the Lost Dutchman."

But his wife and daughter were not so sure.

Dan and Bessie McClatchy moved back into the rooms behind the tavern. The remodeling was almost completed. But there was the equipment to be moved in, and the liquor to be delivered, there were advertisements to be arranged for, and bills to be paid, and there would be the food to be got in, the help to be instructed, and all the rest of it.

And there was the Christmas shopping.

In the midst of all this they received Mayor Schuman's regrets. The mayor wrote that he and Mrs. Schuman found themselves obliged to spend New Year's Eve in San Francisco and so would be unable to attend the grand opening.

McClatchy put on a brave face in imparting this news to his family at the dinner table in the shining new kitchen. He ignored the obvious guess about the real reason for the mayor's change in plans, and said: "That's the way it goes, you know, with them politicians—even on a night like New Year's Eve they can't call their time their own. It's probably a big Party affair they want him at and he can't get out of it." He hastened on cheerfully: "But, Bess, I got an idea. You lead the grand march with Mr. Markham, and I'll get Mr. Reardon to give the address for the grand unveiling. How's that?"

"Sure, Danny. It's all the same. But Mr. Markham knows more about that painting than Mr. Reardon does. Why don't you get Mr. Markham to say the few words?"

"Ohhh, no. Painting's Mr. Markham's business, I know, but talking's out of his line, Bess. And Mr. Reardon knows a thing or two about the fine arts himself, you know. One night there he told me all about Rembrandt, remember? And he's a great talker. Wait'll you hear him. I'd rather listen to Mr. Reardon talk than the mayor any day."

But Arline said: "Oh, Dad! Are you out of your mind? Things are bad enough as they are—but Reardon! He'd ruin everything! Why, he'd probably be drunk!"

"Hold on, now—oh, no he won't! He'll be cold-sober if I ask him. Besides, it'll be too early in the evening. But I'm telling you, now, if he has a few shots in him he'll be all the better."

"No! Ma, don't let him. That old pot!"

"Pot!" her father said. "What do you mean 'pot'? Mr. Reardon——"

"Oh, my God!" Arline said with tears in her eyes. "I won't stand for it, I won't!"

But Bessie said: "Now, dear, the man's an old friend of your father's. And they do say if there's one thing he's got it's the silver tongue. And your father'll see to it he's cold-sober or we won't let him through the door. So we'll leave it at that."

Arline could hardly believe it. Surely her mother knew how much depended on the grand opening, realized that there were already too many obstacles in the way of the tavern's success. But her mother gave her a private look that said: Now, Dad did so want the mayor, and he's got enough to worry him, and the least we can do is let him have his talker. And in that instant Arline knew that this was to be her father's party—that her mother was giving it to him. Restraining herself, she dropped her eyes. "All right, Ma." She felt her mother gratefully squeeze her hand under the table. She looked at her mother and slowly, almost imperceptibly shook her head in baffled pitying admiration, saying without a word: Honestly, Ma, you're a wonder.

And that was how Mr. Reardon was chosen to give the address at the grand unveiling.

The painting arrived from the Markham Galleries, and Johansen's workmen removed it from its new gilt frame, fixed it to the wall behind the bar, and over the edges nailed strips of wood to match the paneling. It was the crowning touch. The tavern was finished.

Beholding the portrait dramatically illuminated by the small spotlight set into the ceiling for the purpose, McClatchy welcomed the wanderer with a grin: "Well, Dutch, what do you think of the place now?"

"Gracious," Bessie said, "I wouldn't know it was the same picture."

"Didn't I tell you? Look at his skin."

"Yes, indeed."

"I bet he don't know it's the same old shebeen, neither," McClatchy said.

The combined restaurant and bar was a spacious room paved with a checkerboard of red-and-white linoleum. Three of the walls were painted pastel green. The right-hand wall and part of the end one were lined with walnut-stained booths. The fourth wall was covered with plywood to match, and the old mahogany bar in front of it had been refinished to look like walnut too. By the entrance door was a walnut-finished counter for the cashier. The double doors to the kitchen were covered with polished sheets of brass. And the kitchen had been repainted white and was equipped with a "new" range, two coffee urns, a ponderous refrigerator, meat blocks, and tables, and with shiny new pots and pans and cooking forks and spoons and ladles and carving knives. And the exterior of the little building wedged between Jack's Auto Repair and the tall warehouse of the Poultrymen's Cooperative, across the street from the railroad yard, was clean red brick with long leaded windows trimmed in delft blue, and from an iron bracket above the delft-blue door hung a small weathered-looking board with the new name of the place, *The Lost Dutchman,* carved into it and stained to look as if it had been burned in with an iron. Not the oldest old-timer would have recognized the historic tavern built for travelers in frock coats and bustles in the early days of the railroad.

McClatchy confidently repeated what he had said fifteen years ago, before the coming of Repeal: "All we got to do is open the doors."

Before eight o'clock on Christmas morning, Arline brought Billy to claim his toys under the tree that his grandparents had set up and decorated in their back parlor the night before. Arline had bought her mother a bottle of perfume, and her father a necktie, and they gave her a calfskin handbag and three pairs of nylons. Bessie's presents to Dan were another tie, some handkerchiefs, and a new Sunday missal; and when she saw what he had given her, she said:

"Lord, Dan McClatchy! What'd you want to go and spend all that money on me for?"

It was a small gold brooch sparkling with garnets and aquamarines.

"Now," he grinned, "it's just a little token of my esteem."

"Mercy, I'm going to take it right back."

"Oh no you don't, now. I got to have my own wife looking as good as the place, don't I?"

"Nonsense, I never heard of anything so foolish; why, it must've cost eighty dollars!"

"It's none of your business what it cost. Besides it wouldn't surprise me if you'd soon be wearing diamonds. And 'Bless us O Lord and these Thy gifts which we are about to receive.' So take it and shut up." He kissed her on the cheek.

Bessie looked at him as if what he had done were shameful, and said: "Oh, Danny!" but could not keep the tears out of her eyes; and then tears came into the sentimental McClatchy's too, and he said heartily: "Oh, it's a great life," which was a general remark meaning nothing in particular, and seeing her parents moved, Arline was moved too, but she was thinking: I wonder how much money he's got left.

Billy was forced to eat his breakfast—the grownups were fasting for Communion. Then the family walked to St. Peter's. Bessie was making a novena of Communions for the success of the tavern: it would end on New Year's Eve morning. Dan was in the midst of a

Rosary novena to the same end. Arline's novena was addressed to St. Jude, patron of the impossible.

And that evening they christened the restaurant by having their turkey dinner in it. They dined in the booth nearest the kitchen. Away from them stretched a floor now crowded with bare tables and empty chairs, but McClatchy turned on all the lights to make the scene more festive, and envisioned for his family the great room thronged with diners. He opened a bottle of wine, poured, and proposed a toast:

"Here's to old Dutch over there—because if it wasn't for him we wouldn't have beans, and Bess, you'd still be reigning over the old stove, and Arline, you'd still be dishing it out on the counter, and the old man'd be hustling the booze in the late lamented old Traveler's Rest, with the termites boring from within and the old boiler blowing us to smithereens some night, and Bill, you wouldn't be nowheres near where you are today neither, the son and heir of a family that's got a place like you see before you, known as the famous Lost Dutchman Tavern, named after his famous nibs over there. So everybody stand up, now—you too, Bill, you take your glass of water there; that's the way to do it. Now we all touch glasses like this, see? Skoll! That's the stuff—that's the way we used to do it in the old days. And," he quoted a gallant hearsay of his youth, " 'A fairer drahft from a fairer hond was never quahft.' "

How will it end? Arline asked herself, taking her son home that evening. Her father was so sure of himself, to hear him; so cocky. But really so worried, she knew, for she had seen him cry. Poor Dad. But oh, she admitted to herself, he was such a fool. He and his "All roads'll lead to the Lost Dutchman." He and his "great talker"—a town drunkard with a huge bloated body and shabby clothes and a "silver tongue" that sounded like a bullfrog's. Oh, why did they have to pretend in the wisdom of her father? Surely her mother could read the signs. But her practical down-to-earth mother, who at first had been so skeptical of the project, seemed all serenity now. Poor Ma. And with bitterness this Christmas night Arline repeated to herself the magic words of a few months ago:

The beginning!

Down at the Lost Dutchman her parents were standing in front of the bar, looking up at the painting, McClatchy's arm around his wife's shoulders, her arm around his waist, and McClatchy was saying:

"They think he was a real man, you know. Rembrandt come along one day and painted his picture—'way over in Holland, three hundred years ago. Gives you a funny feeling, don't it? I wonder who he was."

Bessie shook her head: there was no telling.

And the mysterious Dutchman looked down at them contemptuously. He wore most cavalierly his wide cavalier's hat of worn beaver, plumed, a brown coat, once fine but threadbare now, and stained, a wide belt of plain leather bandolier-wise across his chest, a graying mustache furiously upturned, and a tuft at his chin; his brows were haughtily lifted, there was that insulting half sneer on his lips, and the skin of his fat face was spotted with exploded capillaries. Obviously a man come down in the world. Not a very pleasant-looking man, either. But then perhaps the sneer was explained by his condition, and he might have imagined that by lifting his brows for the painter he was pulling taut the bags under his eyes.

McClatchy said: "I wonder if three hundred years from now they'll be any pictures of *us* around. Maybe some of them pictures the newspapers took. Or maybe they'll find that one you and me had taken the day we got married."

"Oh, gracious!" Bessie said. "*That* one."

"Sure; you can't tell, it might turn up somewheres. And they'll say: 'Now there was a fine-looking woman, but look at the little gink there beside her—who do you suppose *he* was?' And then maybe they'll look to see where it was taken. 'Oh,' they'll say, 'he was some guy that lived in Sampm Cisco 'way back in the nineteen hundreds when they used to dress like that; dead and gone long ago, the both of 'em, and this was taken on their wedding day.' They'll say: 'Who do you suppose they could have been, anyhow?' "

"Yes, I suppose we'll look funny to 'em then, with the clothes and all. And, my, when I think how proud I was of that dress; there was real Irish lace on that dress. But, mercy, it's all out of date. And you with your little tight pants the men wore then, and your little bow tie." She was laughing.

"Yeah. To look at that picture now I suppose some people'd think it was taken during the Civil War. Tinted, it was." Then reflectively: "But it wasn't so long ago. When you come down to it, it aint so long ago they still had the horsecars—I was a grown man; and now they got planes that can beat the speed of sound. Why, it was only a few years ago Lindbergh flew the Atlantic and everybody went crazy thinking it was wonderful. And when Christofferson made it from S.F. to San Diego. And Lincoln Beachy that was killed at the Fair; and Art Smith. We seen a lot of changes in our time, Bess; you realize?"

She smiled at him. This was one of Dan's favorite topics, a thing that he gloried in and never ceased to marvel at, as if unable to grasp it himself, so subtly had it happened to them; and he never seemed to remember that he had said it all to her before.

He said: "We seen the day they still lit the streets with gas; it aint so long ago they put the 'Path o' Gold' on Market Street, neither; and we seen the movies come in, and radio, and now they got television. And we seen the Panama Canal built and the *Titanic* go down, and the *Lusitania;* and two world wars, and Prohibition, and the big Depression. We seen the Kaiser and Hitler and the last of the Russian czars and the Bolshevik Revolution, and I can remember when they shot McKinley. By golly, I was going when they blew up the *Maine,* too, and Dewey took Manila. And we seen the Irish Free State born, and England go broke. Think of that, Bess. I bet old Dutch here never seen that much in his day; am I right?"

"Maybe so."

And they gazed at the Lost Dutchman.

"Poor man," Bessie murmured, obscurely. She was looking at the threadbare coat.

"And now," McClatchy said, as if divining her reference, "they got the unemployment insurance and the old age. That come in our time too. And the income tax—I was a grown man. Oh, the country's changing. Why, Bess, you were a grown woman and had kids before all the women got the vote; and look at 'em now," he grinned, "sitting in the halls of Congress and laying down the law. Yes, sir! We seen Sampm Cisco in ruins, and look at her now. Pretty soon they'll have subways under the streets where the horsecars used to run, like now they got them big bridges across the bay. Remember how they used to talk about bridges across the bay and people used to say they couldn't be built? Oh, they's been changes since them days. Even at the Palace Hotel. Last time I was over there I couldn't find the old bar where I used to work. Seems to me they used to have it where the men's room now stands."

"The Palace"—Bessie repeated the name softly and with affection. She had never been inside the Palace Hotel in her life, but she associated it with all that had been grand and exquisite and "stylish" in a world gone by, for she had heard talk and seen photographs, and now it was almost as if she had been in it. "The Palace," she said. "Have they still got the Court?"

"The Court?" Dan looked at her, at first not understanding the question, then shocked at the realization of how far Bessie had lagged, here in the country, behind the advancing times. Bessie was referring to the celebrated seven-tiered Grand Court into which, once, carriages had driven to deposit their passengers under a great glass dome. "No,

Bess, don't you remember?—the Court, that was in the *old* Palace that they had before the Fire."

—Before that prophetic April dawn of nineteen hundred and only six.

12

GRAND OPENING

New Year's Eve, 1947. The ball rolled on, and as usual no one aboard could feel the slightest movement. Yet many of the passengers were uneasy.

The fissure down the middle of Germany was widening, Russia had hinted that now she too knew the secret of exploding the core of matter, and in London a four-power conference had just ended in deadlock. The Far East was in eruption. Europe was exhausted. Men were fighting in the mountains of Greece. And in Palestine tonight was the spectacle of the wandering Jew come home to wrest back from Islam his Promised Land, where tomorrow Christian pilgrims would keep the Feast of the Circumcision. Manila had been attacked by the fiercest typhoon to blow that way in forty years. New York was in hobbles after the heaviest fall of snow ever recorded there. Across Arkansas and Louisiana raged a tornado.

But it was both peaceful and fine in Llagas this last evening of the year; and at six o'clock from these co-ordinates, where in the recent Stone Age Indians had sat and told how Coyote, Eagle, and Humming Bird had made the world, a ray of light arose and impudently tried to investigate the sky. Back and forth it went, and startled only Llagans: they found it strange to see a searchlight cleaving the darkness that always swallowed the district of the railroad yard at night. But the most interested witnesses of the phenomenon were Dan McClatchy and his grandson, who had just emerged from the new Lost Dutchman Tavern to study the great torch in operation.

McClatchy wore a rented full-dress suit. "How's it going?" he greeted the captain of the light, and indicating the small boy with a gesture of the head, he explained humorously: "Nothing would do but I had to bring him out to see it."

The captain of the light was a tall skeleton of a man wrapped in an old black overcoat and a woolen neck scarf, a dirty checkered cap pulled down over the tops of his ears. He only nodded and went on turning his fat white uptilted lamp back and forth on its swivel, gazing up Hill Street to the little holiday lights of Main; and his bright blue-white mote-filled beam swept hopelessly at the darkness overhead; and his big generator, hooded like the engine of a mighty truck, and parked like a truck at the curb, droned into their ears. With pleasure McClatchy looked up at the turning lamp, taller than he, at the long high generator, on the white hood of which was painted:

APFEL BROS.
SPECTACULAR ILLUMINATION

and up at the beam. And Billy, on tiptoe, gawked through the thick lens of the lamp at the brilliant hissing eye.

"How does it work?" the child asked.

"*Work?*" joked his grandfather. His grandfather had no more idea how the thing worked than how voices happened to come out of his radio, or water out of his faucets. "*Work?*" and he winked at the captain. "Oh, it's all electricity, you see." Indeed, he often said that no one knew what electricity was, a bit of lore that seemed to give him particular satisfaction, and he did not dream that he had not the faintest conception what it meant. "That's the same kind of a searchlight that they spot airplanes with, you know."

"It is?" Billy said.

"Betcha," his grandfather said.

"Is there any planes up there now?"

"Take a look—maybe you'll see one. Or maybe you'll spot one of them flying saucers they're all talking about."

The captain of the light glanced at McClatchy and his mouth loosened in a smile. "Flying saucers," he sneered.

"Yeah," McClatchy chuckled. "That's a hot one, aint it?"

"What's flying saucers?" Billy asked.

"Now that's what we'd all like to know," his grandfather said. "They're supposed to be some new kind of airoplanes that are shaped like saucers. Or maybe," with a wink at the captain, "some little whiz-bangs from Mars."

The captain gave a scornful grunt of a laugh.

"Yeah, by golly," McClatchy said, "it sounds like the boys that've been seeing them things'll be seeing pink elephants next." And for a moment he looked at Billy, who was leaning backward to follow the stately beam in its quest. "But you know," he said more seriously to the captain, having, as it seemed, broken the ice, "it's a funny thing—some of those fellows were avviators, and they're no fools, you know. And I was reading the other day where now they think maybe these flying saucers are something the Air Force is cooking up on the q.t. Something new," he hinted.

The captain looked skeptical.

The child complained: "I don't see *nothing*."

"Keep a sharp lookout," McClatchy advised, "and maybe you will. And then," he went on, "they say it could be something the Russians have got."

"Aaaaaaaaa," the captain jeered.

"Well, now, you can't tell. The Russians have got a lot of them German scientists working with them now, you know, and they say even during the war those jokers had some inventions going that'd curl your hair." It flattered McClatchy to be holding a personal conversation with the captain of the light. Somehow the command of this great engine of radiance and the piloting of its far-seen beacon through the night gave the man, in McClatchy's eyes, a kind of public dignity akin to the dignity of policemen and motormen and conductors; and it flattered him especially because this evening captain and light were under charter to him. He said: "Take them big rockets they had at the end there—the V-2's. And the jet airoplanes. And look at *us* —we're shooting rockets up into the great unknown to find out how the weather is up there, and I was reading it won't be long till they'll be trips to the moon. *Oh*, yeah; they're working on it right now. And I see where they're getting some kind of a radio signal from Mars. Sure —it was in the paper. So, you know, it makes a man think. Maybe the Russians are ahead of us. And if Mars is ahead of us, why, it could even be them with the flying saucers, couldn't it?" But the man only laughed without a sound, still turning the lamp. McClatchy grinned foolishly, shook his head, and said: "Well, the way they're going these days you never know what's coming next."

A car that he had seen come down Hill Street, pass, and turn around had returned and was pulling in at the curb behind the generator; and he said: "Oh! Excuse me. It looks like company. Wait"—a command apparently addressed to himself, for on the point of departure he did wait; he leaned toward the captain confidentially, placed one hand on his arm, and using an inflection that made the question sound like a statement, whispered mischievously: "*Do you ever take a little drink.*"

The captain's lips parted in a full smile, revealing a tooth missing. "Cold night," he admitted.

McClatchy winked and clapped him on the shoulder. "Leave it to me," he said, and was gone.

Two men in overcoats were just getting out of the big sedan, and one of them was Alfred Markham.

"Happy New Year's," a voice hailed them. Markham had been surprised at the light, but the splendor of the owner of the Rembrandt painting in full dress was lost on him: he mistook the suit for a waiter's uniform. "Oh!" he said. "Happy New Year, Mr. McClatchy." He permitted his hand to be pumped heartily. "This is Mr. Ames."

"Pleased to make your acquaintance, sir," and McClatchy seized the hand of a fat man of about fifty, who said jovially:

"Dr. Livingstone, I presume."

"Oh no, don't let the soup-and-fish fool you. McClatchy's the name. Happy New Year's, I'm sure."

"The same to you," the fat man laughed.

"Mr. Ames is an art critic," Markham said.

"Oh, is that a fact! Well, this is a great honor. *First and foremost of the celebrities and dignitaries to arrive were two patrons of the arts,*" McClatchy said as if quoting from a next day's newspaper account of the opening. "And as a professional courtesy I want the both of you to be my guests tonight—it'll all be on the house."

"Well! That's very good of you," twinkled the critic; and the dealer said: "Yes, indeed."

"Oh, not a word. It's what we call a Dutch treat, you know," a joke that neither of the men understood. "Ouch! Don't mind me. Come on inside," escorting them to the door, "while we bake the clams."

"That's quite a display you have there," Markham said.

"Oh, the big searchlight; yes, sir! We're all lit up, we are, as the saying goes. I was just showing the grandson how they spot enemy airoplanes; and here he is in person, the great Bill Lucas, Charming Billy they call him, my daughter's boy. He's a corker. Come on in with us now, Bill, or your mother'll murder me. We'll use the grand entrance." He opened the door. "After you," to Markham and Ames; and to Billy: "Youth before age." And just before he brought in the rear he turned to the captain of the light, raised one hand, shut one eye, and presented a circle formed by forefinger and thumb as a signal that he would not forget.

The opening had been advertised for seven-thirty, but favored ones had been invited early for what McClatchy styled "the inauguration." As yet only four had arrived. On the left, two men were seated at the bar, and in a booth on the right were a man and woman with whom

Bessie, relieved at the cashier's counter for the moment by Arline, was sitting to talk. Waitresses in short blue Dutch-girl uniforms trimmed in white, with starched caps to match, stood about among tables arranged in two rows of four bracketing an aisle which was to be filled with other tables after the grand march. And on a low platform at the far end of the room, between the kitchen doors and the end of the bar, five young musicians in dinner clothes were just taking their places. They were "Herbie Bates and His Gates."

"Why, Mr. McClatchy!" Markham said, looking about. "This is surprising!"

"Oh I tellya."

"It must have been quite expensive."

"Oh, you take it from me. And it don't all show. Take this floor: it's all new. On my word of honor some blame little bugs they call termites chewed up the old one and swallowed half of it, now that's the truth. And you ought to see the kitchen, it's got a big new stove and a big icebox and all kinds of stuff. And besides the help you see before you, we got two cooks and a couple of dishwashers in there; and two bartenders and six uniformed waitresses working split shifts makes twelve, union labor; and the janitor and my daughter is a grand total of fourteen on the payroll, not counting the orchestra there that we got for the occasion, like the spectacular illumination at the door."

Ames asked: "And all this on the inspiration of the Rembrandt?"

"Sir? Oh, sure, that's what give me the big idea. That painting's famous, you know; it's a big asset to a place like this. But we got it all covered up, you see," pointing to a short curtain of red cloth on the wall behind the bar, "till we have the grand unveiling."

"The——? Oh, I see." Ames suddenly began to tremble with mirth.

"Oh, you betcha," McClatchy grinned. "*They had all the formalities of the occasion.*" Just then the band began its opening number: "Where the Blue of the Night Meets the Gold of the Day." He turned toward the musicians. "Listen to that, now. *Music was provided.* And every man in a tuxedo! Oh, believe you me. . . . But give me them hats and coats, now; the party's on." He put the men's things in the rack and hopped back again. Bessie was approaching; she wore a new dinner dress of gray crepe, with a high neck, and in the midst of her bosom gleamed and sparkled the Christmas brooch. "Wait," her husband said; "I want you to meet the wife, and here she is in all her glory. *The elegant Mrs. D. J. McClatchy from Nob Hill was the belle of the ball,*" he merrily composed his running account, taking her by the arm as she came up, and he presented her to their guests. Bessie welcomed them. "She's the queen of the joint, as you can plainly see," he said. "Oh, to be sure. We don't make a move without her. And lo and behold, the raving beauty behind you," directing their attention to the strapping young woman who stood behind the cashier's counter in a black semi-formal on which sequins winked, "is the daughter Arline. She's the official hostess. And as a special honor tonight, Mr. Markham, you're elected to lead the grand march with the missus. How's that!"

"A grand march?" Markham said, looking startled. "Well! I'd be honored, but I've never been in a grand march in my life!"

"No, is that a fact! You haven't? Oh, well, don't worry. All you do is march, and anybody that knows how to walk can do that. Here's the way we do it, now," and with a mock flourish McClatchy took Bessie's arm in his, over her protests, commanding himself gaily: "Forward march!" and stepping up and down without advancing an inch, he sang:

> "We shouldered guns and marched and marched away.
> From Baxter Street we marched to Avenue A.
> With drum and fife, how sweetly they did play,
> As we marched, marched, marched
>   in the Mulligan Guard. . . .

See? And the line of march is up the middle aisle there," he explained, pulling down his vest, "then back between that row of tables and the booths. The missus'll show you. And Mr. Ames and Arline'll be right behind you, only at the top of the aisle they'll branch off and double back between that other row of tables and the bar. . . ."

Arline, already embarrassed by her father's antics, was mortified at being forced on Mr. Ames. "Oh, Dad!" she said.

"De-lighted!" laughed the fat man.

And her father said: "I'll bet you're an old hand at grand marching, Mr. Ames."

"Haven't had a good march for years."

"Now, I declare! Well, it'll all come back to you. All you have to do is parade around, you know, like a peacock. But would you believe it, this girl's never been in a grand march in her whole life neither; I had to show her myself how it's done. She's all trained with the guarantee of the house—service or your money back. So you gentlemen just stick with the ladies and you won't go wrong."

Arline repudiated her father by a sharp little sucking sound of her tongue, glancing to heaven for patience.

"Come here to me till I fix that," Bessie said to him; she straightened his white tie and gave his arm a little finishing pat. "My, don't he look nice."

"Look at who's talking. Feast your eyes on that, would you. Rings on her fingers and bells on her toes. Oh, have you seen Stella! She's a daisy. You're a lucky man, Mr. Markham. And I know something that'll make you light on your feet as a feather, so come on, now, and I'll do the honors. Bill, you stay here. He's a little pillar of total abstinence, you know; he won't be tempted."

"Honestly, Ma," Arline complained of him when he and his guests were out of hearing.

Bessie had come round behind the counter. She chuckled. "Oh, God bless his heart." And with her head laid over on one side, she followed her husband tenderly with her eyes.

Arline had been ashamed of her father before the city men and was vexed with him because he had embarrassed her so. But the soft look on her mother's face touched her. And this was the night—this was the party her mother was giving her father, the symbol of her life in his hands, his big opportunity and probably his last one, the cast that could ruin them. Arline put her arms around her mother and kissed her.

Bessie looked surprised. "What was that for?"

"For luck."

"*Thank* you, dear."

"I'm hungry," Billy demanded.

"Heavens," his grandmother said, "I forgot—you're invited to eat with Mr. and Mrs. Silvestro, child; but you'll like that, won't you? Now," she silenced the pettish objection on his lips, "the rest of us won't get to eat a bite till after you're in bed. But do you know what? You'll be having ice cream!"

"What kind?"

"Chocolate or vanilla, you can take your choice. And I wonder if I can guess which it'll be."

"Which?"

"Vanilla?"

"Nn-o. . . ."

"Chocolate!"

"Yes!"

"Thaaat's my boy."

Arline took Billy to the Silvestros' booth. "John" Silvestro was the prosperous owner of a fish market, a big hearty Neapolitan with a cropped gray mustache, and at the moment with a napkin collar-hung for a bib; his wife Gina was equally big and hearty, with pierced ears from which bright baubles hung dancing, and with a bright soprano which on Sundays dominated the choir at St. Peter's; they had four married daughters and already eleven grandchildren. They warmly took Billy in, making much of him; and his mother, keeping an eye on the front door for new arrivals, ordered his dinner for him.

Leaving him there, Arline looked at her wrist watch. Six-fifteen. Sixteen persons had been asked early, and only six had arrived: maybe some had changed their minds. New Year's Eve was *not* a good night for the opening: there were too many more exciting places to go. Surely no one else would come to this little town from San Francisco tonight. Apart from the favored ones, there were reservations for only eight parties aggregating twenty persons, only twenty. I might have known, she thought, and blamed her father. The beginning! But look at him; and as Arline did, the words her mother had said on the night when they had just learned about their treasure came back to her: "You'd think he was Floodobrienmackayandfair." At the bar her ruddy little father in his rented finery was presenting to Markham and Ames a round-shouldered horse-faced man of bashful mien, and announcing:

"Mr. Jacoby here is one of our public officials."

Oh, God! Arline thought in alarm—No!

But Markham, as he shook hands, was inquiring: "Oh?"

And Mr. Jacoby explained modestly: "City rodent exterminator."

"Yes, sir!" said the jester. "Mr. Jacoby here is in charge of exterminating all the rodents."

Now, honestly! What must they think? But despite Arline's humiliation, her heart suddenly went out to mother her father. (*In the absence of the mayor, whom wild horses had dragged off to another engagement, the City was represented at the festivities by the rodent exterminator.*)

"He's done some fine work right in this place here, too, I can tell you," her father was praising the shy Mr. Jacoby with a grin. "He's a great little mouser."

Phyllis Plover, fresh from the beauty shop, wore her pert waitress's uniform like a part in *The Red Mill*. The slight flare of the skirt emphasized the slimness of her waist and set off her shapely legs, the laced bodice became her well-molded little bosom, and the light blue color blended with her eyes and complemented her pink and white cheeks, scarlet lips, and gilded hair. She moved to Arline's side, chewing gum, and with a lift of her pretty chin to indicate Markham and Ames at the bar, asked: "Who're *those* two?"

"Oh, the one on the left owns the art gallery where we had the painting. Dad just told him he's going to lead the grand march with Ma—imagine! And," with a long-suffering sigh, "the other one drew me!"

"The fat one?" Phyllis asked, laughing. "Oh, brother! That I got to see. Who is he?"

"Dad said he was an art critic."

"Really?" Phyllis looked him over. "Boy, he's *built* for a grand march. . . . Gee, a grand march," she said disgustedly, slapping the air with her hand; "what a waste of good music," and turning toward the band, she began sinuously limbering her body to the slow rhythm, dropping her knees alternately, and snapping her fingers. "But you know who I'd like to draw for a partner, don't you?"

Phyllis's supple pantomime had drawn the attention of Herbie Bates himself; he pointed his saxophone at her as he played, and raised the end of it in salute.

Arline asked: "Herbie Bates?"

Smiling seductively at Herbie Bates, Phyllis said out of the corner of her mouth: "*Him?* Naw! The drum-mer."

Arline laughed.

The trumpet, too, now recognized Phyllis; then the violin, then the piano; and then the drummer saw her, grinned, and raised his head to her. Phyllis answered with a slow blink of both eyes and a wanton smile. And now it was as if the whole band were playing for her.

Arline had a moment of resentment.

Then the band finished the piece, and at the bar McClatchy applauded, calling out to the musicians: "A beautiful rendition."

"Oh, brother!" Phyllis said, slapping the air in the direction of her employer. "What a square!"

McClatchy's compliment had set the musicians laughing. In other circumstances his daughter might have laughed too. Now she felt a little twinge of pain. He was so far outdated at his own party and in his own tavern, and it suddenly appeared so plain that he was incompetent to compete for the patronage of the modern public, and he was so proud and elated and friendly and everyone was laughing at him.

"You," Ames was saying to him at the bar, "are a San Franciscan."

"Me? Well, I hope to tellya. Born in the old South of Market and raised in the Mission. And I was a charter member of Local Forty-one of the Bartenders' Union. I kept bar on the Barbary Coast in the old days, and at the Palace Hotel and the old Techau before Prohibition."

"Is that so!"

"*Oh*, yeah."

"I'm a Mission boy myself."

"*You?* Now, you don't tell me. We-ll, I met with Napper Tandy! And how's old Fifteenth and Valencia?"

Phyllis sighed. "Too bad you're not going to have dancing."

"Oh, I know!" Arline said. For on New Year's Eve people wanted to dance, and not a soul had entered the Lost Dutchman for twenty minutes. She glanced out the front windows and saw the searchlight beam beckoning, beckoning. *Have you seen Dutch!* it said—as if any-one cared to see an old painting on New Year's Eve!

But at six-thirty a stream of new arrivals began—

Ed Primrose, the housepainter, long a frequenter of the saloon of the Traveler's Rest, and his frail timid-looking wife; Frank Johansen, the contractor, and the lively Mrs. Johansen; a liquor salesman named Porter and a pretty companion; Mr. and Mrs. Linnegar; Hump Corkery, freight handler for the railroad, all alone. And although Arline tried to do her duty as "official hostess" her father was always ahead of her with the welcome. Little McClatchy, his red face glowing with cheer, the tails of his dress coat abob against the backs of his knees, went bouncing up to the front door with extended hand, calling out in the lilt of his imitation brogue:

"We-ll, should old acquaintance be forgot! *Then in came the flower of the Old Guard with his one and only, a fine-looking couple they made!* Different? Sure it's different, but we've got your name on the same old mug, Ed, so come on and we'll take off our shoes. . . ."

—"Hap-py New Year's! Come right in and don't be bashful. *The arrival of the famous contractor that built the place was the signal for a rising ovation.* And so this is the wife; I'm glad you could be among those present, ma'am. They're all admiring the fine new tavern and art museum that stands like a monument to your husband's genius. . . ."

—"And here comes the Honorable Mr. Porter now—purveyor to the crowned heads of Europe! *He-e was the envy of all eyes with the missus on his arm.* The compliments of the season to you, Mrs. P., you're as welcome as the flowers in—Oh, Miss Whitter, is it? Excuse my French. . . ."

—"Ah, look at that, now. *A high tone was lent to the opening by the president of the Ladies' Sodality escorted by her ball and chain, and who was he but a prominent member of the Holy Name.* By golly, Mrs. Linnegar, but we ought to get the monsignor here to bless the place on the happy occasion. . . ."

—"Strike up the band, it's the great Hump Corkery! *He-e was the life of the party.*" And stepping up and down in front of the burly grinning freight handler as if marching, while swinging his fists to the time, he sang:

> "Whin we got home at night, boys,
> The divil a bite we'd ate;
> We'd all set up and drink a sup
> Of whisky strong and nate.
> Thin we'd all march home together,
> As slippery as lard;
> The solid min would all fall in
> And march with the Mulligan Guard."

Arline despaired of him; but Noel Ames, watching him in action from the bar, declared with a chuckle: "By George, he's wonderful!"

"What?" said Markham.

"Oh, he is, you know. The real thing. I haven't seen it like this in years."

"I don't quite——"

"The type. It must be vanishing—changing. I hadn't realized."

"Yes, well," said Markham dryly, "the sooner it vanishes the better."

Ames laughed, but said: "Oh, I don't know. He carries me back. He must have been preserved in cold storage."

Markham looked at him oddly. "You really are a Mission boy, aren't you?"

"Yes, indeed."

Alfred Markham had lived in San Francisco all his life, and San Francisco was only seven miles square, but to him, as to many another San Franciscan, virtually all of it that lay below its great divisadero, Market Street, was unknown territory. The part called "the Mission" was the oldest and, surveyed as the spiritual entity that it was, the largest district of the city, but Markham did not know the Mission, nor did he care to. He never went into it except for passing through on blazed trails to the Peninsula, and then it depressed him—a congeries of waning Victorian houses and poor little unhappy-looking flats and ugly industrial buildings and catchpenny shops and tawdry movie theaters, where idlers went shambling and newspapers blew. An area half slum where another language was spoken and where, it seemed, the very daylight had a melancholy tone, as if the only sun that ever shone there were the winter sun. Another world, a limbo, which at night receded and became a galactic nebula of weakly glowing neon gas where sociability huddled in little drinking "clubs" behind former shop windows blinded now with paint, and of deep slumberous fields of blackness out of which flashed, from time to time, a summons to the police.

Once, of course, certain streets of it had been good enough. Some had been fashionable once upon a time. People of means and standing had lived in them. A few old die-hards did still. Certain streets maintained their dignity. And those were the ones that depressed Markham worst of all. But it was a district that he associated chiefly with working-class Irish, the species to which McClatchy, despite his name, plainly belonged. And among these people there existed a native loyalty to the Mission which they passed off as love and pride and which brought out all their peasant clannishness and bad taste and cheap braggadocio. They behaved as if to have been born a Mission boy were something to be cherished, but Markham regarded it as just the opposite. The Mission offended his sense of order and decency and shocked his concept of the beautiful. The Mission repelled him with its pathetic little neatnesses and attempts at brightness and with its Mass-going candle-burning piety as much as with its squalor and dirt and derelicts. And he felt there today that atmosphere of unspeakable loss. It pervaded even the streets that had dignity. And curiously enough it was heaviest of all in the stately old street called by the very name of it, after the Mission church—Dolores; as if the whole district that had grown up around the church, originally named for St. Francis but always called for the Lady of Sorrows, lay in the shadow of her mantle. Had Alfred Markham been born in the Mission district he would have got out of it early, as he supposed Noel Ames had done. But to find in the critic this apparent feeling for the Mission surprised him. He had nothing to say to it, and so he merely grunted.

Old Bob Doughty came in, clean-shaven for once, and wearing a double-breasted blue suit which looked new.

"Glory be to God!" McClatchy greeted him. "Now there's a sight for sore eyes." And capering up to meet him:

> *"Is that Mr. Reilly, can anyone tell?*
> *Is that Mr. Reilly that owns the hotel?*
> *Well, if that's Mr. Reilly they speak of so highly,*
> *Upon my soul, Reilly, you're doing quite well."*

But Doughty, leaning backward, hand at mouth, silently laughing at the full dress, countered: "Who's dead?"

Billy had finished his dinner and bolted the Silvestros' booth, wanting, in his excitement over the growing party, to be everywhere at once; he was right behind his grandfather, and, delighted by the comic recitation, he began to jump up and down, contributing with gleeful whoops:

> *"Brown! Brown! Go to town!*
> *Wear your britches upside down!"*

"Well, listen to that now," McClatchy exclaimed. "He's a poet and he don't know it."

Screaming with laughter, Billy convulsed himself and caught his clasped hands between his knees, then suddenly shot into the air, shrilling hilariously:

> *"Green! Green! You're a queen!*
> *Stick your head in gasoline!"*

McClatchy laughed, and Doughty, his hand guarding his wobbly upper plate, leaned backward again in soundless mirth.

> *"Red! Red! Wet the bed!*
> *Wipe it up with gingerbread!"*

"Oh, not that one." McClatchy playfully roughed Billy's head. "No vulgarity allowed."

The child's whole body was contorted with joy. But at the height of his triumph a startling change came over him. He stood quite still, with a look of fear on his face, and then suddenly embraced his grandfather's legs and hid behind him from the old man. Just then Arline came volunteering: "I'll take him, Dad," and as she reached for him her little boy turned to her at once. He pulled her down to him and whispered in her ear. She straightened and looked at him. "Oh, Billy!" She gave the two men a pained expression, which they found completely enlightening, and William Lucas, Jr. was led to the rear apartment in disgrace.

"He, he, he, he," cackled Doughty, who sometimes went home with his clothes in the same condition.

"Oh, that'll hold him," laughed McClatchy. "He-e's the limit!" But alarmed at a sudden thought, he twisted round both ways to examine the tails of his coat, and Doughty turned the cackle upon him:

"He, he, he, he, he, he!"

"By golly, that was a close call. They're going to put it back in the window in the morning—so don't go throwing no drinks on it, neither." And with one arm hugging the old man round the shoulders, McClatchy bore him to the bar and presented him to Markham and Ames as "the little rascal that threw the booze on the painting."

When Arline re-entered the restaurant with Billy, Walsh Reardon had just arrived; she saw him reach the bar. He was in his familiar brown tweeds, but at least they were newly cleaned and pressed, his thick gray mane was combed and brushed, and to Arline's critical eye he looked sober as yet. Her father turned from the bar, found him towering there, fell back, raising his guard and saying: "Faith, boys, it's the Nonpareil!" and confronted him in the solid stance of the old bareknuckle heavyweights. It was a fair caricature of Reardon, but Arline saw it as more revealing of the caricaturist: her father was impressed by that size and appearance of power even as by the monstrous voice, and having been taken by surprise, had at once confessed this to be at the root of his admiration of the man. But in drawing attention to Reardon's size he had diminished himself. And there came back to Arline the almost forgotten moment of her childhood when, looking up at McClatchy one day as he stood talking on a street corner with two of his peers, she had realized that as fathers went, hers was only a little one, and had wished that he were bigger. Reardon looked down at the miniature John L. Sullivan in the starched white shirtfront of unaccustomed formality, and his Blunderbore laugh attracted the attention of the whole bar. "Well, I'll be damned!" he rasped from ocean bottom. "A penguin!" General laughter. Going by at that moment, McClatchy's daughter tried to revenge herself by despising the staleness of the joke.

And as on that day with Harry Fahs in the park, the claim just made upon her motherhood had caused Arline to feel the burden of her son. What to do with him at this party was a problem. She could not be hostess and mother at the same time; but tonight she did not want to be a mother at all. Attired in the sparkling dress, she fancied herself in a different role. She wanted to escape from her son, wanted to be free, wanted the New life to begin. She left Billy at the cashier's counter with his grandmother, and went to welcome three new arrivals:

Three women, these were—reservations in the name of Mrs. Creevy. Gray-haired women, widowed, perhaps, divorced, or never married, childless, or with a son or two in the service, but unescorted, doing the best they could with New Year's Eve. Strangers; not from the city, Arline thought. And evidently they had misunderstood about the time. She showed them to a table.

At the bar her father, with his giant by the arm, had turned to Markham and Ames, saying: "Shake hands with Mr. Reardon! This is Mr. Markham that owns the big art gallery in Sampm Cisco; he-e's the man that found out the old painting was a Rembrandt. Senator Reardon here is one of our most prominent citizens, and a member of the Old Guard. And this is Mr. Ames, a famous art critic, the pride of the Mission. The senator here is going to give us the inaugural address. Oh I tellya. *Then up rose the Honorable Mr. Walsh Reardon and brought down the house."*

Reardon's commanding aspect did suggest, no less than the old-time prizefighter, the United States senator of a passing type. But Markham, having had some experience of McClatchy's jocosely high-blown style, notably in the case of "one of our public officials," was not taken in. The practiced eye of the merchant appraised Reardon as a prodigious nobody, possibly a newspaperman. But Ames was inquiring as he shook hands:

"*Walsh* Reardon? Not the football player?"

"Oh, you betcha!" McClatchy answered. "He-e's the one."

"No!"

"You've got a long memory," rasped the ex-football player.

"Why, I've seen you play!" Ames said with wonder, and with an enthusiasm that amused Markham. "Walsh Reardon! Of course! *You* remember, Alfred."

"I'm afraid," said Markham, "I'm not much of a football fan."

"Oh, but Walsh Reardon! He was one of the greatest passers that ever lived! And with either hand! I wonder," to Reardon, "if you'd mind letting me see your hands."

Reardon's hands were a football legend. He smiled ironically. "No, they're not big enough to hold a football like a baseball," he said, but he obliged by holding them out once more.

The art critic could not have shown more interest if he had found intact the lost hands of Melos, and the exhibit had set McClatchy beaming: Markham derisively observed their faces, and then, in spite of himself, Reardon's hands. The thick long stub-ended fingers curled like a dockwalloper's, but the palms, he saw, were puffy, soft, and flushed, and the right palm was crossed from the base of the small finger to the heel of the thumb by an ugly scar, and the broad backs were heavily knuckled and large-veined, and under the red hair were freckled but marred also by brown spots too large for freckles, and the nails were coarse and scrubbed-looking and sawn square, with no rising moons visible in their bases, and in several spots along the backs and sides of the big fingers the underskin showed sickly white where the outer layer was broken. Ames too noticed the blemishes, but McClatchy saw only massiveness and power.

"They'll do," said Ames of the famous hands.

And McClatchy said: "Yes, sir!" with a proud grin as he patted Reardon on the shoulder. "The great Walsh Reardon."

Ames asked the former athlete: "Do you live here in Llagas?"

"Oh, sure," McClatchy answered. "He's one of the ornaments of our local bar; a big legal light he is now, and a famous orator—wait'll you hear him. Jerry," to a young bartender, "make it a double gin and water for Mr. Reardon here, no ice, and don't spare the gin; he's an oldlangsyner, I know him for years, a double for anybody else is a triple for him. No, the hell with the lemon, he drinks the plain gin and water. And tell him to keep his money in his pocket, Jerry, we don't want him flashing his roll around here—it's on the house for him the same as for these two gentlemen here."

Reardon rumblingly chuckled off the embarrassment that these revealing instructions to the bartender had caused him to feel, in the circumstances, before the two strangers. "By God," he boomed, "success has gone to his head already. What are *you* drinking, Mac," with a look at the full-dress suit, "champagne?"

(Gin and water! A "triple"! And no ice! To Markham and Ames it had sounded nauseating. They were watching the bartender as he tumbled a glass half full of gin, added water, stirred, and looked up under his brows to take the measure of the man who was going to drink this chemical.)

"Oh I tellya," McClatchy replied to Reardon. "The best is none too good for the Irish. Oh, and I almost forgot—Jerry, when you finish that take one of the big glasses and give me about four fingers of the bourbon for the forgotten man: the unknown soldier," he explained to the others, "on the big searchlight keeping the flying saucers from the door. *He stuck to his post through thick and thin.* Ah," to Jerry as he took up the gin and water, "you're a man after me own heart. And here's to a great speech on the state of the Union."

Almost in the instant when Reardon received the drink from McClatchy, something happened. It was that Reardon, by reason of McClatchy's devoted attentions to his pleasure, suddenly appeared to Markham and Ames in a sharp light and in a character much different from the one McClatchy intended. The bloat of the absolute face and of the majestic figure, the unhealthy look of the hands, the shabby and too well pressed tweeds, the scarred rasp of the basso profundo, all fell into place with the barbarous drink in the fist, with the phrases "member of the Old Guard" and "oldlangsyner," even with "big legal light" and "famous orator," like details in a picture conjured up in the minds of a jury by the subtlest of prosecutors, as if McClatchy had come not to praise the man but in fact to bury him in dishonor.

Alfred Markham could not help but find the picture gratifying. He was not a cruel man, only one who in middle age looked first for feet of clay on every idol and was comforted when he found them; and then, of course, he felt that this tavern had cheated him and that a valuable work of art was being profaned in it, and to be able to despise all that he found here was his only consolation.

But Ames was sorry.

Noel Ames was an art critic who truly hoped to set the bells ringing someday for a new masterpiece, an artist in his wistfulness for perfection, and quite an ordinary man in that it hurt him to see the admirations of his youth degraded. Reardon had been only a football player, but a champion, something of a masterpiece in his field; he was now what the sportswriters called an immortal; and if you had been young then, and going to art school, if you had loved football but not been good at playing it, and if in afteryears of football talk it had given you pleasure to relate his feats and his record—and to relate, for example, that headline in the *Bulletin*—you would by now have acquired a stockholdership in the legend and probably have exaggerated it even to yourself. But there was something else here, too, for Ames, though he could not have defined it. The propensity to hero worship that is born in every man, which has given history all its disastrous heroes, and which is often highly developed where one might think to find it educated out of existence, was in the fat art critic, refined and tempered but unappeased, and to him Walsh Reardon presented semblances of the classic hero in decline. The look of natural rank was in his bearing, the mold of authority in his heavy face, and that fearsome horn in which he spoke might have stood a Roman legion at attention. Yet what was he really but the picturesque ruin of a figure once acclaimed for prowess in a game of college boys? A man (thought Ames, readily fitting Reardon to the conventional image of the football hero in later life) spoiled forever by a taste of schoolboy greatness, clinging to toy triumphs of the past, and destitute of serious achievement. An "oldlangsyner" indeed, of gin and water, curiously marked by false vestiges of grandeur which seemed to have captivated the keeper of the tavern.

And Reardon, as he accepted the drink, cloaked under a bluff humor an emotion that in him took the form of resentment. Like many men whose habit of life suggests that they care nothing for appearances, he cared for them more than a man of his habit could afford. Otherwise he would not have been "a member of the Old Guard" at all; for it had been the opportunity of indulging his weakness in surroundings where appearances appeared to matter least that attracted him to the Traveler's Rest in the beginning. He was keenly alive to appearances where that weakness was concerned, and was aware that McClatchy, having by that worshipful introduction focused upon him the most critical attention, and then exposed his weakness in detail, had succeeded only in pillorying him before the strangers. But Ames had done Mc-Clatchy's giant an injustice: it was not the former football hero that Reardon felt himself to be in that pillory. It was the man of whom so much had been expected after college. It was the prize student and the star of the debating team, the young lawyer of whom it had been said that he was capable of trying a case before the highest court in the land, the lover of books, the thinker of thoughts, the venturer among infinities—the superior man in the round, as, in his great ego, Walsh Reardon conceived of himself. But his resentment was not directed against the stupidity of McClatchy. It was against the critical intelligence of Markham and Ames, against their refinement, against all that they stood for, against their presence at the opening of the Lost Dutchman, and against the passing of the Traveler's Rest. For theirs were the eyes from which he had fled to the Traveler's Rest, but suddenly the old saloon had vanished in a way that he had not foreseen—the world of Markham and Ames, by the value it placed on a picture by Rembrandt, by the claim it exerted on all the goods of culture, had demolished his retreat like a slum and raised on the site this monument to its own genius—and the eyes had followed him and were again marking him an outlaw. But as he received the drink dedicated by McClatchy to a great speech on the state of the Union, the senator disguised his feelings with a chuckle and responded with a hearty air: "Here's to this elegant new skating rink," as he raised his glass. "Mac, it's amazing. May it make you rich."

"Oh I tellya."

And where another man might have tried by restrained behavior to repair the damage that McClatchy had done, Reardon half emptied the glass at one pull. Markham watched with a slightly contemptuous smile, Ames with disappointment. But McClatchy, all unaware that anything had happened, clucked at his molars and said with satisfaction: "Yes, sir!"

Across the room, Mrs. Creevy and her friends had decided on three manhattans; Phyllis Plover left their table to fill the order, but Arline still hovered over them—it was like her to be thoughtful of three gray-haired women dining unescorted in a public place on New Year's Eve. All three were short, stout, and festive. But Mrs. Creevy complained that she did not see the painting. Arline told her that it was covered for the present by that red drape on the wall behind the bar, but in a little while would be unveiled. The women appeared delighted, and Mrs. Creevy said:

"We've read so much about it."

"You have?" Suddenly it occurred to Arline that these three might be members of the Ladies' Service Club. "Do you live here in town?"

"*Oh*, no," Mrs. Creevy said; and one of her friends told Arline: "San Francisco."

"Really?"

"*Oh*, yes," the third woman said, and added: "Mrs. Creevy is with the De Young Museum."

"She is?"

"*Oh*, yes," Mrs. Creevy said, as if she had thought that everyone knew she was with the museum. "We're so anxious to see the Rembrandt."

Arline felt gratified. People, if only three grandmothers, *had* come all the way from the city to see the painting; and one of them from a museum! "Hope you like it," she smiled. "I'll tell my father you're here." And she left them with a pleasant nod.

The waitress was just serving the manhattans when there appeared at the Creevy table a little red-faced man in full dress, exclaiming cheerily: "Happy New Year's! So you ladies are from the old park museum!"

"The same to you," returned Mrs. Creevy. "Well, *I* am."

"No, is that a fact. Well, as owner and operator of the premises I hereby extend my official welcome. McClatchy's the name, and I just want to say, ladies, it's a great privilege."

"Why, thank you, Mr. McClatchy. I'm Mrs. Creevy. Mr. McClatchy —Miss La Font and Mrs. Delmer."

"Happy to make your acquaintance, I'm sure; and you, ma'am," McClatchy said. "I'm an old Sampm Ciscan myself; born in the—— Wait," to Phyllis Plover, "have they paid for the drinks? Well, don't take a nickel; this whole bill's on the house. Oh, don't say a word, Mrs. McCree; courtesy to members of the profession in honor of the grand opening. No, no, it's my pleasure. No, it's all deductible anyhow, the same as for Mr. Markham over there that owns the big art gallery on Post Street, and Mr. Ames, the art critic—compliments of the house on the historic occasion. Oh, don't mention it, Mrs. McCree; we'll chalk—— Oh, Mrs. *Creevy*; excuse me. We'll chalk it up with the damages under 'dignitaries of the arts.' Are you ladies acquainted with Mr. Markham and Mr. Ames, I wonder?"

Was it Noel Ames of the *Chronicle*? All three ladies read him regularly and all three knew the Markham Galleries, but they had not had the pleasure.

McClatchy promised: "I'll introduce you right after the ceremonies —we're just getting ready for the grand march."

"Lovely," Mrs. Creevy said; and then looked startled. "Grand march, Mr. McClatchy?"

"Oh, sure; didn't I tell you? Oh I should say so. *They had everything but the driving of the golden spike*. Oh, and naturally we want you ladies to be with us."

"We? Oh, but, really, I don't see how——"

"Oh," he dismissed the difficulty, "don't worry about that! They's more than enough men to go around as it is. Oh, sure; that's the big inauguration parade—*every*body's going to be in it. We're just going to line up all the ladies on one side and all the bucks on the other, and they'll meet in the middle and march two by two up the aisle like the elephants and the kangaroos—how's that? Are you game?"

Mrs. Creevy said, laughing: "*Well*, I don't know! *Shall* we?"

"*I* don't care," laughed Mrs. Delmer.

Miss La Font merely whooped with laughter.

"Thaaat's the stuff. Sure; I knew you'd be with us from the word go. Just wait, now; I'm going to fix everything. I'll be right with you. Don't go 'way. . . ."

McClatchy went to the cashier's counter. "Now I declare they's a lady here from the De Young Museum in Golden Gate Park!"

"There is?" Bessie's surprised eyes went to the table where the strangers sat.

"Sure; what'd I tell you?—all roads lead to the Lost Dutchman! But come on, I'll introduce you later; it's time for the grand march." He looked at his grandson. "What are we going to do with him?"

"Billy? Oh, *he'll* have a reserved seat. Let me see, child; suppose you sit right up here where you won't miss a thing."

Billy they enthroned on top of the counter, which stood at the head of the aisle formed by the two rows of free tables. McClatchy gathered up wife, daughter, art dealer, and critic, took them to the foot of the same aisle, and stood them four abreast facing Billy from in front of the kitchen doors. Bessie and Markham were paired in the center; Arline stood on her mother's left, the direction of the booths; Ames on Markham's right, toward the bar. McClatchy hopped on the platform behind them and spoke to Herbie Bates. The music stopped. Herbie sounded a trill on his saxophone. McClatchy faced the room, raising out-turned palms above his head, and called out:

"La-adies and gentlemen! Your kind attention *please*."

Heads turned, eyes found the speaker. At the bar Hump Corkery began to clap loudly with a measured whacking of his thick hands.

"Unacc—— I thank you," McClatchy said. "Unaccustomed—— Al-l right. Wait, now. I rise to a point of—— Do-n't mention it." (Corkery subsided, grinning broadly.) "Friends, Romans, and countrymen. Welcome to the famous Lost Dutchman." (General applause; a cheer from Corkery.) "Oh I tellya. And now—— Yes, sir! And now—and now you're all invited to help us break ground: it's time for the grand march!" (Exclamations, laughter, applause.) "And when I—— Wait. And when I say 'break ground' I don't mean the new floor, you know, Corkery." (Laughter.) "But I—I just want to say if there's anybody don't know how we do the grand march, all they got to do is follow the leader. That fine-looking young couple you see in front of me here, the missus and Mr. Markham—— He's the man, he's the—— Wait. The man that owns the—— They'll go first. Then the daughter and Mr. Ames. . . ."

Red-faced, Arline smiled defensively at the laughing, applauding crowd, feeling like a girl on a carnival platform. Bessie was chuckling: "Oh-h, dear. . . ." Markham's smile was forced: he was wondering how he ever had got into this predicament. The fat Ames was again shaking with suppressed laughter.

The master of the revels described the mechanics of the anachronism he was organizing, and with great sweeps of one arm pointed out the line of march, concluding:

"Al-l *right*, then. Al-l aboard for the grand march. Ladies line up on the left there, beside the daughter; gents on the right with Mr. Ames. Step right up and don't be bashful. Al-l aboard. Atchison, Topeka, and the Santa Fe. He-re we go. . . ." Setting the example, he stepped down from the platform and moved toward the men's side of the room, calling out: "Mr. Reardon? . . . Hump? . . ."

Corkery leaped to the sport, bawling: "Let's go, folks; let's go, in there," swinging his arms in front of him and beating his hands together like a baseball coach. "Mix it up! Mix it up, in there. . . ."

"Come on!" Bessie beckoned the Silvestros; and McClatchy called: "Hey, Baccigaloop!" He also flagged Mrs. Creevy and party. "Mrs. McCreedy? Ladies? . . ."

The band played "Hail, Hail, the Gang's All Here."

The observer on top of the cashier's counter was kicking and bouncing and laughing with excitement.

McClatchy gathered his guests by sexes into queues curving round opposite sides of the restaurant. To make up for the preponderance of males, he threw in the waitresses, and then, having created the opposite problem, sent for more men. Cheers greeted these reinforcements —the two bartenders, the chef in his tall white bonnet, the sweating second cook, and two Filipino dishwashers. "What the hell," he said when he saw that there were now too many males again. "But it can't be helped. By golly, it looks like everybody's going to be in this but old Dutch." He squeezed in between Ames and Corkery, signaling to the bandleader.

The overture ceased.

McClatchy called to the marchers: "Ah-re you-u *ready?*"

"Ye-es. . . ."

"Al-l *right!*" Leaning out from the line, he wagged to Herbie Bates— brakeman to engineer. "Al-l-l *aboard!*"

Herbie raised in his right hand an invisible baton.

Down it came. From the instruments blared the lordly opening bars of the triumphal march from *Aïda*. Bessie tugged at the arm of the astounded Markham. "Come on!"

As long as he lived the march from *Aïda* would give the art dealer a moment of revulsion, conjuring up before him yards of red-and-white linoleum along which a dumpy chuckling little woman in gray crepe was dragging him to this preposterous musical accompaniment and the laughter of the whole room.

Arline, too, as she stepped forth next with Ames, was distressed at the incompatibility of the music's royal pageantry with the character of the pageant that was beginning to unfold; she restrained her pace with difficulty to the ceremonial tempo; and the mirth of her partner increased her embarrassment. Then another salvo of laughter went up from the watchers as the third couple fell in behind.

Next in the procession of celebrities and dignitaries came the foremost prima donna of St. Peter's, known as Madam Silvestro, escorted by the esteemed proprietor, who rendered humorously in his inimitable Oxford accent:

> *"As I take me mor-ning promenade*
> *On the boulevard . . ."*

Unknown to him, however, the orchestra had prepared a novelty arrangement for this event, and with a crash the music changed into a syncopated version of "The Stars and Stripes Forever," but instantly taking his cue, Mr. McClatchy jumped as if a cyclone had struck him, saluted, and scampered forward in good order with the Italian nightingale in tow amid the hearty laughter of those present. Mr. McClatchy was the best-dressed man in the parade.

Meanwhile the belle of the ball and the distinguished owner of the art gallery had reached the top of the aisle, or, as it felt to the dis-

tinguished owner, the end of the gantlet: they wheeled left and marched back along the line of booths to finish behind the ladies still moving down to meet their partners.

The official hostess and the famous art critic had branched off in the opposite direction to double back along the bar and finish behind the men.

And as his grandfather and Madam Silvestro came up, the great Bill Lucas jumped, fell, or was pushed from the cashier's counter, confronting them in a squatting position on the floor and shouting poetically:

> "White! White! Come on and fight!
> You're going to be buried in a sewer PIPE!"

Mr. McClatchy's rejoinder was lost in the general hilarity as he turned left with his partner to follow his better half and the distinguished patron of the arts down the home stretch; and squealing with triumph, the little corker fled behind a corner of the counter to peek out devilishly at the couple approaching next.

Next in order of their appearance came the one and only of the eminent housepainter with the representative of the successful railroad, the president of the Ladies' Sodality with smiling Michael Haines, ace truck driver for the Golden West Milling Company, the wife of the famous contractor that built the place with the well-known fish magnate, and the fair Miss Whitter with the prominent member of the Holy Name. The music stopped and left the bass drum booming a dead march: the merrymakers checked their pace too suddenly and were thrown forward by their own momentum, Mr. Silvestro bumping into Mr. Haines, Mr. Haines into Mr. Corkery, and the spectators laughing uproariously at the confusion. Madam delegate from the De Young Museum was launched with the official rodent exterminator, another laugh went up, and madam delegate joined in at her own expense—the orchestra was playing the wedding march from Lohengrin. Behind her with the gallant purveyor to the crowned heads of Europe came Mrs. Delmer, also joining, and on the arm of the gamy houseflower of the Old Guard, Miss La Font, having a fit. The music became the old favorite, "The Girl I Left behind Me," stopped again, and left the drums beating a wooden-legged parade step as the famous contractor himself sallied forth with Hazel Coombs, popular uniformed waitress representing a breath of old Holland, followed by Senator Reardon with Jean Fennell, another, and Bert Goodman, the water company's faithful meter reader, with Bonnie Winekopf, ditto. . . .

The musicians were manipulating the marchers like puppets on strings and everyone was laughing, and Arline thought that it was awful!

But the orchestra was in for a surprise as it swung into another lively hit of sacred memory, for this had been Our Boys' marching song in the Spanish-American War and who should be entering the lists but Fighting Bob Doughty with waitress Phyllis Plover: he came like a drum major, leaning backward and stepping high, and he was shouting the stirring words that had once inspired American arms:

> *"There'll be a hot time*
> *In the old town*
> *Tonight!"*

The spectators were beating time with their hands and cheering the old veteran who during the war with Spain was wounded in a kitchen explosion at the San Francisco Presidio and has been rewarded with a pension ever since. Cheers also greeted the two paid-up union bartenders, Jerry Barth and Leo Carpenter, incorporated, who followed in that order with the last of the ladies from the land of the tulips, Roxie Cox and Doretta Gallagher, respectively. The cheers mounted to a roar of acclaim as marching arm in arm came the world-famous chef and his celebrated assistant, whose names were not obtained, and the rear was being capably brought up by the two merry dishwashers when the orchestra slipped into Mendelssohn's "Spring Song". . . .

"Oh, no!" Arline covered her face with her hands. "I can't look!" The cooks and the dishwashers romped home, and the musicians ended their novelty arrangement with the little novelty tag to which urchins used to sing: *Without a shir-rt. . . .* Laughter. Cheers. Applause. She removed the blindfold, and the chill smile of Alfred Markham across the room left no doubt in her mind that the joke was on the McClatchys. The grand march! Beside her, Ames's voice was weak from laughter. She was heartsick with disappointment and shame.

But only a few steps from Markham her father was applauding the treacherous musicians and calling out: "A fine body of men! Oh, that was a crackerjack."

Laughing, Herbie Bates acknowledged the compliment with a wave of his arm, and out of the side of his mouth observed to the Gates: "Strictly from Dixie."

"*And a good time——*" McClatchy reported to his guests, raising his voice to be heard above the hubbub; "*And a good time was had by all!*"

Bessie was at his side, smiling upon him fondly; she patted his shoulder. "Happy?"

"Oh I tellya. We come a long ways for this night—huh?" One arm took her around the waist and he planted a smack on her cheek. "Happy New Year's!"

Parties were in progress from coast to coast. Crowds were gathering in Times Square, but the fall of snow that had beaten the blizzard of '88 still crippled transportation, deliveries were far behind, and most places were running out of beer; in the White House, Miss Margaret Truman was entertaining at a supper dance, but providing no grand march.

Bessie placed her cheek against her husband's. "The same to you."

"Yes, sir!" he grinned. "All we had to do was open the doors!" Sudden moisture glinted in his pale blue eyes and he gave his head a twist of conviction. "Oh, it's a great night for the Irish!"

Markham thought bitterly that it was indeed; and it galled him to hear this lout boasting like an assured success; and when a few minutes later he met Ames at the bar and the critic exclaimed delightedly "What an art show! Alfred, I wouldn't have missed this for the world!" he was disgusted with Noel Ames.

He asked: "How do you think the place will do?"

"Do? Oh——" Ames shrugged regretfully. "Who knows?" He wished McClatchy well.

Farther down the bar McClatchy found Reardon having another gin and water, and said: "Now for the speech and the grand unveiling! Give us the old eloquence. And look, I'll be there by the painting, see? and the minute you're through just give me the highsign and I'll pull the cord. Just raise your hand like this"—McClatchy raised his, the forefinger and thumb making a circle as in his gesture to the captain of the light—"and I'll unveil the painting. Okay?"

Reardon laughed, reaching for his glass. "All right." He finished the drink. McClatchy escorted him to the band platform, explained things to Herbie Bates, then hurried behind the bar, taking his position beneath the covered Rembrandt, and again raised his hand in the signal that Reardon was to give when the speech was over. Herbie was about to toot his saxophone to attract the attention of the crowd again, but this proved unnecessary. Reardon simply said:

"Ladies and gentlemen!" and at the sound of the great-ogre voice all heads came round. Arline thought: The silver tongue!

"Our host, Mr. McClatchy over there," rumbled the deep hoarse grating organ less loudly, and McClatchy acknowledged this introduction by a vigorous overhead handshake with himself in the manner of the prize ring, whereupon there was a flutter of applause; "Mr. McClatchy is now going to unveil the face of the presiding genius of this new pleasure dome; and he has asked me to say a few words of introduction. . . ."

Suddenly Hump Corkery began to applaud again. He was joined by Haines, Goodman, Primrose, and Doughty—the others of the "Old Guard"; and by McClatchy himself. And all the other Llagans present were eying with curiosity, half smiling, frowning, or narrowly appraising, this town failure in whose oratorical powers and genius at law the whole town believed. Whatever else Walsh Reardon was to these people, whether they held him in good fellowship or regarded him with disdain, admiration, or tolerance, to all of them he was Llagas's man that might have been—mainly, indeed, by hearsay, for it was years since he had practiced in public and no one present had ever been witness to his talents except as he exhibited them in his conversation; and at this moment when he announced that he was going to speak, the old guardsmen took, with their little corporal, personal and collective pride in him.

He raised his great right hand for silence: and silence fell.

"*The Lost Dutchman,* as you know," the dreadful bass resumed, "is a painting by Rembrandt. A portrait of a Dutch cavalier. A masterpiece found behind Mr. McClatchy's bar after having been lost for three hundred years. It has been authenticated by the grand panjandrum of art, Sir Patrick Locklear. And it has lately been the subject of public debate as to whether the place for it is not a tavern but a museum. I noticed that in support of the case for a museum a certain newspaper editor had the stupidity to quote Ben Jonson. It reminded me of something Rare Ben once said about King James. 'He despises me, I suppose,' Ben Jonson said, 'because I live in an alley. Tell him,'" and the voice became a harrowing snarl, "'his soul lives in an alley.'"

This caused but a rustle of amusement and a few tentative claps, more in response to the obvious cue than to the success of the joke. Reardon's friends, while they approved the slander of the king, were wondering who Ben Johnson was. Reardon enlightened them:

"Ben Jonson was a lover of taverns," he roared, "and so am I!"

Cheers, hearty laughter, and applause, led by Corkery. Now he's getting warmed up, McClatchy thought, grinning, and winked across the room at his daughter, cocking his head, as if to say: Oh, he's a great talker. Arline was ashamed of Walsh Reardon. To Bessie it was enough that the man was reasonably sober: she smiled upon her husband, pleased because Danny was pleased. Billy sat before her on the cashier's counter, fascinated by the monster.

Reardon continued: "It was Ben Jonson's delight to sit in taverns eating and drinking and having such talk as would not be heard in any museum under heaven—talk with Shakespeare and with Marlowe. Why," he roared again, "art is born in taverns. Museums," and his volume was down, "are where it lies entombed. Old Rembrandt was a tavern man himself. For all we know it was in a tavern that he met the bully boy whose face you are about to see on the wall behind the bar; and when you see that face you won't have any doubt of it. It is the face of an old Achilles whom we knew. Poor devil, he hasn't had a drink in three hundred years."

Laughter.

"And we know," said Reardon, "that if it could be left to him, he wouldn't even be found dead in a museum."

Cheers.

"And so"—the voice was comparatively soft; a muted foghorn—"we have brought his picture home."

And there descended upon the room a respectful silence.

Markham's frozen smile was ironic. Ludicrous how these fellows bracketed themselves, like adolescents, with the Jonsons and Shakespeares and Marlowes and Rembrandts—as if the great workmen of whom they spoke so clubbily would have hailed them as brothers of the mind and spirit. And how revealing it was that they always recognized one another, even in a picture, and then always romanticized the brotherhood, the drinking, the talking, and the shame, always including in the membership the Rare Bens and the Wills and the Kits and the Old Rembrandts; for Markham had been reminded of the poor tramp artist of the stained-glass window who had sniggered at the lost Dutchman so familiarly and with such diabolical fondness, saying: "The painter must have picked him up in some gin mill." Markham resented and scorned the lot of them.

Ames had noticed that one became used to that voice, and wondered that it could achieve so many shadings in so limited a range; marveled, indeed, though in amusement, at the effect of the muted foghorn coming immediately after two coarse jokes that had drawn laughter—how it had immediately hushed the crowd, as if convincing everyone that bringing the Dutchman's picture "home" was a very touching thing to do.

"Now," said Reardon, "there was never any record of this portrait by Rembrandt until the picture was discovered hanging behind that bar. How it got there, how long it had been there, nobody knows. All Mr.

McClatchy can tell us for certain is that it was there when he acquired the property years ago. But he has a theory. He thinks that someone may have bought it blindly at a railroad auction, then brought it in here, and traded it for a bottle. Fantastic?" he asked when his audience chuckled. "No more fantastic than what we know to be the truth: that three hundred years after this portrait was painted in Holland, the world has just discovered it, and discovered it in this distant town. And perhaps that's not so fantastic after all. We don't know for certain how many pictures Rembrandt painted; or how he disposed of each one. He was a prolific artist, often pressed for cash, in an age when painters in Holland were as numerous as bargemen and a good painting often brought but a few guilders. Many Old Masters like him, little esteemed at one time or another in their lives, and needing cash, sold so cheap that their paintings were bought by peasants. And the only wonder is that in the flux of life, in the shifting fortunes of men and of nations, some of these paintings ever turned up again at all. The Ark of the Covenant itself—we may surmise that it was destroyed with Solomon's Temple, but all we know for certain is that it is still missing. And what ever became of the Holy Grail? Did Joseph of Arimathaea, as one tradition says, take it to Glastonbury, England, and does it today lie buried with the rubble of some Roman ruin beneath the town where the famous thorn tree blossomed every Christmas Eve until some Puritan cut it down? Or on the shelves of some shop in Avebury or Ipswich or Bethnal Green? Or lost with the trunk of some never witting goodwife dead three hundred years in Massachusetts? A chauffeur, strolling a California beach a few years ago, stooped and picked up the calling card of Francis Drake.

"By law and by chance does man live and die, by hap and by stroke, by reason and at random—loving and striving, winning and losing— by work and by windfall, by strength and by weakness. Prey of sickness, conscription, and catastrophe, of knaves, of visions, and of his own senses"—using the mute again he managed to insert in parenthesis: "By hook, crook, the fall of a coin, by rune, zodiac, and charm, by Matthew, Mark, Luke, and John, by faith, by hope, by charity," then picked up in a roar—"he grapples with a whirlwind in the midst of the universe," and softening his voice to a piratical *zitti zitti,* reprised his theme: "By compass and star, current and storm, by ship and by whale!"

Ames was at a loss to think how such language could be put in print so that any sense might be made of it, but as spoken it was all perfectly clear, and the audience appeared captivated by the strange music that the voice was making.

And then in what for him was a normal tone, Reardon growled: "He comes and he goes; the planet remains. He sees, hears, smells, touches, tastes, thinks, imagines; and he acts. He plants a seed, builds a tower to his god, paints a portrait of a brother's face. He loves, procreates, wages war, migrates, gets drunk, labors, cheats, and steals, prays, cries out in anguish, or is dumb. He finds what he is looking for, or not, and then is gone. The attics and basements of the planet are full of evidence that he was here: things he made, souvenirs of where he passed, testimony of how he loved—even pictures of his face. And are there not at every railroad auction relics of the time he meant to go by ship and went instead by whale? The planet is a marvelous place, which we forget at times; and what man finding gold in mere ground, a pearl in an oyster, or a heart in a trunk is not instantly reminded of it?"

What rot, thought Markham; but Ames thought that it was really wonderful what the man could do with that great deformed voice of his; and the audience remained in the spell till Reardon admonished wryly: "But let us look about more carefully in the attic, thou and I."

Chuckles.

Even Arline had been held. Whether it had been because Walsh Reardon was really a good speaker or because he was such a monster she could not for the moment decide, but to her ears the burden of his busker poetry had sounded like profound half-mystic truth.

Bessie was saddened by the philosophy, and gazing at Reardon's face, suddenly perceived in it another expression of something that she had seen in the face of the Dutchman, and pitied him.

Mrs. Linnegar and Mrs. Johansen both had the same thought about Walsh Reardon: There must have been a girl somewhere.

McClatchy was looking about the room with a triumphant grin on his face, winking and twisting his head as if to say: Oh I tellya.

"The question remains," said Reardon: "How came the Dutchman here? But for that matter, how came our friend Mr. McClatchy here? Who was it that led him here to Llagas, or—should I say?—to Latmos? Who was it, Master Keats, that led our beautiful shepherd here, and cast him into a sleep of years, and has awakened him tonight in this enchanted saloon?"

As if declining to insult so well-educated an audience, the speaker did not supply the direct answer to the question. But the big man looked down at the little one, who stood happily, cord in hand, beneath the painting, and the big man smiled, and the smile was full of affection.

"Good old McEndymion," he said.

And raised his hand in the signal for the grand unveiling.

13

BOHEMIA

The art critic of the San Francisco *Chronicle* was a disappointed painter but a born journalist. His chatty Sunday features, sprinkled with anecdotes and quaint but never long words, had a wide following. And on the first Sunday in January there appeared on the *Chronicle's* art page a story that a stranger in San Francisco might have thought a surprising one to be there.

This story ran for two columns on the excuse of a work of art which it dismissed with a paragraph (for Noel Ames had of course dealt with the Rembrandt before). The peg of the story was the opening of a country tavern, or perhaps it was the tavernkeeper, but the space was filled mainly with recollections of the Mission district and the Barbary Coast and of how the art critic as a boy, "one tremendous morning," had climbed the Twenty-second Street hill and "looked down like an archangel on the far smoking ruins of the South of Market."

This kind of thing, it might have been explained to the stranger, was not uncustomary with the newspapers of San Francisco when the opportunity offered, and really all Ames had been doing was publicly filing title to the place in his fashion. But with his opening remark he had shot into the air a slight misapprehension. He had begun:

> And they call him McEndymion—
> this old-time South of Market-Mis-
> sion boy preserved alive by the mar-
> velous climate of Morera, preserved
> intact, pardie, so that he seemed to
> your observer the last of his tribe or
> a throwback to his fathers; a man led
> afield by the moon, they say, and
> courted by her of late with strange
> and wonderful gifts.

Arline, when she had read that far, looked up at her father, who had shown her the story, in alarm, as if it had suddenly been suggested to her that she were the daughter of a freak. But her father was beaming. He enlightened her eagerly: "McEndymion—he was a man in a poem," and told her about the Greek sheepherder. But really her father was flattered less by the allusion than because the newspaper had published *his* title to San Francisco, all San Franciscans being rivalrous of one another and the exiles haunted by an indefinable fear as of claim jumpers.

Across the Golden Gate, old subscribers read the story with a characteristic mixture of nostalgia, irony, irritation, wonder, and amusement—the nostalgia that such stories usually did arouse in them, however faintly; the irony with which they were able to criticize the sentimental tendency of their journalists and their own weakness when it came to this particular subject; the slight underlying irritation that they always felt whenever someone else asserted a tie of old association with their property; wonder because Noel Ames had written as if the South of Market-Mission boy were passing from the scene and because they understood clearly what he meant. They could remember men with great beefy red faces and walrus mustaches, men who really had, it suddenly seemed, been different from those of the identical breed who lived in the modern city; and was it not true that the South of Market Boys' Association was inactive now and dying because the surviving authentic boys who had been the life of it were too old to grand-march? It would be only forty-two years in April since the Fire, and yet, clearly, the South of Market-Mission boy was passing, changing. In San Francisco the fact that the city had changed continued to be a matter of current report, but their attention being directed to a specific example of how its people had changed, Ames's readers experienced a melancholy wonder. And they felt with this a tender amusement; for on his deathbed a new light suffused the South of Market-Mission boy. Characteristics long despised in him could now be smiled at fondly as belonging to the vanished city. He was becoming a collectors' item. And here, according to Noel Ames, was a South of Market-Mission-Barbary Coast boy preserved intact, a real old-timer with, pardie, a Rembrandt painting mysteriously bestowed, in a tavern where there was grand marching still (for some readers assumed that at the Lost Dutchman Tavern it was to be had every night); there was even a picture of him grinning proudly out at them. And his name was Mc-Endymion!

And the timing was fortunate. San Francisco was in another era of gaiety. Restaurants and night clubs were everywhere. The city and its suburbs were swollen by immigration from other parts of the country, and the streets thronged with traffic, with strangers, till matrons declared they dreaded to go downtown these days. At times nostalgia for the city's past became a real and pressing thing.

With the fame attaching to the windfallen masterpiece certified by Sir Patrick Locklear and now linked in the city's mystical mind with the Golden Gate Bridge, Ames's account of his evening at the Lost Dutchman was enough to lure dozens of his readers the thirty miles to Llagas. And perhaps it was not chiefly the famous Dutchman that they wanted to see. They would view with respect and even with a certain reverence the haughty old boozer's face illuminated like the face of Caesar's ghost behind the bar, and then (though Arline found it incomprehensible, idiotic that they should), would ask, smiling: "And where is McEndymion?"

But the novelty must soon have palled. The tavern might easily have failed had it not been for something else.

The aftermath of the war had brought into Morera County a curious drift of outlanders. Not on the farms nor in the towns had these settled, but in shady hollows of the hills and along the rolling ocean that lay just over the little hump of the Coast Range from the Llagas Valley. Most of them were young and from far away—New York, Kansas, Texas. They were discharged servicemen and women studying under veterans' subsidies, or on their own: wanting freedom, rusticity, and cheap rent. Some of them wanted to write; most were studying art. One of them was Rohmer Kinney, whom all his friends called Rover.

The obvious corruption of his first name seemed happily descriptive of Kinney. Not that he had ever been anywhere, to speak of. He was a native of Reno, Nevada, where, after a year at the state university and a choppy career as lifeguard, motel clerk, slot machine attendant, and blackjack dealer, he had been drafted into the Army. He had been sent to Camp Roberts, California, for infantry training, but being equipped with an old stomach ulcer, had achieved a transfer to the service command as a member of the permanent party of the post, and had sat out the war right there. He had not risen above the grade of corporal, but by conducting a small gambling game had accumulated four thousand dollars when discharged. Nearly all that was gone now. At the expense of his grateful country he was now studying creative writing at the University of California in Berkeley, to and from which he got by motorcycle, and creating a novel about army life while "shacked up," as he put it (the army term), with a pretty black-eyed veteran of the WAC in a shack with a view of the sea. He was also cultivating a beard. It was reddish brown and considerably broadened his full good-natured face. He was six feet tall, robust, slow-moving, and soft-spoken. He had a good deal of dry light brown hair with a Celtic skin reddened by sun and wind on the protruding ridge on his forehead and on his cheekbones and the nub of his nose, small but kindly light blue eyes, red lips which seemed continually to flick away a smile, and a rolling gait. With his heavy curved-stem pipe, careless jackets, open collars, and way of slouching in a chair with one leg thrown over the adjacent arm, he was a figure readily accommodated to the image of the shaggy dog and appeared to be perfectly harmless.

The girl's name was Rita Buckley. She came from South Dakota, had Indian blood, and was studying painting at a school in San Javier. She wished to see the Llagas Rembrandt, so one evening Kinney took her behind him on his motorcycle and roared off with her to Mc-Clatchy's tavern. They sat at the bar and ordered beer.

Kinney had noticed several expensive cars parked outside this dis-mally situated though much publicized establishment, and was im-pressed by the interior and by the prosperous appearance of some of the customers. He congratulated McClatchy on a very attractive tav-ern, saying that he had seen a good deal about the place in the papers. McClatchy said heartily that he was glad Kinney liked it. Rita spoke favorably of the Rembrandt, and McClatchy began to inform her about it. She was an intense and serious-minded girl and looked at him queerly when he said that it was handmade and imported, and Kinney told him with a smile that Rita was a painter. McClatchy responded to this with amazement and pleasure; it was plain that he felt an affin-ity with painters; and looking to see what she and her companion were drinking, he ordered, before either could name a preference, two more beers. They thanked him, and Kinney introduced himself—presi-dent, he added, of the Organization.

"President of the—— Well, I'm happy to know you," McClatchy said, and warmly shook hands with the bearded young man.

Kinney presented Rita, who was looking at him with a puzzled expression, and said that she was a star member. McClatchy greeted her again admiringly. The new beers arrived.

"Well," Kinney said.

"Happy days," McClatchy said with a hospitable upward gesture of the hand; and they sipped the beers.

Kinney said: "So you know of the Organization. Looks like people in Morera County take an interest in the veterans."

"Veterans," McClatchy repeated. "Oh, you bet."

"No, but you'd be surprised," Kinney said, "how many are talented painters."

"Painters," McClatchy said, brightening. "*Well*, now."

"Like Rita here." Kinney dropped an arm around the shoulders of the girl, who was looking at him with an ironical smile. "Rita's got a scholarship from the government."

"The government!" McClatchy said.

Rita laughed.

"Yes," Kinney said, "and some of the others have won prizes."

"Prizes!"

"*Oh*, yes. It's been predicted that some of the boys and girls will make names for themselves."

"Be famous!" McClatchy grinned.

Kinney laughed. "With luck, maybe. But," with a twist of the head, "art's a tough racket."

"Yes," McClatchy said, "I suppose it is."

"It really is. You've got to get the breaks."

"You do for a fact. Even Rembrandt—take him. They tell me Rembrandt died broke. Would you believe that? And look at him today."

"Dead," Kinney said.

"Oh, you're right there, too—it's too late. The man is six feet under."

"I'll take mine while I'm still around," Kinney said.

"You said it."

"Yes," Kinney said, "what the kids need is a place where their work can be seen by the public."

McClatchy agreed. "Kind of an official headquarters," he suggested.

"Right. The Committee's been considering the County Museum, the Court House, the Morera Inn. . . ."

"The Morera Inn?" McClatchy said; and on a sudden inspiration he demanded: "What's the matter with this place?"

Both Rita and Kinney laughed, and Kinney said: "As a matter of fact we were just wondering about this place."

"You don't say!"

"Yes, and I don't mind saying I'm favorably impressed. The location is bad, but that Rembrandt sets just the right tone—quality. And I notice the customers are a nice class of people."

"Oh, the best!" McClatchy said. "No bums allowed. . . ."

The tavernkeeper's imagination had caught fire. Was not the Museum his natural enemy, and the Inn a competitor that might draw away the Lost Dutchman's trade if it too should go in for art? It seemed to him that the art trade this side of the Palace Hotel was his by right of original claim. And did he not wish to help the veterans? But principally, the truth was, he wished the veterans to help him. This was Saturday night, the first Saturday night since the appearance of Ames's story, and the crowd tonight was large enough to be encouraging, but during the week he had been worried. What if the place should fail, and all that money owed to the bank? But what, he thought now, if it should become the official headquarters of all those veterans?

Kinney promised to place the Lost Dutchman Tavern in nomination before the Committee. And that night McClatchy enthusiastically told his wife of their prospects.

He spoke of the Organization as the Veteran Painters. "Some of them are prize winners and the girl's got a scholarship from the government; the Inn is after them, and the County Museum, but the president is on our side, I'm counting on him to swing the vote. The proposition has great possibilities. It's a big thing."

"Yes," Bessie said. "Oh, wouldn't it be grand!"

On Monday afternoon Rover Kinney called again. The Committee, he said, was to make its decision the next night and he wondered whether McClatchy had any newspaper clippings and any photographs that might be submitted in behalf of the Lost Dutchman. McClatchy struck his brow. He had! He led Kinney into the rear apartment. Bessie was out, but carefully collected in a box laid in a bureau drawer he found all their clippings together with Frank Johansen's sketches which she had so admired, and he entrusted the lot to Kinney.

Kinney had borrowed a friend's old open Ford car and in the back of it carted down from the marine-view cabin four of Rita's paintings. He mentioned that he happened to have some paintings with him and asked if McClatchy would care to see them. Paintings!—*did* he? McClatchy said that he would by all means. They went outside together and McClatchy helped carry in the large rectangular bundle wrapped in an army blanket. They carried it into the rear apartment and Kinney took out the four unframed canvasses.

As McClatchy looked at the first his brows went up, his lips parting loosely in a wild-oat grin, and he threw Kinney a wink. "*September Morn*," he whispered. He looked at the second and said in the same voice, appreciatively: "Whew! A couple of hot ones." He looked from one to the other and back again, chuckling. There was in fact nothing pornographic about these pictures, but Kinney was content that the merchant should think there was, and smiled. But the merchant's chuckles trailed off, and although he seemed to be still looking at the pictures the rapidity of his blinking indicated a distracted

mind. "Well, now"—he wetted his lips nervously. His face was redder.
Suddenly Kinney realized that the man was embarrassed. It came to
him that the chuckles had sounded forced—that they, the grin, the
wink, and the comments had signified no more than an effort to com-
ply with what the man felt that male convention required of him here.

Kinney asked: "What's the matter?"

"Huh? Well . . ." McClatchy hesitated; he cast a glance over his
shoulder at the doorway, looked at Kinney, and whispered: "I'm
afraid the wife'd never stand for it."

"You're kidding!"

"What? No. Don't you realize? In mixed company—— Hell, we
couldn't have nothing like this in the place anyhow; we'd get arrested
for indecent exposure!"

The bearded young man only smiled again, tolerantly; he scouted
the idea of arrest, and said: "Look, these are legitimate art studies.
They were painted from professional models in a legitimate art school.
Nudes are painted by the greatest artists in the world. Museums——"

"Makes no difference; they's a law, you know. And people bring
their kids in here; I'd be charged with contributing to the delinquency
of the minors. And I got a grandson of my own flesh and blood practically growing up in the joint. Holy Moses, before I knew it," he
finished with a grin, wishing to pass the delicate matter off as lightly
as possible, "I'd be excommunicated!"

Kinney's small light blue eyes flashed angrily with the realization
that this view relegated him to the position of a man offering French
postcards.

And at that look it suddenly struck McClatchy that his scruples
conflicted with his commercial interests. It seemed to him that his
hope of capturing the trade of the Veteran Painters was collapsing,
and he feared that he might be handing over that trade to the Inn.

Both men spoke at once.

"Well, we could select——" began Kinney, ready to compromise.

"But wait, now—wait," McClatchy said, and he turned to the third
painting. He turned to it in the hope of finding something suitable,
something that he could praise. He was relieved to find that this one
was not a picture of a woman; but what he saw surprised him. "What's
this, now?" he asked studiously.

It was a picture of a man lying dead on a slope of ground at sunset,
coatless, bootless, and trouserless, his legs encased in long under-
drawers; a man who had died violently, for his shirt was wet with blood;
he had a sweeping blond mustache, a thin face to which the artist
had given a cruel expression even in death, and long yellow hair.

"Custer," Kinney said. "That was the way they found him."

"Custer! No! With his pants off?"

"Not according to the books, maybe, but according to the Indians. See, Rita's part Sioux. One of her ancestors was in the battle. And that's the way the Indians say they left him."

"In his drawers—is that the truth! Now that's very interesting; I never knew that." McClatchy studied the picture again. "Yes. Now that's the kind of a painting I like, something with a story to it—you know? That's better. He certainly looks like he's in bad shape there, don't he? But now there we have something historical. The low down, you might say, on Custer's Last Stand according to the Indians. That's educational."

Because of what McClatchy had disclosed about himself with the word excommunicated, Kinney wished that he had left the fourth picture at home. He moved to gather up the first three pictures and place them on top of the fourth, hoping that his sleight of hand would cause McClatchy to overlook the fourth as he told him to distract his attention: "Well, we can screen them all and pick the best. . . ."

"The best, yes. Quality, that's what we want. Wait, now, till I take a gander at this."

McClatchy had beaten Kinney to the fourth picture, the largest of the lot; it was as tall as McClatchy's shoulder. He placed it carefully against the wall and stood off to look at it.

"That's not exactly——" Kinney began; but just then McClatchy, with his eyes on the picture, made an awed sound, and Kinney, seeing the expression on his face, did not continue.

The subject of this fourth picture was a crucifixion, but the tortured and bleeding figure nailed to the cross against a stormy sea-green sky was dark-skinned, had long straight black hair parted in the middle with a broken feather in it, and was girded in a loincloth of buckskin. On their knees in the foreground were three soldiers in breastplates; they were playing at dice. And beyond, seen as from a hilltop, stretched a landscape of virgin wilderness. McClatchy was gazing at the picture with reverence. "Oh, say, now, I see. . . . Is she a Catholic, I wonder?"

"Rita?" asked Kinney, surprised. "I—don't know."

"Oh, but I'll bet she is, though, or was raised one. Maybe the sisters raised her in one of the Mission schools. It looks like a Catholic done that."

Kinney's sun-reddened brow furrowed quizzically; at the corners of his bearded mouth a smile flickered.

McClatchy was still looking at the painting. "Do you know what it

reminds me of? Our Lady of Guadalupe. Did you ever hear that story?"
he asked, turning.

"No."

"Oh, that's a beautiful story," McClatchy said. "A couple or three
hundred years ago, it was, down in Mexico, in the geographical center
of the Western Hemisphere—our Lady appeared to an Indian boy,
Diego was his name, and she told him who she was, and he knew her,
he knew she was the Blessed Virgin—but do you know he thought she
was an Indian? The mother of God appeared to that poor ignorant
savage like a member of his own race, the same as his own mother
only younger and more beautiful, a beautiful Indian maiden. And she
left roses blooming in the snow; and on that spot they built a church
that you can see today, Our Lady of Guadalupe, a famous shrine. And
here a few years ago when the Mexican Government tried to close all
the churches in the country, that was one church they couldn't close.
They couldn't close it; and you know why? Because the Indians
wouldn't let 'em. Thousands of 'em come from nowheres, out of the
woods and hills, and stood guard over that church, and the government didn't dare lay a hand on it. It stayed open. Now that's history!"
McClatchy's eyes shone with tears.

Kinney said politely: "Really?"

"Yes, sir!" McClatchy said, turning back to the painting. "Oh, that's
good. You know what I mean? It's inspirational." He knew that the
sublime story that he had tried to tell had been a failure, and realizing
that he had moved no one but himself, he was embarrassed. He had
tried to tell it to the wrong man. But he wished that Kinney had been
capable of hearing it, how loving and beautiful it was.

Rubbing his beard, Kinney said: "Funny—I didn't think you'd like
this one." Having no understanding of the Catholic faith, and finding
to his bafflement that a Catholic liked the picture, he thought that
possibly the picture had a double meaning. If it had, he stood ready
to take full advantage of the meaning that he did not see, but he was
making a clean breast of his innocence in case McClatchy should suddenly see the other.

"That? No, you could hang that in a church," McClatchy said. "*The
Crucifixion According to the Indians—that's* what that is."

"Oh," Kinney said.

"Yes," McClatchy said. "Oh, I wish the wife was here. I'd like her
to see that."

"You would?" Kinney said. Able now to see the picture as Mc-
Clatchy did, he saw at the same time an opportunity to entrench the
Organization in the tavern by winning the approval of the straitlaced

Mrs. McClatchy. He saw too that it might involve some risk, but the irony of the situation, appealing to his sense of humor, was more than he could resist. What a story for his friends! "I'll trust you with it overnight." He waved aside the tavernkeeper's protests. He wanted Mrs. McClatchy to see it, he said, and besides: "Maybe you'll be hanging it on the wall."

"Oh, God willing," McClatchy said, and thanked him for his courtesy.

Bessie, when confronted with the picture, was at a loss before it, but when she heard her husband's explanation of it, when he related it to the story of Our Lady of Guadalupe and told her that Rita Buckley was part Indian, Bessie was touched. She looked at the picture with respect and sympathy and said that it was very unusual.

But Arline said: "Oh, Dad! You wouldn't put *that* one up."

"What do you mean I wouldn't? You could hang that in a church."

"But that's just it—this is no place for it." For it was not that Arline saw in the picture any meaning other than the one that her father had expounded. She, like Bessie, assumed that this was as Kinney had expounded it to him.

But her father would not be convinced.

On Tuesday night Arline had already gone home when Kinney telephoned McClatchy and asked how Mrs. McClatchy had liked the picture.

"Oh, she's crazy about it," McClatchy said.

"She is? Well, you can hang it up! The voting's over and it's the Lost Dutchman by a nose. Congratulations," said Rover Kinney.

McClatchy did not wait to raise the flag of victory. Before the tavern closed that night, up on the wall above the booths, directly across the room from the Rembrandt, went *The Crucifixion According to the Indians,* to signify that the Lost Dutchman Tavern was now the official headquarters of the Veteran Painters.

So when Arline arrived at eleven next morning, there the picture was. Present also were Kinney and a young man in a sweatshirt and silver-rimmed army spectacles, and they were hanging other pictures. Oils, watercolors, etchings; landscapes, seascapes, portraits, still lifes, and abstracts: unframed pictures of various shapes and sizes—she counted fourteen of them; and Bessie said:

"Don't they brighten the place up, though. So colorful!"

Arline thought some of them a bit queer. She could approve the nocturne of the adobe house, the portrait of the little girl, and the two etchings, one of Mudtown and the slough, the other of a Powell Street cablecar. "But, Ma!"—pointing to the crucified Indian.

"Oh, don't bother, now. That's all right."

Arline groaned.

She noticed that the pictures were for sale. The prices were type-written on small cards affixed to the lower left-hand corners. The nocturne was the most expensive, $125, and the etching of the cablecar the cheapest, ten dollars.

When Kinney and his friend had gone the tavernkeeper stood admiring his growing art collection. "Oh, that's a great improvement. It improves the property." He turned and put it with a grin to the silent critic behind the bar. "What do you think of that, Dutch?"

The Dutchman looked at him as if in supreme contempt of a man who did not know when he was being swindled.

At this point in its history the Organization that Kinney had first mentioned to McClatchy four evenings ago was in fact but two days old. Its name was not the Veteran Painters but the Morera Artists' Exhibition and Marketing Association, though it was not in fact an association at all. In fact its president was its proprietor, and its members, as he called them, were his customers. All but Rita. Counting Rita, there were at present only ten members; but Rita paid nothing. The works of the other nine were being hung in the tavern with the famous Rembrandt for an exhibition fee of five dollars per picture, payable to the president. This was understood to cover the rental of wall space in the McClatchys' tavern for a period of six weeks, renewable at $4.50; and in the event of a sale the president was to receive a commission.

But the McClatchys were ignorant of all this. All they knew was that if someone wished to buy a picture they were to sell it at the price marked and turn the money over to the president as part of the tavern's service to the Organization. Rover Kinney was selling the very walls of the building in front of their noses.

Ten days later the membership had increased to thirty-six, and most of the tavern's wall space from the height of five feet to the ceiling, except on the bar side, which McClatchy reserved for the Rembrandt alone, was crowded with pictures. Faces and figures, vistas, interiors, bowls of fruit, pictures that suggested nightmares and Chinese puzzles, with Custer laid out just above one of the brass-plated kitchen doors, but with nothing any closer than that to a case of indecent exposure.

Kinney had pocketed exactly $246, all of it in rental fees except for one dollar commission. Only the ten-dollar etching of the cablecar had sold. The artist had made a net profit of only four dollars on the sale, and that without reckoning the cost of his materials, but apparently he felt encouraged. He had substituted in the same space for the remainder of the six-week period, at no extra charge, another etching of a cablecar: price, $12.50.

But the tavern too had begun to profit from Kinney's enterprise, for the artists came to see their work on exhibition, bringing friends. They came again and again, and they kept coming back, not only for the pleasure of basking in their own glory but also because they found stimulation in one another's company, especially at the bar. It was the old romance of artists and cafés, though the Paris of the story was only the metropolis of the egg.

These anomalous bohemians of the G. I. Bill of Rights lived in country cabins instead of city garrets, and all were well fed, and their attire was disappointing—the men came to the tavern in sports jackets and jumpers, and the women in nothing more picturesque than "pedal-pushers" and head scarves; but they were like art students everywhere. One had only to hear them talking in groups. Not only about art did they talk, but about humanity, philosophy, religion, sex, psychiatry, politics, international affairs, one another, and freely about themselves, over their beer; and the prevalence of large shell-rimmed eyeglasses among these young healthy-looking war veterans was surprising. Most of them were serious, and few ever drank too much, but at times they made the tavern ring with gaiety. And the army game called "shacking up," at which some of them played, was of course an old bohemian arrangement. These, though they might not look it, and might have bolted art rather than starve for it, and might never produce a masterpiece, and spoke with the accents of Texas, Kansas, and Brooklyn, were not very different as a group from their classic prototypes of Montmartre.

But they were recent settlers hereabout, they lived scattered through the nooks and crannies of the county, and until now they had not had a focus, a pivot, a center of gravity. As a group they had not existed. When they descended on the Lost Dutchman they coalesced and became a community. The Lost Dutchman did become their headquarters—their club, their forum, and, with their pictures crowding the walls, their setting. Only now did Morera County awake to the fact that it possessed what it could call an art colony. This queer utopian government-issue bohemia, which at this period of history was repeated in various places throughout the country, in Mexico, and even in Paris, appeared to have materialized in the Lost Dutchman as mysteriously as it seemed the Dutchman himself had turned up in the Traveler's Rest.

Late one February night a few of these veterans, sitting round the
far corner of the bar, had been reminiscing about the war in the far
Pacific, exchanging stories, mentioning places. One told a ridiculous
story about his commanding officer, the others laughed, and one picking up his glass began to sing the ironic ruefully devil-may-care "Bless
'em All," which a few years before had been rolling through the
streets of Sydney and Melbourne. There, in those days, when anyone
in a crowd would begin that song, the whole crowd would take it up,
and that was what happened now, in Llagas, as if in salute to the
memory of the custom. The tavern was suddenly filled with singing.
The veterans of the South Pacific and those who had known the song
in Africa or London (for it had never really caught on in America: in
America perhaps the feelings that it expressed about the war could
not be properly appreciated) were united by a cord of mutual experience; but of course nearly everyone knew what the song was, if only
dimly, and most of the non-veterans present were able to recognize
something of what was passing. McClatchy had a warm sentimental
regard for fraternity among war veterans; he felt a little surge of emotion. Besides, he welcomed this party spirit in his tavern. As the singing
ended he raised his hands for attention amid the cheering and demanded to know whether anyone could play the piano. Shouts of
"Yes! *He* can." . . . "*She* can." He led six volunteer piano movers into
the rear apartment and laid his hand fondly on the old upright of the
Traveler's Rest; they managed to bring it out and set it against the
wall at the head of the bar. "Do you know 'Over There'?" he asked
the young man who sat down to thump it; for he was prepared to
join in patriotically with the voice that might have been the equal of
McCormack's, with the training. But the young man shook his head:
he was continuing with the original theme, and although the piano
was maddeningly out of tune the others supported him heartily: the
whole tavern, it seemed, was singing "Waltzing Matilda."

Next day McClatchy had the instrument tuned, and often in the
evenings after that it was played.

So the old subscribers coming to behold the celebrated moon-given
Rembrandt, and the genuine preserved-intact South of Market-Mission-Barbary Coast boy, although they found here no grand marching,
discovered for themselves an acceptable substitute—a bohemian atmosphere of a kind, in which, as the evening deepened, the talk
became spirited, everyone seemed to know everyone else, and if there
was singing it was suddenly like a party.

Only a few of the artists sold any pictures, but most of the others remained hopeful and kept renewing their tenures of wall space at the bargain rates, encouraged by the success of those who had sold something, and particularly by the booming career of little Moe Freed. He was the modest etcher of cablecars. His colleagues did not consider him a very good etcher, but in twelve weeks he had sold seven cablecars. Then he had begun to expand. He had rented additional space and in the next six weeks sold, in addition to three more cablecars, and at slightly higher prices, the Ferry Building, the Golden Gate Bridge (twice), Telegraph Hill, and Old St. Mary's.

General Custer, though offered for only fifty dollars, and though McClatchy often pointed him out and told the story of the trousers, went unsold. And the crucified Indian was not popular. Arline had seen women turn their eyes from the bloody picture in revulsion and had heard one comment: "Oh! Isn't that horrible!" But her father attributed these objections to a fastidious Protestantism. He was in a dilemma all the same. He feared that the picture might be a liability to trade, while feeling that to remove it now would be an act of disloyalty to his Redeemer. Though in his heart McClatchy might wish that he had never hung the picture, Arline could not persuade him to take it down. The issue was joined on the day Bessie had the Ladies' Sodality to lunch.

McClatchy, having stopped at the long table, composed of six small ones, to greet the ladies, had directed their attention to the controversial painting as to an emblem of their Faith that he had nailed to the mast. But Mrs. Bolger, who had noticed it directly upon entering, warned delicately that in her opinion the picture was sacrilegious.

"Sacrilegious! No, no, no," McClatchy said. "You don't get it." He explained the point of view.

"Yes," Bessie corroborated him from the foot of the table.

The ladies studied the picture. Mrs. Bolger retained her opinion.

"Well, I don't know," said Mrs. Linnegar, the president, who sat to the right of the empty chair at the table's head, "but I think it's unliturgical."

"Unliturgical," McClatchy repeated; "how do you mean? In what way, now?"

"Well, I mean that's not the way it was, of course. It couldn't have an imprimatur."

"Yes," said Mrs. Cusack, "it's unorthodox."

Bessie looked at her husband uneasily. Arline, eying him from the center of the table, sighed, dropped her shoulders, and said: "There!" —meaning that settled it.

But McClatchy said: "Unorthodox, sure it's unorthodox—it's through the eyes of the ignorant savages. For instance what would an Indian think a Roman centurion looked like?"

"I know," said Mrs. Bolger, "but it looks like the soldiers are crucifying the Indian."

"Certainly they're crucifying the Indian; I mean they *think* He's an Indian. The girl that painted it is part Indian herself. Like our Lady of Guadalupe—the young buck she appeared to thought our Lady was an Indian. Sure he did; he made the statement. So there you are. Now do you get it?"

"Well," said Mrs. Bolger, "but it conveys the wrong impression."

"Dad—I told you," Arline said, though in fact she had not mentioned any of the objections raised at this table.

Bessie, the picture being at all suspect, would have preferred to have it down, but her intervention now was for the purpose of saving her husband from the women. "Oh-h, dear. Let's leave it till Father comes; then we can put it up to him."

When Father Cobb came he looked at the picture with a sad smile as McClatchy explained it to him carefully. The old man shook his head. "I'm afraid it's slanderous."

"Slanderous!" McClatchy was respectfully disappointed in his pastor. "But, Father, you get the idea, don't you?"

"Dan, Dan, you poor mick, the idea is the Cross of Christ was used against His children the Indians as an instrument of pillage and murder."

"Murder!"

"Sure, it's the old story."

McClatchy was staring at the picture. "So *that's* the way it looks. I see what you mean!" But he thought it only *looked* that way.

Bessie, soul-stricken herself, was impelled to protect and comfort her husband, but her first concern was for the priest. She rose quietly and went to McClatchy. "Danny, listen to me, now. Wait'll Father goes." She turned to the pastor. "Will you say grace, Father. Your place is there."

"I will." Father Cobb went to the head of the table, chairs scraped as the ladies rose, and McClatchy, on the point of pulling down the painting then and there, stopped, disarmed. The priest bowed his head over folded hands and said grace.

"Amen," said the ladies.

"There," Bessie said to her husband, and whispered: "You'll only embarrass him." Then aloud, giving McClatchy a little push, "Go on, now; we're going to have lunch."

"Yes, don't worry about it, Dan," the priest said.

"But I——"

"Later," said Bessie, pushing him.

So the luncheon of the Ladies' Sodality, with the old priest presiding, went forward under the pretext that the offensive picture was not there, while McClatchy, sent about his business till the luncheon should be over, shuttled glances of consternation between the picture and the priest. Only now, as he sought to excuse himself for having fallen into this pitfall of piety, did it strike him that Kinney had trapped him, that the picture had been intended to mean exactly what Father Cobb had said. Although the idea was incredible to him, for an instant he seized upon it bitterly, but it involved so painful a comment upon his own intelligence that he rejected it at once and reproached himself for ever having entertained such a thought about Kinney. He accepted the view that he was the victim of a hideous accident.

Kinney, as it happened, being short of funds, and hoping that there would be some cash waiting for him at his broker's, came in at four o'clock and McClatchy returned the picture to him privately in the rear apartment, explaining in embarrassment: "It's too unorthodox. I've had a lot of complaints. The Protestants say it's too bloody and the Catholics think I'm giving scandal."

The bearded young man felt relieved in a way. The picture having served its purpose, he had long since come to regret his revenge as imprudent; he had feared that someone would tell McClatchy the truth and that McClatchy, holding him responsible, would break off their arrangement. "I was afraid of something like this," he said accusingly. "I told you—remember?"

"I know," McClatchy said, avoiding his eyes. Later McClatchy thought: He did tell me; but just what Kinney had told him was obscure to him now.

By summer the Lost Dutchman was the leading tavern of the county. In character it was surprisingly different from what Arline in her most optimistic moments had envisioned, but it was no less successful for that. It was attracting trade from miles around, even, as her father had predicted, from San Francisco. Not, she saw, that her father's optimism had been prophetic either, exactly; for it was clear to her, if not to him, that success had come to her father in ways that he had not dreamt of before the grand opening. But Arline could not understand by what logic it had come at all.

"The only thing," he told his wife frankly, "we aint making much money yet."

But this was the paradox inherent in the nature of the triumph. The receipts were sadly disproportionate to the number of customers, and the reason was that one of the tavern's chief assets behaved as if it were part of the overhead. The Organization, it had been noticed, went unrepresented during meal hours. Members might drop in at the bar at four or five o'clock, but then they dropped out again; it was not till eight that they began to arrive in any force, and although they took up a good deal of the room after that, and made most of the noise, they seldom ate anything, and they set up no clamor for cocktails. They bought thriftily of beer.

So McClatchy's vision of deriving a good steady income from the Veteran Painters, as he always called them, was not realized quite as he had expected. On them, it might have been argued, he lost money. But by filling the tavern with their pictures and themselves they produced an atmosphere that attracted more lucrative customers; and the Lost Dutchman became a going concern.

In the evenings the Dutch cavalier looked down on a full bar, and from time to time the pilgrims lining the other side of the counter below would look up at him. In the evenings, with the spotlight shining down upon it, the unpleasant face conjured of oils by Rembrandt in reflection of life three centuries before was the most conspicuous face in the room. Even so, McClatchy developed a little trick of calling attention to his daemon. Passing the bar on his rounds, or stopping to talk, and his eye being caught by the Dutchman's, he would flip one hand off the side of his brow in the urchin salute, and say: "How's it going, Dutch?" or "Everything under control, Dutch?"; or, finding Hump Corkery or some other familiar at the bar, he would tilt his thumb at the man and warn: "Watch out for this guy here, Dutch, he's liable to give us trouble."

San Franciscans who had been here before and knew him would call him over, rally him, laugh at what he said, and wink at their friends. A real old South of Market boy, they said he was; and sometimes, at a table that he had just left after acquainting the occupants with the mystery, known history, and fine points of his Rembrandt, a woman would look at her companion with her underlip compressed between her teeth and her eyes half-painfully, half-humorously pleading with them not to laugh at him.

Reports of what had happened at the Lost Dutchman reached Noel Ames. He came back with two other men and received a grateful welcome. He made a tour of the walls, and gave part of another Sunday feature to the story, under the heading: "North Bank Renaissance." And this time, reversing upon McClatchy the phrase that the tavern-keeper had applied to Markham and himself at the opening, he called McClatchy—more accurately than he knew—a "patron of the arts."

Other city newspapermen began coming to the tavern. A columnist on the *News* recorded an imaginary interview with the Dutchman on the lively topic of the approaching election for the presidency of the United States.

The profits increased a little. But meanwhile there had been another unforeseen expense. Arline had been working till eleven and some-times twelve at night. The McClatchys added a small second bedroom to the rear apartment, and in June their daughter and grandson moved in. The rent was only thirty dollars a month. And by June, McClatchy had repaid three hundred of the three thousand dollars that he had secretly borrowed from his daughter.

And the San Francisco newspaper columns continued to mention the tavern. But Arline noticed that despite the fame of the Rembrandt painting after which it was named, they no longer referred to the place as the Lost Dutchman.

They called it "McEndymion's."

"*Hon*estly," she said.

14

SUMMER NIGHT, II

The New life was all around her now. She received it every evening, placed it at the tables, and moved in the midst of it, and it looked at her and spoke to her and smiled and nodded and said thank you; and yet, that summer, it seemed to be passing Arline by. Not you, it seemed to say, but Phyllis Plover.

That day in Llagas there had been a parade to which she had taken Billy, and that evening her father had taken him to the fireworks dis-play along the "river." Now at eleven o'clock her son was in bed. So was her mother; and behind the cashier's counter was the bouncy mid-

dle-aged waitress Roxie Cox. The Fourth of July trade had been heavy.
But no one had entered the Lost Dutchman Tavern for an hour. There
was really no need for Arline to remain on duty. But she lingered.

She looked, standing high-heeled just in front of the cashier's
counter with a menu in her hand, like a supervisor in a women's shop,
a trimmer smarter "official" Arline McClatchy. She wore a grass-green
frock falling to her shoes in a full skirt and rising in a fitted bodice to
a graceful open standup collar. Her reddish-brown hair gleamed, her
blue eyes were clear, her almost colorless brows and lashes were darkened, her whole face was more vivid. And she was lighter by twenty
pounds; but she appeared no less formidable. That mock-modest
blouse called attention to the great "bust line," and the narrower
waist magnified the breadth of the shoulders.

Roxie said fondly: "Look at Phyl."

In front of one of the booths, small shapely bright-blond Phyllis
Plover, looking, as Arline always thought, more like a chorus girl than
a waitress in her blue Dutch-girl livery, the cap perched ornamentally
at the back of her gilded head, was now behaving more like a chorus
girl, too. In the booth were four young people whom Arline recognized
as Vic Scatina, Dorothy Froelich, Gretchen Scharf, and a young man
known to her only as "Mitch." Phyllis was telling them about the band
at the Mark Hopkins Hotel in San Francisco, where she had gone
dancing one night recently with Ross Miller—that had been an
achievement for Phyllis, and the band was her pretext for making it
known; her head was thrown back, her hands were lifted, and for a
moment she swayed her hips to the melody she was humming through
closed red lips, then she said: "B-rother!" and laughing, slapped the
air.

Roxie said: "Aint she cute," as if Phyllis were her darling.

Arline simulated a tone of knowing sisterly reprobation: *"She's* a
bad girl."

"She sure is," Roxie said, and gave a boisterous laugh. "Aint she,
though?"

Roxie meant that Phyllis had posed for Ross Miller nude—and told
it! Arline had not meant this, although she knew it. She also knew
that Miller, who was not one of the veteran painters but a commercial
artist of fifty-odd with a house in Kentfield, had invited Phyllis to
move in with him; but Arline had not meant just this, either. Of this,
a year ago, she would have thought loyally: Of course Phyllis wouldn't,
though in fact she would not have put it past Phyllis. Now she told herself that the reason Phyllis didn't was that Phyllis was not interested in

Ross Miller. Of one of the young men in the booth, on the other hand, Phyllis had said out of the side of her mouth to Arline one night: "That's for me." He was the tall curly-haired level-eyed young Italian who had painted one of the pictures on the wall, the large abstract that looked like an engineering design in oils and was signed in bold letters: SCATINA. But Dorothy Froelich, tall, ash blond, tanned, and angular, was Vic Scatina's girl, and now right in front of her Phyllis was being "cute" for him. This had been Arline's immediate reference when she called Phyllis a bad girl; but what she had really meant was that Phyllis was too friendly with the customers. Phyllis was popular with the customers, and Ross Miller was not the only one she had been out with.

It was through Phyllis that Arline knew the names and even a little about the private lives of many of the veteran painters and their friends, and this also the proprietor's daughter resented. It was how she knew that Dorothy Froelich was a clothes model in San Francisco—"horsey," Phyllis had called the girl unkindly. And it was how Arline knew that mouselike Gretchen Scharf made "original fabrics" on a hand loom and sold them, too. But who Mitch was Arline did not know. Present tonight also were Moe Freed, the cablecar king, short, concave-chested, and swarthy, his weak brown eyes magnified by powerful government-issue glasses; he was sitting at a table with two other young men, one of whom Arline recognized as Ralph Easton—"He's writing a book," Phyllis had said.

The large rectangular public room was filled with conversation, argument, laughter, and the clatter of dishes. Coffee cups, glasses, and laden ash trays littered white tablecloths, and in the light beam extending from the ceiling to the painted face behind the bar curled the tobacco smoke.

Dan McClatchy in his shirtsleeves stood behind his bar in an animated discussion with Sherman Cook and Paul Vogler, students of art, life, and human affairs.

"What do you mean don't I think he's sincere? Do I think he's a liar? No!"

"Well, then?" Vogler said.

"Well what?"

"Why don't you vote for him?"

"Why don't I—— Wa-it awhile. You're sincere, I'm sincere, and I guess Hitler was sincere. They don't put a man in the White House just because he's sincere, you know."

"No, I mean he's for the common man."

"Oh! He is, yes. But you know why? Because he's a Christian, that's why. He aint like these other jokers, you know. What he wants to do, he wants to get a little Christianity in there."

"You against that?"

"Me? No! I'm only saying that's why he's for the common man."

"Aren't *you* for the common man?"

"Sure I am!"

"Well, then—why don't you vote for him?"

"Oh! I see what you mean! No, I'll tell you why I don't vote for him. I don't think he's smart enough."

"*Smart* enough? You don't know what you're talking about. He's one of the most brilliant men in politics today. He's a scientist, he's——"

"Oh, wait, now, hold on. That aint the way I mean. The thing is I don't think he's smart enough for these foreign nations. Wait—I'll tell you where I think he goes wrong, I'll tell you where I think he'd get us into a hell of a mess if he ever got elected. He reminds me of a fellow I used to know, Tim Huether, 'Father Tim' we used to call him, and he was a walking saint if I ever seen one, a daily communicant and a member of the Third Order and all the rest of it, and a good husband and father that never took a drink, and a good citizen, and he never had a bad word to say about nobody, and I don't mean a thing against him. The only thing, he was a sucker for a hard-luck story. And one night when he was on his way to work—he used to work nights at the old Ferry post office on the Embarcadero there, in Sampm Cisco, and this night when Tim is on his way to work a bum stops him and asks him for a nickel for a cup of coffee. Well, it so happens Tim is flat busted, he aint even got a nickel, and he feels terrible about it. All he's got is his dinner pail, so he says to the bum: 'I'll tell you what I'll do. I've got my dinner here and I'm going to knock off at twelve o'clock and eat it, so you come down to the post office at twelve o'clock and I'll give you the half of my dinner.' But then Tim looks at the bum and the bum looks pretty blame down-and-out, and Tim feels ashamed of himself for taking it for granted the poor old bum would know when it was midnight. 'Have you got a watch?' he says. No, the bum says he aint. So Tim says, *he* says: '*Here*, I'll give you the loan of mine.' So help me, that's just what he did. Now there was a sincere man! And the bum, the bum takes the watch, he takes the watch *and never shows up atall!* No! Now that's a true story, that's a true story and it shows what I mean—I believe in giving food to a hungry man but I draw the line at giving him my watch so's he'll know when it's time to pitch in. And if Tim—wait—

if Tim, if Tim gives away his watch, that's his business, but I don't want him going and giving away mine on me; and with all these hungry nations at the door I'm afraid if we had Tim Huether in the White House he wouldn't leave us the time of day!"

At the Northwestern Pacific station across the street a gaunt old freight train lurched forward, cracking all its joints, and hobbled northward with a long lonely whistle of farewell. Outside the Lost Dutchman silence returned to the industrial district of the town; the tower of the Golden West Milling Company stood sentinel in the moonlight.

A block above the slough, which divided this district from the rest of Llagas, the toy constellation of Main Street had dwindled to the wan solitary lights on corner standards, the little colored neon signs of bars, and the weak bulb still burning over the entrance to Pioneers' Hall. Above Main, on El Camino Real, moved the headlights of cars straggling home through the town on Highway 101 after the holiday, and of trucks, whose work was never done—past the four-story Morera Inn, only a few of whose windows were still awake, past an all-night café, past the Morera Theater, where a man on a tall stepladder was changing the bill on the dark marquee. Above El Camino, on Union Street, the only lights besides the dim beacons at the intersections were the two showing on the ground floor of the old white clapboard City Hall, where the Police Department kept the nightwatch, and the one glowing on brackets above the door of the firehouse. Above Union lay the dark square blocks where the dwellings and schools and churches were, the streets deep-shadowed with trees under the moon; and at the south end of this, but a little withdrawn, rose the four-story Llagas Hospital, thinly laced with light. All around, in the distance, were the dark hills. And on the other side of the western ridge the sea was breaking.

In the best residential district of the town, just around the corner from Traubaugh Avenue, stood number 520 Lincoln Street, a pleasant two-story white wooden house of Monterey style with a lawn in front of it. The upper floor was dark. Through the curtains of the lower left-hand windows a soft light filtered—and was gone. The front door opened, a man came out and shut it behind him gently. He was tall, slim, blond, and in his thirties. He descended the three steps to the walk and was moving toward the street when a door that gave inward from the balcony above was wrenched open; a young woman pulling round her a hastily thrown on negligee stepped to the railing and sharply called his name: "Bo!"

The man only half turned, glanced up at her in the darkness irritably, answered: "I'm just . . . going for a walk," and walked on.

"Bo, come back!"

"Go to bed."

"Bo!" imperatively. Then as he did not stop: "Don't take the car. . ."

He stopped, turned, and said wearily: "Who's taking the car? A walk, I said." Again he walked on.

The woman was about to call again, but checked herself and glanced rapidly to right and left as if fearing there might be witnesses to this scene. The man turned into the street. She stood looking after him with anger in her black Spanish eyes and two deep parallel grooves between her brows; they were thin carefully arched brows, and when drawn into that position gave her strong handsome face a suggestion of the diabolic. The man turned the corner. The woman drew a long breath and exhaled it. She went back into the dark bedroom, shut the door, and lowered herself into a sitting position on the bed, an extralarge luxurious bed with carved head- and footboards of "antique" white decorated with pink rosebuds. Her expression was sad now. For a moment as if to shut out some picture she closed her eyes, and when she opened them they were moist. She let the upper part of her body sink backward on the bed and lay gazing blindly at the ceiling. She was all alone in the house.

True to his word, the man was walking. Having turned the corner, he had even decreased his pace and seemed indeed to have no destination. "Take the car," he scoffed under his breath. The man had had two double helpings of Scotch and soda, but he felt depressed. At the corner of Oak Street he stopped and looked at the moon. The upper air was no doubt full of dust and gunpowder for the moon had a rosy glow, but it did not comfort him. Far away and lonely it looked in the heavens, the preadamite spectator, and he remembered looking up at it one other night, from a ship in Lingayen Gulf, and thinking it was his link with home. His eyes were large, blue, and expressive. His nose was short and blunt. His mouth was large, but the full lips were delicately molded: a "sensitive" mouth, which did not seem to go with the nose at all. He wore a single-breasted suit without the vest, his necktie hanging loose. He thrust his hands in the pockets of his trousers and crossed the street and walked down Traubaugh Avenue under the trees and looked lonelier than the moon.

The dreary aspect of Main Street depressed him still more, and the bars with their lurid little signs of red, blue, and green light repelled him. He pushed open a blue door: demented music and a voice oafishly chanting "Cocktails for Two" assailed him from a juke box as he peered through the murk at the sad complin within. He turned away, letting the door swing to, and walked on. At Hill Street he paused again, gazing down into the sunken industrial district as into a sea of darkness. He plunged in.

When he came up in the softly lighted submarine cavern with all the pictures round the walls and the smoky spotlight playing on the portrait that was set in the walnut paneling behind the bar he asked himself why he had never come here before. There was life here.

Arline was sitting at a cleared table near the kitchen with Phyllis Plover and Jean Fennell, a rangy raw-boned waitress of about forty; Arline was facing the door, saw him come in, and got up to go to him, but he made for the bar. She sat down again, and Jean observed: "That's Bo Satterfy."

"It is?"

"No kidding!" Phyllis said, looking round at him quickly. She added: "I know his wife; she used to eat at the drugstore."

"She did?" Arline said, looking also.

And the three women followed him with their eyes. He was Almon Bowie Satterfy, Jr.; his father owned and edited the *Sentinel*, owned the ice company and the box factory and the Bryan Building and was reputed to be one of the wealthiest men in the county—the man "known," Arline's father had said, "as the worst old hellroarer that ever come down the line." But Bo Satterfy was a figure of additional interest to the women at the table because of his wife. Two years before, having returned to his position with the ice company after his discharge from the Navy, he had eloped to Reno with his secretary, Beatrice Manriquez, born, it was said, in Mudtown. The story had been that his father was furious; but apparently old A. B. Satterfy had become reconciled to this marriage of his only child, for he had built the couple a house, and photographs of his daughter-in-law appeared in the society columns of the *Sentinel*. Arline thought her "stunning" and was charmed by her fairy tale.

She asked: "What's she like?"

Phyllis made a mouth and shrugged. "The Latin type."

Jean said: "*He's* good-looking."

"Gosh," Arline said, "I wonder what the old man would say. He came out against the place, in the paper; remember? He's a prohibitionist or something."

"Don't worry," Phyllis said, "his son's not."

And indeed Arline thought she remembered someone's saying (but that must have been before his marriage) that the son was "a wild one." *Wild one*—poor little Nancy Croan . . . but she put out of her mind the still unsettled murder case.

Jean Fennell was called to the Scatina booth. Then Phyllis was summoned by George Easton and dispatched to the bar for three more beers. Arline watched Phyllis cross the room and stand (Deliberately! she thought) next to Bo Satterfy. Jerry Barth was mixing a drink for him. Phyllis placed on the bar her tray of empty bottles and glasses and sang out her order. McClatchy interrupted his conversation with Cook and Vogler to fill it. At the same time Satterfy turned and looked at Phyllis. He raised his brows at the sight of her, and spoke, but Arline could not hear the conversation.

He said: "Hi."

"Hi." Phyllis received his gaze with a faint knowing smile on her lips. (*Hon*estly! Arline thought.)

He asked: "Buy you a drink?"

"*Uh* uh."

"Why not?"

" 'Gainst the rules."

"Rules!" He turned to McClatchy. "Can't a gentleman buy a lady a drink?"

"They'd be saying I had B-girls in the joint," McClatchy said. "They take your license away for that, you know."

"Is that what they take your license away for? They took mine away long ago." Again he looked at Phyllis. "Do you mind?"

"Not at all, Mr. Satterfy."

"All right, what's *your* name?"

But Phyllis only gave him a teasing smile, picked up the tray on which McClatchy had just set her order, and left him.

She delivered her order to the Easton table. As she finished serving it Vic Scatina and his friends, having settled their bill with Jean Fennell, got up to leave. Seeing this, Phyllis went and spoke to them. Then she came hurriedly to the table where Arline was sitting alone. "Hon, I'm off in fifteen minutes, but if I go now I can get a ride," she said. "Okay?"

The ride meant safe passage through the industrial district. "Go ahead," Arline said. But she did not like Phyllis's imposing on the customers for rides, and particularly she did not like her thrusting herself on Vic Scatina when he was with Dorothy Froelich.

Phyllis was off with a "Thanks, hon." She turned her checks over to Jean, called to Scatina: "Meet you outside," and flew into the kitchen. The Scatina party walked out. Phyllis came out of the kitchen putting her coat on over her uniform, her waitress's cap still on her head. As she ran past the bar Satterfy swung round on his stool, glass in hand.

"Hey! Where you going?"

"Why? Want to take me home?" and a mocking laugh trailed back at him as she ran out.

A male voice hailed him banteringly: "What's the matter, Bo?"

He looked across the room and evidently recognized the speaker, one of two men of about his own age who were seated in a booth. He called a greeting, strolled over, taking his glass, and sat down. Arline looked at him. A handsome man. But she wondered where his wife was, and if perhaps Bea Manriquez was not living happily ever after. And the memory of Phyllis's departing laugh at him irritated Arline. And now the little poacher was riding away with Vic Scatina. . . . After a year of new hope, of diet and exercise and facials and hairdos and extravagances for clothes, of a new hold on the youth that she had been letting go by forfeit, Arline was left sitting at a cleared table in her smart green frock at midnight, all alone; and there was really no reason she should not have gone to bed two hours ago. . . .

"Like the night," McClatchy was saying enthusiastically at the bar, "like the night that Schmitz beat Partridge—oh what a night that was. Schmitz and Ruef, you know, that was the old Union Labor crowd that controlled all the saloons and fancy houses and run the Municipal Crib—Abe Ruef was the boss, he went to jail in the Graft Prosecution; but the night that Schmitz beat Partridge it looked like half the town got drunk. The whole Coast turned out, and the uptown tenderloin, and the Chronicle Building caught fire, and it took a wagonload of cops to protect the Bulletin, and they had a big torchlight funeral parade with brass bands and firecrackers, and they laid McNab's coffin at the door of the old Occidental Hotel—*Gavin* McNab," he explained, as if this cleared up the mystery of what McNab had to do with it; "before your time, just before the Fire, that was—I was a kid selling papers. I stayed out all night that night and caught Hail Columbia when I got home. I guess I was only about thirteen then because the Fire come right before my birthday; but I'll never forget the night of that election."

And they looked at him, Cook and Vogler, men of twenty-odd, vaguely fascinated by this half-incoherent rumor of a world they could scarcely imagine. Cook asked: "Were you in the Fire?"

"Who, me? I was all through the Fire."

"Fire," Vogler said with a laugh. "What about that little matter of an earthquake?" He was from Philadelphia, Pennsylvania.

"Well, sure," McClatchy said, "that was what started it. I hope to tellya. It woke us up at five in the morning, and you know what I thought? I thought it was a tidal wave! I never felt an earthquake like that before or since, or heard anything like it, neither, except the ocean, and I thought the bay had busted loose and was coming down on the house. Yeah—that's just what it sounded like, and felt like it, too. *Earthquake?*" he repeated. Far from being ashamed of that mighty heave, he was boasting of it. "It threw the whole Valencia Hotel into the middle of the street and killed everybody in it, and it pulled down the shot tower and the Grand Opera House, and it put a crack in East Street big enough for a brewery wagon, and it tore up the cartracks in front of the post office, and it wrecked the City Hall! They said if that quake had hit a few hours before or a few hours after, when people were on the streets, it would have killed off half the population. It buried a herd of cattle under a pile of bricks ten feet high in the middle of Mission Street. And over in Marin County, over in Marin County the ground opened up and swallowed a cow. No, but it wasn't the quake that done the damage, it was the Fire!"

Vogler laughed.

"Sure it was," McClatchy said. "The quake tore down the chimleys, and a couple of hundred fires broke out at the same time, and it threw the California Hotel on top of the firehouse and killed Chief Sullivan in his bed before he knew what hit him, and it broke all the water mains so they wasn't no water to fight the flames with; and that was the trouble, that was why all the ministers down in Los Angeles were saying it was the wrath of God, you know—it started the fires, killed the fire chief, and cut off all the water first crack out of the box. That Fire burned for three days, you know."

"It did?" Vogler said.

"Sure it did. Oh, that was a Fire. That Fire," McClatchy said, touching Vogler on the arm impressively, "that Fire was so hot it melted the sash weights in the windows before it burned the frames. And it got into steel safes with walls a foot thick and burned up the money; right in the banks, I mean. And the air was so full of flames and black smoke—— And the sun, the sun looked like a red-hot stove lid; and at first nobody could get a drink of water, even—they *wasn't* no water."

"Gee," Cook said mildly.

"Oh I tellya," McClatchy said. "And no food! Some of the stores give away their whole stock, and the ones that didn't give it away, the people broke in and took it; but then the authorities got the relief wagons going, and the soup lines. . . . And no gas or electricity—nothing. They had to fight that Fire with dynamite. And half the time that only made it worse. You could hear the blasts going off all over town. And then they'd be another quake. And the Gas Works blew up. And they shot fourteen men trying to break into the Mint."

"Who did?" Cook asked.

"The soldiers did. Half of 'em were drunk, you know. Oh, they shot lots of people," McClatchy said. "And they had to take the dead and injured down to the old Mechanics' Pavilion, till that went too; and one undertaking parlor had to move so many times they finally had to turn their bodies over to the Army, and the Army put 'em in one of the trenches with a lot of others, and I remember that was where Mr. O'Connell found his mother; the old lady'd died of a heart attack or exposure or something in the middle of the Fire, but he didn't know where she was, and he went looking for her at the Morgue and the funeral parlors and every place he could think of, and that was where he found her, lying dead in a trench with all them others. Oh, they was a lot of stories like that. Like when nobody remembered to feed the dogs and the dogs started eating the bodies out in North Beach, and when they found out about that they went hunting the dogs with guns before the rescue work and the digging for bodies went on again. Because people were buried under buildings, you know, and caught in the wreckage."

Cook shook his head, and Vogler asked: "What happened to you?"

"Oh, we had a hell of a time. The old man wasn't home yet when the quake hit, and we didn't know where he was. And the door stuck and we couldn't get out of the house, we had to climb out a window. Everybody was out in the street half dressed—five o'clock in the morning, you know—the eighteenth of April, nineteen-oh-six. Oh I tellya. And after a while we went in next door with the Breeneys for a cup of tea, but the stove was busted, and pretty soon some of the houses was on fire, and the first thing you know somebody comes along and tells us to get the hell out of there. I clumb back through the window and got us some clothes and blankets and my mother's purse and stuff, and we started up to-ward town. Union Square!"—he pointed, straight-armed, at Vogler: "That was where we spent that first night. And the next day we tried to get down to the waterfront to get over to Oakland, but we wound up down in the P'trera some ways. They had a camp there, and that was where we stayed, in the open. And that was where the old man found us, in the P'trera Camp. Everybody had to sign up, you know, and that was how he found us. I remember he wanted to take us to Oakland but by that time my mother wouldn't go. 'They'll be plenty of work here now and here's where we'll stay,' she says; and we stayed. The old man got a job digging trenches at Bernal Heights and later throwing bricks, and I was selling the old

Morning Call again—the papers had moved across the bay then, you know; and when the relief boats come my father was back at his old job, unloading 'em. The Oakland real estate boys were advertising, you know, the go-getters, you know, saying Sampm Cisco was all washed up and trying to get the people to buy property in Oakland, you know. But the people of Sampm Cisco said the hell with Oakland and stayed right there in the City That Knows How and built her up again; and look at her today. You betcha. *Fire?* That Fire took everything south of Market Street from the waterfront to Mission Dolores; and north of Market, from the bay to Van Ness Avenue; and from Fisherman's Wharf to the P'trera: all the downtown, all the South of Market, North Beach, the Barbary Coast, Chinatown, Nob Hill, Russian Hill, the whole business—five hundred city blocks; and as far as the eye could see they was nothing but devastation. It was the greatest Fire in the history of the world."

In the new bedroom off the back apartment, where Billy Lucas was fast asleep, Arline undressed in the dark at half past twelve. Across the silent town she heard the bell of Milton Groom strike once.

15

AMERICA

Up Main Street came a bawling parade of political irregulars led by a big brown-bearded young man on horseback. But it had merely inserted itself, somehow, in the Saturday afternoon traffic so that at first there was no telling who was leading this parade.

Last week the William L. Todd Parlor of the Sons and Daughters of the Pioneers had canceled an agreement to let its hall this evening for a rally in favor of Henry A. Wallace for the presidency of the Union. The reason given had been that the parlor feared its property might be damaged if used in such a controversial cause as the Wallace candidacy had become; for the sincere man, to his own consternation, had suddenly received the endorsement of the Communist Party. The cancelation, noised abroad, had brought upon the Pioneers, the mayor, and the City Council a clamor of protest from as far abroad as New York City. The Pioneers had stood firm, the public officials had not been able to do anything, and the local committee of the Independent Progressive Party had failed to get another hall for the rally. But no one had been more surprised than the committee when Llagas, on awakening this morning, had found itself decked out in Wallace posters, all hand-painted; nor had there been any advance notice of this stentorian parade, which came demanding:

"HEAR THIS! HEAR THIS!" over an electric amplifier. "THIS IS THE VOICE OF THE *LITTLE* PEOPLE. . . ."

The grand marshal, who was having trouble with his horse behind the slow-moving traffic, wore a white cowboy hat, a red shirt, blue jeans, and cowboy boots. Behind him two young women in red caps, white sweaters, and blue shorts were marching abreast; each carried upright a long pole, and stretched between the tops of the poles was a strip of white canvas lettered:

WALLACE (in red) FOR PRESIDENT (in blue)

Next came an open Ford car, old and battered; it mounted a loud-speaker like a cannon on top of its windshield and was manned by a crew of three: driver, sound engineer, and the announcer, who was small and swarthy and wore powerful G. I. spectacles. Then a slight impropriety: Old Glory came next, carried by a girl dressed as Uncle Sam. Behind the colors came two young men, one wearing an army overseas cap, the other the white cap of a naval enlisted man; like the first two girls they were marching abreast, carrying poles, and stretching a banner between them: it read:

WIN THE PEACE

They were followed by a squad of other young men and women with individual signs which said: Outlaw the A-Bomb, No Peace Time Draft, The Marshal Plan Means War, and other things. Abreast behind these marched two more male banner bearers; their burden ran:

COME TO THE RALLY

Next another open car, as old and battered as the first; one girl drove it and in the back rode two others who waved to the crowd and called out: "Come on along!" Three paces behind marched a young woman clothed in white buckskin; she marched alone, as befitted the representative of a minority group, with a sign that said: Justice for the Indians. The parade ended with a crippled veteran of a black sedan; this car had lost its hood and its wheels were wobbling, but between two poles lashed to its sides it flaunted over its peeling top the motto of the United States Infantry:

FOLLOW ME

Merchants were coming out of their shops to stand in the arrested streams of passers-by, looking on.

"Who *are* they?"

"Never saw *none* of 'em before."

A motorcycle came roaring down between the lines of traffic to meet the parade. Police Officer Carl Yates slid to a stop and waited till the grand marshal rode up.

"Pull over!"

The grand marshal, raising his free hand, called: "Hold it!" His followers passed the order, the parade halted behind him as he reined up, and Yates demanded:

"You got a permit for this parade?"

"I guess so," the grand marshal said.

"What do you mean you guess so? Who's in charge?"

"I don't know."

"You don't *know?*" But the words were drowned out by the Voice of the Little People:

"WE DEMAND FREE SPEECH!"

"Shut up!" The policeman's motorcycle gave a roar, the horse reared, and Officer Yates cycled down to the car. "You in charge here?"

"NO, SIR."

"Shut that thing off!"

"Yes, sir."

"Who's in charge of this parade?"

Announcer turned interestedly to Driver: "Who is?"

Driver looked surprised: "Search me."

Sound Engineer said he didn't know either.

"Oh, yeah?" Yates said. He rode down the line asking: "Who's in charge?" "Who's in charge?" while behind the parade horns were honking; but in response to his question the paraders only shook their heads, grinning; and he muttered: "Wise guys."

"Arrest us," a girl shouted gaily, and other voices repeated the challenge.

But the police officer, knowing the capacity of the Llagas jail, recognizing that this was a political situation connected with the controversy about Pioneers' Hall, and suspecting that these people were trying to trick him, had decided to report his position to headquarters and request instructions.

First he managed to get the parade around the corner into River

Street, below Main, where, it being Saturday afternoon, there was hardly any traffic. A crowd of onlookers followed.

"Why," a woman said suddenly, "there's Bernie Webster! Bernie Webster!" she called to him. "What're you doing in that parade?"

A bright-faced youth carrying a sign that said Repeal Taft-Hartley responded: "Hi, Mrs. Ackerman. Come on along." He was the son of the Reverend George Daniel Webster of the Baptist Church.

An authoritative voice demanded of the policeman: "What's going on here, Officer?" and turning, Yates found himself face to face with Mayor Schuman.

Yates explained to the mayor, who appeared upset, and the mayor turned sternly to the grand marshal, who had dismounted. The grand marshal said all he knew was that there was going to be a rally in the park.

"In the park!" the mayor said. "You've got to have a permit to have a rally in the park; you've got to have a permit to have a parade. No permit has been issued."

"Why hasn't it?" the grand marshal asked.

"Why *hasn't* it? Because no permit was applied for, that's why hasn't it."

"*Oh* yes," the grand marshal said.

"What? No! What do you mean oh yes? I guess I'd know if a permit had been applied for. I'm the mayor, the president of the City Council. . . ."

Up spoke the giant killer: "WHAT IS HAPPENING TO FREE SPEECH?"

"Shut up!" Officer Yates started for the car.

"HERE COMES THE STORM TROOPER NOW!"

But the mayor stopped the policeman and went himself.

"*Give* me that." He seized the microphone. "LADIES AND GENTLEMEN! THIS IS THE MAYOR SPEAKING. . . ."

"Booooooo."

"THERE'S BEEN A MISTAKE. HEAR WHAT I'VE GOT TO SAY." He said that whoever was responsible for this, this demonstration, had bungled it, that under the law, the law, for which no one had a greater respect than their own candidate, the former Vice-President of the United States (cheers) a permit—just a minute, please—a permit, a permit—no permit had been applied for. He said he honored the Honorable Henry A. Wallace and (cheers) that if, if, if, if a permit had been applied for in his behalf under the law, the law as it was administered in Llagas, where the rights of free speech and peaceable assembly had *always* been respected, it would certainly have been (boos) granted.

"Boooooooooooooooo."

He held up his hand: He would prove what he said. As mayor, as mayor of Llagas, he was going to order here and now that they be allowed to proceed with their parade and with their rally, too. . . .

"Hooray!" a girl sang out victoriously.

—He was going to guarantee on his authority as mayor that a permit would be issued even though no permit had been applied for, because, because he had enough confidence in his colleagues of the City Council, in their fine Americanism, in their fair and, and democratic spirit, enough confidence to know that they would back him to the limit in upholding the inalienable rights of all citizens of whatever race, creed, color, or political affiliation.

The paraders cheered, feeling that they had won the day. The mayor waved affably, feeling that he had saved it. He asked that they show their good faith by conducting their parade and rally in an orderly manner; he thanked them.

And the parade resumed its march. Officer Yates cleared the way on his motorcycle. Two other policemen who had arrived on the scene in a patrol car fell in behind the black sedan. A dozen citizens tagged along. The parade reached and entered the park. The grand marshal and three or four others mounted the bandstand.

An hour later the rally broke up in a fight.

Bernie Webster, Sherman Cook, and two members of the audience who gave their names as David Bigelow and James T. McBride were taken into custody by the police, and the patrol car led an informal parade of the champions of Henry Wallace to the City Hall, in front of which a demonstration of protest was held while Chief of Police Roy Lally was hearing the case inside.

As the chief reconstructed the fight, the minister's son had struck the first blow, catching Bigelow on the side of the face while Bigelow was heckling a speaker, whereupon the two had closed and Cook, in attempting to separate them, had been misunderstood and flattened by McBride, who stated that he had been motivated by the spirit of fair play. But Webster charged that Bigelow had provoked the fight by trying to disrupt the rally, adding: "Nobody can call *me* a communist," a position that the chief was glad to hear him take. Besides, the chief had received his orders regarding the rally: "Show them every courtesy, handle them with kid gloves," the mayor had said, "because these people are dynamite." And the chief was aware that two of his patrolmen were outside trying to clear the sidewalk of these people, a situation that he feared might develop an explosion; and he saw that the situation might never have arisen if Bigelow had kept his mouth shut. It was the chief's duty, furthermore, to show the world how free speech was protected in Llagas. He therefore released the others and jailed Bigelow, with whom he was very angry, on the charge of disturbing the peace.

When Webster and Cook came out of the building they were cheered, their hands were pumped, their backs clapped, and they were borne off to McEndymion's, where there began a victory celebration which lasted till midnight. The beer flowed. There was singing. There was cheering, in which McEndymion, though he was for Truman and feared that Wallace would ruin the country, joined heartily. But shortly before eleven o'clock Bernie Webster was found flat on his face on the floor of the men's room. Certain townspeople who were present that Saturday night saw him being assisted out by two other young men, who took him home in the black sedan, on which the motto of the infantry yet waved, held him up while they rang the parsonage bell, and delivered him safe to his father.

The episode left Llagas with a grudge against the veteran painters; for by the next day of course everyone knew who the demonstrators had been.

Before the demonstration many citizens had been pleased to claim the art colony for the town. But the artists had stepped out of character. In the first place they had made it inescapable that they did not belong to the town—as electioneers they struck the electorate as presumptuous strangers. In the second place property owners were indignant because the walls of their buildings had been papered with Wallace posters. In the third place it was thought preposterous that a lot of artists should have interfered in an election; nor could the fact that these artists were war veterans justify them in Llagas eyes: on the contrary, it was turned against them by the report that they were living at the taxpayers' expense. They were called parasites and smart alecks. Even the Wallace committee disowned them. But this did not help Henry Wallace in Llagas.

And on the day after the Llagas demonstration, the hapless man himself was pelted with eggs by a crowd in Durham, North Carolina. President Truman called this un-American, which surely was not the right adjective, but the citizens of Llagas accepted it. They were against throwing eggs at candidates. Yet many of them could not help but feel that their sentiments regarding this one had been confirmed by the citizens of Durham. The incident hardened their distrust of the veteran painters.

And so a little of the mud of the presidential election of 1948 came off on the tavern.

Then there was the case of Bernie Webster.

"That boy," Dr. Dow, the one-time principal of the high school, had said of him to Mr. Webster one evening, "has not been in Switzerland for nothing"—although in fact Bernie Webster had never been in Switzerland in his life. Robert Dow was a scholar of the old school and he abominated the new one; he had a jargon of his own to express his ideas about his enemies, and "Switzerland," an obscure allusion which no one understood, was in this case meant to stand for the state university, which Bernie was attending. For it had reached the ears of the Baptist congregation that the minister's son no longer believed in God. When Bernie identified himself so spectacularly with the veteran painters, some of the scandal attaching to him naturally came off on them, but in the end many of his father's flock, wishing to excuse him for his father's sake, and never dreaming of Switzerland, got it backward, imagining that the scandal had come off the strangers on Bernie Webster.

When in November the nation had re-elected Truman, Wallace, overwhelmed in every state, retired to private life and silence, possibly stunned by the strange character of his defeat as much as by its violence. Simultaneously many of his loudest champions stopped mentioning his name. But it stuck in the mind of Dan McClatchy that so many of them had asked the same question about him: "Don't you think he's sincere?" This had made an impression on the tavernkeeper because he had never properly understood what the question was about, and had found it irritating on being confronted with it so often. Looking back, he thought that it had always been asked hopefully, and this struck him as the more curious. Dimly he sensed that something of more than political interest had happened. And although he still shared the majority opinion that the man was a dreamer and imprudent, and would not have changed his vote, he felt uncomfortable about what he had helped to do to Henry A. Wallace.

Christmas again, another tree, family dinner at five o'clock at a table specially set up in the back parlor. And McClatchy's gift "to the family" was a table-model television set: he played with it all evening and all through the holidays, and after New Year's installed it behind his bar, because, as he explained, every little cocktail parlor in town had a television set these days and you had to keep up with the competition.

"How's that for a picture, that's a picture no artist could paint, am I right?" he said, unveiling to Hump Corkery the animated spectacle of two wrestlers wrestling at that very moment in San Francisco.

And actually beholding the newscasters as they read the news, he felt closer to world events in the self-conscious age that repeatedly entitled itself "our time":

Berlin had been cut off from the West by a Russian land blockade; the United States and Britain were supplying their zones of the partitioned city by air. The Reds were winning in China. At home twelve communists were under indictment for conspiracy to overthrow the government; a man named Hiss, of the State Department, accused by a man named Chambers of passing secret documents to the Soviet underground, and denying it, was awaiting trial on two counts of perjury; there was talk of requiring some professors to take an oath of loyalty to the country.

He caught the fever.

The waitresses, bartenders, cooks, dishwashers, janitor, hostess, and cashier of the tavern, in the kitchen assembled, placed their right hands over their hearts and repeated after him: "'I pledge allegiance to my Flag'"—he was not aware that since his day the phraseology had been corrected to specify which flag—"'and the Republic for which it stands; one nation indivisible, with liberty and justice for all.'"

Bo Satterfy came to the tavern now and then, at night, and alone, and at the bar became acquainted with some of the art students. Once he said to Phyllis: "How about taking you home tonight?" but Phyllis put him off banteringly, and from his tone indeed she did not know whether he meant it. He drank a good deal of whisky when he came, and would be gay or dreamily amiable, but once McClatchy had to call a cab for him and assist him out to it.

But Dorothy Froelich no longer came to the tavern, and one midnight Arline saw Phyllis leave with Vic Scatina, and the next day she asked her about Dorothy Froelich.

"Oh, her! Vic shook her." Giving Arline a second glance, Phyllis added: "He was trying to shake her anyhow," and laughed the little-devil laugh that Arline had begun to find vain and lewd and maddening.

But Phyllis told Arline no more, which was not like her. Arline thought at first that this might be because Phyllis was serious about Scatina, or because she felt guilty about Dorothy Froelich, but later it seemed to Arline that the laugh had contained a mocking note.

Between Arline and Phyllis a barrier had arisen. It was there because of the changes in their relationship. Arline was now in a position of authority over Phyllis, and Phyllis resented both this and the good fortune in the McClatchy family that had lifted Arline above her; but it was there chiefly because Arline now regarded Phyllis as a rival, and therefore as a trespasser, and envied the younger and prettier woman, and resented Phyllis's brazen successes with the New life in contrast to her own protracted failure—and because Phyllis of course had sensed Arline's changed feelings toward her long ago. But on the surface the two women remained friends.

Maybe (Arline kept on thinking) I'm *not* very attractive, but I'm better looking than some women, than lots of women my age who have good and attractive husbands. And it's not just looks that men want in their wives. I'd be a better wife than Phyllis would. I've *been* a better wife. . . .

But that was behind her, brief and unreal as a dream. Besides (she admitted) I was younger then; and with Bill I never—— (She stopped, conscience-stricken, asking that his soul and the souls of all the faithful departed rest in—— and broke off again, fearing that it might be only the Bill Lucases who were attracted to the Arline McClatchys.)

Then she would be standing before the glass in the women's room, and that would bring back standing before the glass in the same room at the Willow Tree, and Harry Fahs waiting, and *Stacked!* and how he had held her dancing and had looked at her. . . .

But that would bring back her son too, even as the glass in the Willow Tree had.

And sometimes at night, after her mother had looked in on Billy sleeping and had said the Rosary and gone peacefully to bed, when her father would be leaning across his bar in conversation, his little florid face shining as though all were right with the world, or would be standing at a table telling the occupants about his Rembrandt, when Arline would see in a booth some amorous couple careless of propriety, or would overhear a ribald word or laugh, or passing the bar would catch faintly the familiar sickly-sweet odor that had begun to creep through the walnut finish of the old mahogany, she would be attacked by a strong feeling of aversion, of antipathy to her surroundings, even for a moment tormented by a need to escape. The warm mist of smoke would afflict her like a miasma, and the scene would appear to her like one beheld in some noxious cellar where all was depraved, diseased, and baleful, or in some terrible dream that would not let her go.

And she perceived what she had never perceived before—that the face of the Dutch cavalier was obscene.

16

THE BANKS OF THE MOCHO FAR AWAY

One spring day a story in the *Sentinel* set telephones ringing in the houses of the leading families of the town. Evelyn Traubaugh had come home.

The late Senator William H. Traubaugh had owned more of Morera County land than anyone else since Don Roque himself. He had left his holdings to his three children. One portion had been dissipated. Half the second had been sold. The third and largest share remained intact and had doubled in value, and this was the share of the senator's only daughter; but she, except for one brief visit in 1929, had been a stranger to Morera County for nearly twenty-five years.

In 1924 (not a year after her father's death, as remarked at the time) she had left for Europe as the bride of Hunt Farrelly of the crested pioneer San Francisco Farrellys of Hillsborough. The couple had stayed abroad until the Crash did for Peter J. Farrelly II's pile and for his heart on the same day. Everyone had heard when Hunt and his wife came home that the senator's daughter was now the sole support of old Grubstaker Farrelly's grandson. But only a month later the Hunt Farrellys had returned to Europe. This time they had stayed till the sound of stukas drove them back again, but no farther back than Washington, D.C., where Hunt had immediately enlisted in the State Department. Two years ago he had been killed in action when a plane crashed in Canada. He had left his widow childless. He had been buried in Arlington Cemetery. Then Mrs. Hunt Farrelly had sailed for Europe again, alone. Now she was reopening the great stone "Traubaugh place," which stood in its own little park at the head of Traubaugh Avenue.

Llagas remembered Sis Traubaugh as its princess. Remembered still the French governess and the ponycart, the red Dusenberg roadster, the formal debut to which San Francisco society had come, and the big parties later, jazz "orchestras" and dancing in the elegant ballroom, the royal funeral of her father, and the wedding. Women acquaintances of her youth looked forward hopefully to dinner parties in the high Parisian or Washingtonian style as soon as she was settled. . . .

Walsh Reardon was eating breakfast at the counter of the Buckhorn Café on Main Street when he read the news. For a moment when he had finished the story he sat there with the print receding and the image of her flitting in front of it. Till now, except when the *Sentinel* had jotted some hearsay of her doings, or when he looked at the jagged scar across the inside of his hand, he had not thought of her for years.

"Annytin elch?" The man standing on the other side of the counter in the soiled white apron spoke round the wet stub of a burned-out cigar.

Suddenly beholding the frycook, Reardon felt anger rise in his throat as if at some indignity; he took his eyes away, giving his burly silver head a shake, and rasped: "Just the check." And on an absurd impulse he turned his head and glanced through the plate glass front of the café. He had not thought of her for years but it had suddenly occurred to him that she might be passing by and looking in and seeing him there. He paid the check, got up, pulled on the rakish brown felt hat, and clamping the folded newspaper under one arm, walked into the warm spring morning.

He was an everyday figure on Main Street, and neither a gentleman from sole to crown nor imperially slim, and everyone knew that he counted for nothing, but people always looked at him when he went by. This was not because of his faded football fame, nor because of the folk tale that he knew law and had the silver tongue, nor because he had disgraced himself with drink, nor simply because he was so big and mighty-looking, but, not so simply, because in spite of everything he had such authority in his heavy red face and in the carriage of his great head and bloated body. The town had a niche for its rumpled giant as it had for its every butcher and baker, for Sam Schuman and A. B. Satterfy and for Link Cotter, one-eyed, malicious, and eighty-four, who sat observing life from his post on top of the ashcan at the corner, and as it had for each man's wife and for Josie Cantrell, but Reardon, seen sober and steady-nerved, mocked the niche it had for him. There must have been something else, too. It was curious. There were men who looked at him with sly derision, though he had never harmed them in his life; and wives with whom he was scarcely acquainted would look at him with veiled eternal hostility. These he despised. He felt that he was capable of breaking the niche asunder and that they knew he was and feared he would do it. But there were also men whose eyes measured and ingenuously admired him, and some who in passing actually ducked their heads and touched their foreheads in salute. No doubt he awoke at sight, in most people, the ghost of some primitive memory. He was used to being looked at on the street, and sometimes he drew strength from it. But what, he thought this morning, if he should meet her face to face?

He had not met her when he reached the block where she would never be, the blind end of Gore Street which ran against the slough. In the O. K. Machine Shop an acetylene torch was sputtering flame as he passed. He turned into the narrow opening next door, out of the fragrant morning, and climbed the stairway to his lair.

The room into which his door opened off the dark landing doubled back over the front part of the machine shop: a narrow room, crowded and unkempt. In the long front wall was one big dirty window, which on its outside bore his name and the proposition "Attorney at Law" in peeling gold leaf. The dusty sunshine fell on the back of the kitchen chair that he used for a desk chair, and on the flat top of his battered oak desk with its clutter of papers, books, pot of pens and pencils, inkbottle, cheap brass lamp, and scarecrow telephone, and crossed the room and fell on a low cabinet placed against the wall opposite the window. On top of the cabinet were books, shaving things, groceries, and a damp bath towel. Above the cabinet and the sunshine hung the only picture, a little gilt-framed photograph of a man seated and a woman standing beside him with her hand on his shoulder. Against the same wall on the far side of the cabinet, out of the sun, stood a gas stove with two burners; on one burner a coffeepot, on the other a skillet in which some spaghetti had been left. In this wall also, but on the near side of the cabinet, was a door. And in the shade beyond the window, between the desk and the short far wall, were a wooden table and chair. The table held dirty dishes, salt and pepper, yesterday's *Chronicle*, and some books. Attached to the far wall were a small white washbasin, a mirror for shaving, and a rack on which a hand towel had been thrown; and beneath the rack was a kitchen garbage can, covered. The bare pine floor of the room, which creaked when the tenant walked on it, was piled with books—books of law, history, literature, the volumes of an old encyclopedia, in a jumble. The rough walls were a muddy tan through which the white plaster showed in cracks and gouges. In the middle of the dirty white ceiling hung a large naked electric bulb.

Behind this room he had one that was more to his measure: a gargantuan bedchamber extending over the greater part of the machine shop; but although sparsely furnished for its size, this too was crowded. The unmade bed was pushed against the distant end wall, and above the bed was the only window, half open now, its green blind drawn, stirring lazily, and blinking a thousand tiny slits of eyes against the morning. From a socket in the ceiling (the only electric outlet here) a long cord drooped to a plug by which it was connected both to a small heater and to a lamp standing on a table beside the bed. And in this room were a slovenly armchair, a chest of drawers with books on top of it, a wardrobe with one door hanging open and Gargantua's red flannel bathrobe hanging over the edge of the door, and in one corner a heap of soiled linen, in another corner a broom, on the floor knee-high stacks of books, hundreds of books. And in the left-hand wall was a door which led down to the backyard of the machine shop, a boneyard strewn with the rusty iron bones of mechanical monsters.

Between these two rooms was an unvented closet unlawfully housing a toilet and a bathtub. On the floor were more books. Wherever the tenant walked he waded through his library, and he went down on his knees when he consulted it.

For these quarters he paid eighteen dollars a month, the landlord never having raised the rent. Leonard Beiderman, proprietor of the machine shop, was the landlord, and if the rent was overdue he was patient. He was one of those who admired Reardon. Although sorry for him, he took pride in being his friend. Besides, he reasoned that another tenant would demand heat, legal plumbing, painting, and other improvements, and probably would object to the hammering. Sometimes even Mr. Reardon would complain about the hammering. When he had a headache a window would be yanked up and the horrisonant voice would bellow:

"God Almighty, Leonard, what are you doing down there?"

But Reardon put up with the Vulcanian hammering. He accepted it as one of the penalities for the low rent and the never being interfered with otherwise. Except for the hammering, and at times the cold, he had got used to these quarters.

But coming back to them now, he was revolted by the meanness, dirt, and musty smell of the loft that was his home. He slammed the door behind him and stood looking about him in disgust. He snorted. He tossed the newspaper onto the desk, pulled off his coat, dropped it over the back of the desk chair, and tramped into the watercloset, undershouldering his suspenders with his thumbs.

When he came back he had brooded. It was a small town, eventually he would meet her on the street, and by then of course she would have heard. He came back scowling. He went to the basin, washed the Olympian hands, and dried them with the towel on the rack. His telephone rang. He walked to the desk. "Yes?"

"Hold the phone, Mr. Reardon"—a girl secretary's voice. "Mr. Parker calling."

He thought: To hell with Mr. Parker; and slammed down the receiver.

But Earl Parker was one of his most important clients, if clients he could call the practicing attorneys who secretly engaged his talents from time to time and paid him little enough, God knew, for the privilege. Little Earl Parker, little weasel-faced Parker—He used to lick my boots at Stanford, he was thinking—was city attorney now. Walsh Reardon stood enraged but half fearing that the phone would not ring again. When it did he let it ring three times before he answered it. But he still had to stand attendance till Earl Parker came on.

"Hello, Walsh?"—he could picture the little weasel leaning back in his swivel chair with that dirty smile on his face. "How're you feeling, Wal——?"

"What's on your mind?"

"What's that? Oh, got a few things here, Walsh. What's on yours?"

"I'm busy."

"Busy? Yes?" Parker chuckled. "Well, now, that's my trouble, Walsh. Thought I might throw a little of it your way."

"You did, uh? What is it?"

"Better come see me, Walsh. . . ."

Silence.

"Walsh?"

"Can it wait?"

"What? Oh, well, now," with another chuckle, "if you're that busy. Guess it might wait till Monday." This was Friday. "Drop in Monday morning, Walsh. Lemme see, here"—pause indicating that Parker was consulting his crowded desk calendar; then peremptorily: "I'll see you at nine o'clock sharp. . . . Walsh?"

Through his teeth Reardon said: "I'll be there." He hung up savagely.

As he did so his eyes fell on the newspaper lying beside the telephone. It accused him of having sold out to Earl Parker again.

He raised his head.

Beyond the window the Morera County hills were green. They looked the same as he remembered them springs and springs and springs ago. A faraway look came into his face; but the backward lettering on the windowpane interposed itself between him and his dream. "Ozymandias," he misread his name aloud, bitterly, and he growled: " 'Look on my works, ye Mighty, and despair!' "

Just then the hammering began.

"God Almighty!" he roared.

In reaction from these causes he arrived half an hour later at his obscure decision to go fishing.

He borrowed Leonard Beiderman's rod and reel. Beiderman was a mad fisherman: that he was willing in this case to lend any part of his equipment was the highest proof of his admiration for his tenant. At first he was even enthusiastic. Having handed over the items, he said with the joy of having discovered a brother:

"*I* didn't know you were a fisherman, Mr. Reardon."

"Oh, I used to fish a little," Reardon said. He was tinkering with the reel. "How do you work this thing?"

"Here"—Beiderman showed him. "Oh, that's a dandy."

"Is, uh?" Reardon put the reel back in its case.

Beiderman offered: "Don't you need no flies or nothing?"

"No, thanks. Well, Leonard . . . Bring you back some fish."

"Good luck," Beiderman grinned, and called after him: "Where you going?"

"Little place I know. Up here on the Mocho."

"Mocho Crick?" Beiderman looked incredulous. "Why, hell, Mr. Reardon, there aint no trout in the Mocho."

"I'm not particular," Reardon called back.

"*Huh?* But—but that's a *trout* rod you got there."

Reardon was gone. Too late it came to Leonard Beiderman that of all the men he knew his tenant was the last one he would have taken for a fisherman. "*Christ!*" he said.

Reardon bought some fishhooks and a sinker at Apperson's hardware store. He went to the Green Gardens floral nursery and got a boy to dig him some worms, which later the boy delivered in a can at his door. For transportation he bargained with Ollie Krause, who drove an independent taxi—this little place he knew, he said, was only a mile or two out of town. He bought some bread, ham, cheese, bologna, dill pickles, and beer at Fife & Piver's market, went home, prepared a sportsman's lunch.

At six o'clock next morning the taxi called for him; and driving out on the highway in the long light and chilly air of that hour, with dew glinting in the fields, and Mr. Reardon in the back seat, Ollie Krause felt the eccentricity of the expedition. "Goin' fishin' in a cab—hallelujah!" he grinned to himself, shaking his head over the wheel. Reardon was not even dressed like a fisherman. He was wearing his old gray worsted business suit, vest and all because of the morning cold, a necktie, and the brown felt hat. Ollie heard him yawn, and thought: I bet he aint been up this early in years—I know I aint.

"Slow up here, Ollie," Reardon said. They were coming to a crossroad. "Seems to me this ought to be the road. . . ."

"That's the Mocho all right," Ollie told him, waving his hand in the direction of a line of trees that cut across some fields to the right.

"*Must* be," Reardon said doubtfully.

"Yep." Ollie turned right onto the crossroad.

"Paved the road," Reardon concluded.

"Huh? Sure they paved the road. This here road's been paved for years."

"Has, uh?"

"Why sure."

"What are those houses down there?"

"Where? Ahead there? That's Lynfield."

"*Lynfield?*"

"Sure."

"Hm. Didn't realize this was where they built Lynfield."

"Yep, that's Lynfield."

Lynfield was a suburb built since the war. And so the little place that Reardon knew, or thought he knew, was never found. But they drove through Lynfield and turned onto another road, an unpaved one this time which paralleled the Mocho at a distance of thirty yards, till they came to another place that Reardon thought might do. The passenger got out, pulled his equipment and lunch after him, paid the driver, and told him to be back at four o'clock.

Ollie asked: "You figure to stay out that long, Mr. Reardon?"

"I do."

"Well, I'll make it close to four as I can. Need any help with that gear?"

"Hand it to me when I get through the fence, will you?"

"Sure thing."

Ollie got out. Reardon tried gingerly to pass between two strands of barbed wire with six cans of beer weighting the pockets of his coat and trousers. Ollie stretched the strands apart with one foot and both hands. When Reardon had got through, Ollie handed him his lunch, can of worms, rod and reel, and the large paper sack that was to do for a fishbasket; and the sportsman nodded, smiling confidently. "Four o'clock."

"Sure thing. Good luck, Mr. Reardon."

The driver got back in his cab, lighted a cigarette, and turned his head for a curious last look after his departing fare.

It takes a farmer to walk with any gainliness across a plowed field. The laden giant was used to pavement. He was picking his way unsurely over the great damp clods of slippery-tufted earth, leaning this way and that to keep his balance, and stumbling a little. In that field he looked no bigger or more powerful than a ship foundering in the open sea.

17

FULL MOON

He remembered a girl with light yellow hair caught round behind her head in a bun, light blue eyes, an irregular nose, high cheekbones, and slightly sunburned cheeks: looking "like a little Swede." Not a beautiful girl. It's that way she's got with her, he had explained to himself. But in fact he had scarcely known Evelyn Traubaugh.

The landgrave's daughter had never gone to school in Llagas, but after being tutored by the governess had attended Miss Cannon's School in San Javier: and he remembered a child in a long white coat, with a veil over her head, being conveyed home in a great open "touring car" by a begoggled chauffeur. He remembered her as far back as the ponycart but he had not spoken a word to her till after his freshman year in college.

Jim Traubaugh, though, had gone to public school in Llagas at the same time as he. The younger of her brothers had been two years older than he and a year ahead of him, but Walsh Reardon had once fought and whipped her brother Jim. . . .

Seeing him on his first day in high school, Jim Traubaugh whoopingly called attention to the short pants for which, at not quite fourteen, he was far too big though not yet old enough, his mother said, for long ones; and there in the schoolyard the fight began. He beat the senator's son all but unconscious. Afterward he would sooner have been punished alone than tell the part about the pants. Jim Traubaugh told it and they were punished together; but the winner of the fight was left humiliated and still in short pants and condemned, he felt (lest anyone think he cared), to wear short pants to school all term even if he should acquire a pair of long ones. Tears of baffled rage came into his eyes.

On a Sunday morning three years after that incident he and two other boys were rambling along the slough. Toward them on the opposite bank came a girl on a fine horse galloping, a yellow-haired girl in riding clothes: she lifted a hand in a wave as she passed, and little Aug Yeager called: "Hi!"

"You know her, Aug?" Howard Espey asked.

"Evelyn Traubaugh."

"Yeah, but do you *know* her?"

"Me? She don't know us neither but she waved, didn't she?"

Walsh Reardon thought: I wonder if she knows who I am!

On his graduation, with his parents in the audience, he received from the senator himself the William H. Traubaugh Scholarship to Stanford Law School. After the exercises he shook hands with the senator again, and looking up at the young red-headed giant gravely, the senator asked:

"How old are you?"

"Seventeen, sir."

"Seventeen—hm."

Dr. Dow, the principal, said regretfully: "Promising boy, Senator."

"Yes?"—almost sadly. "Played on the football team, too, I suppose."

The question embarrassed the promising boy, who had always worked after school. "No, sir."

His father, a tall gray-haired man in his fifties, with a weatherbeaten face and great humped shoulders, spoke up, and there was a rascally twinkle in Matt Reardon's eye. "Our boy was on the debating team, Senator." Among his cronies Matt Reardon was a formidable debater himself. He stood with Henry George against the landlords, with Eugene Debs against Big Business, particularly the Southern Pacific Railroad, with Thorstein Veblen against the leisure class, and with Robert Ingersoll against the preachers. But the landgrave, a director of the Southern Pacific and a trustee of Stanford University, a leader of the Republican Party in the state, and a stanch Lutheran, knew him only as the man who brought the morning mail.

"Debating team—I see; yes, you can talk, young man, you can talk." But perhaps in the circumstances the bellicose patriotism of the valedictory address had saddened the senator. It was June 1918. . . .

Stacked rifles in the inner Quad, drilling on the athletic field, beds in Encina Hall made square-cornered and tight enough to bounce a quarter on, the army haircut everywhere, and everywhere the uniform, the khaki uniform with choke collar, wrap leggings, and flat-brimmed campaign hat—that was Stanford as he found it in the fall; and out of uniform the Stanford man still wore high stiff collars; and the elite Five Hundred had long hair, wore middy blouses with sailor ties, ankle-length skirts, and heavy cardigan sweaters, and did not paint, and had never been seen to smoke, and although the saxophone moaned in the distance there were still some Stanford girls who played the mandolin.

Walsh Reardon got a job, a real one, washing dishes in Palo Alto because he would not descend to menial tasks performed for the benefit of his peers, and he repulsed overtures from fraternities with the explanation that he did not believe in fraternities. He joined the Students' Army Training Corps, wore a gauze mask over his nostrils and mouth against the epidemic of Spanish influenza, and looked forward to the day when he would march off to war. But the war stopped on the brink of his eighteenth birthday.

He first distinguished himself in the freshman-sophomore battle, during which he was careful to avoid Jim Traubaugh.

But his first real glory came from debating after all. By April he had been selected to compete with two other Stanford men, one a senior and the other a junior, and with three California men, for the Médaille Joffre. He boned on the general subject from which the specific question for debate was to be taken: The Reconstruction of France; but not till two hours before the contest was the specific question announced: Resolved, that the policy of national ownership of industry in France should be extended. A mischievous question to select, that was, in the spring of 1919, when in the United States the government was being accused of nearly ruining the railroads by mismanagement during the war and of driving express companies out of business with the Parcel Post, when Business was denouncing the high cost of labor and Labor was girding to fight for still higher wages and shorter hours in a series of strikes from coast to coast, when Debs was in prison and so was Tom Mooney and Labor was howling to have them both out again, when Lenin and Trotsky were prosecuting their red terror in Russia, and the United States was distraught by socialist demands and fear of the Bolsheviks, and Wilson was still in France. The affirmative side of the question was not the obvious one to maintain that night in Wheeler Hall, Berkeley, with three justices of the State Supreme Court sitting in judgment. Yet the judges awarded the Médaille Joffre to Walsh Reardon. Later he gave the medal to his father, declaring: "Dad, it was really you that won it"; and his mother said to him when they were alone: "Son, no matter what

you do in life you'll never do a finer thing than you did tonight for
your father." But on the night of the debate Senator Traubaugh was in
the audience, and although he abominated the decision he said to the
winner:

"Young man, you can talk!" apparently forgetting that he had said
the same thing to the young man before. "What's more, you can think
on your feet, I see. How old are you?"

"Eighteen, sir."

"Eighteen—don't say. That's a fine voice you're developing there.
People are going to listen when you talk. Suppose you're thinking of
politics, eh?"

"I've thought of it, sir."

"So? This vacation you come see me—hear?"

So one day, having made an appointment, he put on his best suit,
pressed by his mother for the occasion, and walked up Traubaugh
Avenue and through the iron gateway and up the drive to the great
stone house, even more magnificent inside than he had dreamed, and
the butler showed him into the study.

Senator Traubaugh was a stocky man with a bull neck, white hair,
and a clipped white mustache, which, until the recent unpopularity
of the Kaiser, had been a full one. He had a large bluff nose and thick
white brows, and there were deep creases at the corners of his eyes,
blue eyes which had the sharp focus that comes, usually, with years
of peering over great distances, as though he had spent most of his
life patrolling his real estate. He said:

"They tell me they think a lot of you down there, Walsh. Say you've
got a future ahead of you—hm? By the way, do you really believe in
public ownership?"

"In public ownership of natural resources and public utilities, I do."

"What? Plum Plan, for instance?"

"No, sir."

"Why not?"

"The Plum Plan would only benefit the railroad brotherhoods at
public expense."

The senator drew him out for an hour. Young Reardon believed in
Woodrow Wilson and in the League of Nations. He was opposed to
Governor Stephens, a Republican, in favor of a pardon for Mooney,
and against Prohibition. He approved of woman suffrage, which the
senator deplored. He was for labor unions, collective bargaining, and
the right to strike, he balked at the closed shop from fear it would lead
to the closed union, which he said would abridge liberty of opportunity, but he predicted that Capital would have to yield to Labor a

share in the management of industry. He spoke with enthusiasm of
Justice Brandeis, whom the senator could not abide. And he sympa-
thized with the Bolshevist cause in Russia. The senator snorted.

"Sounds like I bought a pig in a poke."

The young man flushed. "Senator, I don't think you bought anything. I *won* that scholarship."

The senator gave him a sharp look, but said sportingly: "Tha-at's
right. Board's a play, uh? Well, my boy, you can talk, but you can't
vote. Ha! You're young yet, you'll get rid of those radical ideas. I'm
not complaining. I'll tell you something. I don't think you're a radical
at all. What do you think of that?"

Reardon found the suggestion presumptuous. "I'm not for 'back to
normalcy' anyway."

"No? Progressive, eh? We-ll, in politics maybe that's a good thing
these days. I doubt if we'll ever see normal again; not as it was. Easier
to swim with the tide than against it. But," with a frown and a shake
of the head, "I don't know which way the tide's going, in or out. . . ."

The door opened suddenly.

"Come in, come in, 's all right," her father called, brightening and
beckoning, as she stopped on the threshold at sight of the giant rising.
"Young man won the scholarship last year, Sis. My daughterevelyn."

She said: "Congratulations."

He had never been shy with girls, but having been surprised by this
one in her father's palace, he felt mountainous and clumsy and unre-
fined. All he said was: "Thanks."

"She'll be ready for the Farm herself pretty soon.—Too bad he
doesn't play football, eh, Sis?"

Stanford had just turned back to American football after some
years of Rugby, and had been humbled by California, 67 to 0.

She asked: "Don't you play?"

His size had never embarrassed him so, but if he colored it was half
because of the guilty knowledge that he worked for his room and
board. "No," he admitted.

"Heh, heh. Got a future, though," her father said.

"Dad—can I take the Marmon?"

"Oh, so that's it. Well," her father said, digging into a trousers
pocket for the keys to the princely car: "Here."

"Thanks," taking them as she would have plucked a flower; and she
turned on her heel, her long skirt wrapping itself around her legs.
"'Bye." Apparently she had dismissed young man Wonthescholarship.
Her mother's dead, he thought, and her father spoils her. But at the
door she turned again, impishly. "Mr.——?"

She knows who I am. . . .

"Reardon," her father said first. "Walsh Reardon—don't you ever let 'em forget it, Walsh."

"—Mr. Reardon."

"He may be governor of the state some day—mark my words."

"*Governor,*" with light blue banter. "W-*ell!*"

And the door closed.

"My daughterevelyn. Heh. Well . . ." The senator looked at his pocket watch. "Well, I've helped lots of boys through Stanford, Walsh. But I'll tell you what. It's always up to the boy. Learn everything they can teach you. And when you're through come see me again. We'll have another talk—hm?" The senator rose. "Meantime you're on your own." He held out his hand, smiling. "Good luck to you, Governor."

Who does she think she is? he growled to himself in the night; but what was really troubling him was who she thought *he* was. He feared that she thought him both a charity case and an oaf. Governor: with a man like William H. Traubaugh behind him—— But he wouldn't want a Republican behind him; he could do it on his own. Governor Reardon. Governor Walsh Reardon. But that would take years. Years! And she would be "ready for the Farm herself pretty soon"—whose father was paying his tuition. And he did not even belong to a fraternity. Somehow, he decided that night, he would play football.

The odd thing was that this determination, made upon such trifling overt provocation, still persisted after he had worked in a hatchery all summer, bought what he needed, and found himself with less than a hundred dollars' capital.

At Stanford he went to Doc Atterbury and bluntly stated his problem.

"Think you can play football, do you?"

Reardon picked up a football. "Come outside." Outside he threw the ball with all his strength, and Doc Atterbury watched it fly through the air.

It was too high and it wobbled all over the place, but what got me soon as he threw it was the boy threw it like a baseball, and it must have gone over fifty yards at that before it hit the ground.

But Doc Atterbury at the time seemed unimpressed. He said: "Now go get it—fast."

He was fast all right for a boy that big, but, Lord, the power! I said: That boy was born to be either Richard the Lion-Hearted or a fullback.

But to the boy all Doc Atterbury said was: "Uh huh. Lemme see your hands . . . All right. Turn out for practice. If you look good in scrimmage maybe we can find somebody'll help you."

On the first day of scrimmage he plunged through the first team three times for seven yards, and once, breaking through for thirty-five, crossed the goal line dragging two men with him, and his team made sixty-five yards more on two of his lubberly passes, one of them thrown, to Doc Atterbury's surprise, with the left hand, and then he tackled a ballcarrier as big as he was, and when the man had been assisted from the field Doc Atterbury said to him:

"You better not turn out to be an Englishman, boy. That was a fullback you just crippled."

Walsh Reardon had played football from childhood, but never before on a coached team. At Stanford his long passes became bullet-like, he learned how to charge and run, following his interference, and to veer, dodge, and spin round like a halfback, evading or throwing off tacklers. But he did not know who was depositing ninety dollars a month to his account in Palo Alto. "Member of the Alumni—wants it anonymous," Doc Atterbury had said on giving him the bankbook; and this arrangement providing him with an illusion of some independence he was content to think of the man impersonally as "good old Alumnus Anonymous, the noblest Roman of them all."

In his first season his passes and line bucks gained 235 yards against U.S.S. *Boston*, he won the accolade of "brought the stands to their feet" with an eighty-yard run in the Santa Clara game, he bucked through St. Mary's for two touchdowns, through Oregon Aggies for another, and through California for five first downs, and in the Big Game it was his spectacular sixty-yard pass that gave Stanford its only touchdown—California won, though by the greatly reduced margin of 14 to 10.

During the winter and spring quarters he continued to study hard, but he frolicked a good deal, too. He felt the need of excitement and reward. But in the summer he worked at physical labor in a Llagas warehouse to toughen himself for the coming season. Even his home town had hailed him a hero. But Walsh Reardon missed something. There had been no word from the great stone house.

Then in October he saw her at Stanford. In the crowded arcade of the inner Quad between classes a voice called: "Hello, Llagas!" and he turned, surprised, as she went flashing by his shoulder. "Oh—how are you?" he said, and she, smiling round at him, waved an arm as she hurried on with two other girls. He thought: She knows me now, all right.

And during the games of his second season it gave him pleasure to think that she was watching or, if the game was played on some distant field, would hear. He believed that she was the reason he had turned to football; and in the heat of the Washington game he suddenly thought: Someday I'll marry that little Swede.

Yet even after that he never courted her so she could notice it. It was a strange courtship; and, strange to say, he never in his life knew anything to compare with the excitement of it.

Taking into consideration what he could do himself and what the team could do WITH *him, I still say he was the most valuable player I ever had. Personally he had more color than any other fullback I ever saw—he kept reminding me of that King Richard smashing up and down the beach at the Battle of Jaffa in Ridpath's* History of the World. . . .

But in Llagas on the night of the Washington game the senator's daughter was presented to society at a ball to which King Richard had not been invited.

. . . And they rallied round the Big Guy. They'd go to town with him in there. The trouble was they just couldn't give him what it took against California those seasons. . . .

In the California game of that season Stanford met the first of Andy Smith's "wonder teams." Time and again holes were smashed in the prodigious Bear line by Walsh Reardon, but the line always held at the goal; and all but one of his passes were knocked down or intercepted. The San Francisco *Bulletin* headlined the score:

CAL 38, REARDON 0

The Wonder Team went on to the Rose Bowl and attracted national attention by defeating Ohio State, 28 to 0. When Walter Camp selected his All Americans he named McMillan tackle on his second imaginary team, and Muller, Reardon's rival as a passer, end on his third. But in 1920 the East paid little notice to Pacific Coast Conference football; and that season the fabulous George Gipp had played fullback for Notre Dame. Gipp was Camp's first choice for fullback, but Reardon was not even mentioned. A howl went up from Stanford. Reardon silently promised them all: Wait till next year.

But in January he was called home by the death of his father. Getting up from breakfast one morning, Matt Reardon had been killed by a heart attack.

As a child Walsh Reardon had thought his tall great-shouldered father probably the strongest man in the world, and later the "smartest" one in town. Then he had come to feel a little ashamed of his father sometimes, but to pity him with a fierce defensive pity which recognized that his father had lacked opportunity and which determined someday to vindicate him. That had been the triumphant meaning of decorating him with the Médaille Joffre; and at his son's insistence the medal was buried with him. The funeral was held at Groom's, with the postmaster officiating. The senator sent flowers, but none of the Traubaughs came.

And now it seemed to Walsh Reardon that his college days were over. He felt it his duty to leave Stanford and assume the support of his mother. But Jessie Reardon had a small pension and a little insurance, and she would not hear of that. "Your father wouldn't want that any more than I do. He'd say get the thing he never had while you could get it, a real education; now wasn't that what he was always talking about?" It was. "So another year and a half for our sake, won't you, son, and then you can make us proud of you."

He went back to Stanford with renewed determination to become governor of the state, at least. He was elected president of his class and also of Nestoria, the debating society. But the campus lion took a mysterious room in Palo Alto, refused all invitations, and, partly from pride, partly from a new sense of responsibility, kept to himself in leisure hours, which in some quarters was thought very "stuck up" of him but which in fact was against his nature and hard for him. Secretly he had got his old job back and was sending his subsistence allowance home: he did not want his Roman to know about that, nor Evelyn Traubaugh to hear that Walsh Reardon was dishwashing his way through college. His hands took on a raw and puffy look. He studied and read more than ever.

Pride prevented him from paying court as yet to the daughter of the man who was paying his tuition; but the thought of her would gnaw at him. Who was queening her? He was sure that someone was, someone with money and social position, someone who had been to her coming-out party; and perhaps that made him fancy all the more intensely that he wanted her; nor would he "queen" any other of the Five Hundred. He took to prowling at night. He sought comfort with girls of the towns (Bought Red Lips, he called them—Dowson was in fashion again), but with alcohol he achieved a glorious new confidence in himself. On the night of the Junior Prom a sheriff's posse raided a blind pig and arrested, drunk, after some difficulty, the president of the junior class.

It was in the papers that Walsh Reardon had been arrested, and because of that he telephoned his mother from the jail. His mother cried. His shame was all the deeper because of the certainty that Evelyn Traubaugh also knew. Her father must have read the papers too, but his patron sent no word, not even a rebuke. If it had not been for

235

his scholastic record and for Doc Atterbury he might have been expelled.

But he finished the year at the head of his class.

And still from the senator only silence. Reardon resented that.

In the summer he worked in the warehouse again, and one hot night found himself standing in the darkness across the street from the Traubaugh gate. Through the trees he saw several cars in the drive and light flooding the steps as though the front door were open, and he could hear a private orchestra playing "Margie." The royal musicians, he thought, and he wondered whether she was dancing with Bob Noble, because by this time he had learned who was queening her: the banker's son. Bob Noble and other nobles were in there no doubt. But he was not unconscious of a certain inconsistency in the situation, and it pleased him to imagine what they would say if they should suddenly come out of the house and discover who happened to be passing that way. "Hey, look who's here—Walsh Reardon! Come on in, Walsh Reardon—gather round—have a drink, huh? Aw, come on." And she would say—what would she say? What would Llagas say? In Llagas if it came to dancing with the landgrave's daughter in the landgrave's house he was still the letter-carrier's boy who was going to college on her father's money.

I suppose he thinks he owns me—he and the munificent Roman.

Then there entered his mind a monstrous possibility.

No . . . *But Traubaugh was a trustee, he wouldn't dare do it in the open; and it was known that the senator was paying his tuition— that would explain the silence: it made sense. . . .*

That night's suspicion that the senator and Alumnus Anonymous were the same man, and the feeling of rejection that he had experienced there in the darkness outside her house, took hold of his imagination. He was sure that Doc Atterbury would not tell him who the Roman was, and doubted whether he could discover at the bank, but he could not bring himself to make inquiries because—because if his suspicion was correct he would not be able to stand knowing it or having the fact out in the open between the Traubaughs and himself if they should hear that he had been told (because then he would have to accept, or to act). So he tormented himself. He growled: I ought to have a T on my jersey; and the conviction that the senator expected to help, to *use*, him after college made it worse. He felt as though he were in chains. Stanford in the fall was amused, then troubled, and then angered by his wild efforts to be free.

. . . *And then he got hard to handle.*

Three times he broke training for drinking bouts, and once was gone two days. Doc Atterbury protected him, tried reasoning with him, then stopped speaking to him, and during the whole Washington game left him sitting on the bench. The Stanford rooters shouted for him, and Atterbury let them shout; and the sports writers commented; and everyone knew that Walsh Reardon had been disciplined.

But leaving him on the bench was worse punishment than Atterbury knew. In football he found release. That was as close as he ever got to her—when he could feel that her eyes were on him, that there was no one between them, that now she could see who he was. Smashing up and down the beach King Richard would have his hour. On the fifteenth of November he turned twenty-one years old.

And four days later Stanford's new stadium was "dedicated" with his last Big Game.

Sixty thousand spectators got to their feet in the first few seconds of play when Crip Toomey, having caught Stanford's kickoff, was tackled so hard by Walsh Reardon that the ball flew out of his hands, and Reardon, on his feet again in an instant, recovered it, ran it to the three-yard line before Erb caught him, and dragged Erb to the two-yard line before McMillan brought him down. And the spectators remained on their feet while Walsh Reardon four times charged the center of the California line. The first time he gained a foot, the second time another foot, the third time he gained half the remaining distance to the goal line, but the play was called back, and the fourth time he went over for a touchdown. But the ecstatic Stanford crowd was silent again in a moment. The hero had not got up.

A great impact of applause broke upon the afternoon air from the still standing sixty thousand as Walsh Reardon was carried from the field on a stretcher, and the Stanford rooting section cheered him. But Reardon had lost consciousness. He was taken to the hospital with his right leg broken. Stanford kicked the goal after his touchdown, making the score 7 to 0, but it never scored again. At the final gun Stanford had been crushed, 42 to 7. But Reardon, hurt or not, had gone out of football in glory.

Only his wildest Stanford admirers pretended that if he had played the whole game the Wonder Team might have been beaten; but Andy Smith chivalrously admitted that the score might not have been quite so one-sided if he had, and added: "I always wished he played for me," which was considered a magnificent compliment at the time. But he was not consoled.

His team and his school had been humbled again, and the Wonder Team, which indeed he had viewed as a personal challenge, was again triumphant, and that was the way it would go down in the record, and he had been cheated of doing all he could have done, and he would never have another chance—he was finished. But, besides, he knew that he had been chasing an illusion; he had known it all the time. Football glory was nothing. With all his efforts he had not wiped out his inferiority to the Traubaughs, or his debt to them. And he was more resentful of his patron than ever, because, having broken his leg "for dear old Traubaugh," as he put it to himself, he still had not heard from the man.

But when he re-entered the life of the university it was as though he were consciously determined to make up for all he had missed of it.

He discovered that even on crutches, with his leg in a cast, he could get dates with coeds. In old trousers that had one leg cut off, and in rented dinner jackets, he went gaily to parties and was made much of, collected girls' autographs on his cast, and being unable to dance, made it up to the girls in parked automobiles. The Jazz Age had over-taken Stanford: two members of the Five Hundred had been expelled for smoking on the campus and climbing trees, and fraternity men were saying they wanted pledges who had "cellars." Harding was President: short skirts were in, and bobbed hair was a daring innovation: it was the day of the flapper and the hip flask, of dancing cheek to cheek and the "petting party."

But at the St. Francis Hotel on New Year's Eve he saw her for the last time.

In San Francisco, Fatty Arbuckle was between manslaughter trials for the death of Virginia Rappe after a party in that same hotel, and girls were sighing over Rudolph Valentino in *The Sheik*, and trumpets were wailing "The Wabash Blues." The young giant on crutches amid the serpentine and confetti in the St. Francis that night was wearing for the first time his own dinner suit (with a piece sewn into the right leg of the trousers to make room for his cast); and he was more affected by gin than appeared at first glance. His date was a little TriDelt named Edna, from Los Angeles, who had not yet bobbed her hair but was not averse to vivid makeup off the campus, and who petted, and who laughed too loud, and who called him Walshie. With them were Johnny Peers, a substitute Stanford end, and Mike Owen, a law student and Nestorian whose stepfather was St. George Newton, the San Francisco corporation lawyer, and two girls called Peg and Di. Their table was against the wall.

On the rim of the dance floor a large round table had been laid for a dozen other revelers, and there he saw her in a light blue dress of shiny silk, her hair gleaming in the light of the chandelier. Bob Noble

was on her right and Hunt Farrelly on her left. He did not want her to
see him there with Edna, or at the inferior table, and suddenly he
imagined that she would be amused if she saw him there at all, the
home-town mailman's son, her father's fullback, in black tie at the
Hotel St. Francis. At the same time he wanted her to notice him,
wanted to show her. He thought that if it were not for his leg, his
damned leg, he would go and make her dance with him.

Afterward he vaguely recalled that state of mind, but he could not
remember much of what had happened next. The place had been
filled with Stanford and California, and people had kept coming to
his table, and he had been slapped on the back and asked how he
was coming along (he had thought that she was noticing now all
right), and more drinks had been poured openly from flasks, and there
had been kidding and argument, and they had been pretty loud, he
supposed, but it had been New Year's Eve, hadn't it? And all of a
sudden the headwaiter had been telling him he would have to leave.
Who? What for? You're crazy. Go 'way. And Mike and Johnny (they
must have been drunk too) had been taking him by the arms. No!
And then he had hit somebody——

It was the policeman he had hit, the first one, Mike and Johnny
told him next morning.

And he had a horrible memory of standing at bay in the middle of
the dance floor all alone and brandishing a crutch at some policemen
and defying them, with everyone watching, with her watching, and
the whole place quiet, and then a girl screaming or something and
the orchestra striking up and suddenly a light blinding him——

"The spotlight," Mike explained. "They turned the spotlight on
you. That was when the constable threw the billy—*that's* why your
head hurts. Then they rushed you. . . ."

Like an animal, he thought, like a wild beast; and she had seen it all.

". . . And Johnny and I tried to pull 'em off you."

Which explained why they were all in the City Prison together this
morning.

But his hand, his right hand, was bandaged: they said he had cut it
badly across the palm but they could not tell him how. That must
have been why the girl screamed, she must have seen the blood when
he raised the crutch, they said. There was dried blood all over his
cuff.

They were sitting on the floor of the crowded drunk tank of the
jail in their evening clothes, their backs against the wall, Reardon's
broken leg stretched straight out in front of him—he had to keep

warning other prisoners not to fall over it; and Johnny said with a rueful grin: "I wonder what became of the girls."

Reardon leaned his splitting head back against the wall and closed his eyes. "I wonder what became of—any of it"; so mysteriously did it all seem to have slipped away from him, like a motion picture scene that at one moment is clear and the next a blur and then is something else again, or like a dream that suddenly goes into a nightmare from which one wakes, shaken and astonished, in a strange room.

It was in the newspapers again, but this time of course it was worse. This time it was on the front page and illustrated with Walsh Reardon's picture from the files. And for Reardon there was added bitterness. The same issues of the papers announced Walter Camp's All Americans of 1921 and he was not among them but, with what seemed to him double irony, he received "honorable mention."

It was Sunday and a man sent down by Mike Owen's stepfather got them out on bail. Reardon telephoned his mother to reassure her again, but he could not face her yet: he stayed the night in San Francisco. Next day the three young men appeared in court. The first thing the police judge wanted to know was where they had got the liquor: as though it were a matter of surprise that any liquor could be got in San Francisco; but when they said that friends had treated them he did not pursue the matter. The judge lectured them but then (perhaps for St. George Newton's sake) let them off with fines and in Reardon's case a suspended sentence of thirty days, saying threateningly that he hoped they had learned their lesson.

But academic justice in Reardon's case was this time not tempered with mercy. Walsh Readon was expelled from Stanford.

"I tried, Walsh," Doc Atterbury told him glumly after the case had been heard and disposed of. "But this time they wouldn't listen."

"No; what did you expect?" Reardon said. "I couldn't play football any more anyhow, could I?"

Dreading the goodbyes of his friends, he left Stanford within an hour. He never went back. He left Evelyn Traubaugh ignorant that he had ever courted her. But he tried not to think of the girl in whose eyes he would only see himself the wretched figure he had cut on the night of his disgrace. In San Francisco he hobbled about the waterfront inventing ways to tell his mother. But at the Ferry Building he found that the news of his expulsion was already in the papers. When he got home it was dark. His mother already knew.

She did not meet him with tears of sorrow and reproach. At the door he seemed gathered by some mother's feat into her arms, and she laid her head on his chest and for a moment held him as though it were enough to have him back again; and she said they were not even going to talk about it because it was finished and he was wiser now, but that they were going to start all over again. That night he told her his plans: he was going to get a job and complete his studies at night school, and when he had been admitted to the Bar he was going to open an office right here in Llagas, and when he had established himself as a lawyer he would enter politics here, too, because the Llagas Valley was a great political constituency in this state; and she said she liked his spunk and, did he know something? she had never been so proud of him. He resolved that he would take her out of that rented cottage into a palace, and darken Stanford, Llagas, and the house of Traubaugh forever in the shadow of their name.

And the next day the senator sent for him.

At last, he thought.

When he was shown into the study the senator did not rise, but merely glanced up coldly from the papers on his desk and said: "Sit down."

Walsh Reardon's face as he hobbled across the floor on crutches and lowered himself into the chair opposite the desk was dead white, but the older man, if he noticed that at all, perhaps misread the sign. The senator did not seem to notice the broken leg, either, or the bandaged hand, but he looked his visitor sternly in the eye and began: "Last time you were here I guessed something about you. So I let you alone——"

But Reardon, in a voice that he managed to keep down and deliberate, but that filled the room like surf, cut him off. "I know. I led my class alone. I was president of it alone, too, and I was president of Nestoria alone. I won that medal alone. I made the football team alone. And then I was expelled alone. Is that what you wanted to see me about?"

The senator's eyes had flashed. The boy was impudent. He looked at the boy. Physically the boy had filled out and broadened; he had an overpowering amount of what the senator called presence; and that deep voice had power. "How old are you?"

The boy looked back at him. "I'm a full citizen now, Senator." It was as though he had said: "I'm as good as you are."

The senator put his hands on top of the desk and pushed himself slowly to his feet as if to dominate the boy.

But using one crutch, the boy also got up, and dwarfed him. "I *won* that scholarship—remember? Before that you didn't even know me. You didn't know I could play football, either, till I'd made the team. You've got your money's worth, Senator. You haven't got a cent of change coming, and you know it."

The senator's lip twisted. The boy was an ungrateful whippersnapper. But deep beneath this perhaps were other things that the senator felt: consciousness of age, jealousy of the strength of a younger male, and fury at the passing of youth: what the king bull moose grown old must feel when, after a lifetime of victorious battles which count for nothing now, he is challenged on equal terms by a younger and stronger bull whose battles are all ahead of him—a whippersnapper. With far more energy than the action required the senator reached for the button on his desk and pressed it.

But Reardon picked up his other crutch and with long strides of leg and crutches left the room. He passed the butler in the hall, strode out the door and down the drive. His sense of triumph was disturbed by the conscience of an ingrate but he exulted that he had broken the chains and thrown them in the senator's face, that he was free of the senator and his little snob of a daughter, his little snob of a daughter. . . .

At home there awaited him a telephoned message from St. George Newton's office inviting him to drop in on Monday. He guessed that the leading corporation lawyer wished to offer him a job.

So on Monday morning he went to San Francisco, and found Mike Owen's stepfather in a large private office on the top floor of the Phelan Building—a roly-poly man who seemed delighted to see him, asked after his wounds, and talked about the California game before coming to the point:

"Doc Atterbury tells me you're looking for a job."

"Yes, I——" Reardon stopped. He would have expected Newton to know that from Mike Owen. He asked: "Doc Atterbury?"

Newton smiled. "So he never told you." He laughed, and answered the look on Reardon's face: "Yes," nodding, "I'm the man."

So Reardon did not accept the job that Newton offered him. No more chains: he wanted to be free. But being an expelled student, he was glad to let his munificent Roman help him get into a good night school. He was enrolled in the Hall McAllister College of Law, and leaving home again, he moved into one room in the flat of an Italian family on the lee slope of Telegraph Hill, and when his leg had healed he got a daytime job as a stevedore.

Often at night he would fall asleep over his books. But, except for a few lapses, he stuck this out for a year and a half. In that time he won his credits and took his degree. He passed the State Bar examinations. And with what money he had saved and some that his mother pressed on him as a loan—it was the same three hundred dollars he had sent her from college that term—he opened his office in Llagas. Jessie Reardon and her son stood arm in arm on the sidewalk and looked at the sign, and she said how proud his father would be; and then she cried.

Months before, Llagas had read that Senator Traubaugh was in the hospital, and one day Reardon watched the landgrave's funeral pass through town from the Lutheran Church. Behind the hearse came two black limousines with blinds drawn, an open car carrying Governor Richardson, Mayor Kidd, and Dr. Ray Lyman Wilbur, president of Stanford, and then a long procession of other automobiles from the most expensive to the cheapest. To the young lawyer it seemed the funeral of an era. Harding too had just died and Coolidge was President: the steel industry was changing from the twelve- to the eight-hour day (Capital was having to listen to Labor), woman suffrage was in effect throughout the nation, churches were losing disciples to Darwin, Freud, and Margaret Sanger, the mind of John Dewey was capturing the schools, and people were learning to look at towns like Llagas through the eyes of Sinclair Lewis. Well, Reardon thought, he died in time.

And when, ten months later, just after her graduation from Stanford, the senator's daughter became the bride of Hunt Farrelly, Walsh Reardon felt nothing but a mild relief that the little snob would be leaving Llagas now. She was in possession of a shameful picture of him.

Already he had begun to succeed at the law. First he had managed to get a few small cases assigned to him by judges in the county seat. His knowledge of the law, his clear presentations, his looks, and his voice had made an impression at the Court House. Clients had begun coming to him. He had been winning all his cases. And he had got his mother a hired girl.

It was in 1925 that the wealthy miller Henry Jancke died, and to break the will the disinherited son Lloyd retained a San Francisco lawyer of some reputation. Martin Dickey, the family lawyer, was an old man, and he wanted help; but he did not want to yield prestige in the case, or to sacrifice any more of the fee than he had to. He took in young Reardon at twenty-five per cent; and Reardon, sure that his first big chance had come, went home jubilant that night.

"Walsh?" his mother's voice inquired when he had closed the front door; and when he answered that it was he: "Oh . . . Take off your skates, dear."

"*Skates?*" He laughed, guessing that she had been dozing again

and dreamed he was still a child; and going into the parlor, he found
her in her rocker with her eyes closed. His mother dozed a good deal
since he had got her the girl. Jessie Reardon was only fifty-six, but
she had never been strong, and all her life had worked hard; she was
tired. He did not guess that her heart was giving out. "Mom?"

With a start she opened her eyes again. "Oh." She smiled and took
his hand and patted it faintly, her lids drooping. "*That*'s a good
boy. . . ."

He said: "Guess what."

But there was a sound in her throat and her head went back rigidly
and she was dead.

18

THE COMPLEAT ANGLER

Of his obsession for Evelyn Traubaugh apparently nothing remained
to upset him when she suddenly returned to town. But in his best
days she had been the goddess of all he meant to do, have, and be,
and in 1919 had heard the landgrave say: "He may be governor of the
state someday—mark my words," and it was thirty years later. He had
suddenly been confronted with himself, that was all. He had looked
round his flat, and at his face in the glass, and then his telephone had
rung and he had sold out to Earl Parker again, and the newspaper
had accused and the hammering mocked him. And it was spring. He
had rebelled against his failure. He had resolved that it was not too
late. But it had seemed necessary for him to get clear at once of that
loft; he would go somewhere else—and think. Where? And he had
seen the hills, green again with new wild oats, looking the same again.
And so he had come fishing.

He was forty-eight now, and white-haired, with the body and voice
of Blunderbore, and he had fallen back to replan the conquest of the
world, equipped with fishing tackle, some worms, lunch, six cans of
beer, a certain education, and an empty paper bag.

When he descended the bank to the creek he saw to his disgust that
the sands were defiled with food cans and scraps of wrapping paper.
Lynfield people, he supposed. And the creek was narrower and lower

than he remembered it. But it made the same pleasant sound flowing around its rocks under the arches of its trees.

The things in his arms he placed secure on the flat top of a boulder. He took the cans of beer out of his pockets and put them on the sand at the water's edge. He got down on his knees and set the cans in the cold water, working them a little into the mud and buttressing them carefully with stones. He got up, dried his hands on his handkerchief, and dusted his knees.

Take coat off? Too cold yet.

He looked about him and scowled at the reminders of the Lynfield people. Tidiness was not characteristic of him but he gathered up the debris and hid it from himself behind some brush; and standing hands on hips, he rested. Except for the purl of water he could hear no sound yet. He told himself that it was peaceful, the perfect place to think. Far off a bird called. A sudden sound at his feet made him start, and looking down, he saw a little black tail disappear beneath a rock.

Lizard.

He put his rod together and attached the reel and tied sinker and hook to the end of the line and took a worm out of the bait can with his fingers and looked at it. He did not like what he had to do next, but he did it. Then, rod and baited hook in hand, he went climbing round the bend in search of a good hole. But from round the bend he could not see his lunch or the place where the beer was, so he came back. He simply cast his line into the water and sat down against a tree, and in solitude addressed himself to the problem that he had come to solve.

He considered San Francisco. For it had been in his mind that he would rebegin his career in another place. But he remembered Mike Owen and several other Stanford classmates of his who were successful attorneys in San Francisco now; they would think it strange to see Walsh Reardon at the bottom of the ladder after all these years; and this distracted him from the problem—it reminded him of matters that were painful to him. He pulled his mind away from the painful matters and back to the problem: San Francisco was overcrowded with attorneys, he decided. Some city farther away was where he would go, a city where he would not be remembered, a city that was booming after the war. Reno, Las Vegas—but that would mean studying to pass the Nevada Bar. Los Angeles: two million people down there now, they claimed. But Los Angeles reminded him of other Stanford-educated lawyers, and that brought back the painful matters; and by this time, through the seat of his trousers, he was feeling the clammy touch of the earth. He got up rubbing himself.

Damp here.

A few yards upstream a low sunray that had found a path through the trees on the east bank lighted the end of a fallen tree trunk that jutted a few feet over the water, and attracted him. He reeled in the line, took the hook in his fingers, and looked intently at the worm.

Dead.

He detached it and threw it into the creek. But where it sank there was a sudden disturbance of the water which could not have been made by a dead worm. He scrambled back to his can of bait on the boulder, hooked on another worm, cast it after the dead one, and waited. When nothing happened he tried trolling it. Up and down . . . up . . . down . . . up . . . sidewise. But he fouled the line in some twigs, freed it only after a struggle, and then it seemed probable that he had frightened away whatever fish might have been down there.

Gone.

He climbed out on the sunny tree trunk. It was a broad one which offered the up-curling stump of a broken limb for a seat. He sat, cast again, and waited. Nothing happened. He took out and filled his pipe, lit it with a great kitchen match, and puffed. Immediately a painful question came into his mind. He banished it and bent his mind back to the problem. Oakland: that was too close to home; and in Oakland he would be remembered. Eureka: he pictured the little port fog-bound behind the big woods of the northern cape: Ultima Thule. Sacramento, Stockton, Fresno, Santa Barbara, San Diego . . . San Diego. . . .

But the sunray moved off the tree trunk and left him in the shade, and it was damp again, and the light had an unearthly quality, and he thought that except for the murmuring of the stream it was unnaturally quiet. Where were the birds? Then there penetrated to him the hum of insect life; but beyond that and the sound of the water the silence somehow remained. He reminded himself that it was peaceful here. But a sense of strangeness, of unreality, of eeriness had come over him; and a feeling of panic. He knew it was absurd. He got up and tried trolling again, but without success. He sat down again. He remembered that the taxi was coming for him at four o'clock. He took out his watch and looked at it. He put it to his ear, but it was going. It said five minutes to eight.

An hour later he had beat a hundred yards down the stream and back again, and fished in half a dozen places more. He was still without a fish; but he had made some progress with his thinking. He had faced the fact that an attorney setting up in business in a strange city would need capital: he had arrived at the problem of how to raise a thousand dollars. He had also drunk a can of beer.

By ten-fifteen he had abandoned the impossibility of borrowing the thousand dollars. He had considered seeking out clients in jails and hospitals, and declined to be so unethical. He had remembered his beginnings at the law: how judges at San Javier had assigned small routine cases to him. He had thought of soliciting cases from Judge Díaz, who had always been friendly to him; but knowing his own reputation and the judge's high sense of public responsibility, he had thought better of straining the friendship. He had even weighed the possibility of saving the thousand dollars, by rigid discipline, out of the money he earned from the hackwork that other lawyers gave him. He had not yet arrived at a decision.

But he had made some progress with his fishing. He had beat a hundred yards along the stream in the other direction and caught a fish five inches long. But in the excitement he had stepped into the water up to his ankle.

He came back stiffly, his tackle in one hand and the dead fish in the other, his right trouser leg dripping and the foot squishing in the shoe. He leaned his rod against the flat boulder and put the fish in the paper bag. Walking about as if with one foot in a gutter, he gathered brush, twigs, and the scraps of paper he had hidden, and made a fire. When he saw that the fire was going he limped to the creek, bent over, and took out a can of beer dripping mud. He washed it off, found the beer opener in a pocket of his coat, punched a hole in the can, and drank a mouthful of beer. He returned to the fire, placed the can carefully on the sand, and sat down beside it.

Then he took off his great sodden brogue, shook it, and put it to the fire.

Then he peeled off the wet sock, wrung it out in his fists, pushed a rock to the fire, and hung the sock over the face of the rock to dry.

Then he dried his bare white foot as best he could with his damp handkerchief, then wrung out and brushed off the wet cuff of his trouser, and then, swinging round on his rump, extended the leg to the fire.

After a moment he looked at his watch again, and with a deep growl of a sigh returned it to his pocket. He took up the beer in his left hand, reclined at full length upon his right elbow, drank again, and lay there staring into the flames. A mile away a train whistled.

And the painful thoughts that pursued him swooped down on the disabled giant.

He remembered himself as he had been, Stanford, and winning the Médaille Joffre, and the medal pinned on the breast of his dead father, and his mother's saying: "Then you can make us proud of you." Senator Traubaugh and his daughter, and the St. Francis Hotel on New Year's Eve, 1921, and Evelyn Traubaugh Farrelly just come back to town. Brutally he asked himself:

What was the matter with me?

He meant that, endowed beyond most men, as he believed, educated at Stanford, and having made a promising beginning at the law, he had somewhere given up: why? He knew that drinking had not been the reason, only the method. The associated word "escape" came into his mind—nowadays it was a word associated with nearly everything; and he thought that he had been trying to escape from boredom. But he was being mercilessly self-analytical, as objective as possible, using his education as intelligently as he could, trying to apply to his own case the clinical ideas surrounding that word characteristic of the century—Escape; and he asked himself whether it was not from reality that he had been trying to escape. Maybe it was lately, he cautiously allowed. . . . Yes, lately. Then he owned: Even this morning!

For a moment he stared at that discovery. Yes, it was true. Still, he thought it did not answer the riddle. Why had he quit in the first place?

He sneezed—the fire had dwindled. He blew his nose powerfully. He got up and threw more wood on the fire, felt his wet sock and shoe, turned the sock over, heaped still more wood on the fire, and stood there till the fire was roaring. The smoke made him cough and wipe his eyes and sent him limping over the damp compact sand for another can of beer. He came back, sat down, brushed the sand from his bare foot, and again extended the foot to the fire.

He remembered: *Last time you were here I guessed something about you.*

What was it old Traubaugh had guessed, or thought he had guessed? Reardon wished he had let the senator finish that day. Seeking a clue, his mind went back to the previous interview in the great stone house, and he remembered:

I don't think you're a radical at all. What do you think of that?

He had recently had another occasion to remember that remark of Senator Traubaugh's. It had been during a political discussion with some of the artists at the Lost Dutchman Tavern. "Roosevelt worship-

ers," he had called them, and declared: "Roosevelt cheapened everything he touched."

"*What* did he cheapen, for instance?"

"For instance, the Congressional Medal of Honor. He gave it to
George M. Cohan."

That had stopped them all right, he thought—they were war veterans. But they had been willing to overlook that. "What else?"

"The penny, the dollar, currency, stamp collecting, states' rights,
property rights, the right to work, liberty, his own Party, and he tried
to cheapen the Supreme Court and the Constitution of the United
States."

The penny, the dollar, currency, stamp collecting, and property
rights they had scornfully dismissed. They had tried to refute him
about the other things. They had cited Roosevelt's fight for civil
liberties, his championship of Labor, his raising of the minimum wage,
his social security and public housing programs, his abolition of child
labor; and then—beaten, in Reardon's opinion, but unsurrendering
—had only looked at him in sneering silence. He had known that they
thought him the worst kind of reactionary. And in the presence of
their invulnerable youth he had remembered. He had felt old. He
had suddenly wished that he could take back all that he had said.

Well, what did those children know about America? But it pained
him to remember that in the last election he had voted Republican.
He growled disgustedly: "Dewey!" But he had voted Republican because the Democrats had forced him to. They had turned the government into a bureaucracy. Government itself was Big Business now.
Cynical, too, and full of corruption. The citizen was its servant. Congress had lost place. The Administration and the Supreme Court
made the laws now. And the military—engaged in a conspiracy to
exalt itself: and the perfect symbol of the conspiracy was that damned
labyrinth called the Pentagon. But the people couldn't see the Krem-
lin Annex going up, either, on the banks of the Potomac. The people
were blind. Ignorant. Uncaring. No principles any more. Standards
debased. All cheap now. The same all over the world. And he wondered whether this was why he had given up—because the world had
gone cheap and lost its charm.

He got up and renewed the fire again. He turned his sock. He examined his shoe. He looked at his watch. It was only eleven o'clock.
But he was hungry.

He got his lunch and opened another can of beer and sat down
on the beach in the sun. With his mouth full he remembered Evelyn
Traubaugh. He swallowed, and in the same tone he had used for

Dewey he addressed the passing stream: "Governor Reardon!" But it seemed to him outrageously unjust, a violation of his natural prerogative, his birthright, that returning to Llagas after all these years she should find him the . . . a . . . bum, he told himself blackly, just a . . . damn . . . bum. And I'm a better lawyer than any of them. Live on their handouts. In a rat's nest. She'll hear. . . .

And again the imminent presence of that stranger forced him to turn his mind to the enterprise of reconstructing his life. He was sitting with his knees drawn up, a sandwich in one hand, a can of beer in the other, and concentrating again, he sat quite still. Around him on the sand were several distinct imprints of one great bare foot.

He thought that possibly seven hundred and fifty dollars would do; or even five hundred. He would draw up an estimate. And get the money. And go to San Diego. He accused himself that this would only be running away again. But he knew that even now he was evading the truth.

The truth was that the idea of settling in a strange place, among strangers, filled him with misgivings. Was he afraid? No, but—*he didn't want to leave Llagas.* But he had always despised Llagas. That small town? But he realized that he had little desire to conquer a world from which Llagas would be subtracted. It was that small town that he had always wanted most to impress. King Richard had always wanted to be king in Llagas. He would have liked to be the landgrave. Was that true? He supposed it was; he supposed it was that way with most men, really. And yet—he had never liked Llagas. He concluded: It was for my father's sake. Then it came to him that his orbit had got considerably smaller than the town. He did not dwell on that. Well, he thought, he had failed his father. Llagas was lost. So it seemed to him that going to San Diego would not be cowardly but rational. Resolute. Courageous.

But he finished his food and with it another can of beer and he still had not hit on a plan for raising the money. He looked at his watch again. There remained four hours and forty minutes till his taxi would be due. He drank his last can of beer. He noticed a bug in the sand, the leaves faintly stirring, the greenness of the hills, and the sky, the calm blue, he thought, impenetrable sky. A white butterfly passed quietly, but, he considered, it was not the same butterfly. Not the same green on the hills. Not the same spring. Only the process was the same. "The majestic procession of the equinoxes." The System, the inexorable mad inscrutable System from which there was no escape; no escape but one. And then? . . . The sun was warm and the passing water lulled him; he yawned, lay back flat, and closed his eyes.

The sun rose to the meridian and looked down on him fast asleep, one shoe off and one shoe on, on a beach littered with papers and six empty cans.

19

MOTHER OF A GROWING BOY

In June of 1949 the United States withdrew the last of its troops from Korea. But the newspapers gave more space to photographs of young women in bridal veils. June was the month of weddings.

On the twelfth of June, 1942, for instance, Arline McClatchy had married William Lucas. But to Arline that seemed much longer ago than seven Junes.

This June the wedding talk in the McClatchys' tavern was of Vic Scatina and Dorothy Froelich.

Gretchen and Mitch had brought the news. But Arline got it from Phyllis Plover. That night Arline had found the pretty waitress crying in the women's room.

"Phyl—what *is* it?"

"What?" Phyllis tossed her head and went to the washbasin. "Nothing."

"But . . . did somebody insult you or something?"

"No!" Phyllis, with her back turned, began to bathe her eyes. "Leave me alone, can't you?" But the next moment her head wilted on its tender stalk and she was sobbing over the basin.

Arline took the girl in her arms. "What hap-pened?"

"Oh . . . it's just that damn . . . sc, sc, Scatiiiiina. . . ."

Phyllis had just heard. Scatina had gone off, she said, and married that *horse!* And he hadn't even told her he was going to. She hadn't seen him for two weeks. And everybody out there was talking about it, had been asking her about it because they knew that she . . . that he—— "Oh," she broke off, "that *heel!* That dirty *w-wop!*"

June.

Once Phyllis had recovered from her shock she rejected sympathy, slapping the air. "*I* didn't want him; it isn't *that. I* told him where he could go two weeks ago."

All the same she appeared to respond to the return of Arline's affection for her.

Arline had instantly forgiven Phyllis everything. What had happened to the little devil had been her own fault, of course; but Vic Scatina shouldn't have led her on. Again she had picked the wrong man. Her flirtatious ways with the customers, even the concise and shapely figure in the livery that she wore like a costume, the obvious little swagger committed on the premises, the gilded head, and the pretty leer, when considered in the light of her history, seemed less dangerous than pathetic.

It was almost as if the two women were friends again. Almost as if Phyllis could not sense that there was something in her defeat that gave Arline satisfaction. Arline could not help it. Men might amuse themselves with one kind of woman but they always married the other kind. Sometimes even when the other was a "horse."

On the twelfth of June, the widow, the son, and the parents-in-law of William Lucas assisted at Mass for his soul at St. Peter's. And afterward they took the bus to the cemetery and put flowers on his grave. June was the month of the Sacred Heart.

The small granite headstone identified him as "Beloved Husband of Arline McC. Lucas" and "Father of Wm. Jr." As though he were Napoleon, it also dated his sojourn on earth: "1913–1943."

"Nineteen-thirteen," his father-in-law said to his mother-in-law. "That was the year we got married. This same month, it was—June the first." And to the widow: "What date was he born?"

"August third."

"August third. I was tending bar at the old Potrero Saloon when he was born." The historian added sadly: "And we still had the old Traveler's when he died. He never seen the New place. He had a short life." And to the son: "Well, he was a fine man, your dad, Bill. And a real hero. He give his life for his country. That's *your* name—see?" pointing to the gravestone.

"Is ut?"

"Nonsense," the mother-in-law said.

"Sure it is. William Lucas, Junior," the father-in-law filled out the name.

"Never mind!"

"What?"

"Don't *frighten* the child. Just kneel down now, Billy, and we'll all say a prayer."

And then the family knelt and prayed for him again; and the

widow of the beloved husband and father was wondering whether he
heard and saw them at his grave. The slight moisture in her eyes was
partly for her son and partly for him, but for him only because his life
presented itself to her as so pitiful and his death as so sad. For herself
she could not mourn him; and she feared that he knew. She knew that
God knew.

And then they went home to lunch.

She felt that she was falsehearted because at this distance it appeared
to her that she had never loved the dim Bill Lucas at all. She never
could have loved him; not that way. She had married him, she thought
now, while only pretending even to herself that she loved him.

So maybe that was why Bill Lucas had been taken from her like
that, so soon, so suddenly, leaving her with his son still to give birth
to and bring up. But leaving her also with the means of atonement—
motherhood. And with the love of his child to console and sustain
her. And with nothing else.

Such thoughts would come to her in the presence of some solemn
expression of human dependence on the supernatural Government
in which she believed. They would come to her in church. But even
in their own world at times they would seem to her as fantastic as:
Cut a window and you cut a grave. Yet the irreligious world seemed
to her unreasonable. It behaved as if willing to settle for a good deal
less than she thought human existence was worth. Some of its allure-
ments attracted the lusty young widow powerfully but she saw in it no
plausible tolerable large enough explanation for life. Such as the simple but sobering statement: *We are here to work out our salvation.*

You came into the world endowed with immortality, mortal flesh,
mind, and somewhere in the immortal soul a heart, and it was the
heart you worked out your salvation with. You did it, if you could, with
love. It was that simple, that complicated and perplexing, involved
with a world that you could see and touch, and a world invisible, intangible, unknown: that easy, that hard. It was beautiful or it was
hideous, all depending on your heart, on what you did about love. To
Arline it was austere and difficult but it was what she would expect of
infinite Goodness, and it made life reasonable, and it was large
enough, and something in her nature answered it and said that it was
true.

But all I want, she pleaded, is to find him a stepfather.

She knew that she loved her son, Bill Lucas's son, and looking at
the photographs of young women in bridal veils, she reasoned
(though it made her feel still more perfidious to Bill Lucas) that the
child *ought* to have a stepfather, one who would be good to him, one

whom he would love and admire, and by whom she might, yes, give him half-brothers and -sisters—she was only, she argued, thirty-five.

But more weeks passed, and then it was September, the twenty-first month after the grand opening of the New life, and no one came forward to be his stepfather. And he was getting bigger. A man would think twice about marrying a woman with a six-year-old son. And Billy was so conspicuous in the tavern in the evenings, and everyone knew he was her son. Poor Billy, she would think, he had no place else to go; but he did seem an obstacle to her getting him a stepfather.

September was the month she had been dreading. It marked his entrance into grade school.

He was a Big boy now, her father praised him admiringly, pretty soon he'd be taking over the place; and her mother, preparing his lunch on his first day of school, sighed: "My, it don't seem no time at all since he was a baby. Well, they have to grow up sometime, I suppose."

"Oh, Ma!" Arline said. "He's *only* six. Besides, he's been to school before, hasn't he?"

Bessie looked at her daughter, but said nothing.

Before the boy left for school with his mother, his grandmother gave a few dexterous pulls and pats to the new clothes he was wearing, said how nice he looked, kissed him, and told him to be a good boy and mind the sisters, and then she accompanied them to the tavern door and stood smiling fondly but sadly after them and waving slowly, under the sign of the Lost Dutchman.

William Lucas, Jr., set off bravely enough. As Arline had reminded her mother he had spent three years in nursery school. But when, in the parish school, he saw all the unknown Bigger children and the sisters in black and only a few small fellow beginners of his acquaintance, some of whom looked lost, his courage began to fail. When it came time for Arline to leave he clung to her, tears starting to his eyes. But Sister Humiliata, a mere girl who had the face of an angel, talked to him soothingly, took his hand, and promised to look out for him. Then he let his mother go, and he did not cry. Arline, walking home, realized that she was disappointed. She told herself that he was growing up.

She told herself that it was nothing. A little boy starting grade school: what was that? But she knew that it was one of the great benchmarks of his career. It was as big as graduation. She admitted to herself that he was really six and a half. She felt that he was emerging into the light as a person and that, as he ascended, his shadow would cover her.

She knew that she loved her son; only——

Only now she could not be sure what she would do if there came another moment like the one promised in the Willow Tree, with another Harry Fahs.

But in the same month when Billy started grade school a shudder passed over the world into which he was growing. President Truman announced that Russia too had exploded an atomic bomb.

On the third Sunday in December, special prayers were offered at St. Peter's. Not a drop of rain had fallen since spring. And the next day Billy came down with the whooping cough.

"Land," Bessie said, "what next!"

The boy was coughing in a thudding bass that shook and racked his body, and for minutes at a time could not stop, so that it seemed he would choke or go into a convulsion. The doctor prescribed a sedative and a soothing cough syrup, but there was little that could be done for him beyond making him as comfortable as possible while the cough wore itself out. Regularly he slept on the couch which had been moved into the new bedroom from the parlor, but being ill, was put into his mother's bed.

After he had fallen asleep on Christmas Eve, a seven-foot tree was brought into the parlor by his grandfather and one of the Filipino dishwashers, and set up at the direction of the women. His mother and grandmother decorated it and arranged the presents beneath. Then his grandparents put on their best clothes and, although the tavern was thronged with revelers, set off across the town to adore the Saviour born into the world again at midnight Mass.

Arline was alone in the apartment with her son.

She prepared herself for bed, entered the sickroom, softly closed the door, and without switching on the light tiptoed to the bed and looked down at him by the dim glow from the window. He was still sleeping. But there was a fretful line between his brows, his mouth was open, and his breathing sounded chesty; his face was thin and pale; he had lost weight; and the tissues of his lungs, she thought, must be inflamed and raw: the whooping cough was no joke. Suppose it weakened his lungs permanently? *What if he died?* But that was silly. All children got the whooping cough. She had been through it herself as a child . . . and now it was *her* child who had it. As she stood alone beside the sleeping boy in the darkness, with the sounds of revelry coming to her muted from the tavern, how strange that seemed.

She knelt by the bed for her night prayers.

She prayed more fervently than usual tonight because Billy was sick, and because of what was passing in her heart, and because it was the night before Christmas. *Hail Mary.* She did not feel so close to Mary as she had when a child. She was a woman now and sensible of corruption, and Mary was a woman and pure. Sometimes she thought that when God bequeathed Mary he was thinking chiefly of men— men always needed a mother and so He had given them His own to make it easier for them to come to Him. When they were too much ashamed to approach Him, they would go to her, and she would lead them to Him by the hand, and they felt safe. God knew men, all right. Notice how in church so many of them would hang far back from the tabernacle, but how they would all go right up to Mary. Arline felt drawn direct to the Sacred Heart of Jesus. When you prayed to His Sacred Heart you approached God through His love and mercy. But then you did the same thing when you approached Him through His mother; and Arline felt herself a hypocrite, and knew that into every creature's heart He saw—"Under the fig tree" or in a darkened room; and Mary, it was said, had interceded even for Judas. *. . . now and at the hour of our death.*

As she got up from her knees a pattering on the roof made her turn to the window and she saw that it was raining. It would be raining, she thought disappointedly, on Christmas. She remembered the prayers for rain, and thought: Well, we asked for it. But then of course this was the rainy season. And she remembered: *I will give thee rain in due seasons,* and for the moment was filled with hope.

She got into bed on the couch.

She lay there listening to the rain and thinking how the sun drew the water out of the oceans, lakes, and rivers, so that sometimes you could see it rising, but drew it up just so far, and held it there in clouds, and how the clouds moved inland and when the time came watered the earth again. But sometimes the rain was long overdue; and she supposed gloomily that there were deserts where it never rained at all.

Someone in the tavern was playing the piano. Staring into the dark, she listened to that, and to the rain, and to the boy's thick breathing. *Suppose he did die?* But he was not going to. . . . But someday when Billy was grown he would marry. Some girl would take him. And her parents would die. Alone! Unless . . .

The pianist began to play "Silent Night," and a few voices took up the hymn. All at once the sounds of carousal in the tavern died out temporarily, and except for the pattering rain and the boy's thick breathing, there was only the muted hymn.

Round yon Virgin Mother and Child,
Holy Infant so tender and mild. . . .

She listened. But she was not picturing the scene at the manger.
She was curiously picturing the scene in the tavern: customers,
waitresses, bartenders all turned toward the piano, all silent except
for those who were singing, some of the listeners no doubt with tears
in their eyes, especially those who had got drunk on the vigil of His
birthday—and the spotlight playing through the smoke on the face of
the Lost Dutchman.

The hymn ended, there was a round of respectful applause, and the
pianist began to rattle off "Jingle Bells."

She remembered her parents gone to Mass at midnight, and asked
herself how they would get home through the rain.

And of her mother, because of what else had been going through
her mind, she wondered: Is Ma happy? Her mother worked as hard
as ever now, perhaps harder. How much had her mother got out of life,
really? What had she wanted once? Had her mother ever been in love
with anyone else? Had her mother always loved her father, and been
loved by him, as every woman wanted to love and be loved by a husband? The thought struck Arline as indecent. But she remembered her
parents as they had come up the aisle in church on Ash Wednesday,
each with a little cross of ashes on the forehead. Symbol of mortality,
but also of penance. Sinners. And she remembered how she had inwardly giggled because that had struck her as so ridiculous in their
cases. But she knew that it was not ridiculous.

"Jingle Bells" received rousing approval in the tavern. Then the bell
of Milton Groom began to tell her it was midnight, began to toll that
it was Christmas, through the rain.

20

THE UGLY DUCKLING

Nineteen hundred and fifty! Technically, it was true, the second half
of the century would not begin till '51, and McClatchy conceded the
point when it was explained to him, but he saw nothing in it, and as

for Bessie it only put her in mind of the golden wedding party of the Healys:

"Old Mr. and Mrs. Healy lived upstairs from us when I was a girl, and they were both in their eighties, and all the relatives from miles around were going to come for their golden wedding, when at the last minute their old-maid daughter Nellie went nosing in the old family Bible and come to find out they were a year ahead of time, and if she didn't go and tell them. Oh, she was a busybody. The whole thing was postponed for a year. And one day my mother met old Hap Healy on the steps and he was crying. 'Why, what's the matter, Mr. Healy?' she says. 'Oh, Mrs. Moyles,' he says, 'I seen that old black wagon coming down the hill again without any horses.' It was the third time he'd seen it; and sure enough the year wasn't out till they were all there at his wake."

Bessie's husband was not one to be put off by a technicality. The arrival of the fifties naturally stimulated him to recitals of what he had "seen." It brought to his bar the shades of Cleveland and McKinley and Dewey and Terry Mustain and Indian Smith and old Bob Hogan and Steam Schooner Ruby and Gyp the salome dancer, and evoked from him curious outlines of history: Jim Corbett, whom he had once seen in person, knocked out by Jeffries in 1903, and Stanley Ketchel dealt the same fate by Jack Johnson at Colma six years later, the Fire, the great streetcar strike when Calhoun had brought the Easterners in and every car had been a fortress, the mysterious death of a police chief named Biggy, Halley's Comet, the *Titanic* and the *Lusitania*, the Panama-Pacific International Exposition, the bombing of the Preparedness Day parade, speakeasies, Idora Park. . . .

And Bessie, indulging one morning in recollections of her own as she and Arline sat darning in the parlor, remarked with a sigh that there were "no songs any more."

"Why, of course there are," Arline said. "There are plenty of good songs."

"Oh, they're not like the ones we used to sing."

"Like what, for instance?"

"Oh"—Bessie put her head back recollecting for a moment; then rocking her head from side to side with the tune, softly in a thin voice she began:

"*Yip I addy, I ay, I ay . . .*"

Arline gave a whoop of laughter, but her mother, half smiling, kept on singing, rocking her head, and on her mother's lips the tune sounded so pitifully merry, and her eyes were so gentle, that, for all the incongruousness of song and singer, or perhaps because of that too, and for all the absurd devilishness of the words, Arline in the next instant wanted to cry. The song struck her as more like what was sung in her own day than she would have expected, which was because the popular music of the present had turned to the past for some of its types, but she knew that her mother did not realize how "like" it was, and sung in her mother's quaint style, it seemed to be resurrected from the dead. What did it mean to her mother? Why had she chosen this one? With whom had she sung it? What had she looked like then?

> "*Sing of joy, sing of bliss*
> *Home was never like this.*
> *Y-ip I addy, I ay.*"

"Oh-h, dear," Bessie laughed, "that was one of 'em. We used to sing that one when I was a girl."

Arline, with tears in her eyes, jumped up and kissed her, saying "Dear Ma!" out of a painfully loving, inarticulate desire to protect her mother from all that had come into the room with the song, and out of a need for closeness with her mother in the presence of those great sorry things that made the two women sisters. She would never forget her mother's singing that foolish song of the first decade of the century.

Indeed, no one was waiting till the second half of the century should really begin. As the fifties opened people everywhere were gazing back to 1900 and beyond; you would hear them telling one another how the world had changed. Historians, statesmen, and philosophers varied the theme: they spoke of the bewildering acceleration of the rate of change: they showed how in less than a lifetime the world had changed more than it had previously changed since Columbus. When you listened it sounded curiously as if they had presentiments of the black wagon of Mr. Healy descending the hill without any horses.

As the fifties opened the peoples of the earth were simplifying themselves into two antagonists, each armed with Excalibur. At home there were rumors and accusations of traitorous activities in high places in the government, and there had been exposures of graft in the government and in the Army, and the insane asylums were overcrowded, and the telephone books offered lengthening lists of psychiatrists, and the police blotters discovered increasing numbers of drunkards, and the divorce rate was roughly one to every four marriages, and the courts were alarmed about the extensiveness of depravity among children, and Business was exceedingly busy, and jobs were plentiful, and on the last day of January, President Truman announced that he had directed the Atomic Energy Commission to manufacture and explode, if possible, the hydrogen bomb.

That was the state of the world and of the Union when in February there entered Arline's life a face.

The customer was of medium height and perhaps in his late thirties. The hair always looked as if it had been combed by a kind of dead reckoning, but the whole figure gave an impression of neatness, due perhaps to the tab collars and the fit of the quiet suits, to the quick precision of the movements, and to the narrow symmetrical structure and alert intelligence of the face. The hair was brown, short, tough, and dry. The skin was tanned, and the light gray eyes in contrast were like sudden lights. They had laughter lines at the corners. And the plane of the forehead extended unbroken to the tip of the nose. An unusual and, she thought, attractive face.

When he came to the tavern he usually sat among the veteran painters, but he did not appear to be one of them. Arline thought that he looked like a city man. She did not know his name. He had never shown the slightest interest in her until this evening.

It was late and she was tired. A yawn overtook her as she stood inactive just inside the tavern door, and she stretched. Suddenly she saw those two gray lights turned full upon her. They brought her to herself with a shock. Then his gaze moved away. But several times afterward she saw him looking at her. It was not the way Harry Fahs had looked at her. There was no ribald grin in it—it made no use at all of the laughter creases around the eyes; and there was no boldness in it, nor challenging male vanity. His eyes appeared as impersonal as two gray lights. But they embarrassed and annoyed her.

When next he came to the tavern, a few weeks later, repeatedly again she saw him looking at her in the same way; and again the next time. Once, she confronted him with an expression that demanded irritably: What is it? He gave a quick little smile and nodded, which conveyed his apologies but implied that he had not been conscious that his eyes were on her, and then he turned to his bar companion and went on talking.

She was not deceived. Yet he had never shown any interest in her till that other night, and there were so many women in the tavern whom she thought more attractive than herself, and he never spoke to her.

One night in March he was sitting in a booth with Bo Satterfy. Phyllis, their waitress, after serving them and lingering to talk, sauntered over to Arline, who was standing where the man with the gray eyes could not see her without turning around. Arline began the conversation jokingly as Phyllis came up idly folding her arms:

"Going to let Bo Satterfy take you home tonight?"

Phyllis glanced at her; then with a careless laugh: "I might."

Instantly Arline suspected that Bo Satterfy had taken Phyllis home before, and then Phyllis perceived that she had been wrong in supposing from the question that Arline already knew he had.

Arline said: "Oh, Phyl! Have you let him before?"

"Oh," Phyllis shrugged, "he's lonesome."

"He's married!"

"*Lots* of people are married. I was married too, wasn't I?" Phyllis's little mouth looked disgusted; she lifted the forepart of one folded arm and slapped the air above the other elbow with her hand. "He's married to a bitch."

"Did he say that?"

"*I* said it. He's a sweet guy." Phyllis looked into space and swayed on her crossed ankles. "I feel kind of sorry for him—you know? He likes to read poetry and play the banjo." Then she laughed.

All of which was interesting, but it was leading Arline away from the information she wanted. She looked at Satterfy. "He always comes alone." Then she asked: "Who's that sitting with him?"

"Who, the Professor?"

"*Pro*fessor?"

"Sure; didn't you know? He's a prof at Fremont." Dancing-eyed, Phyllis clucked twice, and winked. "Cute, huh?" She laughed again. "Don't worry—he's the uncooperative type."

Arline did not yet know his name or whether he was married or anything else about him, but she was glad that just then Phyllis was called away.

A professor at Fremont Institute: Arline could hardly believe it. She had always thought of professors as elderly, but this one was young and quick and attractive, and he always looked at *her*. It was a wonder to Arline that she could attract a professor, a young professor. But Phyllis's "Don't worry—he's the uncooperative type" made it almost incredible to her, sounding as though Phyllis herself had tried to attract him and failed. Maybe, Arline thought, the way he looks at me only shows that he's . . . absent-minded. Maybe he really doesn't see me at all. But no, she knew better than that. Maybe the reason he never spoke to her was that, being a professor, he was . . . shy.

And when at midnight Phyllis left, sure enough, with Bo Satterfy, Arline felt no resentment. All she thought was:

That little devil'll get hurt again if she doesn't watch out.

It was Phyllis's night off, a Monday night in April. Arline had sat down at a cleared table in a booth, facing the door, so that she did not see him coming from the men's room. He stopped beside her in an attitude of mock formality, his heels together, his body bent slightly forward from the hips, his gray eyes crinkled, and said:

"Miss McEndymion, I believe."

She flushed a shade, correcting him with a smile: "McClatchy." She did not want to say Mrs. Lucas.

"Tom Heath—friend of your father's," he said, and she saw that he was not entirely sober. "May I?" All at once he sat down opposite her and folded his arms on the table and was facing her with an impudent smile.

She said: "Well! Come in!"

He said: "It's my birthday and you remind me of a woman."

"Not really!"

"No, I mean it. Magnificent. Have you ever been in the jungle?"

"The jungle!" She laughed. "No, Professor, I never have."

"Who told you I was a professor?"

"Well, aren't you?"

"We were discussing this woman."

"We were?"

"Definitely."

"Oh."

"Yes." He sat back against the booth, his hands on the edge of the table, and said: "Now, then. The School of Forestry of the University of the Philippines is situated at the foot of a hill that was once a volcano. . . ."

She laughed. "Is that what you teach?"

"What? No." He waved aside the interruption. "Back of the college, on the slope of the hill, is an arboretum which merges farther up with the jungle. The jungle. Trees that look as if they've writhed up out of the earth in pain. Overhanging palms. Giant ferns. Elephant's ears. Tangled vines. Thick, that jungle. And deadly." He folded his arms on the table again and leaned on them, looking her in the eyes. "Trees poisonous to the touch. Plants with a sting like the bite of a snake. Plants that trap insects and eat them. Insects that eat one another. Predatory. Voracious. Walk in the jungle and the first thing you know a leech has fastened itself to your skin."

She made a face. "*Please*, Professor."

"Tom."

"*Are* you a professor or aren't you?"

He shook his head. "Mere instructor."

"Instructor? At Fremont?"

He nodded. "Addressed as Mister there; here, Tom."

"What do you teach?"

"Say: 'What do you teach, Tom?'"

She laughed. "What do you teach, Tom?"

"Physics, Arline. May I continue?"

She thought: He knows my name. She was impressed that he did teach at Fremont, and pleased that he wanted her to call him Tom. But the alcohol on his tongue made her uneasy. On the other hand she was curious about the woman of whom she reminded him, and she thought that if he were sober he might not be talking to her at all. She shrugged. "Go ahead."

"Yes. Well. You reach the top of the hill, go down, and you're on level ground. You're walking on the crater of the sleeping volcano. All around you is the green forest of the jungle. You see? Hot. Humid. The earth is soft, alive with insects and bacteria, renewing itself with humus, with death. And clinging to the trees are parasites, epiphytes. All around you, birth, growth, predacity, death, and decay: birth for procreation, death for birth again: roaring at you like the surf, like the surf in a seashell that you hold to your ear. . . ."

She was thinking: What a line! She was looking at his narrow brown face with its unindented nose, his light gray eyes, his short tough untidy brown hair, his tab collar, and finding him handsome, but she was thinking that this was the queerest approach she had ever heard. His eyes were not smiling now. He was saying: "You have the feeling that the jungle is all of a piece, alive, and watching you. And then in the thickest part of it you come onto a pond of boiling mud. Simmering on the fires below. The jungle overhangs it all round. Hides it from the sky. Droops down and almost touches it. The air is full of its evaporation. And you don't hear the seashell any more. Here and there on the pond a bubble bursts; now and then from the banks a little geyser rises, and falls again. The steam drifts off. And you hear the slow irregular dripping of water from the overhanging leaves onto the surface of the pond. There is not another sound."

She gave a little shiver. "Terrible."

"Yes. It is. Terrible. When Japan invaded the island the American members of the college faculty and their wives and children went up there. Hid in the undergrowth behind that cauldron, among the leeches. And sometimes the Japanese soldiers would come up to see it, and the Americans would be crouching in the jungle on the other side. And the mothers would hold their children tight and put their hands over their mouths to keep them absolutely still."

"Oh, how awful! Were you there?"

"No. Three years later."

"What happened to them?"

"Came out and gave themselves up."

"And then what?"

"Imprisoned, of course."

"Oh, the poor things."

He waved them away. "Not talking about them."

"What?"

"Don't interrupt. The jungle. Nature dramatized, epitomized, made comprehensible. Listen." Leaning forward on his folded arms and looking into her eyes, he said: "The narra tree. A giant. King of the jungle. One day a seed, a little seed, falls out of the wind, falls on the narra tree. From the seed a plant begins, a vine, a tender vine which draws its food out of the air. It twines its tendrils around the trunk and branches of the tree. And grows. It covers the tree. And from the lower branches of the tree it drops its tendrils down. They hang from the branches of the tree. Grow longer. Reach the ground. Take root. Out of the ground they draw strength for the whole vine. They expand and support the vine. And the tendrils twined around the tree expand into huge coils that have the tree in a death grip. They strangle the tree. The narra dies. It dies but it can't fall. It disintegrates in the coils that killed it. And the coils that hold the trunk fuse and become the trunk of another tree that puts forth branches of its own that sprout leaves of their own. The giant no longer exists, but in its place stands another tree, a gigantic wild fig. The natives call it the baléte tree."

During this monologue, spoken in a low intense voice, his eyes never leaving hers, the color in her face had deepened. It was clear to her that natural history was not the subject of his discourse.

Then his eyes crinkled, but without really smiling, and he said: "That's all."

She did not ask him to explain. She gave a little mirthless laugh and said: "Very interesting, I'm sure," getting up from the table.

He looked surprised. "What's the matter?"

"I'm off duty now."

"Stay and have a drink with me."

"No, thanks."

"Oh, sit down—please."

"Some other time."

"Arline!"

"Goodnight."

She went to bed. But she could not sleep.

She lay wide awake, seeing and hearing him again. She reasoned that the alcohol had given him a compulsion to tell her that he wanted her, and a confused notion of how to be subtle about it. Any sailor could have done better. Maybe he didn't know how to talk to women about such things anyway. But she still felt the force of his assault.

She was lying on her back, open-eyed, hearing with the third ear the gentle breathing of the boy on the couch, and half-conscious of her own deep, slow, powerful breathing.

She lay for a long time thinking over the riddle of what Tom Heath had seen in the jungle.

21

JUSTICE AND MERCY

"They *got* him," her father shouted. It was the first morning of May. Arline was making her bed and her excited father was coming across the parlor toward the open doorway of the bedroom, his breakfast *Examiner* thrust out before him. "They got that fellow they been after for killing the cop! But he claims the girl done it."

"The *girl?*"

"He claims he was doing the driving. Here."—Her father pointed out the story in the newspaper.

She read that Raymond Dirigo had been arrested in a raid on a pool hall in Tulsa, Oklahoma, not for murder but for possession of a gun and marijuana cigarettes, and identified through his fingerprints after he had given the police an alias, and that his defense in the murder case was "based on the contention his girl accomplice could not operate an automobile."

"Oh, that's ridiculous!" she said.

"Did you——"

"Just a minute."—She was reading on. Bessie entered the parlor and McClatchy called out the news to her. Exclaiming, she came into the bedroom as Arline was finishing the story. Dirigo said that he had taken the wheel of the getaway car and given his gun to Nancy Croan, telling her "just to keep him off us." He said that *she* had killed Harry Fahs. But the sheriff of Morera County did not believe him. Raymond Dirigo was to be extradited and tried for murder. Arline raised her eyes and found her mother looking at her with compassion.

She knew that she would have to testify.

That afternoon Lee Braden and another deputy came to see her.

Braden asked: "Who was driving the car?"

"The girl was."

"You saw that, did you?"

"No, I didn't see it. Nobody saw it but Harry Fahs."

"Then how do you know the girl was driving?"

"Harry said she was. Or somebody did, and it must have been Harry because he was the only one who saw it."

The deputies looked at each other. Braden told her: "That's not good enough, Mrs. Lucas. We want you to be sure it was Harry."

"Well . . ." She tried to concentrate: Harry Fahs coming back through the door of the Willow Tree and going to the telephone on that night twenty-nine months before. Suddenly she remembered something else. "Wait a minute! Harry said he shot 'him'—a man. Yes, I'm sure that's what he said, because I remember I thought the boy was the one who was wounded. Everybody did. And wasn't that the way it was in the papers?"

"Our report says Harry *thought* he hit him," Braden told her with a frown. "But it says 'he' shot Harry. You remember Harry saying that?"

"Well, I guess so. I know I never thought it was the girl who shot Harry."

"At the inquest you testified Harry told you: '*He* just winged me.'"

"Oh—yes! I remember."

"Good. Now the report says the girl was driving. Try to remember about that. Didn't Harry say the girl was driving?"

"He must have. I know I thought she was driving. I still think she was. . . . Didn't she have a license?"

"We don't know that yet."

"But he could have taught her anyhow, couldn't he? And weren't her fingerprints on the wheel?"

The second deputy said: "He wiped 'em off."

"Oh. Then . . . weren't there *any* fingerprints on the wheel?"

Braden said: "The wheel was clean as a whistle."

"I see. And that makes it look like he was driving, doesn't it? I mean because he was wearing gloves."

The second deputy said: "There would have been prints somewhere. The job was too clean."

"Oh."

"Look, Mrs. Lucas," Braden said. "You want to see him convicted, don't you?"

"If he's guilty."

"*If* he's guilty?" the second deputy said. "We know he's guilty. He's guilty of the girl's death, too."

"He certainly is! Oh, when I think how he left her to die in that boathouse!"

Braden said: "But he'll be tried for killing Harry Fahs—murder in the first degree. And now he's trying to pin that on her. . . ."

"Oh, I know. It's contemptible."

"He's down there," Braden continued, "in Tulsa thinking he can pin it on her and maybe get off with prison. But Harry said it was him that shot him. And he said the girl was driving. Now you try to get that straight in your mind before the district attorney talks to you."

"I'll do anything I can," Arline promised.

"Thank you, Mrs. Lucas," Braden said. "And don't do any outside talking. You're an important witness in this case."

The deputies left.

So at last it had come. A thousand miles away and nearly two years and a half later it had overtaken the kid, the cowardly, she thought, contemptible kid, overtaken him as if by accident, by means of a blind police raid and some marijuana cigarettes, and she would be going to court to accuse him. However inconclusive the testimony she could give, her responsibility weighed on Arline heavily. And there was something else. The case disturbed her for reasons that went beyond Raymond Dirigo and Harry Fahs and Nancy Croan and the state, reasons that as yet were not clear to her, and these subtly influenced her thinking about it. To Arline it seemed a very cloudy and complicated case indeed.

In the first place the kid had fired at Harry Fahs because Harry Fahs was firing at him, had fired not because he was a murderer, she still reasoned, but because he was a robber in fear of his life; and in the second place Harry Fahs had not *died* of a bullet in the shoulder but of the movement of the clot, the little clot that hours after the shooting had moved from the wound into the pulmonary artery. A man guilty of an attempt at armed robbery had been forced, by danger and fear, into a gunfight, and then had been guilty also of shooting a man in the shoulder, but on the next morning he had been turned into a murderer in the eyes of the law, and so made liable to the penalty of death, by an improbable miscarriage in the process of healing. In the case of Harry Fahs it was as if the kid had been unable to help himself from the moment he walked into the Willow Tree to rob at the point of a gun; it was almost as if he were a murderer by accident. But poor little Nancy Croan's life might have been saved if the kid had taken her to a doctor, and instead of doing that he had abandoned her. (He had even stolen her handbag!) He had put his own safety above the life of his girl, and run away, and that was why she had died. Alone! Yet Harry Fahs had been the one who had shot her. And the certainty that Harry Fahs had said that he had shot "him" nagged at Arline.

If Harry Fahs had been wrong about which of the two he had shot, might he also have been wrong about which he had seen driving? No, she did not see how he could have been wrong about that. But now it struck her that a person shot while frantically driving a getaway car would very likely lose control of it, especially if the person were an inexperienced driver and a girl. But Harry Fahs had said that the girl was driving; and if he had seen a girl in the car with the kid he must have seen which was in the driver's seat, mustn't he? But mustn't he also have known which was shooting at him, and which he was shooting at, and whether the one who appeared to be hit by his bullet was the one he had aimed at or the other one, the driver or the passenger, the boy or the girl?

But suppose—suppose Harry Fahs had suddenly found himself in a gunfight with a girl, and the girl had shot him, and he had shot the girl, and he had not made any mistake about it at all! Mightn't a man like Harry Fahs have wanted people to think he had mistaken the girl for the kid?

Suppose Harry Fahs had lied!

Early one evening she was at her post near the door of the tavern when Tom Heath came in.

"The very person I want to see," he said. "Let me buy you that drink I owe you."

She met his eyes with amiable comprehension in her own, and contradicted him: "You don't owe me any drink."

"But I want you to have one with me."

"I can't."

"Why not?"

"I'm on duty."

"Last time it was because you were off duty."

"No it wasn't."

"Meaning I'd had too many; I know. It was my birthday. Tonight it isn't. Will you show me to a quiet table for two?"

"Are you expecting someone?"

"Yes. A woman."

Smiling faintly, she led him to a table. He pulled out a chair for her, and with the same little ironic smile she declined it. "No, really."

"But I want to ask you something."

"What do you want to ask me?"

"Will you sit down for just a minute?"

"I can't."

He sighed. "Well, then"—he pushed the chair in. "There's a picture I want to paint."

"You? I didn't know you were a painter."

"Sunday painter. But I think I can get a real picture out of you, Arline."

"*Me?*"

"*You.*"

She gave a short derisive laugh, and left him.

He did not call after her, but as she walked away he gazed at her broad back. Then he turned and went to the bar.

She did not believe that anyone would want to paint Arline Mc-Clatchy, and the idea that Tom Heath thought he could use her cheaply, in the way Harry Fahs would have done, was far more offensive to her than it would have been if Tom Heath were a policeman. But at the same time she was disappointed. He had said that he wanted to ask her something. If after his indirect apology for his behavior at their first meeting he had asked her to go dancing some evening, or out somewhere for dinner, she might have agreed. She told herself bitterly that he must not know anything about women at all.

Billy was plunking at the keys of the bar piano.

"Billy, you know you're not allowed on this side."

"I'm not doing nothing."

"Never mind. You go in and get ready for bed."

"It's not tiiiiime yet."

"Well, that's what you get for disobeying. Go on."

"No! It's too earrrrrly."

Several of the bar customers had turned around, amused. Arline insisted, but had to lead him off sternly by the hand. They were halfway to the back apartment before she realized that Tom Heath might be seeing her in the role of mother. She kept herself from glancing around, so she never knew. But in a little while he left the tavern without pursuing his request.

May was the month of the Blessed Virgin, and on its second Sunday, which was Mother's Day, Billy received his first Communion. He had reached the age of reason.

All the McClatchys were there. So were the families of the other children whom the sisters of St. Peter's School had been instructing for months in the mystery and ritual of the Sacrament. The little girls, in white dresses and bridal veils, occupied the first three pews on the right of the center aisle of the church; the boys, in blue flannel, the first three pews on the left; and all the children looked extraordinarily good.

Father Cobb spoke to them from the pulpit. He told them the famous story of Napoleon—how, looking back over a career that had shaken the world, the Emperor of the French had called the day of his first Communion the happiest day of his life. Not one of his victories, not the moment when he had crowned himself Emperor, not all his worldly glories together had given Napoleon such happiness as he had known when he had first received his God and Saviour; and in the end Napoleon's vainglorious career had brought him woe and bitterness. Today it was the children's turn to begin receiving our Lord; not, Father Cobb reminded them gently, because of their merits, but only because He loved them so. The innocence of their immortal souls was a gift from God that until now they had been incapable of destroying. Now they had the responsibility of preserving it. Their lives stretched out before them; the ways of the world were not the ways of God; many temptations and trials awaited them. If, by God's grace, and with greater wisdom than Napoleon's, they preserved their innocence all their lives, then they would be heroes, then they would be saints. Jesus would always be there to help them. Let them remember His invitation: *Come to me, all you that labour, and are burdened, and I will refresh you*; let them always stay close to Him in the Sacrament of His love. Father Cobb closed his sermon to the children with the quotation that closed all his sermons: "And on the last day may our Lord say to you: *Come, ye blessed of my Father, possess you the kingdom prepared for you from the foundation of the world.*" Making the Sign of the Cross over them, the old priest gave them his blessing.

And when the time came, the first communicants filed, first the girls, then the boys, one by one, reverently, with hands joined in front of their breasts and pointing to heaven, and with eyes downcast, through the central opening in the communion railing and up to the top step but one of the altar, and received the Host on their tongues, and turned, and filed back to their places, and knelt, and bowed their heads, and with closed eyes adored, while the school choir of mixed sopranos sang "O Lord, I am not worthy" and then "On this day, O beautiful mother." The grownups watched through mists.

And after Mass the children filed, three feet apart, again with joined hands and lowered eyes, up the aisle to the front door. But there was some interruption and the procession halted. In one of the pews stood two boys smiling at William Lucas and whispering together. Hearing the whispers, he covertly looked sidewise and saw them. It was too much. He broke out in a grin. His mother, watching him, knew well enough that it was only childlike, but because of her state of mind it stirred vague fears in her. Then the procession moved on. The children were trooped to the front steps of the school, where a photographer began taking pictures of them. Their relatives followed. Bessie began to cry again.

"I can't help it," she said, "he has to work out his own salvation now and he's so *little*."

The words gave Arline a shock, although she had been thinking along the same lines; shocked her indeed for that reason. During the sermon she had remembered, but imperfectly, a passage of Scripture not mentioned by the priest: Better that you should be thrown into the sea with a millstone around your neck than that you should scandalize a little one.

That week Raymond Dirigo was brought from Oklahoma to San Javier by Lee Braden, and there was more about the murder case in the newspapers.

So far as her father knew, they reported, Nancy Croan had never driven an automobile up to the time of her leaving home. But the father had belittled that admission with the same comment Arline had made: Raymond Dirigo could have taught his daughter to drive. The father recommended that Raymond Dirigo be tarred, feathered, and hanged. But Emmett Croan had been "done with that girl from the day she left." Arline could not conceive of such a father. She thought: No wonder his daughter ran away. If he'd been a good father to her she might still be alive. "If" again. Inches. Minutes. Years! Moments: *roaring at you like the surf in a seashell that you hold to your ear.*

And Raymond Dirigo, whom the newspapers described as good-looking and dapper, said that he had brought the girl to California because she asked him to. They had left Nebraska in a stolen car, and to throw off pursuit had abandoned that car for another in Salt Lake City, and the second stolen car for a third in Placerville. But that night he had not known that one of her bullets had hit the man, he said, or that the man was a policeman. He told of a wild flight in the car with

Nancy Croan unconscious beside him, of coming upon the boat-house, and of carrying her inside. All that night he had sat with her in the dark, telling himself that she was dying and that a doctor could not save her. By morning he had resolved to bring a doctor to her. But in the morning he had listened to a news broadcast over the car's radio. He had heard that he was being hunted for murder, for the murder of a policeman. "I wasn't the one—she was the one," the *Examiner* quoted him as saying. "I figured if she lived they might kill her anyhow; but she was dying, so I might never be able to prove it was her, and they'd kill me." Far down the beach he had seen some fishermen. "I guess I lost my head." He had fled on foot, caught a bus——

By compass and star, current and storm, by ship and by whale. And the mothers would hold their children tight and put their hands over their mouths to keep them absolutely still.

Then Braden came again. He drove her to the county seat, and she met the district attorney, a tall robust man with gray hair and a florid face. His name was Willard. He handed her a transcript of the testimony she had given at the inquest, and asked her to read it. Seated in front of his desk, she did; then he questioned her about the holdup and shooting. He asked whether she had fainted, and when she said she had not, congratulated her. Sometimes, he said, the trouble with women witnesses in such cases was that they had gone to pieces and did not remember clearly. And sometimes on the stand, he added, they were timid about remembering. He hoped, with a smile, that Arline was not going to be a timid witness. She said that she would do her best. He thanked her and said that without the co-operation of the public it was often impossible to bring criminals to justice. He spoke of Raymond Dirigo as a murderer.

"Now," he reminded her, "you said you could recognize Dirigo by his voice."

"Well, it was a long time ago, of course——"

"Yes, and at first I didn't believe you could do it, but when I heard him talk I changed my mind. He has a very distinctive voice, hasn't he?"

"Well, I don't know. . . ."

"Oh, yes. That flat throaty quality."

"I remember he talked very tough."

"Yes, that too. Excellent. Now. We'll see how good you really are."

He said that he was going to take her into the next office and leave her alone. First, she was to try to recall the holdup man's voice exactly. Then he would have Raymond Dirigo brought into his office. The door would be open, but Dirigo would not know she was behind it. She was to listen to him talk. She was to try to associate the voice with the man she had seen wearing the handkerchief over his face—the voice with the image. Was she willing?

She did not ask why, if Raymond Dirigo admitted the holdup, it mattered whether she could recognize his voice. She conscientiously accepted her duty as it was presented to her. She said that she was willing. And Willard led her into a small office adjoining. It was unoccupied. He seated her in a chair behind the door. He went out, leaving the door slightly ajar. For five minutes she sat recalling the kid and, to the best of her ability, what he had said and how it had sounded. Willard returned and asked whether she was ready. She said she was. He left again. Arline was tense. After a moment she heard another door to his inner office open, and voices, the voices of Willard and Braden, and then the voice of one they called Dirigo.

At first the Dirigo voice was low and laconic, a young voice, buried deep in the throat, and surly. It answered questions about the gun. It said:

"Threw it away."

Where had he thrown it?

"Ina field."

A field near the boathouse?

"No."

Where, then?

"Donno."

Then Willard sharply: "Speak up! What are you afraid of? Nobody's going to hit you."

Mumble: "Not afraid."

"No? What are you cowering in that chair for? You look scared stiff. Why, I thought you were tough." And Willard laughed. "Come on, stand up."

Then Braden: "Stand up!"

And Willard: "All right. Over by that door. That's it. Now show us how you held up that place. What did you say?"

"Said: ''S a stickup.' "

A burst of laughter from Willard. "*That* way? Is that the way you said it?"

"Naw, not that way. ''*S a stickup!*' "

So Willard badgered the young man into talking tough. And Arline knew that the voice was the voice of the kid. How she knew may have been debatable. She had of course been certain beforehand that Dirigo was the kid, for he had admitted the holdup, he had told about the boathouse and about Nancy Croan, and his fingerprints matched those the officers had found; then the district attorney had assured her that the voice was distinctive, and had deprecated women witnesses and challenged her memory, and now Dirigo, prompted by Willard, was telling what had happened in the Willow Tree. But as she sat listening with closed eyes, holding in her mind the image of the robber, she was convinced that the voice she was hearing now was the robber's voice. And she thought: I've got to tell.

Willard returned and closed the door. "Well?"

"Yes," she said. "He's the one."

Willard said that this might prove invaluable. Then he asked her to confront Raymond Dirigo and repeat her identification.

"Do I have to do that?"

"Are you afraid?"

"No. If I have to, I'll do it."

"Good. I want you to look at him and say exactly what you said to me: 'He's the one.' No more. Have you got that?"

She said she had. He left her again, closing the door, and she waited nervously.

Then he returned and took her into the other office.

It startled her to see the prisoner wearing a handkerchief mask and a hat, just as on that night. His hands were cuffed together in front of him. The deputy stood beside him. Her heart was thumping as the district attorney led her straight up to him, saying: "Well, Dirigo, you've seen this lady before, haven't you?"

Then she was face to face with him, and if there had been any doubt in her mind that this was the kid it would have disappeared. His black eyes were bright with alarm. In answer to Willard's question he gave his head a shake and said: "No."

"Oh, I think you have," Willard said. "She's seen you before. She remembers you perfectly, don't you, Mrs. Lucas? Take another good look at him. Is he the one?"

The district attorney had talked too much. The black eyes had begun leaping meaningfully up and down between her eyes and her throat, her hand had gone to her throat, and as Willard finished speaking a sensation as if she had touched an electric wire went through her body when her fingers found the small gold cross that she was wearing. She suddenly turned and walked to the window. At the window she turned back. Willard's eyes and tone tried to enforce his will. "Well, Mrs. Lucas?"

She said to the prisoner: "I'm sorry—I have to." And to Willard: "Yes, he's the one."

"Thank you, Mrs. Lucas. All right," to Braden, "that wraps up the case. Take him out."

The deputy removed the handkerchief from the prisoner's face. It was a dark attractive boyish face but it wore an expression of desperate thought, the eyes fixed on the floor but focused inward. Braden took him by the arm. "Come on."

Dirigo resisted. "Wait." He looked at Willard. They saw him swallow. "Suppose . . . I mean . . . what'll happen if I say I did it?"

"If you confess?" Willard said, and sighed. "Frankly, Dirigo, I'd rather you didn't. But the law does give you that opportunity."

All at once Arline realized what had happened. She blurted: "I didn't see you shoot him."

Willard said: "That's all, Mrs. Lucas."

"No! I just said he was the holdup man." She told the kid: "I didn't see the shooting. Nobody did."

"We've got enough on him to send him to the gas chamber," Willard shot back. "Dirigo, the only chance you've got is to throw yourself on the mercy of the Court. Is that what you want to do?"

Relief had spread over Raymond Dirigo's face, then he had dropped his gaze to the floor again. "No."

Willard glared at him, the muscles of his jaw working. "Good— good! I want to see you get all that's coming to you." He gestured to Braden. Braden left with the prisoner. Willard turned on Arline. He was furious. "Mrs. Lucas, you had no right to interfere."

She looked him defiantly in the eyes. "It was a trick."

"It was a trap for a guilty man. An innocent man wouldn't have fallen into it."

She realized that he was right. Raymond Dirigo had shot Harry Fahs. He had shot Harry Fahs and was trying to save his own life by blaming the shooting on the girl whom he had left to die, and he had tried to protect that cowardly slander of the dead by asking Arline in Christ's name to lie for him, and then had turned away from the Cross and grasped, instead, a straw, the little straw that she had held out to him.

But she thought afterward that she had been right in not letting the district attorney trick him. He had to do it of his own free will or it would not be any good. The district attorney had tried to cheat him of his birthright as a human being, his highest right on earth: the right to make the choice. He was a man and entitled to the truth.

A few days later she testified briefly before the Grand Jury, and Raymond Dirigo was indicted for murder in the first degree. The trial was set for August.

22

HEATH

For a long time there had been that feeling in the air, and in various ways it was affecting conduct and behavior. It was as if everyone expected something to happen. Something terrible. Like a cataclysm.

Then in June the Korean War broke out; and suddenly American troops, fighting under the flag of the United Nations, under the command of General MacArthur, were retreating down an East Asian peninsula before a communist native army which Russia had trained and equipped and was advising in the field, and it looked as if they would be driven into the sea, it looked as if this might be the beginning of that third world war. There had been no real peace for eleven years, and little sense of security, real or not, for twenty-one. Now the country's leaders doubted whether either would come again for another generation, if indeed man survived that long. Cause enough for anxiety, particularly among boys casting about for starts in life, and girls coming of age to marry. At times the outlook afflicted even mothers of the small.

In a few years, she would think, even Billy might be going to war as his father had; like his father he might be killed before his future really began. And she would think how generations came and fought their wars and vanished, leaving the earth to other populations, other wars; she would remember the face on the wall behind her father's bar, and gaze into darkness after the mysterious generations that were gone.

In June too her son had finished the first grade, and in July he took another step in the world, his first away from home and family. The parents of one of his school friends, Albert Kramer, invited him to their cottage at Clear Lake, and Arline let him go. No sooner had he left than she regretted it. *What if he drowned?* She knew it was foolish to worry that way. She worried all the same, especially at night when she had got into bed and the couch was empty. She had told herself that because his future seemed so gloomy and because he was "not even having a normal childhood" she ought to let him go. Now, in bed, she would question whether she had been honest with herself, honest with him. She would think of Tom Heath. And while her son was away she met Tom Heath at the fair.

The Morera Art Fair was the latest promotion of Rover Kinney. The bearded young man had heard of the bazaar that Mrs. Frederick Lewis Nichols of San Francisco gave each year on her old country estate on the Choquali road for the benefit of a charity hospital. The residence on this estate had burned down long ago and never been replaced; there remained the gatekeeper's lodge, the garage, the stables, a pergola, and twenty acres of land, and under some trees Mrs. Nichols had installed wooden tables and benches for use at the bazaar. All this had inspired Kinney, and on hearing of the cause of the veteran painters, the old lady had charitably consented to lend her property for the event, which he hoped to make an annual one for the benefit, chiefly, of himself.

He had organized the veteran painters into committees so that the hard work of organizing the two-day fair was done by his clients; he sold them the privilege with exhibition space, and they agreed to pay him ten per cent commission on all sales of their art to the public. He sold space also to several business firms, including a plumbing company. He sold a parking concession on the property. He sold a hot dog and soft drink concession. He got up a program that was to sell for a quarter; it was filled with advertising solicited by members of the ways and means committee in the spirit of raising funds for expenses, and one page of it advertised the Lost Dutchman Tavern.

Dan McClatchy was as enthusiastic about the project as anyone, and when the Silvestros proposed a picnic he suggested that they have it at the fair. So on opening day he and his wife and daughter and the Silvestros attended. Bessie had insisted on supplying the lunch because they were going in the Silvestros' car; and her husband took a case of beer on ice, and Mr. Silvestro a demijohn of wine.

They drove onto the Nichols estate just before noon that Saturday; a large leisurely crowd was already there. They left the provisions locked in the trunk of the car, McClatchy bought programs, and for an hour before lunch they roved the fields of art, looking at pottery, woodcarving, a photography exhibit, costume jewelry, handloomed cloth, and the Bathroom Beautiful; and wandering through a grotto of statuary, they came on Noel Ames. The fat man was alone and in his shirtsleeves, his jacket over his arm. He appeared surprised but delighted to see them, and when Bessie invited him to lunch with them he accepted heartily.

They picnicked at one of the long tables under the trees. Seeing the art critic, Kinney came over, bringing Rita Buckley; they too were persuaded to taste a little something. Then Heath was passing by, and to Arline's embarrassment her father seized him, introducing him to Ames as one of his most distinguished customers: "He's a science professor at Fremont."

The brown-faced slim and agile Heath was wearing gray slacks and a Hawaiian sports shirt. "Instructor," he corrected McClatchy, smiling as he shook hands with Ames. He was presented to the Silvestros. He greeted Arline with a friendly "How are you today?" as if their acquaintance were of a merely cordial and impersonal nature, and spoke to Kinney and Rita, whom he knew also. Then McClatchy was pressing a can of beer on him, and Bessie had another paper plate out and was asking him if he liked stuffed egg and potato salad, and Tom Heath was yielding to their entreaties. Arline was uncomfortable. But seated across the table, Heath entered into the general talk. It was about the food and the fair and the weather. Then it turned to the war, and Ames asked him:

"Do you think the H-bomb can be made?"

Heath said he would like to think that it could not.

Rita looked at Heath with a furrow of concern between her black part-Indian eyes and asked if it was true that the bomb might start a chain reaction that would consume all the hydrogen on earth.

Heath smiled at this rumor. "No. That's impossible. But a war fought with the H-bomb," he said, "could charge the earth's atmosphere with enough radioactivity to kill every living thing—that's not impossible."

"Goodnight is that a fact!" McClatchy said, putting down his beer; and Bessie shuddered and Mrs. Silvestro ejaculated in Italian.

"You see?" Heath said to Ames, referring to their surprise. "They don't know. That's the trouble. If the people knew what forces we were dealing with here we could outlaw war." He spoke with the earnestness of the crusader, tapping the table. "The people have got to be educated. That's what Urey of Chicago has been shouting about."

"By golly," McClatchy said, "I second the motion. How does it work?"

Arline protested: "Oh, Dad!"

"Well, we ought to know. You ought to know yourself how it works. You wouldn't know what hit you."

"Thatsa right!" Mr. Silvestro said.

"But——"

"You pay attention," her father said. "Go right ahead, Mr. Heath."

Noel Ames was shaking with laughter. He said to Heath: "Go ahead, give it a whirl."

Heath laughed; but feeling perhaps that he owed something to the public after what he had just said, he attempted a simple explanation. Matter and energy were interchangeable. All matter was composed of basic substances called elements. An atom was the smallest piece of an element. The trick was to convert parts of countless atoms into energy in one big explosion. In the A-bomb it was done by splitting the centers of the atoms; in the H-bomb it would be done by fusing atoms of one element into atoms of another element, assuming a way could be found to set the H-bomb off. If that could be done, it would be possible to make an H-bomb a thousand times as powerful as the A-bomb.

"Whew!" McClatchy said. "No wonder they call it the Haitch-bomb." He turned to the others. "And I see where they can put a couple of million atoms on the head of a pin. A pin! That's the secret." He returned his attention to Heath, plainly expecting him to continue. "Excuse *me*."

The instructor looked drolly at the art critic, who laughed: "Shoot."

But Arline said to her father: "Oh, Dad, you wouldn't understand it."

"I know that myself, but he could give us the general idea, couldn't he?"

Heath asked him, smiling: "Do you know anything about the structure of the atom?"

"The structure," McClatchy repeated studiously; "I don't, no."

"Well, in the simple mechanical construct an atom would look like the solar system."

"The solar system; how do you mean, now?"

"I mean like the sun and the planets; the earth and the other planets travel around the sun."

"Oh, the sun—sure," McClatchy nodded. "I know that, yes." He told his daughter: "Everything goes around the sun; that's the solar system."

"Oh, really!" she said with irony.

From the pocket of his sports shirt Heath took a silver pencil, and from his hip pocket a notebook from which he tore a leaf, and he made a sketch of the hydrogen atom. He explained that the "sun" was a particle called a proton, which had a positive charge of electricity, and that the lone "planet" was an electron, which had a negative charge. If, instead of one solar proton and one planetary electron, the atom had two of each, he said, its nature would be changed and it would be hydrogen no longer, but helium, which had the atomic number two. So helium, in a manner of speaking, was twice hydrogen, and all the other elements also were multiples of that first one.

Then he turned the paper over and made another sketch. He began with two circles touching. One represented a proton, and in this he put a plus sign to show a positive charge. The other circle represented a particle called a neutron, which was electrically neutral, and in this he put both a plus and a minus because in one theory, he said, the neutron was composed of one proton and one electron whose charges canceled each other. Now, he said, the two circles in this sketch represented the sun of another atom; and he explained that the proton and the neutron were held together by tremendous cosmic energy, called the binding force, which in the laboratory had been materialized, to a limited extent, into a particle called a meson; and for emphasis he said that a meson was part of the energy of the universe converted into matter. Then at a distance from the two circles he drew an electron planet and described its orbit.

Notice, he said, that this atom, like the other, had only one proton and one electron. Only the mass and weight of the sun were different. The electrical charge was the same as the other's; the atomic number was the same. So this too was an atom of hydrogen. But this was a different kind of hydrogen, a variety called heavy hydrogen—and he went on to explain as simply as he could the fusion bomb. There was a round of head-wagging comment when he had finished.

Bessie had pulled the paper to her across the table and was studying the second sketch. Suddenly she said: "Why, yes! There! Of course! Why, it's just like the Blessed Trinity!"

"What?" said Heath.

"Oh, Ma!" her daughter rebuked her, and Rover Kinney laughed, and Heath smiled defeatedly.

"Why, it is!" Bessie insisted. "Look! This one with the cross in it, here——"

"That's a *plus* sign," Arline corrected her, red-faced.

"Well, this one's like God the Father. And this one with the two signs—that's like the Son, the divine nature and the human nature in one and the same Person. See?"

"Lea' me see," her husband said, getting up to look over her shoulder.

"And look here, now," Bessie went on. "It's just like it says in the Last Gospel: 'In the beginning was the Word, and the Word was with God, and the Word was God.' And didn't the Father say: 'This day have I begotten Thee'? And the Last Gospel says: 'All things were made through Him, and without Him was made nothing that has been made.' And it says in the Creed: 'Sitteth at the right hand of the Father,' don't it?"

McClatchy asked: "Where's the Holy Ghost?"

"The Holy Ghost is the Spirit of Divine Love that 'proceeds from the Father and the Son'—He's what binds the Father and the Son and Himself together in the one God. Aint that right, now?"

"The energy," Heath suggested dryly.

"Why, yes," Bessie said, "that's it."

"Now I declare!" McClatchy said. "Sure! He come as a dove and a big wind and tongues of flame."

"And as a meson," Heath said; but his voice was lost.

"*Looka*," said Mr. Silvestro, who with his wife by this time was also looking over Bessie's shoulder, and he thrust a great forefinger at the electron planet of the atom of heavy hydrogen. "Whosa dat?"

They stared at it, confounded.

"San Michele!" he announced triumphantly.

"Who?" McClatchy said.

"San Michele Archangelo! Stanza before the face of God!"

"St. Michael the Archangel!" McClatchy said. "No. Wait, now. That shows the system. The same as the solar system. Everything goes around Almighty God. Maybe *that's* what that is."

The little group that had suddenly turned a nuclear physics class into an open forum in speculative natural theology was full of enthusiasm and delight over Bessie's notion. Heath put his pencil back in his pocket with a smile of resignation. Kinney was chuckling in his beard. Rita was looking from one theologian to another as some women look at caged baboons, in half-fascinated disgust. Arline was mortified.

A thin ribbon of smoke rose, curling in the placid air, from a cigarette which Noel Ames held between two of his chubby but graceful fingers, and his eyes rested softly upon Bessie. "'And the light shines in the darkness,'" he quoted another verse from the mystical first chapter of John, "'and the darkness grasped it not.'"

"*That's* right," Bessie said. "Why, it's as plain as day!"

He smiled. "The signature of the Artist. Well, all anyone else seems to have discovered in the atom is death and destruction or a bigger and better power plant. Who knows?—you may be right. Or perhaps, Mrs. McClatchy, what we see when we look into the heart of matter is only the reflection of our own hearts. In either case, I think you're to be congratulated."

"Oh, nonsense," Bessie said. "St. Patrick seen the same thing in a shamrock."

"So he did," Ames laughed, snuffing out his cigarette in his paper plate; "so he did."

And Arline was struck by what he had said about her mother's heart.

The art critic got up from the table saying that much as he regretted having to leave the picnic he really had to see some more of the fair. Kinney said that he and Rita would show him round; and when these three had taken their leave Tom Heath addressed Arline for the first time since he had greeted her so impersonally: "Have you seen the fair?"

"Some of it."

"I haven't seen any of it. Shall we have a look?"

On the wave of her relief that the gathering was breaking up, she assented. Besides, she was grateful to him, and then of course he had asked her politely, raising no barriers, but in fact she was only too glad to lead him away from her people before they should disgrace themselves further.

As she got up her father asked: "Where *you* going?" and she overheard her mother say to him: "Mind your own business"—which surprised Arline and made her ask herself, turning away, whether there had been anything her mother could possibly have noticed.

Tom Heath took her to an avenue of pictures. It stretched down the long east-west drive of the estate under tall eucalyptus trees which formed an arch overhead and foiled the sunshine. She could see that he was much interested in pictures, and wondered whether he could have been sincere in asking her to pose for him. He was being quite decent, congenial, and attentive. She thought perhaps he now understood that she was not the sort he had taken her for, and she forgave him.

Half a dozen times on the walk down one side of the avenue and up the other they stopped to talk with artists. Tom Heath knew them all. Arline knew most by sight and some by name, and they knew her as McEndymion's daughter, headwaitress at the tavern, but she had always been an outsider among them. Meeting them now with Tom Heath, she found herself treated as if she belonged. But although they talked and laughed with Heath as equals she felt that they deferred to him. Not as an artist, perhaps. He had told her again that he was only a Sunday painter. No, it was probably because of his knowledge and his position at the institute.

He took her back to the grotto of statuary. After that they watched a dozen artists, one of them a girl, playing craps behind the stables. Arline marveled at the girl's adept handling of the dice, and even more at her proficiency in the magical cant of the game. As they were leaving there Heath's name was called in a high croaking voice:

"Tom! Oh, Tom!"

The little old man was perched on the top rail of a high board fence in the shade, holding his hat on his knees, and waving a cane. Tom Heath grinned, called a greeting, and told Arline: "Old Dr. Dow." She recognized the name of the former principal of the high school, "principal emeritus," the *Sentinel* always called him—a kind of patriarch. Heath took her over to meet him.

Robert Dow's body was shriveled, hunched, and frail, his white head had a senile tremor, and his face, which all came to a point at the nose, was the color of chalk, but his blue pink-rimmed eyes were marvelously bright. "How do you do, my dear," he said to Arline when Heath introduced them; and to Heath keenly: "Not Swiss, I'll bet you."

"No," Heath laughed, "not Swiss."

Dr. Dow nodded. "I thought not. Not a Llagas girl, though."

"Yes I am," she smiled. "I went to St. Peter's."

"Oh, St. Peter's. That explains it. I didn't remember you. I remember him, though. Oh my, yes. How's Switzerland?"

Still grinning, Heath said: "All right, sir."

"Switzerland?" she asked.

"Oh," the old man said, "that's just a pet name, my dear. An allusion to the cantons of the New Illuminati, as I call 'em. *He* knows. Well?" he asked Heath, leaving Arline bewildered. "How about it, eh? Have you signed?"

"Not yet," Heath said.

"What? Why not? Witch hunt, I suppose. Tut. Don't talk Swiss to me. Academic freedom, I suppose. More Swiss."

"Academic freedom? Oh, not Swiss, sir."

"No? Old American principle, is it? Rubbish. Read the history of your country, boy. But the term's been tampered with—reduced to a cheap slogan for a monstrous hoax, that's what. Pure Swiss now. Go back to the classic meaning. Truth—do you mean to tell me communists believe in that? Look at the history they teach. Look at their genetics. Read their propaganda. You've got intelligence. Can you plead the sanctity of truth to justify a plot to murder it—what?"

"I *don't*," Heath remonstrated. "I'm not defending communists."

"Who's talking about communists? It's not them I'm afraid of. It's demagogues in caps and gowns, by George, who stand for that kind of academic freedom. Oh-h, I know," Dr. Dow said, waving Heath down with his cane, gently, "I know what you're going to say. You won't find the word teach in that quotation unfortunately, and I'm old enough to see through Voltaire anyhow." He winked at Arline. "Listen to him—hasn't 'been to Switzerland for nothing,' has he, eh?"

Heath laughed.

Arline, by a flash of genius if not by sheer female intuition, gathered that the subject under discussion, if discussion this could be called, was the loyalty oath controversy at the institute, about which there had been so much in the newspapers lately. But the allusion to Voltaire and the obscure quotation from Dostoyevsky meant no more to her than New Illuminati had. She understood "Swiss" better than she did the jargon of Dr. Dow. But she smiled back at him merrily because he looked like a white rabbit hunching on top of the six-foot fence. And gesturing toward her with an elbow as if to dig her in the ribs, Dr. Dow continued to address Arline:

"Oh, but it's the principle, you understand. Yes. So they've *got* to protect the communists; they've got to keep the trustees and the people from interfering in order to establish the principle. See that? Heh!"

"Yes," Heath smiled, "but that's not the whole story."

"No, by George, not by a long shot," Dr. Dow said. "They're not teachers at all, they're pedagarchs! Power, that's what they're after. I known 'em. Some of 'em are even against teaching the people to read. They despise the people. Control of society by an intellectual elite, that's what they want. Selective education. Standardization. Regimentation of the masses. Another 'new order.' You'll see. The schools are only the beginning. The State Department, all those insolent bureaus —UNESCO, or whatever the ridiculous name of it is—what are those?" He waved his stick. "Cantons of Switzerland! A rrreg——" He broke off in midair. "Here she comes. Help me down from here."

A small gray-haired woman was hurrying up to them, trailed by a tall workman bearing a large package which presumably was hers. "Oh, Robert, you ought to have better sense!" she deplored as Heath and Arline helped the old man down. "Heavens, I left him sitting right there on that bucket. Be careful! Oh, it's a wonder he doesn't kill himself." Indeed, it was a wonder to Arline that he had managed to get up there at all, so shaky was he in the descent.

"My wife," he explained sourly as the woman brushed him off. "Stop fussing!" he said to her. He presented them. Mrs. Dow smiled at

them anxiously with a face that was all wrinkles, complained of not being able to leave Dr. Dow alone for a minute, and said she was glad
they had been with him. His last words to Heath before his wife carried
him off were:

"Mind—don't be taken in. Sign it! Sign it! A little daylight will
do that place good. If I were you I'd sign it as big as John Hancock."

Hobbling away, he shook his cane overhead in farewell; and Heath
said, chuckling: "He's pretty sharp yet but he doesn't understand the
issues."

And as they walked across the fields Heath told Arline some of his
side of the story. He likened the great communist hunt now in progress over the land to the Bolshevik scare of 1919. He said it was everywhere breeding suspicion, inquisition, and slander, giving credit to a
form of lynch law, and intimidating conviction. He said if not resisted it
could turn America into a police state. He spoke of the academic
principle of tenure, of professors who he said had given their lives to
education and were now being asked to sign an oath that was an insult to their records and an abridgment of American liberty. But you
had to begin, he said, with what an institution like Fremont was. At
its heart it was a society of scholars founded, endowed, and equipped
for the study of man and his environment and for the dissemination
of knowledge, in the name of truth and for the benefit of humanity.
So it had to be regarded as above ideologies and politics. It had to be
free to pursue the truth. And without free colleges and universities
the nation would not be free, nor in the modern age could it continue to remain a nation. For these reasons they had to be defended,
he said, against the mob; and what real protection did they have if
not the right to govern and police themselves? "You see," he said,
"the problem's not so simple."

And now Dr. Dow's thesis, or as much of it as she had been able to
follow, echoed in her mind as shallow and cantankerous. Tom Heath
had been indulgent of the tirade, but she understood that this matter
was on his mind, that he was deeply concerned about it. This was a
side of him that she had not seen before. She respected and admired
it. "And you're not going to sign?" she asked.

"Do you think I ought to?"

She answered: "I think you ought to do what you believe is right."

"Thanks," he said.

And she was pleased. She was pleased that he had explained his
views to her, that he had asked her opinion, and that she had encouraged him to follow his convictions bravely whatever the cost, and
that he had thanked her; and she was pleased because it seemed they

were on a better footing now, and because, with all that, she knew he wanted her.

They saw some more of the fair. The crowd thinned out. The artists began to gather at the large white pergola, leased from Kinney by Moe Freed for a display of his famous cablecars and other San Francisco etchings, many of which by this time had sold. It was here that McClatchy found his daughter.

"Where you been, I been looking all over for you, come on," he said, "they're waiting to go home."

Heath objected: "But I was going to take her to dinner," and turned to the surprised Arline: "If she'd come."

"Oho!" her father grinned. "Why didn't you say so?"

"Oh, but I can't," she told Heath. "Not this way. I'm not dressed." She was wearing a linen dress with a scarf but no coat, and low-heeled shoes.

But Heath said: "Nonsense, it's summer, isn't it?"

"Sure," her father encouraged her. "Nobody'll look at you anyhow, go on and I'll put Roxie on in your place, no no," waving her back with his hand as he retreated, grinning, "I'll see you later."

"See?" Heath said. "I got you off work tonight. Is it a date?"

Her father was hurrying off. She smiled. "All right."

The girl crapshooter called to them: "Come on with the gang, why don't you? We're having a barbecue at Jinny and Wick's." Cupping her lips with her hands, she shouted to the assembly: "Everybody bring their own rations."

"Not tonight," Heath said, looking at Arline.

"Oho!" the girl crapshooter said, and Arline laughed.

Then somebody mentioned having heard that Arline was a witness in the Dirigo case, at which Heath expressed surprise, and for a little while Arline was the center of attention. Answering questions, she told something about the holdup, but from what she said it did not appear that she and the policeman had been together that night. She explained that she had not seen the shooting. "I'm not supposed to talk about it anyhow." She did not want to think about it, either.

It was only about half past five, daylight saving time, and the sun was still far above the rim of the hills: it was too early to go to dinner. Heath and Arline lingered. The gathering increased. The veteran painters discussed the fortunes of the day, exchanging experiences and ideas, envying, pitying, and rallying one another. A boy stood with one arm around a girl; Arline saw the girl turn her face to him and their lips touch; no one else paid any attention. Others of the group sat on the floor or on the benches that lined the lattice walls: girls in shorts or "pedal-pushers," young men in suntans, in denims, in colored sports or white T-shirts, and nearly everyone in sunglasses; a dozen conversations flourished.

It was a spontaneous gathering of youth united by a common interest after a day of confederated effort. For a widow of thirty-six who had lived so long with responsibility, routine, loneliness, and disappointment, it had charm. This was the closest she had ever been to the life of these bohemians. She thought of the barbecue they were going to have—at some cabin in the hills, probably, or on some beach, in the moonlight. And she wondered why, with so many young pretty girls in this crowd, Tom Heath had invited *her* to dinner.

The sun was dropping behind the western ridge of the continent when they left the fairgrounds. Heath's car was a gray Ford convertible, the top was down, and Arline was glad she had brought her scarf. The sunset was paling into twilight as they entered San Javier. Heath drove into a large parking lot, vacant as yet, and the red neon sign of the restaurant was turned on before their eyes:

MARCO POLO

The place was cool and quiet, with a red tile floor in the vestibule, with a square dining room of spindly tables each mounting a candle in a Chianti bottle, with a dance floor, and with a platform for a band which had not yet arrived. There was also a narrow bar where she joined Heath after refreshing her appearance in the washroom, and sipped a manhattan. Then they were shown to a table by an Italian in a red stocking cap who presented each of them with a large bill of fare decorated with a drawing of a Venetian galley, ceremoniously lighted their candle, and took their order. When the waiter left Heath leaned with folded arms upon the table as he had that night when he introduced himself in the Lost Dutchman, and said:

"I didn't know you were a Llagas girl."

"I'm not. We lived in San Francisco till I was fourteen. But did *you* go to school in Llagas? Honestly, I never would have believed it."

"Oh yes. I was born in Llagas."

"Not really!"

"Mm hm. My mother kept a boardinghouse. I still own it."

"A boardinghouse? You don't say. And you still live in it?"

"No; I lease it out. It's one of those old-fashioned monstrosities with a lot of ground around it; when my mother died I fixed up a three-room cottage she'd built on the place, and moved in there."

"You *did?*" She looked at him queerly.

"It's comfortable," he smiled, "cheap, and quite nice really. Private walk and everything."

He was not at all like Llagas. His manner was quick, urbane, sophisticated; she could have pictured him in one of those penthouses she had seen in the movies, all glass, overlooking New York. And she thought of his life at the institute—a professor; for to the tavernkeeper's daughter it was all the same. The waiter brought their dinner; they ate and talked. She found it strange that they should be dining together. But the twilight faded from the windows, and looking at his dark face by the light of the candle in the wine bottle, at his gray-lamp eyes and the place where the indentation of his nose should have been (which fascinated her), she remembered that other night and the wild fig tree of the jungle; and the intellectual repugnance that she felt for the tree, but less for the tree in fact than for the metaphor, was quietly overborne and drowned in a warm exhilaration of her blood.

They were having their coffee when the band arrived.

They danced. The music was slow, the floor dark. He was only a little taller than she was in her low heels, and of a slight frame, and Arline was trying not to be "hard to lead." But it was as if he were not leading at all; it was as if his body were magnetized by hers, held by hers; and she did not draw back. Experiencing her attraction for him, she exulted in it, and wondered, the ugly duckling, holding him as if with open hands. His breath touched her ear: "*Arline!*" Then the music stopped, and it happened just as it had with Harry Fahs—he whispered: "Let's go."

Without a word she turned and walked back to the table. She picked up her scarf and waited while he paid the bill. She walked out ahead of him into the darkness of the parking area. At his car she turned and waited till he came up after settling with the attendant at the entrance. She asked:

"Home?"

"Home?" he repeated in surprise. "No; my place."

"No," she said.

He took her in his arms. "What's the matter?"

"Don't!"

"Arline!" His arms tightened.

"No!" Straining, she broke away. She got into the convertible. Then he was leaning over her, his face touching her hair, and his hand closed upon her upper arm; his voice was urgent, pleading:

"Arline, I need you."

"Oh, stop it!" She wrenched free. "Take me home."

He straightened, angry. "You . . . bitch!" But his eyes were full of tears. He turned and walked round the rear of the car.

His tears had disarmed her; she was suddenly sorry and ashamed. Then he appeared on the driver's side of the car, slammed the door, started the engine, and did not look at her. The car pitched backward and stopped, the gears clashed, the car lurched forward and swung round, and then they were speeding up the road with the wind tugging against her as she fixed the scarf over her hair.

The speed and the wind calmed him, and the landmarks warned him that in a few more miles they would come to the end of the imperfect day. As he slowed down he said bitterly: "Sorry."

"Forget it."

"No. You don't know what you do to me."

"Oh, any woman would have done the same thing to you."

He gave a snort. "You want me to tell you that isn't so, don't you?"

"No I don't."

"All right, it isn't." His eyes were on the road, his jaw was set, his words came through his teeth. "There's a quality I need in a woman. Something I've never had. And you've got it. You've got it for me more than any other woman I know."

She was both thrilled and humbled by this confession, understanding it not at all but convinced of its truth because of the way she had seen him look at her, of what Phyllis had said of him, and of his half-drunken allegory of the jungle, and because her body had felt its attraction for him, and because it had made him cry. She asked kindly: "*What* do you need in a woman, Tom?" But he made no reply. She said: "Tell me."

He glanced at her. "Let me paint you."

"Paint me? No."

"Why not?"

"Because."

"Because you think I want you to pose without any clothes on. No. I'll paint you in a skirt and blouse; and I'll show you what it is. I'll show you a great peasant, an earth-goddess, a giantess! Yes! I'm like Baudelaire: I wish I'd lived in the time of giantesses!"

"*Giantesses?*" She was horrified and stung.

"Will you?"

"Of course not."

"You know what's the matter with you, Arline? Your head is crammed with a lot of middle-class ideas. And you're full of inhibitions. You're living in the Victorian age. Arline, you're a prude and you're frustrated and I think you're a very unhappy girl."

She took refuge in irony: "Really?"

They entered Llagas in silence. But he had no sooner stopped the car in front of the tavern than he turned to detain her, flinging his left arm over the wheel and saying: "No, wait." He stopped, made a wry mouth, and wagged his head. "I'm the one that's frustrated. And you're not a prude. While we were dancing—— But why, Arline? Why?"

"I'm sorry, Tom."

"Arline, you're not happy. I've seen it in your eyes. You've got beautiful eyes; did you know that? But they go sad, they go a million miles away."

"Do they?"

He looked at them. "Michelangelo's goddesses have eyes like that."

"Don't be silly."

"Silly? I'm making love to you, Arline. What do I have to do, propose marriage?"

"What makes you think I'd have you?"

"You're religious, aren't you?"

"Not particularly . . ." She started to get out of the car.

"Wait," he said.

"No. It's no use, Tom. Maybe I am Victorian; but I know one thing. You and I don't even talk the same language." She got out. As she did so he said: "We could communicate."

She flung him a contemptuous look. "Thanks for the evening." The pale smile faded from his face as he watched her go.

Inside the door Roxie greeted her in surprise: "I thought you were taking the night off."

"Not all of it," she tried to say lightly, passing on. "Be out as soon as I change."

And her mother called to her from the cashier's counter: "Back so early?"

"We had dinner; I knew you'd be busy."

She went into her bedroom and, leaning back against the door she had closed behind her, let her face twist in pain. Through the door came the sounds of the tavern. She pushed herself into the room. She dropped her bag on the bed and pulled off her scarf with little regard for her hair. When she had taken off her dress she turned and looked in the glass of the low chest of drawers, looked at herself as at a stranger. Her face was perplexed. Then slowly she came erect. Her features smoothed themselves. She filled her lungs with air. . . . Beneath her reflection was the letter that she had received that morning from her son. Slowly the air escaped. She took the letter in her hand.

The scrawl was grotesque, and the paper, from the signature to the bottom, was covered with X's.

23

THE MERCIFUL JUDGING OF THE KID

He was the youngest of four children of a laboring man and his wife, of Kansas City, Missouri. His mother had died when he was ten. In the packed courtroom at San Javier when he was tried for the murder of the policeman were his father and one of his sisters.

The defense attorney, a man named Naughton, tried to becloud the case against his client. The policeman's mistake in supposing that he had shot the boy, when in fact he had shot the girl, demonstrated that Officer Fahs had been confused in the darkness, Naughton said, and made worthless his report that he had been shot by the boy and that the girl had been driving the car. And were there any eyewitnesses to corroborate the policeman? No. The defense, on the other hand, he said, offered the deposition of the girl's father that up to the time of her leaving home she did not know how to drive a car. The state could adduce no evidence that she did know how to drive, or that a driver's license had ever been issued to her, and it admitted that her fingerprints had not been found on the wheel. Presumably the state accused Nancy Croan of having broken the law by driving without a license, but the state was unable to prove that she had, or even that she could, and because of that, Naughton said, the case against Raymond Dirigo collapsed. He moved that it be dismissed for lack of evidence.

The judge ruled: "Denied."

For the supposition that Raymond Dirigo had driven the car would not remove all doubt that he had done the shooting, and District Attorney Willard had already established, first, that Nancy Croan had been shot in the shoulder from behind, so could not, at the time, have been in position to be engaging the policeman in a gun duel, second, that a trace of blood matching the blood on the dead girl's clothing had been found on the back of the driver's seat of the car and that someone had tried to wash it off with salt water, and then, that the holdup man had threatened to kill the bartender, that he had shot at the cook, that he had promised to shoot anyone who followed him through the door, and that Harry Fahs had followed him through it immediately with drawn gun.

Arline marveled that in the face of the evidence against him the kid would stake so much on the flimsy story of having driven the car. She remembered what the district attorney had said to the prisoner in the office that day: "Dirigo, the only chance you've got is to throw yourself on the mercy of the Court." And on the mercy of God, she thought.

She was not asked to identify the defendant by his voice. Since he admitted the holdup there was no need of that; and Walsh Reardon gave it as his opinion to her father afterward that her testimony on the point would not have "stood up in court" anyway. Willard's hoax, then, had been calculated to deceive her along with the prisoner; which made her wonder if such immoral devices were common practice among enforcers of the law. But when Arline was on the stand the district attorney treated her with a show of sympathy and kindness, as if in the death of Harry Fahs she had lost the man she loved; and that perhaps was to counteract the sympathy that the jurors must feel for Naughton's pathetic exhibits, old Mr. Dirigo and his daughter.

Mr. Dirigo, with his bowed shoulders, gray head, deep-graven features, grizzled mustache, weak eyes, and big warped brown hands, gave the impression of being old as the rocks. His daughter was a married woman of about thirty-five, small, dark-skinned, and beaten-looking. Naughton, by thanking the judge for permitting them to sit with his client at the table, had contrived to let the jury know who they were. From time to time Mr. Dirigo would draw from his hip pocket a red bandanna and with that flag of poverty and toil wipe the tears from his eyes, provoking Willard to exclaim to Braden during the lunch hour: "Damn it, people in Kansas City don't carry bandannas any more, do they? I'll bet Naughton gave him that goddamn bandanna."

Arline, testifying in a low voice, tried to avoid the eyes of all the Dirigos, but especially those of the old man; and in cross-examination Naughton did no more than ask three gentle questions to establish that she had not seen the shooting and did not know who had shot her policeman or who had driven the car.

Naughton never called on Mr. Dirigo or his daughter, but left them to make a purely visual appeal. His last witness was the defendant.

Raymond Dirigo told his version of the holdup and shooting. He denied having wiped off the wheel of the car. He denied having tried to wash the blood from the driver's seat, but he said he had not even known the blood was there, and so in trying to make his story stronger he made it weaker than it might have been, for he thus denied himself the opportunity of explaining how the blood had got there if the girl had not been driving. He said he had abandoned his wounded girl because he believed there was no saving her and feared he would be condemned for the murder that he laid to her. He said the holdup was the only one he had ever committed. He answered questions about his undistinguished war service and said he had received the good conduct medal. And he told that he had met Nancy Croan by mail while serving with the Army in Trinidad during the war. He had seen her photograph above another soldier's bunk and had written to her and she had answered, and so they had begun a regular correspondence. After his discharge he had written to her from Kansas City, and she had written back inviting him to meet her in Omaha. He had done so. Then, telling him that she had left home and was afraid to go back, she had begged him to take her to California. Naughton, Arline saw, was trying to stamp the record with a picture of a temptress and her prey.

But with Dirigo, Naughton had changed his style to unhappy effect. He had not merely called Dirigo to the stand but had escorted him to it with an arm around his shoulders, talking to him soothingly as though he were a lamb among wolves, which struck everyone as ridiculous; and Naughton was asking his questions in a tone of pity and tenderness, many of them with no other purpose than to depict the witness as by nature good, gentle, even noble, as a victim of society, of circumstances, and of Nancy Croan. The trouble was that no one could forget the girl's dying alone in the boathouse, and that Raymond Dirigo presented the wrong appearance. Sitting nervously on the stand with his head sunk between his shoulders and his black eyes positively furtive, the slim olive-skinned weakly handsome defendant recalled a figure that everyone had been taught to recognize on sight in gangster films. Naughton's pathos therefore lost him the confidence of his audience, the jury. It made Naughton himself suspect. And it deprived the boy of whatever dignity he might have had while speaking, truly or not, for his life. Naughton was literally killing his client with kindness.

Then Willard stepped in with a hammer.

It was the shabbiest of murder cases, and not even the facts that two human lives had been taken and another was in jeopardy could save the trial from being ludicrous. But Arline was disturbed by the profound mysteries that underlay it all and were not being discussed here, not being even acknowledged. She was convinced that Raymond Dirigo had shot Harry Fahs and she was puzzled by nothing within the jurisdiction of the man on the bench, but she had been puzzled and disturbed all along by what to her mind was the fatal theme of the case, the element of cruel, it seemed, and relentless destiny. For Raymond Dirigo had not killed Harry Fahs. The clot had done that. Yet Raymond Dirigo had been marked with the blood; and it was as if he had been doomed from the moment he entered the Willow Tree. But in Arline's philosophy there was no such thing as a cruel and relentless destiny. God did not do things like that. It could not be true. It frightened her. And she wanted to see it contradicted. That was why she silently asked her merciful God to let Raymond Dirigo live. But Willard, in his address to the jury, asked the Court for the death penalty.

Then Naughton was addressing the jury. He charged the State with the motive of revenge; he declared that the reason the State would not be satisfied with anything less than the death of "this boy" was that Harry Fahs had been a policeman, and with a dramatic sweep of the arm he pointed into the spectators' section, snarling: "Look at them out there—bloodhounds! Thirsting for blood!" as though the benches were filled with policemen, and in fact three or four were present. A little later he spoke of Raymond Dirigo's father and dead mother, of his brother and sisters, and of a temple in the sky that he said had the word mercy written on it, and his speech degenerated into tender Irish bathos. Willard objected that there was nothing in the record about any temple in the sky that had the word mercy written on it, and asked the judge to instruct counsel to keep within the record, and the judge did. But Naughton was delivering a prepared address, and just as he would begin to draw tears from the jury he would come to the temple again, Willard would rise with another objection, and the whole effect would be ruined.

In rebuttal Willard said:

"Ladies and gentlemen of the jury. When we were hand-picking twelve citizens to weigh the evidence in this case the State's aim was to select people who could not be made fools of. In that I believe the State succeeded. I have confidence in the intelligence of this jury. I don't believe there is any doubt in this jury's mind about who killed Officer Fahs. But the jury has just heard the defendant described as an injured lily. So now let's see what kind of person the defendant really is. But let's judge him by the facts. Let's keep within the record.

"You've heard that as a boy he was arrested for stealing a bicycle, received a suspended sentence from a merciful judge, and was released in the custody of his parents; and you've heard that when he grew up he stole three automobiles. Ask yourselves whether, when he began to correspond with Nancy Croan after seeing her picture overseas, he was not in effect stealing a buddy's girl. And we know he tried to take money at gunpoint from the Willow Tree Inn, masked to the eyes and wearing gloves.

"He thrust his loaded gun in the bartender's back, threatened to kill him, and would not hear his prayer. He tried to kill the cook. Then, threatening to kill anyone who followed him, he ran. He ran in panic, a gun in his hand and the policeman at his back. We submit he killed the policeman.

"His girl was wounded and he did *not* take her to a hospital. If his girl had killed the policeman, as he wants this jury to believe, her recovery would have given him his best chance of proving it. But he didn't lift a finger to save her. First, in the contention of the State, he wiped off the wheel of the car and tried to wash his girl's blood from the driver's seat; he was already planning his alibi. Then he deserted her. He left his girl in that cold and lonely boathouse, bleeding to death! Her blood is on his hands and he accuses his girl of the murder because she cannot speak. That, we submit, was how he planned it.

"And the record tells us that when he was arrested in Tulsa he gave a false name. He lied. But his fingerprints betrayed him. And I ask the jury to remember this: there were marijuana cigarettes in his pocket and he was carrying another gun!

"No. Raymond Dirigo is no injured lily. There is a true picture of him in the record. He is a thief, a robber, and a coward, and Raymond Dirigo is a liar. The record tells us that this defendant has no moral sense whatever. That he has no loyalty. That he is incapable of love. That he is viciously selfish, without respect for the rights of others, with no regard for any human life but his own. That he can feel no pity. That he will show no mercy. That he feels no remorse. He is that barbarous freak of nature, a man without a conscience. And I ask you to see that Raymond Dirigo is dangerous. Ladies and gentlemen, it is all there in the record. It is the picture of a monster."

Arline did not believe that Raymond Dirigo had no moral sense or conscience, but because of what Willard had said she began to see the case in another light. Everything Raymond Dirigo had done that night—his attempt to rob, his threats, and all his responses to the circumstances that had been forced on him: his firing at the cook, his firing back at Harry Fahs, his abandonment of the girl—appeared to her as logical though irrational acts, logical because consistent with his character. She saw that if he had been unable to help himself it had been because of what he was, because of what he had become. And she suspected that to blame Raymond Dirigo on society would not do. For at sight of the little gold cross at her throat he had instantly pleaded with her in the name of Jesus Christ, and his own name sounded Italian or Spanish, so she thought it not unlikely that he was a Catholic, and if that was so, he had known the law and rejected both that and the help of God. By his life, by countless acts of choice, he had created this destiny himself. You couldn't blame it all on society. You couldn't blame the circumstances or Nancy Croan. And this was not the doing of God.

And yet—there was still the clot. He was still not by choice and free will nor in a medical sense the killer of Harry Fahs. There was still the dark affair of the next morning, the mystery of the pulmonary embolism—the very name of it rumbled like a formal curse; and it came into her mind that God might suddenly have withdrawn His mercy and disowned him because of what he was, because of the *what* that was engraved in his heart even as the *who* was engraved in the skin of his fingers, the fingers that had told the police who he was, and who, she believed, he would be forever, in eternity, in heaven or in hell. But to think of this as the justice of God was no less chilling than to think of it as the work of a cruel and relentless destiny. To think that divine mercy might ever be withdrawn was unbearable. Silently again she prayed for him.

The trial had lasted five days. The jury was out less than an hour. And then the kid, at the judge's command, was on his feet and facing the jury, isolate and frightened-looking, and she thought how far he was, if he was a Catholic, from the day of his first Communion. There was a hush, and the foreman read the verdict. "We find the defendant guilty of murder in the first degree." There was no recommendation of clemency.

There was a low moan which everyone recognized came from the old man, and then the old man and his daughter were hanging on the neck of the son and brother, the convicted murderer. The judge waited a moment before he asked for order. Naughton led the mourners back to their places. The kid faced the bench. The judge ordered him to appear on Monday to hear his sentence. Monday washday came senselessly into her mind: the beginning: beginning without end. And court was dismissed. The father wept on the shoulder of the son, and the daughter and sister was trying to mother both at once, trying to console both at once even while lamenting with and over both, and Arline wanted to go to them but knew she would be rejected as an enemy, though at that moment she too was a mourner, even a sister. The bailiff led the prisoner away and Mr. Dirigo sank into a chair and buried his face in the red bandanna.

Arline got back to the tavern in time for the dinner trade.

She dreamt her son was dead. He had drowned in Clear Lake and they had brought him back to the old flat on Fell Street in a little coffin lined with white satin and Tom Heath was trying to console her and Mayor Schuman was making the Sign of the Cross over the body but saying "In nomine proton, neutron, meson," and beside the coffin stood a big floral horseshoe and rain was streaming down the windows because it was Christmas Eve, and her parents were not there, her parents would never be there, and in the distance the Municipal Band was playing drearily off key:

> Yip, I addy, I ay, I ay,
> Yip, I addy, I ay. . . .

She awoke in tears, her flesh cold and her body tingling with dread; she tore off the covers and stood up. Then she remembered that Billy had come back from Clear Lake, and went to the couch and found him sleeping. Thank God! All on account of that awful trial, she thought. One of his feet protruded from the bedclothes and she covered it. Then looking down at him in the darkness, she remembered Christmas Eve and Billy sick with the whooping cough and herself thinking: What if he died? That was why it had been Christmas Eve in her dream, she reasoned. But in the night one does not so quickly shake off the effects of a nightmare; there was a feeling of ill omen in her heart, and that was why she stood trying to put together the pieces of her dream. Tom Heath and then Clear Lake again, and then she remembered that other night, Billy gone and herself thinking: What if he drowned? And it came to her with a shock: Maybe I was wishing him dead! No, she thought, I didn't! I couldn't! But again she remembered Tom Heath in her dream, and was appalled. My own child! O God! She went down on her knees at the bedside.

In the daylight she was able to reassure herself. The grief she had felt so keenly in her dream and the dread she had felt on waking were comforting now; and the sun was out.

But it had taken her a long time to get back to sleep; she had slept late this Sunday morning. Her parents had gone to the children's Mass with Billy at eight-thirty and when Arline arrived for the last Mass at eleven Father Cobb was already beginning the sermon.

"I wonder," he said, peering over his spectacles, "I wonder if I asked how many of my parishoners had crosses on the doors of their houses, how many hands would be raised. I wonder would I see any hands at all. But suppose I asked how many of my parishoners had doors with panels. You'd say: Is he crazy?—*all* doors but the modern dustproof sanitary kind of a door have panels. True for you. But look *between* the panels of nine tenths of the doors and what do you see? Crosses! Sometimes one, sometimes two, sometimes three. Don't ask me why they were put there. Maybe a pious custom of our ancestors or their carpenters, God reward them; or only a good, sound principle of construction. The point is everybody sees the panels but only one in ten sees the cross on the door of his own house. Now there's not one of us born isn't carrying a specially designed custom-made cross of another kind, and what I want to drive into your heads today is if it isn't sickness or a nagging wife or a drunken husband nine out of ten of my parishoners don't know a cross from a hod of bricks." And he went on to preach on the subject: No salvation without a cross.

She recoiled from the thought that had come into her mind. No, Billy was not her cross. She loved him, he was part of herself, he was her joy and her hope and if anything happened to him she would die. It was because of her dream she had thought that. And then the talk of crosses brought back Raymond Dirigo mutely begging her for a lie in God's name, and all at once it seemed to her that she understood the meaning of what had happened to him.

In the light of crosses it seemed to stand out clearly that if God had suddenly arrested him in full career and placed him on trial in that courtroom, it could only have been because God had compassion for him, for the immortal boy whom the district attorney had called a monster. As if God, though He would not interfere with free will, had mercifully forced the issue, saying: *Look into your heart. See what you have become. It is the hour of your death. You must make the choice forever. Be still and see that I am God.* And it appeared to her that the day she had worn the little gold cross to the district attorney's office she had carried to Raymond Dirigo the message of God: *Pay with Me for what you are. Confess, and ask for heaven, and I will give it to you, and God's justice will be done; because this is also the mercy of God: take up your cross and follow Me.* So it appeared to her mind that if Raymond Dirigo's soul was lost it would not be because God condemned him, but because distrusting and fearing and refusing mercy, he condemned himself. And she thought of the end of the two thieves on Calvary, applying to it the merciful words of the Psalm: *Be still and see that I am God.*

The sermon, or what she took for the sermon, for she had not missed a word of it, had moved her. The conception she had drawn concerning the nature of mercy stripped from the idea the sentimentalism in which till now she had always clothed it, and warned her, and yet she felt relieved and full of gratitude to God. After Mass she remained for some time in prayer, and when she left the church through the front door the pastor had just said goodbye to the last of the congregation but her. He spoke to her, and she said gravely:

"Father, that was the best sermon I ever heard."

"Was it, now. Well, I don't hear that every day," the old man said, leaning backward in his soiled and greening cassock to look at her keenly through his drooping spectacles. "What was it impressed you?"

"That God's justice and mercy are the same thing. I never knew that before."

"That God's justice and mercy are the same thing—oh no, not at all, you don't understand. In pure justice every one of us would be damned to hell. But God *tempers* His justice with His mercy. You see that, don't you?"

"Yes, but I mean it's the same thing, isn't it?"

"The same thing," he repeated, looking baffled, "no. How do you arrive at that conclusion? It's two different—— But what you say is true in a sense. In the sense that God's justice is founded on love in the first place. And in the sense of His Oneness. In *that* sense."

"Yes, that's what I mean."

"Now you don't say. Where did you hear that?"

"It's what you said, isn't it?"

"What *I* said?" He shook his head. "No, I'm too far from the seminary to be spouting that kind of theology." But seeing her embarrassment, "Oh, but it's all right," he said, taking her hand in both of his, "and I'm going to tell you something."

"But, Father——"

"No, no, but I'm going to tell you a little theology of my own. It's been my experience nobody is ever converted from a pulpit. The priest talks and it's generally true what he says never penetrates or is forgotten as soon as he's said it. But here or there may be a pair of ears where something he says or doesn't say at all strikes home. And that's nothing but the grace of God. So think of it this way: I didn't tell you but maybe God told you. And if you like I'll get you a book about it."

Afterward she was able to understand something of what had happened, and there appeared to have been nothing supernatural about it at all. In attributing her insight to the grace of God, Father Cobb had apparently been wrong. And yet the natural explanation appeared only to illuminate the mystery of grace. In an entirely natural experience she had found a supernatural truth: the justice and the mercy of God were one and the same thing!

And the next morning Raymond Dirigo was sentenced to die in the gas chamber.

24

WOMEN AND MEN

That Monday night Tom Heath returned to the tavern and found Arline just inside the door again.

"Don't you ever get a night off?" he asked.

"Of course." Sometimes she would take a night off and go to the movies.

"When?"

"Why?"

"I thought we might go out that night."

She looked at him levelly and asked: "Where?"

"What's the matter?"

"I thought you knew."

"Oh, drop it."

She turned to leave him.

"Arline!" He detained her by catching her arm. "What is this, an act?"

"What do you mean?"

"What about that policeman?"

Then she knew that he had read about the trial and drawn conclusions. Her lip curled. "I told you—we don't even talk the same language," she said, wrenching free.

She went into the rear apartment and ordered Billy to bed. She threw on her coat, found Roxie Cox in the kitchen, and said: "Take my place for a couple of hours." Without a word to either of her parents she went down the back alley to the street and headed for the movies.

But on her chest of drawers at home was a library book dealing in popular fashion with atoms and the stars.

That night had been Phyllis's night off, and the next morning Arline received a message from her. It was delivered over the telephone by a nurse. Phyllis was in Llagas Hospital. No, it was nothing serious, the nurse said, but Miss Plover wanted a nightgown and some clothes. The nurse would say no more. Arline hurried to Phyllis's apartment. The woman manager of the building, who knew her, let her in. Arline packed a suitcase and took it to the hospital.

Pretty Phyllis Plover lay in a ward bed, her lips as brightly made up as ever, with a black eye, several square inches of her scalp shaved and covered with a bandage, a splint in one nostril, a strip of adhesive over her nose, and a swelling on one side of her tender jaw.

"Phyl! What happened?"

"Don't *look* at me," Phyllis said, turning her face away.

"Oh, you poor thing!"

Phyllis asked weakly: "Did you bring the gown?"

"Yes. Everything you said. Do you want to change?"

"First I got to get permission. They make you wear these." Raising her upper lip in disgust, Phyllis plucked at the hospital sail canvas she was wearing.

"But what happened to you?"

"Oh, he was drunk."

"Who? Did he beat you or something?" Arline sat on the side of the bed.

"Beat me?" Phyllis turned her head on the pillow to look at Arline. "You mean you don't know?"

"No. I don't know a thing!"

"It was an auto accident."

"Oh, Phyl! Are you hurt bad?"

"No, I'm just a mess! But *his* neck's broken."

Arline caught her underlip between her teeth deploringly.

"He's not going to die, though; they can fix it," Phyllis said. "He'll have to wear a brace for a while, that's all." Then looking straight before her, she said: "I guess you got a surprise coming."

"Why?"

"Because he's Bo Satterfy."

"Bo *Satterfy?*"

"You'd hear anyway. The whole town will."

"Oh, Phyl!"

"There wasn't another car on the highway," Phyllis said. "He had to hit a telegraph pole."

Arline gave a suck of the tongue. "Where were you going?"

"We were coming back from the city."

"From the *city*?"

"Oh, he's left his wife already. He's going to get a divorce."

"He is?"

"Know something else? I'm going to marry him."

"Phyl!"

"Aeh," Phyllis said, raising her fastidious upper lip again, "don't give me that. Is it my fault she made his life miserable? That bitch! You don't know. What do you want him to do, drink himself to death?"

"Now, Phyl! Maybe it's none of my business——"

"All right, it isn't. So forget it. I just wanted you to know."

There was a pause, and Phyllis said: "I guess I won't be coming to work tonight."

"Well, naturally. Nobody would expect you to."

"Maybe I won't be coming to work there at all no more, huh?"

"Why, what do you mean?" But Arline knew that Phyllis meant she might be fired. "You just get well."

"Oh, I'll be out of here in a few days. But"—tears came into Phyllis's eyes—"my nose is broken," and again averting her face on the pillow, she began to sob.

"Oh, honey," Arline said, stroking the gilded hair.

When Arline got back to the tavern both her parents followed her through it to the back parlor.

"Well?" her father asked her.

"She was in an automobile accident."

"I know that."

"Is it in the papers?" Arline asked.

"It don't have to be," her father said. "Is he going to die?"

"No. . . ."

"Thanks be to God!" her mother said.

"But he's got a broken neck. He'll have to wear a brace. Phyl's all right, though. She'll be back to work in a few days."

Her mother asked: "Here?"

"Ma!"

Her father said: "What were they doing five miles down the road in party clothes at three o'clock in the morning? He's a married man, you know."

Arline said: "He's *left* his wife. They're going to get a divorce. And he and Phyllis are engaged. Are you satisfied?"

"Engaged?" her father said.

"Satisfied?" her mother repeated. "Are you out of your mind?"

"Listen," Arline said. "Bo Satterfy and Bea Manriquez were un-

happily married in the first place. What do you think he drinks so
much for? Why do you think he always comes in here alone? Phyl
isn't to blame."

"No?" her mother said.

"No! Because if it wasn't Phyl it'd be somebody else. And what business is it of ours, anyway? Who are we—God? And it's legal, isn't it?
People all over the world are getting divorced and remarried, aren't
they? All over the world! That's the trouble with us, all of us—we're
living in the Victorian age!" Arline went into her bedroom and
slammed the door.

"What's the trouble with *her?*" McClatchy said.

Bessie looked at the slammed door. "Leave her alone," she said.

It was a time when Phyllis needed a friend, Arline felt. The whole
town would be against her now. Arline pitied her and excused her because Phyllis did not know any better and had only acted according
to her nature. The pity was a half-vicarious pity. But Arline was sorry
for Bo Satterfy too, remembering: "What do you want him to do,
drink himself to death?" And for Bea Manriquez.

The subject of Phyllis's job was being held in abeyance at the
tavern; not because of any indecision but simply because Phyllis was
still in the hospital. McClatchy invoked the mercy of the market
place: "You can't kick 'em when they're down."

On the third day Phyllis was released from the hospital, and Arline
escorted her home. Before they left Arline asked: "Aren't you going
to see Bo Satterfy?"

"Like this?" Phyllis said bitterly. She was wearing dark glasses, which
Arline had bought for her, and her nose still had the splint in it, and
adhesive over it, and the contour of her little jaw was not yet down to
normal. Her head was covered with a scarf and she wore the collar of
her coat turned up.

Home again, she took off her coat and scarf and lighted a cigarette
and looked at herself in the glass, turned, and said: "I just want you
to do me one more favor."

"You know I will," Arline said.

"Tell your father I won't be working there no more."

"Whaaat?"

"Oh, I'm getting out of this town."

"You are? Why?"

"Why do you think."

Arline thought: Because of the gossip. She asked: "Where will you
go?"

"Back East."

"*East?*"

"Uh huh." Phyllis gave a mock sigh. "And I'll never be Mrs. Bo Satterfy."

"You won't?"

"I don't think it's a good idea, do you?"

"But what happened?"

"I just thought it over."

"Have you told him?"

"*Uh* uh. I'm just going to get out of his life—clear out—forever. Make a clean break. That's the best way, isn't it?"

"And not even tell him? You can't do that."

"All right, so maybe I'll write him a letter." Phyllis flung herself into a chair, drew at her cigarette, and expelled the smoke.

Arline stared at the girl. "But he's left his wife for you."

"Ah, he never left her for me. He'd have left her anyway."

"Phyl! You can't do that to him."

"You're the one didn't want me to marry him, remember?"

"But you said——"

"*I* can't reform a drunk. And I'm not going to spend the rest of my life with one. I won't have my looks forever—if I ever do again. Look at my nose, busted! All on account of him!" Phyllis got up and crushed out her cigarette in an ash tray, conscious that Arline looked scandalized.

"Phyl I don't understand you."

"*You* don't understand *me?* That's a laugh. What's the matter, now you *want* me to marry him? You want me to break up his home?"

"You've done that already, haven't you?"

"*Me? She* did, you mean. And don't worry, she'll take him back!"

"So he can drink himself to death?"

"Could I stop him?"

Arline said: "You didn't even love him."

"Love," said Phyllis, "look who's talking. Your father owns the Lost Dutchman. You got a son to take care of you when you get old. I got to take care of myself, see? Love. Oh, brother! What do you know about men? You never had a man in your life. Oh, sure, Bill Lucas. Aeh!"

Arline had drawn herself up, turning crimson. "Oh, yes? Maybe you don't know as much about men as you think you do."

"Oh, Arline, I'm sorreee."—Phyllis rushed to Arline and threw both arms around her, bursting into tears. "I didn't meeean it."

But the tears told that she *had* meant it.

"You're the best friend I ever h-had. . . ."

"Never mind," Arline said, disengaging herself.

Phyllis wailed: "Shall we have a cup of coffeee?" But Arline was walking toward the door. "Well, if that's the way you feel about it . . ."

Arline went out.

When she told her parents that Phyllis had quit her job and broken her engagement and was leaving town, Bessie sniffed: "It's a good thing."

"Well . . ." McClatchy said, "I owe her for Sunday and I was going to give her two weeks'. I'll send it to her; and we can take it off the income tax."

"You'll send her no two weeks'," Bessie said.

"Well, a week, then. I guess she needs it."

"Oh, dear," Bessie said. "Make it the two if you must."

"Sure; the government pays for it anyhow," McClatchy pretended.

But the letter with the check in it came back. Phyllis Plover had already gone, and without leaving a forwarding address.

Phyllis's insult cankered in Arline's mind. The "great peasant" and "giantess" could not help wishing that Phyllis had known about Tom Heath. But not, of course, what he had said. Phyllis would have laughed. Yet Phyllis could not attract him: the revenge of the ugly duckling. Yes, a lot Phyllis knew about men. But Arline herself could not understand. Peasant was insulting too, and giantess was crazy, and it seemed incredible that any man would want either. She wished she were small and pretty, as Phyllis was.

But he needed me, she thought when she remembered that night, he did need me, he needed me so. And nobody ever wanted me that much before. It never happened before. . . .

Then she heard over the radio that some faculty members at Fremont Institute had been suspended for refusing to take the loyalty oath; and the next day the *Sentinel* confirmed her surmise that one of them was Tom Heath.

She was indignant and sympathetic. Evenings, she found herself looking for him in the tavern. A month passed and he did not come.

But one night Bo Satterfy came in. His blond head was held erect by a great leather collar cradling his chin and the base of his skull. Followed by Arline's pained eyes, he walked to the bar, sat down rigidly under the insulting eyes of the Dutchman, and ordered a drink from Jerry Barth. She did not know him personally and thought better of speaking to him now. But an hour later, on his way out, he stopped and spoke to her.

He said: "Hello, Phyllis's friend."

"Hello, Mr. Satterfy. I'm so glad to see you back again."

"Where did she go?"

"Phyllis? Back East, that's all she said."

He gave a twisted smile of disbelief and would have passed on, but she insisted: "No, really. The post office returned the check my father sent her. Even the manager of the apartment doesn't know where she is."

He looked at the hat in his hands. "Back East—sure. The bright-lights. That's Phyllis." Then, as if with an effort of will, still without looking at her: "You know why she left, I suppose."

"She just said . . . she thought it was best."

He glanced into her eyes, and said: "Well, goodnight."

"Goodnight, Mr. Satterfy."

She had always thought he had a "sweet" face, but tonight it was bitter, and for some reason, as he went stiffly out the door, there came back to her what Phyllis had said about him once: "He likes to read poetry and play the banjo." Still, it seemed to her afterward, he didn't look like a man who was going to kill himself. And it would never have occurred to her that Phyllis's desertion could have left him in such a state of mind.

Less than an hour later a bus hit him and killed him, and the story was that he had deliberately thrown himself under the wheels.

His death shocked and scandalized the town. It was no secret that he had separated from his wife and been recuperating at his father's house, or that a waitress had been in the car with him when he hit the telegraph pole, and now everyone heard that the waitress had taken him away from Bea Manriquez and then jilted him, and the *Sentinel*, after reporting his death as an accident, announced that the funeral would be private, and these things lent color to the story that Bo Satterfy had died a suicide. The coroner's jury, it was true, returned a verdict of accident, but that was put down as a kindness to the family. And the Lost Dutchman Tavern reaped an increase of trade at lunch time, and there was much curiosity about the departed siren.

Arline reasoned that if Bo Satterfy had wanted to take his own life he surely would not have chosen such a method. Yet, she remembered, some people jumped off buildings. Perhaps he had done it on a desperate impulse. The idea of self-murder was appalling to her: despair was a crime against mercy.

But Bo Satterfy's death also had another effect on Arline, a strange one. It was a personal resentment of his death. It was an intensified resentment of the traitor, the squanderer, Phyllis Plover, whose insult the tragedy seemed somehow to make worse. And it was thinking that Tom Heath's obscure bit of self-revelation made him sound as unfulfilled, as lonely as she, and reflecting on the proposition that whatever the quality was that he needed in a woman, and had never had, she could give it to him. She might not want to have it, whatever it was, but not every woman could be small and pretty, and that, mysteriously enough, was not what he wanted, and it might never be this way again, and October had come and her son was in the second grade. Then it struck her that she could be to Tom Heath the woman he needed above all other women on earth. And she thought: It doesn't happen that way very often, does it? That must be something rare. . . .

That, she realized, was not a property of ugly ducklings. It belonged to the swans.

On the morning of the funeral she had bought a polo coat at Willis's and was walking down Hill Street to the tavern when she became conscious that an automobile at the curb was keeping pace with her. She glanced its way, said: "Oh!—Hello," and stopped; and Tom Heath stopped in his open convertible.

"Hello, Arline."

Spontaneously she moved to the car, saying: "I heard what they did to you at Fremont; I think it's terrible."

"We're taking the case to court."

"You are? Good! Will the Court make them take you back?"

"I'm not worried. I was just on my way down to see you."

"You were?"

"I want to talk to you, remember?"

"Oh." Then her eyes faltered.

But he never dreamt that he had not to do with the same woman. He pleaded: "This is important to me; I want you to believe that. But we can't talk here, or down there either. Get in the car and we'll drive somewhere. I'll bring you straight back. Will you?"

She met his gray gaze for a moment, then, dropping her eyes, simply opened the door and got in.

"Good girl!" And he started the car.

Then they were turning around, then driving westward out of town, and the road wound up into the hills but she did not object. He drove in silence and she did not ask him to begin. She half dreaded the moment he would. She thought of God and Billy and Phyllis Plover and her mother and father and what he would say to her and she would answer, fighting all at once conscience and pride and hunger.

It was a morning of faded sunshine, with figures of soiled cotton floating in the sky; the rains had not yet begun and the yellow grass in these hills where, in the Stone Age of California, Indians had gathered acorns from those live oaks, was tarnished and trampled-looking; then the car mounted the summit and below them, blue and calm and sheening to the brink of universal space, were the waters from which the *Golden Hind* had lately disappeared, and in the sky again a gull was wheeling.

"Here's what you need," he said, pulling off the road: "perspective." He stopped the car with the ocean dead ahead, and turned to her as she filled her lungs with the cold salt breeze. "And fresh air to clear your head," he added.

"It's beautiful," she said.

"Now the Philippines would be just about there. That's where the——"

"I know."

He smiled. He stretched an arm along the top of the seat and looked at her embarrassed profile. "Arline?"

"What?"

"What would you say if I asked you to marry me?"

The suggestion nearly stunned her.

"Arline?"

She had not turned her face to him. "Are *you* serious?"

"Perfectly serious."

An answer sprang to her lips: You don't have to marry me, Tom; but she checked it.

"All right," he said, "I *am* asking you."

"Tom!" And she almost said it.

"Well?"

That Tom Heath might ask her to be his wife had been in her mind from the day of the fair. But not that she had really believed he would. And now that he was offering marriage both her pride and her judgment said no. Marriage was not what he wanted, and if he was willing to marry her, marriage probably did not mean to him what it meant to her. There would be religious obstacles, too. And she a professor's wife—it was crazy! But the first thing she said was: "Do you know I have a child?"

"Certainly. I've talked to him. Why—do you think he'd mind?"

Talked to him? *Mind?* That Tom Heath knew of her almost eight-year-old and yet was asking her to marry him nearly overcame all her objections at once. At the same time it put another check on her moral deportment with Tom Heath. "But, Tom! I'm not the wife for you."

"How do you know you're not? I've never wanted any woman so much in my life. I haven't been able to get you out of my head."

Then remembering that he needed her, she was grateful again and full of compassion. But marriage! She said: "But that's not . . . love." ("Love," Phyllis had said, "look who's talking.")

"It could be," he said. Then he asked: "Aren't you going to say: 'But we hardly know each other'?"

"But we don't. Tom, we're practically strangers."

"Exactly!"

She looked at him. "What do you mean?"

"This. I got off to a wrong start with you; I realize that. I'm just beginning to know you. But you don't know me at all. I don't want you to answer me now. But give it a chance. Let's get acquainted. Let's go out a few times. Arline, I'm asking you like a schoolboy to let me court you. Fair enough?"

There was nothing immediate about his proposal now. There would be time enough to think about the objections, time enough to discuss the obstacles. And she felt humbled. "If you want."

"Arline!"

But she gently drew back, asking: "No. Wait."

His eyes crinkled. "This is so sudden?"

"Something like that."

"What's your night off?"

She smiled. "Any night but the week end."

"Dinner tomorrow night?"

"All right, Tom."

"Seven o'clock?"

"Seven o'clock."

"Fair enough."

On the way home she thought: I'm practically engaged; and hardly knew whether she was glad or disappointed.

She parted from Tom Heath at the tavern door, entered, and saw that something was wrong.

The lights on the bar side were turned off, all but the spotlight on the face of the Dutchman—except for him the bar was deserted. She stopped, turned, saw her mother at the cashier's counter, and went to her, alarmed.

"What's happened?"

Bessie's eyes were red. "Well . . . they arrested Jerry Barth."

"Arrested him?"

"And they're after Leo Carpenter—for bookmaking."

"*Book*making?"

"And we got a registered letter this morning from the State Board. Dear, they want to take your father's license away."

"Ma! The liquor license? What for?"

"For serving liquor to a drunken man. And there's talk they mean Mr. Satterfy the night he was killed."

"What! *He* wasn't drunk. I talked to him. Not drunk."

"Well, they say he was drunk when he was run over, and they say he got it here. And they say we're keeping a disorderly house, and Billy——"

"*Billy?*"

"Ohhh, dear. They say it's no place for a child."

"That's a lie!"

"Oh, and there's more. A whole rigamarole. It's all on the paper your father's got. Signed by the mayor and the City Council."

"No! Oh, Ma! Where's Dad?"

Bessie wearily closed her eyes for a moment before she replied. "He went out to get a lawyer."

"He did? Well, I should think so." A terrible suspicion came into Arline's mind. "*What* lawyer?"

Her mother told her grimly: "Mr. Reardon."

"Oh, God!"

"Well, I tried to stop him, but you know how your father is. He thinks the sun rises and sets in Mr. Reardon."

"Ohhhhhh," Arline said, "men!"

"Ohhh, dear."

"But, Ma! Isn't there still something we can do?"

"There is," Bessie said. "We can get down on our bended knees and pray."

25

THE MEN

Dan McClatchy ran up the dark flight of steps in the doorway next to the O.K. Machine Shop and rapped on Mr. Reardon's door. Nothing stirred. He rapped again. Not a sound.

The knob turned in his fingers. He looked in. A bell went off and nearly frightened him out again. It was the telephone. And then beside the instrument on the cluttered desk he saw, aureoled in the light from the dusty naked window, a gallon jug made of clear glass and containing only half a gallon of colorless liquid. He held his ground while the telephone jangled. From the back room came a growl. The telephone gave up, but the little tavernkeeper picked his way through the library heaped on the floor and knocked at the bedchamber.

"Mr. Reardon?"

A blast of the hoarse bass voice: "Wha'?" followed by two thuds that shook the floor under his feet, and a roaring challenge: "Who's there!"

"It's me—Mac—Dan McClatchy," he said, opening the door in his hurry.

Toward the back of the dusky cave that stretched fifty feet over the machine shop, outlined against the riddled blind that fought against the light of noon, and rooted in books to his knees, stood the giant in his shorts. "Mac? Oh," and convulsing himself, he burst into a fit of monstrous coughing.

"Excuse *me*, Mr. Reardon, but it looks like the whole town's after me," McClatchy said, advancing with a paper in his hand. "They're trying to close me up, Mr. Reardon. They claim we got Mr. Satterfy drunk and they arrested——"

Reardon, coughing, staggered past him into the bathroom. The stricken man hung over the toilet honking and hacking and roaring, and the earth trembled, and McClatchy stood distressed in the doorway. When the cataclysm subsided Reardon turned on the faucet in the tub, for the only handbasin was in his office, and laved his eyes and face, and drank from the tumbler of his famous hands, and blew, and with wet palms and fingers pushed back and smoothed his furious gray mane. Then he turned again to the toilet.

McClatchy retired into the bedroom. Going to the end of it, he reached across the havoc of the bed and raised the window blind and looked down on the boneyard of rusty mechanical skeletons. A clanging began in the machine shop. Down the room came Reardon. He landed on the bed with both hairy knees, nearly smashing it, and hurled open the window.

"God Almighty, Leonard, get away from that anvil!"

It seemed even the clanger's blood must have curdled at that unhuman roar, but the clanging continued. Reardon banged the window down again. McClatchy thought: It's a hell of a note he has to live in a dump like this—a man like him! And Reardon threatened: "I'll move!" Drunk but majestic, towering above his visitor, massive of front, red hairs flashing on his mighty arms and shoulders, and a stubble of white ones on his face, he stood indignantly hitching up his shorts.

"Mr. Reardon?" McClatchy recalled his presence, shouting to be heard above the din. "The State Board wants to close the bar on me; they're trying to revoke my license. Here's a copy of the Accusation signed by the mayor himself and the whole City Council; they're going to hold a hearing; they claim——"

Reardon stared down at him. "*Close the bar?*"

"That's what they're trying to do. They claim we got Mr. Satterfy drunk the night he got hit by the bus. And they claim——"

"Bo Satterfy?"

"But he never got it there, Mr. Reardon. Jerry Barth swears he wasn't drunk at all that night so he must have got it somewheres else. But they arrested Jerry for making book on the races, and they're looking for Leo Carpenter, and if it wasn't for Jerry telling them I had nothing to do with it they would have hauled me in too. They tried to claim I was running a betting joint. The police did. Would you believe that?"

"Certainly I would. You were! Everybody knows that."

"No, on my word of honor, Mr. Reardon, if I was, it was news to me. It must have been a little game the bartenders run on the side. I never knew a thing about it."

"Why you damn fool, is that the truth?"

"Well," McClatchy said, "I might be a damn fool but I was never a bookie, now I'll take an oath. And the boys'll tell you the same. But that aint the half of it. Here—here's the official Accusation."

Reardon took the paper. He poked his feet into his slippers. He put

on his great red bathrobe. He tramped into the front room, followed
by McClatchy. He found his weighty eyeglasses on the desk. He put
them on. With his back to the light he held up the paper and glanced
at it, then extended it to arm's length and glowered at it, then scornfully handed it back, saying: "Read the charges," and went round the
desk and lowered himself into the chair.

The tavernkeeper put on his spectacles and read, while, with elbows
on desk and hands clasped in front of mouth, the robed lawyer gazed
with concentration into the crystal jug. Downstairs the clanging
stopped, and through the floor came the hissing of an acetylene torch.

McClatchy began: " 'Conducting and operating a resort that is contrary to public welfare and morals in violation of section forty, California Alcoholic Beverage Control Act'—that's a lot of malarkey, I run
a respectable place there, don't I? You know that yourself, now. They
aint a picture on the wall you wouldn't show to the Ladies' Sodality
—I've had *them* there; and look at the class of people I get from the
city——"

"Read the charges."

McClatchy continued: " 'Conducting and operating a disorderly
house'—what the hell, that's a *whore* house, aint it? Where do they
get that stuff, anyhow? Let's see, here. . . . 'Selling and furnishing
intoxicating liquor to an obviously intoxicated person'—that's young
Mr. Satterfy, they say, and he wasn't drunk by a long shot, you can
ask Jerry; not when he left my place; I'm an innocent party, Mr. Reardon. 'Selling and furnishing intoxicating liquor to minors'—and they
can tell *that* to the Marines. I never done that in my life. But wait'll
you hear this, now—here's the last one: 'Contributing to the delinquency of a minor, to wit'—you won't believe it—'to wit, bringing up
a small child in the atmosphere of said resort in, in conjunction with
home and domicile'—little Bill! My daughter's boy. My own grandson. Now what do you think of a thing like that?" He waited anxiously.

Growling, Reardon said to the jug: "Old man Satterfy."

McClatchy asked: "Will you take the case, Mr. Reardon?"

Reardon raised his eyes, then dropped them. "I . . . I'll send you to
somebody."

But McClatchy said: "I want you, Mr. Reardon."

"I don't take cases any more," Reardon said roughly; "haven't for
years."

A pause. Then in a low voice McClatchy said: "Don't you think I
know that?"

And looking up at the solemn face, Reardon saw that his greatest admirer did know all there would have been to say. Everybody, he thought, knew.

McClatchy had not come to Reardon because of admiration only, but also because in the world to which McClatchy belonged one always gave one's business, when that was possible, to one's friends. It was part of a code, with obligations on both sides. That was what his wife knew and his daughter did not. Reardon knew it. But this offer nettled Reardon like an impudent challenge. He saw, still drunk though he was, that this little tavernkeeper wanted to use his own trouble to give Walsh Reardon another chance. Presumption! And it nettled him because he knew that underneath it all he was afraid.

"They say you're the greatest lawyer in town, Mr. Reardon."

For Reardon there was more irony in the statement than anyone else could have perceived. He sneered but could not resist asking: "Who says that?"

"Hump Corkery. Ed Primrose. They all say it."

Reardon did not miss the irony in those names, either. Yet on hearing them he was touched. He said: "The Old Guard."

"Yes, sir!"

"Well . . ." Reardon said, putting McClatchy off as he reached for the telephone, "I'll see what I can find out," and he began to dial with some difficulty the office of City Attorney Parker. But before he finished dialing he hung up on the little weasel with a bang. He tossed McClatchy the telephone book. "Look up the ice company." McClatchy found the number and Reardon dialed it. But George Huggins, member of the City Council, was out to lunch. "They'll *all* be out to lunch," Reardon said, disgusted with their clockbound lives and their frittering. But he dialed the Police Department and the chief answered.

"Walsh Reardon," he identified himself. "What's this about closing the Lost Dutchman?" . . . "Who—McClatchy?" . . . "Then what are you closing him up for?" . . . "Well, what *about* the Board of Equalization?" . . . "You don't believe that, do you?" . . . "Who says so?" . . . "How much?" . . . "And what does that prove?" . . . "Thought so. Much obliged." . . . "Yes." . . . "That so?" . . . "Uh huh . . . I see." . . . "That's about what I thought. Much obliged." He hung up; and it came to him that the reason Roy Lally had asked "McClatchy a friend of yours?" was that it had not even entered the chief's mind that Walsh Reardon might have a client. The bastards!

"Are you going to take the case, Mr. Reardon?"

Reardon's big red face had suddenly turned purple. "Take the case?" he said. But he paused, confounded. "It would be you and I and the Old Guard against the City and A. B. Satterfy. No, Mac." Depression wreathed him. "You've heard I was good once, but what you don't know is," he confessed, "I'm rusty."

"I'm asking you to take it, Mr. Reardon—for old lang syne."

For Walsh Reardon at that moment the phrase had magic beyond McClatchy's meaning. "For auld lang syne I'll take it!" he roared, raising his fist in the air. "And for auld lang syne I'll win it!"—the fist nearly drove the desk through the floor, and he rose to his feet misquoting Charles Kingsley with all the power of his lungs: "When you and I were young, lad, and all the hills were green!"

"You tell 'em—atta *boy!*" McClatchy cheered him, leaning forward from the hips, "I knew you'd *do* it."

The giant looked down at him in a kind of wonder. "*You*—you little son of a bitch! Little McEndymion! The last man in the world!"

"Oh I tellya."

"McEndymion—the beautiful shepherd!" Reardon said. " 'Arise, good youth, for sacred Phoebus' sake.' "

"Yes, sir!"

"McEndymion!" Reardon said again, for it had struck him from what part of Keats's poem came the line he had quoted. It was where the old sea god Glaucus recognizes in the beautiful shepherd the one appointed to free him from the witch's curse; which struck Reardon as a good omen. He said: "The man I christened!"

"Now you did for a fact!"

Reardon thundered:

> "I was a fisher once, upon this main,
>   And my boat danc'd in every creek and bay;
>   Rough billows were my home by night and day—
>   The sea-gulls not more constant; for I had
>   No housing from the storm and tempests mad
>   But hollow rocks—and they were palaces
>   Of silent happiness, of slumberous ease.
>   Long years of misery have told me so.
>   Ay, thus it was one thousand years ago."

And throwing out his arm, he pointed at McClatchy. " 'Thou art the man!' "

"You said it."

"Put some coffee on the stove."

"You betcha!"

Reardon shaved at the small mirror hanging on a nail high above the washbasin, and cursed when he cut himself. He was in the tub when McClatchy brought him his first cup of coffee, strong. Out again and dry, he put on clean shorts, a shirt, and, with the help of his client, his trousers. He sat on the bed to pull on his socks, and the client knelt to help him with his shoes. Suddenly Reardon stood up, looking wild. "Got to get back," he said.

"Back where, Mr. Reardon?"

"Back!"

"Yes, sir!" McClatchy said, bending over the shoes again; he sang:

> "*Wanna go back to my little grass shack in Kealakekua, Hawaii,*
> *Where the Humuhumu Nukunuku a puaa goes swimming by. . . .*"

He looked up again, his face shining with humor, and Reardon stared down at him. Then Reardon threw back his head and hurled at the roof his alpenhorn laughter:

"Hrrrrrrrraw! Hrraw! Hrraw!

"You tell 'em," grinned the clown, bending over the shoes again—

> "*Where the Humuhumu Nukunuku a puaa goes swimming by. . . .*"

"Hrrrrrrrraw! Hrraw! Hrraw!"

26

DELILAH

Within a few hours the news about the tavern had spread through the town, and it met with considerable approval.

The Ladies' Service Club had of course opposed the tavern from the start, and the veteran painters had made enemies with their demonstration for Henry A. Wallace, and businessmen begrudged the very existence of those butterflies, and wives deplored the way some of the females would display themselves on the streets in warm weather. And it had been observed by certain eyes that if you read the San Francisco newspaper columns you would think Llagas existed to be the setting for the tavern, and it rankled in certain breasts that the columnists

were always quoting the proprietor, as if *he* were the prominent citizen, and it had reached certain ears that the veteran painters were now
having the effrontery to criticize the approved and accepted design
for the new City Hall, and it was believed by the Baptist congregation
that the tavern was to blame for the atheism of the minister's son,
Bernie. The tavern was widely regarded in Llagas as a corrupter of
youth, and the separation of the A. B. Satterfy, Jr.s, had suggested it
might be a trap for husbands. So, on hearing that Bo Satterfy had been
drunk when run over, and that he had got it at McEndymion's, many
Llagans agreed it was time that bar was closed.

Such was the tavern's fame that within a few hours also the news
about it was in the San Francisco afternoon papers and there had
arrived in Llagas a feature writer for the morning *Examiner* to dig a
little deeper into the case. William O'Rourke was his name, and he
was a big upstanding man with a fine beefy convivial face. Reading
his story next morning, Llagans discovered their feeling against the
tavern to be nothing less than public indignation. But he had treated
McEndymion with hearty affection, and the tavern in the traditional
Mermaid manner, and he had made light of the town, so they discovered further that this was more than a case—it was a cause.

In vain Arline had insisted to her father, on his return from Reardon's
yesterday, that Reardon was "nothing but an old barfly" and "a bum"
and "a windbag" and would ruin them. And to her amazement her
mother had kept putting in for Reardon with the best she could mus-
ter, such as: "Well, they say he was good once, God help us," and:
"They say he knows law, at least," and: "He's got the silver tongue
anyhow," and: "Well, we can offer him up, whatever." And later her
mother had said to her:

"Now I don't want you worrying your father. He's got enough on
his mind."

"Worrying *him? His* mind? What about us? We'll lose everything
we've got."

"Oh, don't be so sure."

"But this place won't be any good without a liquor license; we'll
have to close up! If we lose the license we'll lose the place; and with
Reardon we won't have a chance—we'll go bankrupt. Dad'll have to
go back to tending bar for somebody else. And what about you? What
about Billy?"

"Now you listen to me. He's got Billy and the both of us on his
mind as much as you have. And he's doing the best he knows how.
And you won't change him. And two nagging women in the house

won't help him or Billy neither. And I want you to remember this"—sternly: "It's his license. And his bar. And his business that he built up from nothing. And he's your father and my husband and the head of this house. And I won't have him interfered with. Now. Do you hear? I won't!"

And Arline, with the ground swept from under her feet, asked herself what was to become of them.

Last night she had dwelt on the proposal of Tom Heath. Could she be his wife? Wouldn't all the other professors' wives laugh at her? But couldn't she read and study, couldn't she learn? *He* would see that Billy got an education and didn't become a bartender or anything like that; and she would form his character, see that he kept his religion; and there would never be a Nancy Croan for Billy, never a Phyllis Plover, and he could never do what Bo Satterfy had done, and she would teach him never to drink—she would tell him about Reardon. And maybe he would grow up to be a professor.

But if she married Tom Heath, would it last? They were so different, he and she. They belonged to different worlds. They didn't think alike. They didn't speak the same language. There was only—that. And what that was she scarcely knew. Was it strong enough? Would it hold?

In the morning Reardon came down to the tavern to interview family and staff, and Arline suffered herself to be pumped. But then she saw that he thought she didn't like him, and felt mean. It wasn't that. She was sorry for him really. He was so big and gruff and shabby and such a failure. ("Offer him up.") Everybody would laugh at them for having Reardon. And with the town against them they would lose the license and have to sell the tavern, or as much of the tavern as they owned. Sell the Rembrandt, too. And then what? Oh, her poor foolish mother. But Billy, little Billy with his life before him, child Billy being sacrificed to the blindness of his grandfather—what about Billy?

That afternoon she went to the beauty shop, and that evening put on the new semi-formal of crimson silk that she had worn only once before, worn only as hostess in the tavern. But Tom Heath took her to a French restaurant on Main Street, and she was disappointed because there was no dancing. He had heard the news of course, and while they ate they discussed the case.

He said: "I hear you've got Walsh Reardon."

There! The whole town had heard it. But having admitted it was true, she found herself having to defend Reardon: "They say he's really good, you know."

After the least hesitation Heath answered politely: "Yes, I know."

And he said no more about Reardon. He said he wished there were
something he could do to help, and she thanked him and said there
was nothing—nothing, she was thinking, that anyone could do, now
they had Reardon.

In an old-fashioned house on Union Street just then the city
attorney and his wife were also having dinner, and it happened that
he was saying:

"Where would he be today if it wasn't for me? Never liked Walsh
Reardon, either. Thrown him work for years just for old times' sake.
He's biting the hand that fed him."

Sympathetically his wife asked: "Are you worried about the case,
dear?"

"Worried! *I* should say not. We've got that tavern dead to rights.
Open and shut. Nothing Walsh Reardon can do. He's the one ought
to be worried. He's only taking the bread out of his own mouth."

But having been married to Earl Parker for twenty-three years, Mrs.
Parker knew he was worried all right, and having lived in Llagas all her
life, she knew why.

In the French restaurant Arline asked Tom Heath about his own
case.

"Well," he said, sitting back with a smile, "the institute's in disgrace and the fight's a *cause célèbre* throughout the academic world. I
think the trustees are finding out they made a mistake."

Cause célèbre, which she recognized only as French, discouraged
her.

She asked: "You think you'll win?"

"In court, yes. Those dismissals were entirely illegal."

"You had courage, Tom, to do what you did."

"Oh nonsense. Whether I lose that job doesn't matter very much. I
could get another; this country's not all fascist yet, you know. But it's
in danger of being. And we simply can't let it happen. None of us.
That's why intelligent liberals everywhere recognize the case as important. It's no mere intramural matter concerning a few rebels. It
strikes at freedom of thought and conviction everywhere."

"All the more reason," she said.

"For what?"

"Why I think you've got courage."

He smiled again, but in a different way, and asked: "Have you
thought about us?"

She nodded. "Mm hm." And sighed. "But Tom, how could we——
What would we talk about?"

"*Talk* about?" He laughed.

"No, I mean," laughing too, though coloring. "I mean I don't *know* anything. Oh, Tom, what would your friends say?"

"That's ridiculous. Is that what's worrying you?"

"That and other things."

"For instance?"

"Oh, I don't know. For instance——" Knowing quite well the instance she would mention, she bowed her head for a moment as if to recall one, gathering her courage, then looking up, said: "Religion, for instance. I'm a Catholic, Tom."

"Catholic! I don't care if you're a Mohammedan. Unless you mean you can't marry a heathen."

"But for instance you'd have to promise not to interfere."

"All right. That's your business. I have nothing against Catholics." She repeated: "A *heathen?*" and asked: "Weren't you ever baptized?"

"Oh, yes. A Baptist. The works," he grinned.

"But you have no religion now?"

"The Golden Rule, where possible."

"You don't believe in God any more?"

"Arline, I'm a physicist, not a philosopher. Certainly I believe in God. The universe is governed by a Mind, an inconceivable Mind—God, if you like. But not an old man with a white beard. No man at all. We can't make God in our image."

"But you just made Him in *your* image. 'Mind,'" she smiled. "Tom, you made Him a Scientist."

"Oh, no. Mind, yes, but no human mind; and Scientist undoubtedly, but no Scientist that I made."

"Divine Mind?"

"If you like."

"And Will? And Heart, Tom, don't you think he's Heart, too? Because if He can't love," she rushed on to say before he could interrupt, "He's not as much as people, is He?"

"That, Arline, is what is known as anthropomorphism—God in the image of man."

"No, Tom, we believe God made us in His image, with minds and wills and hearts."

"Do you believe in hell?"

"Yes."

He looked at her with curiosity and smiled.

She asked: "Do you believe in heaven?"

"Oh, there may be some form of survival after death. Strömberg has satisfied himself there's even pleasure and misery."

"But, Tom, don't you think it's important?"

"Very important—especially if Strömberg is right."

"Who's he?"

"Astronomer. Worked it out scientifically. Very interesting job."

"But you think what I believe is superstition, don't you?"

"I think it's a fable."

"But don't you care what I believe?"

"Why should I?"

"Well, because you believe in truth, don't you? And if it isn't true, then it's bad, isn't it?"

"Some people think so. But I think religion is good for some people. Jung maintains that people who lose it are in danger of psycho-neurosis. If you need it and can accept it and it helps you, then for you it may be good. Besides, freedom of worship, which is a form of freedom of conviction, is protected under the Constitution, so what you believe is constitutionally none of my business. Does that answer your question?"

Smiling with closed lips and nodding, she said: "*Mm* hm," and let him change the subject.

But it had upset her plans that there was no dancing, and when he had driven her home early, as promised, she had not accomplished half what she had set her mind on. She welcomed his invitation to sit in the car and talk awhile.

He said: "I want to know what else is on your mind about me. Let's get it into the open. What else is bothering you?"

"Oh," she sighed, "well, for another thing," she told him hesitantly, her eyes on the dashboard, "an important thing," she pointed out, "I'm not pretty or anything."

In a tone of gentle reproach he repeated: "Pretty," and asked: "Pretty as in what? Pretty as in doll baby? Pretty as in glamour girl? Pretty as in Sigma Chi? No," he said, "you're not pretty."

"I know," she admitted, dropping her eyes to her handbag. "And I'm not educated or intelligent or—— So I don't see why you want me."

"Arline, I don't want to marry a Ph.D., and I don't care for peaches and cream. But you!" His arm was on top of the seat back and she felt his hand brush the hair on her neck. "You know what you do to me."

"But I don't know, Tom, I don't know!" And suddenly she turned her head and their eyes met, and she looked at him, and he was astonished.

"Arline!"

Sinfully she permitted him liberties that aroused him to a pitch of passion, and in the midst of it he heard her saying: ". . . a priest. Not in the church but in the priest's house. A priest——"

"Hang the priest."

"Would you be married by a priest?"

"Yes, a priest!"

Then she made him stop, and he was furious and there were tears in his eyes. . . .

And then she was standing in the dark beside her sleeping son, erect, triumphant. She was thinking it was strong enough and that there would be no difficulty about any of the other things. She was thinking: He'll have to. I'll make him. I will!

27

IN THE SIREN'S WAKE

The little white-clapboard City Hall of Llagas, where the Lost Dutchman Tavern was to go on trial for its life this bright November morning, sat well back from the street behind a lawn, its shingle roof crowned by an open belfry, vacant now the swallows were away, and its walk flanked on each side by a low pyramid of black iron cannonballs. And this morning the veteran painters were picketing it. They carried signs reading:

**SAVE
McENDYMION'S**

**DON'T RUN ART
OUT OF TOWN
ON A RAIL**

**GIVE VETS
A CHANCE**

As usual in liquor control cases where a city like Llagas was the complainant, the hearing was to be held in the City Council chamber.

Arline and Bessie, arriving together, found men standing about the corridor outside it, smoking, and the chamber already fairly crowded.

The chamber resembled a courtroom. At its head stood the mayor's raised desk of dull brown mahogany, very like a judge's bench, but shorter; George Washington gazed out from the wall behind it—to his right the American Flag hanging loose on an upright standard, to his left the Bear Flag of California arranged the same; and on a platform beside the mayor's desk a chair had been placed—the witness chair. Directly in front of the mayor's desk and below it three long tables formed a squared U, and there was another long table ranged parallel to each side of the U, and a small one by the witness chair. All this a wooden railing cut off from five rows of scuffed benches, painted brown, where the public sat, itself bisected by an aisle. And there was brown-painted wood six feet up the walls, and above that faded tan paper which in places on the ceiling was waterstained. Fastened to the ceiling over the Council section were six fluorescent lighting tubes; over the public's aisle hung an ugly iron chandelier on a dusty iron chain. In the left-hand wall were six windows, tall and thin, with a view of cannonballs and the picket line.

Even the official side of the railing was pretty well filled up by now. Mayor Schuman and Chief of Police Lally conferred with City Attorney Parker at the table that formed the left leg of the U, while Coroner Milton Groom listened; several policemen stood about, talking; and both tables flanking the U were occupied by members of the press, which was amazing. Hubert Ritter of the *Sentinel* and Alice Fritz of the *Leader* were there of course, but the other newspaper people were all from San Francisco, which was more amazing still and was distracting Parker. Why in the name of common sense, he wondered, should San Francisco be so interested in this case as to send such a delegation of its press to Llagas?

But then what sensible man ever could make sense of such a city as that? Once, when a Chinese houseboy residing in it was arrested for the murder of the white woman who employed him, that city rose up indignant to defend him, in the face of the most damning sort of evidence, on the principle that no Chinese houseboy was capable of such disloyalty—and got him off. And this was the same press that, flocking to the once-upon-a-time gold town of Columbia on the Mother Lode for the trial of a mountain woman accused of having poisoned her husband, had wanted the judge to signal the opening of court by ringing the old vigilante bell. There they sat—the hearty O'Rourke of the *Examiner*, the cynical-faced sensual-lipped bemonocled Wickshaw of the *Chronicle*, and the *Chronicle's* art critic, fat

Noel Ames, and the small-black-mustached Kipp of the *Call-Bulletin*, wearing, of all costumes, a hiking one, and the wild-black-haired Polly Eichler, looking the born defender of civil liberties, of the *News*, not to mention four photographers, one with cheeks like raspberry jam, another with a hogshead belly. Parker had the feeling they were all against him.

Arline too was troubled by birds of omen. She had recognized Mrs. Henry H. Crown, whom the *Sentinel* called "civic leader," in the audience, and there was a clergyman present, a kindly-looking one, but his suit was gray, and Link Cotter, the octogenarian Eye of Main Street, had a seat in the front row. And a chill went through her as she recognized the old carrion bird Josie Cantrell, dispatcher of girls and hoverer at funerals. ("Was Josie there?" "Josie was there.") She was knitting.

Arline did not know that half a dozen of the men waiting in the corridor were lawyers attracted here by the scheduled appearance of Walsh Reardon. And she did not know Judge Díaz when she saw him, but wondered who the distinguished-looking and picturesque old gentleman with the cane was. He was sitting just across the aisle, tall, gaunt, large-beaked, and stately, with light tawny skin, black hair barely touched with gray, and grizzled black mustache: descendant of Don Marcos Díaz and, on his mother's side, of the gentle Sancha, sister of the now half-legendary Toríbio Tortoléro, friend, rival, and conscience of Roque Moréra. Retired now, Salvador Díaz had been for many years one of the most highly respected superior judges in the state. Even he was here to see Reardon.

Reardon was coming down the aisle; and at first hardly anyone noticed that his client was coming behind him. The giant with the heavy red face, silver mane, and thick rusty brows, in the freshly pressed brown suit whose shabbiness only lent an air of kingly indifference to that figure, took every eye but Bessie's; and the city attorney thought bitterly: Walks in like he's used to appearing in court five days a week. The client, neatly turned out in blue serge, and walking rapidly to keep up, followed him through the railing to the table that made the right leg of the U, where they took seats facing the battery of officials at the left leg; and the eyes of the two attorneys met. Smiling slightly, the giant rasped: "Morning, Earl."

The city attorney answered: "Why, good morning, Walsh," as if in good-natured amusement. Earl Parker was a bony man with a slight hump, in a suit of hard gray worsted; he had sandy hair gone thin, two unhealthy-looking pink spots at his cheekbones, a tight mouth which he was wont to purse when absorbed or irritated, keen blue eyes, and spectacles.

"Full house," the little client whispered to his champion uneasily. But, locating wife and daughter by means of the handkerchief that his wife shook at him, he bravely grinned and hoisted the O-signal of forefinger and thumb. Four flashbulbs went off in his face. Next the photographers posed him with his lawyer. Then he saw Noel Ames at the press table behind the officials, and shooting clasped hands into the air, shook the union cordially at his friend—the cameras recorded that one also.

Two men with topcoats over their arms were coming down the aisle, the older one carrying a briefcase, the younger something that might have been a portable radio. The older led the way through the railing. The mayor approached him inquiringly; they shook hands; the mayor presented the other officials; they chatted and then laughed and all turned their heads to look out the window at the picket line. Meanwhile the younger man had sat down at the small table by the witness chair and arranged before him his black burden. It was a stenotype machine and he was a court stenographer. The older man put his topcoat and hat on a chair, and keeping his briefcase, mounted to the mayor's desk.

Conversation in the chamber waned; the bell of Groom's Fine Funerals was heard tolling, two blocks away; the man behind the mayor's desk took some documents out of his briefcase and put on great horn glasses. He had corrugated gray hair and loose white cheeks which hung on his face like drapes, and it happened that on this day he was turning sixty years of age. He was a lawyer and a lifelong Democrat who in his youth had run for the municipal bench in San Francisco and been snowed under, and it was a source of chagrin to him that the quasi-judicial post he now held with the State Board of Equalization was one that hardly anyone understood and the general public did not even know existed. He looked up, over his glasses.

Generally speaking, he disliked these hearings in small towns. You never knew what you might get into where liquor was concerned. You might even have the Bible read to you; and when that happened you'd better let it be read into the record—indeed, there had once been read into the record for the guidance of the Board the entire sixth chapter of the First Epistle to the Corinthians. The policy was to be tolerant and make no enemies for the Board. And there would be pages of irrelevancies, mere accusations, and incompetent hearsay to wade through afterward when you were preparing the proposed decision which the Board, in ninety-nine cases out of a hundred, would adopt and hand down as its own. You did the work and the credit went to the Board—what credit there was. Ninety-nine out of a hundred of these cases were never heard of outside the town. But this case was being written about in the San Francisco papers, and the man behind the mayor's desk knew the metropolitan press when he saw it. He smiled paternally on his throne and rapped twice with the mayor's gavel, and the City Council chamber became a courtroom. He read the specifications of the case aloud and asked, rather as an afterthought, whether the respondent licensee was present.

Reardon got up and sawed on the great bullfiddle: "He's here, your honor. I represent him in this matter. My name is Reardon."

The man looked at the representative of the respondent licensee, impressed by sheer size and sound and by that absolute mien. "Very well, Mr. Reardon," he said, and to the courtroom at large addressed a statement such as he customarily used on opening a crowded liquor hearing in a small town. It was intended to assure everyone of the good will of himself and the Board, put everyone at ease, and explain a little of his function and authority, and in this instance it served to insure that the press would not be at a loss for his name.

"My name," he said, "is James J. McGann, and I may say for the benefit of all that technically I am not a judge. My title is hearing officer. And this is not technically a court of law. The Administrative Procedure Act, which we follow, is, to cite its preface, 'designed to afford a fair hearing before an impartial and qualified tribunal,' and our procedure here is 'more liberal and less restrictive than in proceedings before courts of law.' The duty of the hearing officer is 'to exercise all powers relating to the conduct of the hearing,' review the evidence, and recommend a decision to the Board of Equalization. We are governed by the Alcoholic Beverage Control Act, but under Article Twenty-two, Constitution of the State of California, the Board has broad powers of discretion. All of which, of course," he finished with an apologetic little wave meant to indicate the attorneys, "you gentlemen know."

Reardon didn't know it, Arline thought. She had the impression that the Silver Tongue had thought the hearing officer a judge. She glanced at her mother, but her mother's face was placid. Arline supposed *she* had offered Mr. Reardon up.

Half a dozen of the veteran painters, having left but a skeleton of a picket line in front of the building, crowded in among the attorneys in the standing room behind the benches as the City called its first witness, a swarthy young police officer named Cardinelli. And the trial of McEndymion's began.

28

KING RICHARD

At about eleven o'clock on the night of October 14, Officer Cardinelli testified, he had seen a man step into the street from the Lost Dutchman Tavern. He had driven his prowl car slowly along the curb, turned his spotlight on the lone walker, and recognized him as Almon B. Satterfy, Jr., whom he knew by sight. Parker asked him why he had looked at the man so carefully.

Answer: "We keep a watch for drunks that time of night."

"But you don't turn your spotlight on every citizen you see, do you?"

"No, sir."

"Then why did you do it in this case? Was the citizen walking in an erratic or unusual manner, or would you say Mr. Satterfy was walking normally?"

"He had a brace on his neck, sir."

"A brace on his neck—you mean a surgical brace? The kind a man wears when his neck is broken?"

"Yes, sir."

"Did you know that Mr. Satterfy had a broken neck?"

"I heard he broke it in an automobile accident."

"And you thought that accounted for his strange manner of walking; was that it?"

"Yes, sir."

"Now, did you, on that same night, investigate a traffic accident on El Camino near Oak Street, and find that at approximately eleven-forty o'clock, or about forty minutes after you had seen Mr. Satterfy leave the Lost Dutchman Tavern, he had been hit by a Greyhound bus?"

"I did."

"Will you describe how the accident occurred."

"According to my investigation the bus was proceeding southbound into town on El Camino at a lawful speed when the victim walked in front of it."

"Mr. Satterfy walked in front of the bus—I see. And what happened to him?"

"He was killed."

A chill ran down Arline's spine and Parker said: "That's all."

Reardon got up slowly, removing his glasses, and rumbled: "Now, I take it the testimony we have just heard is preliminary to something else; and I presume that the first part of it, remote and inconclusive though it may be, is offered as bearing on the issue whether an obviously intoxicated person was served liquor in the Lost Dutchman Tavern. But it isn't clear to me whether the second part of the testimony, bearing on the man's death, is objectionable or not. Is that offered as evidence that the man was obviously fuddled with liquor served to him in the Lost Dutchman?"

"It is," said Parker.

Reardon shrugged, and to the mild surprise of the attorneys in the back of the room said: "No objection." He addressed the witness. "Officer, when you turned your spotlight on this man what did he do? He didn't just ignore a thing like that, did he?"

"Well, no. He stopped and looked kind of scared for a minute there, I guess, and asked me what the trouble was."

"So you saw him walk, looked at him under your spotlight, and also heard him talk. Did you arrest him?"

"No, sir."

"If you saw a man staggering on the street and heard him talking thickly and knew he were not in control of his faculties, it would be your duty to take him in charge, wouldn't it?"

"If I knew that, yes."

"But Mr. Satterfy you did not arrest. Were you personally acquainted with Mr. Satterfy? Were you a friend of his?"

"No, I was not. I was not acquainted with him personally."

"Thank you, Officer," said Reardon, and turned away.

Mr. McGann asked: "Have you anything else, Mr. Parker?"

"Yes, sir," said Parker, rising again. To the witness: "You didn't know Mr. Satterfy personally but you knew who he was, didn't you?"

"Yes, sir."

"You knew him to be the son of Mr. A. B. Satterfy, Senior, the owner of the newspaper called the *Sentinel*, a wealthy and influential man in this community?"

A pirate roar shattered the calm: "Mr. Referee!" said Reardon.

Referee was the title for which hearing officer had only lately been substituted by law, a change which Mr. McGann thought ridiculous. Who could say "Mr. Hearing Officer"?

The pirate voice was demanding: "Is the city attorney impugning the integrity of his own witness? Is he suggesting that this young officer did not arrest the son because he was intimidated by the wealth and influence of the father? Is he suggesting that the son went to his death because of cowardly dereliction of duty on the part of this young officer?"

"No!" shouted Parker, almost jumping up and down in his agitation. "No, no, no, of course not. I am suggesting, I am trying to show that the officer, that although he didn't know the man personally, there was no mistake in the identification."

Reardon said dryly: "I think that's already been established, Mr. Parker."

"Very well! All right! Since you agree to the identification, I have nothing further."

"In that case, I have!" said Reardon as Parker sat down, and he returned to the witness, whose young face had flushed during the exchange. "Officer Cardinelli, if you had thought this man drunk you would have arrested him no matter who he was, wouldn't you?"

Witness (indignant): "I certainly would."

"Then, after seeing him walk, looking at him closely under your spotlight, and hearing him talk, why did you not arrest him?"

"Because I did not think he was drunk."

There it was, clean-cut and definite. Whispers and chuckles among the standee attorneys, to whom it was plain what had happened. Reardon had set a trap for Parker, Parker had leaped into it, then Reardon had taken Parker's witness away from him. Parker was sitting with his mouth screwed to a point, his eyes snapping, the two pink spots at his cheekbones considerably enlarged and dyed dark red. Arline felt a bit more hopeful, though the trickery had escaped her and she could have died when the family lawyer called the hearing officer a referee.

"Thank you, Officer," Reardon said again, and turned for the first time to the testimony about Bo Satterfy's death. "Now, when you were investigating the traffic accident did you *then* discover you had been derelict in not taking Mr. Satterfy into custody forty minutes before?"

"Not necessarily. He could have been to another bar in the meantime."

It was a point that set Earl Parker back where he had begun; and yet Reardon did not appear to care for it. He said: "But no bottle was found on him?"

"No, sir."

Reardon pulled thoughtfully at his chin. "Now," he said, as if beginning again, "did anyone observe the victim between the time you saw him leave the tavern and the time of the accident?"

"Yes, sir. The ticket man at the bus depot observed him walking up and down in front there till about fifteen minutes before the accident."

"I see. The bus depot is how far from the place where the bus hit him, and in which direction?"

"Approximately one hundred yards south."

"Then he walked north from the bus depot, in the direction the bus was coming from; is that your understanding?"

"Yes, sir."

"As if on his way home? I mean, was that the direction of his home, or of his father's home?"

"That would be the opposite direction."

"Opposite from both addresses?"

"Yes, sir."

"I specify both addresses because I understand he was making his home with his father on Traubaugh Avenue at the time, and not with his wife on Lincoln; is that correct?"

"That is correct."

"How long did he walk up and down in front of the depot?"

"About five minutes, the ticket man said."

"And how long would you say it would have taken him to walk from the place where you first saw him to the depot if he went there directly?"

"Oh . . . about ten minutes."

"Are there any bars between the depot and the place where the bus hit him?"

"Nn-o, sir."

"All right, then. He spent five minutes walking in front of the depot *until* fifteen minutes before the accident. That accounts for twenty minutes. And ten minutes to walk to the depot make thirty minutes. That leaves ten minutes he could have spent in another bar if he went to one. How many drinks would you say a man would consume in a bar in ten minutes from the time he entered the door?"

Parker objected and Reardon withdrew the question.

Mr. McGann was baffled. It appeared to him that Reardon had been taking Parker's side by suggesting that if Satterfy was drunk when the bus hit him, he was probably drunk when he left the tavern, so that the officer *had* been derelict in not taking him into custody—and *Parker* had objected.

Then Reardon threw the officer a lifeline: "Officer Cardinelli, I sug-

gest to you that this so-called accident was not an accident, and ask
you whether in the course of your investigation you heard the word
suicide."

A rustle swept the benches, and immediately the courtroom was
quiet again. But the Llagas attorneys at the back of the room were as
confused as the hearing officer was. For out of Bo Satterfy's death the
City, thus far, at least, had made only the flimsiest circumstantial case
against the tavern, and Reardon had already demolished it, and wasn't
that enough? Then why should he risk a libel suit? Why go out of his
way to make an enemy of Bo Satterfy's father?

The word suicide had made the black eyes of the young policeman
flicker once. He glanced at his chief, then quickly away, and shifted
in his chair. "I heard the word, yes."

"You heard the word. Did you question the busdriver?"

"Yes, sir; he said the victim dashed out in front of him."

" 'Dashed' out? I believe you previously testified the victim 'walked'
out."

"The busdriver used the word dashed."

"And he also used the word suicide?"

"Well, I can't say he used that particular word, no."

"But you did, as you have just testified, hear the word suicide at that
time?"

"I heard it at that time; I heard it from an eyewitness, Manuel
Salazar. He was passing by at that time. He said it looked like suicide."

"Manuel Salazar?" Reardon went to his table, consulted some papers, and returned with them. "Did the eyewitness Manuel Salazar
later give a different version?"

"Well, at the inquest he called it an accident."

"At the inquest he called it an accident but at the time he said it
looked like suicide. *Thank* you, Officer. Now, returning to the ticket
agent in the bus depot: you testified that he saw the victim walking
up and down. He did not say 'staggering' or anything else to indicate
a state of obvious intoxication?"

"Said he looked kind of nervous; that's all."

" 'Kind of nervous.' Thank you; no more questions."

Hubert Ritter of the *Sentinel* went out hurriedly to telephone his
office as the spectators began to chatter. Bessie said to Arline: "Now,
I think Mr. Reardon's doing pretty good." And Arline had to admit
that it seemed he somehow was.

Never before in his career with the Board had anything half so interesting as a question of suicide come before Mr. McGann; better
yet, this particular question evidently concerned a person of conse-

quence—and there sat the metropolitan press. He was not sure that the question could influence the proposed decision in this case but he hoped all the same, upon his sixtieth birthday, that if Satterfy *had* committed suicide, this man Reardon could show it. He asked if Mr. Parker had any more questions. Parker wanted no more of this turn-coat policeman; he said with disgust that he had not. And for his next witness he called the coroner.

Dr. Milton Groom, who testified that he was a doctor of medicine, was white of hair, ruddy of complexion, and mild of countenance, and looked, in his blue suit and wing collar, more like a doctor of divinity. Parker asked him what percentage of alcohol in the blood would produce drunkenness, and he answered: "Why, I believe the National Safety Council estimates the amount at fifteen hundredths of one per cent." Parker asked him if he agreed with that estimate, and he admitted that he did. Parker asked him if an analysis of Satterfy's blood had been made, and he owned up that it had. Parker asked him what percentage of alcohol had been found, and he sighed: "Fifteen hundredths of one per cent." Parker asked him: "Then, Dr. Groom, would you as a doctor of medicine conclude that the victim was under the influence of alcohol when he was killed by the bus?" And he made a clean breast: "I regret to say that I would." Turning to Reardon, Parker finished on a mucous note of triumph: "Your witness!"

"Well," Reardon grumbled, getting up, "again I can only suppose that this is preliminary to something else. But what is its purpose? Is it adduced to support the contention that the man had been made drunk in the Lost Dutchman?"

"It is," Parker said again.

Reardon smiled and turned to the witness. "Come, now, Milton, you certainly don't believe that all human beings have the same tolerance for alcohol, do you?"

"Well, the National Safety Council——"

"I didn't ask you about the National Safety Council. The National Safety Council's estimate applies to when a person of either sex is not in a safe condition to drive an automobile, doesn't it?"

"True——"

"This man wasn't driving the bus, Milton; he was walking. Furthermore, he did not appear drunk to either Officer Cardinelli or the ticket agent. How do you account for that?"

"Well, but even walking—I think fifteen hundredths of one per cent is a fair estimate of when a man is under the influence. We must have some norm," the coroner insisted, looking at the prodigious body

of the notorious toper before him. "I am assuming Mr. Satterfy was
an average human being."

"*Assuming?* Wasn't there an autopsy in this case?"

"*Oh no*, it is not the practice to perform an autopsy in every traffic
case. But we do take a sample of the, ah, blood."

Reardon lowered his eyebrows menacingly. "You did not examine
the liver?"

"No."

"What! But if this man was a heavy drinker, wouldn't his liver have
shown it? What basis have you for 'assuming' he had no more than the
average tolerance for alcohol? Did you know he'd been in the Navy?"

"Browbeating the witness!" Parker cut in, jumping up. "I object to
this kind of cross-examination."

"If I lost my temper," Reardon said to Mr. McGann, giving no indi-
cation that he had regained it, "it was because this unprofessional testimony is apparently going to oblige us to exhume the body!"

The benches gasped at the idea of exhuming Bo Satterfy. Parker
repeated: "*Exhume the body?*" There was a mass movement at the
press tables as the reporters bent forward to scribble, and two cameras
exploded in the coroner's eyes. "Good heavens," he said.

Parker retorted: "That's preposterous! What would an autopsy
prove?"

"*Prove?*" Reardon said. "I will remind counsel that the question before the Board is not how much liquor was in the man's blood. It is
not even whether he was intoxicated. Under section sixty-two of the
Alcoholic Beverage Control Act, it is whether he was furnished liquor
in the Lost Dutchman while *obviously* intoxicated. The City argues
from the circumstances of his death that he was obviously intoxicated
forty minutes after he left the tavern, and persists in contending that
this was due to liquor he had drunk there. We have shown that when
he left the tavern he did not appear intoxicated to Officer Cardinelli,
and to support that testimony we intend to show that he was in command of his faculties when the bus hit him. The amount of alcohol
in his blood therefore raises the question of his alcoholic tolerance, of
which this witness is in total ignorance!"

Possibly the city attorney had no confidence in Bo Satterfy's liver,
or had visions of trying to explain to the old hellroarer of a father
how it happened that the son's body was to be exhumed in order to
discover if it had been a human tank, for Parker looked as if he were
wrestling with the problem whether this troublemaker Reardon would
go to that extreme; and possibly the mayor thought that Reardon

might—he grabbed the city attorney's coattail, hissing: "Sit down!";
and the city attorney sat with a thud. Hubert Ritter of the *Sentinel*
returned from the telephone, heard what was afoot, and went out
again swiftly. Mr. McGann only cautioned: "Keep your voice down,
Mr. Reardon."

"Your honor, I'll try!" Reardon said as he planted one great foot
on the witness platform. "Dr. Groom. Isn't it a fact recognized by
the United States Government that tolerance for alcohol is generally
greater in a white man than in the American aborigine?"

"In the Indian? *Oh* yes."

"And isn't it a fact that some difference is normally to be expected
between the capacity of the Italian or the descendant of hard-drinking English lords, on the one hand, and the capacity of the man who
comes of a long line of abstemious Mohammedans? In other words,
Dr. Groom, some of us inherit greater capacities than others to begin
with—isn't that a fact?"

"Ye-es," the coroner admitted uncertainly. "Heritage can be a factor."

"All right! Now taking two men of the same blood and heritage,
isn't it a medical fact that under identical circumstances the system
of a man who consumes a quart of liquor every day will absorb and
oxydize alcohol faster than the system of the occasional highball
taster?"

"Ye-es."

"Isn't it a fact that besides being able to throw off alcohol faster
than the other man, the seasoned drinker is better conditioned to
living with it, so to speak, and can hold more without showing signs
of its effects while walking along the street or sitting at a bar?"

"Gen-erally."

"Then do you or do you not question the testimony of Officer Cardinelli?"

"Question it? Oh no!" said the coroner. "No indeed! The officer
detected no signs that Mr. Satterfy was under the influence; that is
quite possible."

"Yes. And yet the officer used a strong light. Now, then, Mr. Coroner, I presume you discussed this case with Officer Cardinelli, since
he was the investigating officer?"

"I did."

"Did you in your investigation of this case hear the word suicide?"

Dr. Groom stiffened. "There was absolutely no suggestion of such
a thing at the inquest. The jury returned a verdict of accident."

"I asked whether in your investigation you heard the word."

"I did not hear it officially."

"Didn't you talk with Officer Cardinelli in the line of duty, Mr. Coroner?"

"I mean I did not hear it at the inquest. I am not required to discuss cases with the investigating officers. This case it happens I did discuss, yes, but only informally, and I heard the word informally. At the inquest the witness he referred to did not use it. The witness used the word accident. The jury must go on the testimony, of course!"

"Of course. Didn't Officer Cardinelli use the word at the inquest?"

"Absolutely no one used the word at the inquest."

"Well, that's interesting. Do you also recall that there was no testimony the man was drunk, nor any statement of his alcoholic content?"

" 'Had been drinking,' " the coroner said irritably. "It was testified he 'had been drinking.' That was sufficient, I think. This is a small community; his family is well known."

"Yes, I remember the city attorney spoke of his father."

The coroner said firmly: "There was nothing to be gained by going into the matter any further."

"Well, we're going into the matter now, Mr. Coroner. Someone apparently thinks there's something to be gained now."

"Yes! The closing of that bar for the common good!" There was a murmur of approbation from the benches: the coroner felt encouraged. "And as for the testimony at the inquest, I should like to say for the record that in Llagas we have hearts. We do not believe in persecuting one another in time of sorrow. It would only have deepened the wounds of those who mourn."

" 'Those who mourn.' Ah, yes, I was forgetting you were not only the coroner but in private life an undertaker. You conducted first the inquest and then the funeral—a private funeral. Didn't you?"

"Well, it so happens that I did."

" 'Those who mourn' must be very grateful to you, Milton. That will be all," Reardon said.

Hubert Ritter returned from the telephone again. Alice Fritz filled him in. He rushed out again.

And on the stand now was another man, small, wrinkled, bald, and almost toothless. He was perched forward on the chair, elbows on the arms of it and hands joined nervously in front, grinning like a willing soul, ducking his head, and now and then snuffing as if he had a cold. He gave his name as Hugh D. Weiser and his occupation as odd jobs, and he offered the first direct evidence that Bo Satterfy had been served liquor at the Lost Dutchman while obviously drunk—he testified that on the night of October 14 he had been at the bar and seen it.

Parker addressed him as Mr. Weiser, but Reardon called him Hughie, explaining to the hearing officer that everybody in Llagas knew Hughie—"Don't they, Hughie?" he said, and Hughie grinned and ducked and said he guessed about everybody did.

"And you knew Mr. Satterfy, Junior, did you?"

"Oh, sure. Knew him since he was that high."

"Well, well. Did odd jobs for his father, did you?"

"Yep."

"Did odd jobs for his father. Come to think of it, I've never seen you wearing a suit before. That's new, isn't it?"

Parker snapped that the suit was irrelevant, and the objection was sustained.

Then Reardon asked about the address Hughie had given, and Hughie said he had a room there. Had he lived there long? About two weeks. When was the last time he had slept in the County Jail? Indignantly Parker objected again and Mr. McGann sustained him and admonished Reardon.

Reardon continued: "And so you were in the Lost Dutchman on the night of October 14, were you? Isn't that a rather expensive place for you?"

Here was the thing that was sticking in the minds of the lawyers at the back of the room. They would never have expected Hughie Weiser to be in the Lost Dutchman. It did not fit. But Parker must see that, and he was a reputable attorney. Therefore Hughie must be telling the truth. Unless . . .

Hughie ducked and answered: "Kind of. But I just drink wine, you know, just wine."

Reardon asked him if he went to the Lost Dutchman often, and he said oh no, no, he'd only been there twice, just two times. Reardon asked him if he knew of anyone now living who had noticed him there that night, and Hughie said he didn't reckon he did 'less'n maybe the bartender. Forth from the back of the room at Reardon's request came Jerry Barth, out on bail. Hughie identified him shyly. Then Hughie failed to identify Leo Carpenter. Then he identified McClatchy and then Arline and Bessie, but whether any of them had been on duty that night he said he couldn't recomember.

During the direct examination Hughie had described Satterfy as "not staggering, maybe you wouldn't call it, but kind of weaving, you

know, weaving, and talking drunk, too." Now Reardon asked him what
Satterfy had talked about, and Hughie said he didn't recoremember
what about. Reardon helped him:

"Well, you say you'd known him since he was a boy—didn't you
ask him how he'd been? Didn't he say anything about that?"

"Oh, he said he'd been fine, and asked me how I'd been."

"He said he'd been fine. And he looked all right, did he?"

"Looked all right 'cepting he was drunk."

"Anything else about him attract your attention?"

"Not particular."

"You didn't notice he had a broken neck?"

"Oh! He had a broken neck! He had a big leather collar on his
neck."

"What color, Hughie?"

"Huh? . . . Leather color."

"Black leather? Brown? Light tan? Yellow? Dark red?"

The wide range of colors in leather appeared to confound the witness. He said he couldn't recoremember that, either.

"Well, now, it seems you ought to remember if it was light or dark.
Or had you taken a few too many yourself that night, Hughie? Was
that it?"

Hughie grinned and ducked sheepishly. "I guess I had a few too
many," he said.

And having made this point, Reardon turned away, saying: "All
right, Hughie. I won't ask you any more questions. As the coroner has
put it," he added with a glance at Parker, "we do not believe in persecuting one another."

Parker had been following the cross-examination with visible ten-
sion, and at the last words his face flushed with anger; but he did not
rise to rebut the point. This puzzled the watchful Mr. McGann, who
was highly suspicious of this witness but could not believe that the
city attorney would have suborned him. Not the worst kind of scoun-
drel would suborn a witness in so small a matter unless he were a
fool, and only the worst kind of fool would have chosen as the witness
a Hughie Weiser. Parker must have foreseen what kind of impression
Hughie would make—that would explain why he had not called
Hughie first, but had called him after the policeman and the coroner.

To the standee lawyers also it appeared as if perjury had been done,
and they could not suspect Parker either. But to them it was clear
that from the beginning Reardon had been sketching into the background of this case the figure of old man Satterfy. And to some of
them it occurred that the purblind prohibitionist who owned and

edited the *Sentinel* was one man who would not have seen that Hughie Weiser, known bibber though he was, did not fit into the Lost Dutchman. But what did that prove? And would old A.B., whom all esteemed an honest man, use foul means to have the tavern closed? No. And if, as Reardon had suggested, A.B. had caused his son's drunkenness and all hint of suicide to be suppressed at the inquest, which was not inconceivable, would he stir up the scandal now, in public? Of course not.

A jumble of similar impressions set the whole courtroom going again as Hughie left the stand, which gave Mr. McGann the impression that nobody believed Hughie but that everybody else knew more about the matter than he did; and this was another thing he detested about hearings in small towns—there were times when you felt you didn't know what was going on under your nose. This was the second time that had happened to Mr. McGann this morning. Reardon looked at McGann and faintly smiled to himself as if satisfied that for the present he had accomplished exactly what he wished.

Surprisingly, Hughie Weiser was the City's last witness on the Satterfy count. Parker turned grimly to the other charges against the tavern.

He called a policeman named Butterson and asked him if it was not a fact that on October 18 he had arrested the two bartenders of the Lost Dutchman "for receiving horse-racing wagers and feloniously conducting a betting joint there."

Reardon quickly objected.

But Mr. McGann, determined that no more of the background of this case should escape him if he could help it, said peevishly: "Well, we're not bound by the strict rules of evidence here; an arrest in itself is no ground for a finding, no, but the Board is interested in getting some idea of the character of this place. I will therefore hold the objection in abeyance pending further testimony, Mr. Reardon."

Officer Butterson then testified that on October 18 he had arrested both the bartenders for bookmaking and recovered from them some marked money which had been used in placing two bets with them at the tavern. In support of this Parker offered in evidence the affidavit of a witness named Kovic that he had placed the bets, one with Barth on October 18, the other with Carpenter the day before.

But it happened that the two bartenders, although they intended to plead guilty when their case came to trial, had, at Reardon's request and for McClatchy's sake, pleaded not guilty at their arraignment; and Reardon now countered with a court record showing that they had pleaded not guilty.

Mr. McGann said he would admit the testimony and receive both exhibits.

And Officer Butterson went on to describe the tavern, which he said was frequented by artists.

In cross-examination Reardon brought out that the bets charged and the arrests of the bartenders were dated within a few days after the death of Satterfy, and that the witness Kovic had been acting as an agent of the police; and Butterson, when asked why he had not arrested McClatchy, too, for bookmaking, answered: "Insufficient evidence."

But preventing his tavern from being used for illegal purposes was McClatchy's responsibility. Insufficient evidence that he himself had practiced bookmaking might prove of no value when it came to keeping his liquor license if it could be shown that bookmaking had been carried on there. The two pleas of not guilty preserved the legal presumption of innocence for the time being and checkmated Parker, but it was the consensus of the lawyers at the back of the room that on this count the tavern was in trouble.

Motorcycle Officer Carl Yates told of the Wallace parade and rally and the fight in the park, and identified the demonstrators as artists who resorted at the Lost Dutchman. Reardon objected that none of the events described had occurred on the premises of the licensee, but Parker came back:

"Section fifty-eight of the Alcoholic Beverage Control Act, pertaining to disorderly houses, specifies any premises to which people resort to the disturbance of the neighborhood. We contend that these artists constitute a disturbance not merely to the neighborhood but to the entire community!"

A hoot from the back of the room. Mr. McGann tapped with his gavel while Parker was going on: "This testimony is clear evidence of that fact." (Someone was heard to say: "Free speech!") "It shows that they are a lawless hoodlum element inimical to the public peace." (Angry murmurs.) "And for the record, they are at this moment"—Parker pointed an arm out the window—"picketing the City Hall!" (Jeers. McClatchy turned around nervously and made calming motions with his hands.)

"Order!" Mr. McGann said, rapping for it. "Objection overruled." (Muttering.)

Reardon treated the testimony lightly. "Well, Officer, so these young hotheads neglected to get a permit for their electioneering. But you've testified that when the mayor had investigated he authorized them to go ahead; so it turned out to be perfectly legal, didn't it?"

"It turned out that way, yes."

"And whom did you arrest for the fight in the park? Any of the young electioneers?"

"Well, we arrested one of the bystanders."

"Bystanders? You don't say so. On what charge?"

"Disturbing the peace."

"All right, Officer. I think that fixes the blame for the fight."

Chief of Police Roy Lally, a squat thick-chested man whose pock-marked face had a permanently roasted look, testified that the Lost Dutchman was "a police problem." He said that the tavern drew a large trade from San Francisco and that out of twenty-nine drunken drivers arrested in Llagas in 1949, five had been arrested while coming from the Lost Dutchman. And the Lost Dutchman, he said, had no parking area, so its patrons had to park their cars on the streets, and the district, being an industrial one and dark at night, was the wrong part of town for a resort like that to be in, and last year two parties of the Lost Dutchman's patrons had been held up and robbed, and recently three cars parked in its vicinity had been stripped of tires, wheels, and other parts. He finished: "We have to keep a car cruising down there all the time."

Reardon began: "Roy, you testified that five of the Lost Dutchman's customers were arrested for drunken driving in 1949. Now you know better than to talk like that on a witness stand. How many were convicted?"

"Four were convicted; four out of five."

"Convicted of drunken driving?"

"I believe one charge was changed to reckless driving."

"That leaves three persons, not five, convicted of driving while too much affected by alcohol to handle an automobile. But not convicted of being drunk by any other standards; isn't that right?"

"I was talking about drunk driving—being a hazard on the road."

"Can you testify that to your certain knowledge any of them had been served liquor in the Lost Dutchman while obviously intoxicated?"

"Not to my certain knowledge."

"Have you ever had any trouble *at* the Lost Dutchman—any fights or anything of that kind?"

"We may have. I don't recall."

"You can't recall any. Yet you 'keep a car cruising down there all the time.' As a matter of fact, Roy, it's an axiom of police work, isn't it, that any place where people congregate at night constitutes 'a police problem'?"

"Well, but I say this place is in a bad part of town for a place like that."

"Oh. Now that's curious. Doesn't the City license Mr. McClatchy to conduct his business at that address?"

"Yes——"

"Have you, as chief of police, ever suggested that his business license be revoked, or that abatement proceedings be instituted against his tavern?"

"No," the chief admitted, crossing his legs restively, "I have not."

"Then why haven't you?"

"Well, I—— The situation never came to a head before."

"You're referring to the death of Mr. Satterfy."

"Yes," the chief said unwarily.

"Oh, so that's it—the death of Mr. Satterfy! That's very illuminating. Now let me ask you whether in your investigation of that death you heard the word suicide."

The benches had quickened. And Mr. McGann was glad to hear that word again. He had feared that the question of suicide was getting away from him.

But Chief Lally smiled scornfully and answered: "I guess everybody in town heard it."

"Really?" said Reardon. "It was common talk that Mr. Satterfy had committed suicide, was it?"

"That's what it was—just talk."

"Didn't your investigation show that Mr. Satterfy had threatened or been contemplating suicide?"

"It did not."

"His wife was questioned about that, was she?"

"There was no call to question his wife at all."

"Then you didn't know he had left his wife?"

"Mr. Hearing Officer!" Parker objected. (*He* could say it.) Parker objected that the record contained no foundation for the supposition that Mr. Satterfy had left his wife. He objected further that this was not the place to go into details of the investigation into Mr. Satterfy's death.

Reardon replied patiently: "Well, it's been established that Mr. Satterfy was living with his father and not with his wife; but if the Court wishes I will rephrase the question. As to the second objection, the Administrative Procedure Act provides that a witness may be cross-examined on any matter not covered in direct examination provided it be relevant to the issues." And he began another of the lucid arguments with which he was befogging the case. "Now the City contends that the circumstances of Mr. Satterfy's death establish that he was obviously intoxicated at the time; and the City is here attempting to hold the licensee answerable to the Board for what it contends was the cause of that death. We deny that Mr. Satterfy was fuddled when he left the Lost Dutchman, and contend that his death does not establish that he was fuddled forty minutes later. We intend to show, on the contrary, that his death proves he knew what he was doing. Therefore the facts about his death are certainly relevant. And the record contains ample foundation for the supposition that not all the facts came out in the investigation. The licensee has a right to all the facts. And if the Board is to accept the verdict of the investigation, which counsel has just asked it to do, it is entitled to know what kind of investigation there was."

The spectators made sounds of approval. Though most of them were against the tavern, they were eager to get at the truth of Bo Satterfy's death and also, now, of the investigation. And the newspaper reporters had leapt to their note-making again, seizing on the picturesque conception that McEndymion was being held to answer as if on a manslaughter charge. The tavernkeeper looked as if he were trying to straighten the thing out in a shocked mind. And the standee lawyers were asking themselves what Reardon could be thinking of, hammering away at Satterfy's death again, challenging old man Satterfy, harassing the coroner, and bullying the Police Department, all at the same time, just as if he didn't have to go on living in the town.

Judge Díaz was mentally insisting on the hole in the argument: whether Satterfy had committed suicide had nothing to do with the case—unless, of course, it could be shown that he had done it cold-sober, and the coroner had shut the door on that. Moreover, since the real issue turned on the testimony of Weiser, Reardon appeared to be attacking the City's case at a false point, uselessly. But Judge Díaz did not doubt that Reardon was using the fog in order to attack just here; which left the old man disapproving but mystified. He was indignant when Mr. McGann said:

"Yes. Just rephrase the question, Mr. Reardon."

And Parker, to the surprise of Judge Díaz, angrily turned on his heel and went back to his place. What!—didn't *he* see that to prove suicide would not be to disprove drunkenness?

Reardon said courteously to the hearing officer: "Thank you, Judge." He turned back to the chief of police and asked: "Did you know that Mr. Satterfy had not been making his home with his wife?"

"We knew that, yes," the chief answered.

"Did you know the reason?"

"No."

"Yet you did not question his wife. Did you or any of your officers question his father or anyone in the tavern where he had spent part of his last evening on earth?"

"We did not."

"Then the truth is there was *no* investigation, isn't it?"

"There was an investigation. It showed he was drunk."

Reardon snorted. The photographers moved up and began taking pictures of the witness. Reardon accused him: "Manuel Salazar said: 'It looked like suicide.' The busdriver said the victim 'dashed' in front of him. You knew he hadn't been living with his wife but you did not know why. It was 'common talk' that he had committed suicide. Yet when the coroner found alcohol in his body you *dropped* the investigation—was that it?"

"We were satisfied it was an accident. That *completed* the investigation."

"That's all, Mr. Chief of Police."

An angry drum-roll of comments and asides from beyond the railing accompanied the departure of Roy Lally from the stand, and Mr. Mc-Gann, privately rejoicing in the suspicion that the investigation had been what the newspapers called a whitewash, frowned after him censoriously and used the gavel.

Arline and Bessie fumed while Mrs. Crown was on the stand.

Mrs. Crown identified herself as past president of the Ladies' Service Club, and she said it was a public scandal that a small boy was being brought up in that tavern. She had not been able to believe it until she had seen it with her own eyes, and then it had reminded her of Dickens.

"The air," she reported, "was positively blue with tobacco smoke, and people at the bar were drinking, and one woman, I know, was intoxicated, and there was this poor child in the midst of it. They say he's there every night—he lives there. Imagine! I tell you people like that have no right to a child."

Arline, her face white with anger, growled "*Ohhhhh*" between her teeth; and Bessie commented stiffly: "She has little to do."

Mrs. Crown also attacked the tavern as a meeting place of undesirables, and said yes, she did mean the artists. (One of them sniggered on hearing so.) But, she said, they weren't real artists; their pictures proved they hadn't the slightest talent. (They sneered in silence.) She said it was just that they had a good thing in that tavern—they were using a priceless masterpiece as window dressing; and she told of the Rembrandt and of their own pictures' being displayed for sale around it. And they drove noisy cars and motorcycles up and down the streets at night, whooping and shouting, she said.

"Madam," Reardon opened the cross-examination, "you say you were *formerly* president of the Ladies' Service Club."

"No, I am past president. In fact I am twice past president; I served two terms as president of the ladies'. The present president, I regret to report, is recovering from an operation she had on Thursday. She has asked me to speak in her place. The present president, I should mention, is Mrs. Trainor. *I* am Mrs. Crown."

"Could it be that you were president of the ladies in December 1947?"

"In December 1947 I was president, yes. I was president for the second time."

Reardon showed her two copies of the *Sentinel* for that month. He directed her attention to the report of her club's resolution condemning the exhibition of the Rembrandt in the tavern as a crime against art, and to the editorials on the subject. He asked if the report of the resolution was accurate, and she said that it was. With Mr. McGann's permission he read the report into the record. Then he asked Mrs. Crown if she recalled the editorials, and she said that she did. He asked if she had agreed with them at the time they were published, and she answered: "With every word." He read them into the record. He asked if she had changed her mind about them in any particular, and she answered: "Not in a single particular." Did she mean to say that her feeling about the situation was exactly what it had been before the Lost Dutchman Tavern opened for business? She answered: "Ex-actly."

"All right; so much for the painting," he said. "Now you are also interested in the child, madam. You have brought that matter to the attention of the welfare authorities?"

"Well, no, I haven't. But I suppose I should have."

"Oh, I don't know. You saw the mother with the child, didn't you?"

"I was informed that the headwaitress was the mother; yes."

"Yes. You have children of your own, have you?"

"No."

"No. Well, you do your bit in other ways. *Noblesse oblige.* You are obviously a woman of means; you have never worked for a living, have you?"

"That has never been necessary."

"No, obviously. You are a woman of culture, a civic leader; a strong-minded woman, I should say, Mrs. Crown, but a womanly one, or I wouldn't ask you the question I am going to put to you now. The mother tells me that her child is forbidden the bar side of the tavern. Now I ask you to think carefully and tell me if you saw her child on the bar side."

The witness was frowning queerly. She was puzzling over why Reardon should be counting so heavily on *womanliness* here, and why he had brought *that* up at all. "Well!" she said. "He might as *well* have been."

"But he was not? Take your time, Mrs. Crown."

She seemed to struggle with herself. "I don't remember."

"I thank you for an honest answer. That will be all, Mrs. Crown."

Reardon was equally mild in cross-examining the Reverend Richard E. Kittridge.

The gray-suited clergyman turned out to be from the Presbyterian Church, and the gist of his testimony for Parker was that the tavern exerted an insidious attraction on many of the young people of the town. He called it a nest of atheism and immorality. But the servant of God was ill-equipped to make a case under the rules. Addressed as Reverend by the cross-examiner, he admitted that the State Board of Equalization was not authorized to deal with atheism. But he said that atheism led to immoralities and was itself immoral. Reardon asked of what other immoralities he accused the tavern. He spoke of the drinking. But drinking was not illegal. He said carousing, then, and mentioned also the bookmaking matter. But he could offer no qualified evidence whatever on any count, and then it came out that he was a teetotaler and prohibitionist, and Reardon thanked him, and that was all. Noon was Grooming, and the hearing officer asked the city attorney:

"Have you any more witnesses, Mr. Parker?"

"Well, I don't want to prolong this," Parker said. "I'll call just one more—his honor the mayor."

"We'll hear his honor now, then. And Mr. Reardon can present his case after lunch."

Sam Schuman took the stand. Asked about the Wallace demonstration, he said that he had found a policeman trying to cope single-handed with a wildcat parade and being heckled by the marchers, and he explained that as mayor of Llagas he had there taken the responsibility of authorizing the demonstration in the hope of averting a riot. (Laughter from the back of the room. Mr. McGann demanded: "Order!") The mayor continued that for a week afterward complaints had been received that "these people" had defaced private property with their posters—"even stuck them on store windows"; and he declared: "There's no doubt the whole plot was hatched down there in that tavern." And the San Francisco traffic that the tavern brought into the dark streets of Llagas at night, he said, placed an intolerable burden on the town. Llagas did not want the Lost Dutchman, and it particularly did not want "this gypsy band" that the tavern had introduced "from nowhere."

"They don't belong here; I don't believe a single one of them is a registered voter here," the mayor said. "I don't know where they live—nobody does. They come down from the hills in old jalopies and make a public nuisance of themselves. I doubt they even work for a living." ("Order!") "Nobody knows *how* they live. By betting on horse races, probably. Some of them look like minors, too. And they tell me the man who keeps this tavern used to keep a dive on the Barbary Coast. We don't want anything like that in Llagas. I've had many complaints about the place."

Reardon made no objection to any of this, but when it came his turn he asked severely: "Have you any proof that the artists put up those posters?"

"Well, if they didn't, who did?"

"Ask your Police Department, Mr. Mayor. Have you a shred of evidence that the artists put up the posters?"

"No evidence that would be acceptable in a court of law; but everybody knows——"

"Not a shred? Have you any evidence that a plot was hatched, as you charge, on the licensed premises in question?"

"No evidence, no."

"Or that these artists don't work for a living?"

"No."

"Or that they bet on the horses?"

"No."

"Or that any of them are minors?"

"I said they look like minors."

"Or that Mr. McClatchy 'used to keep a dive on the Barbary Coast'?"

"That's been in the newspapers repeatedly. But that's not evidence, I admit."

"You testified that you had received many complaints about the tavern. Can you say *what* complaints?"

"Yes. Those posters——"

"You just admitted you had no evidence to connect the posters with the tavern. Anything else? You're under oath, Mr. Mayor."

"*I* realize I'm under oath. Yes—people have complained to me continually. But I'll have to think a minute here."

"You received a complaint from Mr. Satterfy, Senior, did you not?"

The mayor looked at Reardon. Parker shouted: "Objection!" But the mayor said:

"Now wait a minute. I think I ought to answer that. Certainly Mr. Satterfy complained to me, and I don't blame him. A man who lost his son the way he did? I think this Board will agree that Mr. Satterfy had every right to complain. And I want to say that we don't want anything like that happening in Llagas again."

"Anything like what?"

The mayor glanced at Reardon indignantly. "Gossip," he said, "I don't pay any attention to gossip. And I want to say that I have full confidence in our chief of police."

"*Confidence?*" Reardon barked. "After hearing his testimony?"

"Mr. Hearing Officer!" Parker objected.

"Not necessary," Reardon said, turning away. "I'm speechless!"

The hearing recessed.

Outside it was like a day in June.

29

KANGAROO

The hearing officer had just mounted to the mayor's desk after lunch when he saw Reardon and McClatchy coming down the aisle with two nuns. Mr. McGann looked startled. He immediately descended, went to the railing, held open the gate, and was presented to Sisters Madeleine and Regis of St. Peter's School.

Sister Madeleine, the principal, he learned, was to testify. He handed her onto the witness chair, remounted the bench, declared the hearing in session again, and apologetically administered the oath, noting with relief that there were no photographers this afternoon.

Sister Madeleine testified that William Lucas, Jr., was in the second grade of her school. He was a good boy. An average student. Deportment: good. And she did know his mother, oh yes, Arline had attended St. Peter's herself and the witness herself had taught her.

Thought her a good mother. Knew his grandparents also. Very good people. Yes, she would judge that the boy came from a good home. In cross-examination Parker asked her if she approved of a child's being brought up in a tavern. That, she answered, would depend on the kind of tavern, and on what was meant by 'being brought up' in it; she added that she did not disapprove of taverns as such. Parker asked her if she approved of drinking. That also depended. She explained: "We believe that God made wine for man's pleasure; and our Lord turned water into it for the wedding guests at Cana; it is drinking to excess that is wrong." Parker asked her if God had made whisky.

"Heckling the witness!" Reardon objected.

Down came the gavel. "*Mr.* Parker."

"Why," Parker said, "I think that's a proper question. I'm trying to discover what credibility——"

"*Credibility?*" the hearing officer exploded.

"Responsibility—reliance, I mean; what reliance we can place on this good lady's judgment as to what constitutes a good home."

"I don't think you need disturb yourself, Mr. Parker," Mr. McGann said. "And I caution you to be more respectful. And no blasphemy."

"*I* intended no blasphemy, and certainly no disrespect. I don't happen to be of this lady's religion but I will say that I have always entertained the highest respect for her profession."

"Vocation," Mr. McGann corrected him distastefully.

"Pardon?"

"Vocation is the word."

"Oh."

"Yes."

"But," Sister Madeleine put in, embarrassed, "I don't think Mr. Parker was heckling me. And it's a *good* question. And the answer, Mr. Parker, is that man has made many things with the intelligence and materials that God has given him, and the only thing good or bad about them is how he uses them; some of them can give him relaxation and pleasure, and that can be good for him; and whisky can't offend our Lord, only men can do that; and God permits man to be tempted and will give him the grace to resist it, but the decision is everyman's and you can't take that away from him without making him less than he is, without depriving him of his freedom and his power to give glory to God; so I have nothing against poor little whisky, but only against intemperance, which is a sin, and against the use of whisky by those poor people for whom it is an occasion of sin. Does that answer?" she asked with concern.

Parker cleared his throat and said: "Yes. Thank you."

Mr. McGann said challengingly: "Anything else, Mr. Parker?"

"No—no. That will be all."

Mr. McGann stood up and bowed the nuns through the gate, and McClatchy escorted them to the door of the building.

Mrs. Linnegar was here this afternoon; she had been sitting with Arline and Bessie, and was on the stand when the tavernkeeper returned. The president of the Ladies' Sodality of St. Peter's told that the ladies had lunched at the Lost Dutchman twice and that she and her husband had dined there several times. She said that she had never seen anything reprehensible in the place, and volunteered that she had seen children dining in it with their parents. She called Billy well brought up and Arline a good mother, and spoke highly of Mr. and Mrs. McClatchy.

The city attorney was uncertain what the Ladies' Sodality might be. He respectfully asked but two questions of this dignitary. The first brought out that she had never been in the Lost Dutchman late at night. The second was meant to suggest that she was biased in favor of the McClatchys; but afterward he feared that it had been a mistake to bring out that they were personal friends of hers. He hoped that Reardon had no more of these witnesses.

Then Reardon called Noel Ames.

The popular journalist, too, spoke highly of the McClatchys, and he said that he had never seen anything reprehensible in the tavern either, and he begged to differ with Mrs. Crown about the artistic abilities of the veteran painters—in his opinion some of them showed promise. And he thought that the Lost Dutchman, to coin a phrase, he said, filled a need. It gave these young artists a place where they could show their work; and he would like to see that kind of thing encouraged. He said he had never understood the hostility that had so long existed in Llagas against the tavern. He saw no crime against art in the exhibition of the Rembrandt there. There it was seen by many people who would never set foot in a museum; it was not, to borrow a word that Mr. Reardon had once used, entombed.

The veteran painters at the back of the room cheered him.

Parker smiled tolerantly and said: "No questions."

Reardon boldly put Jerry Barth on the stand, and then Leo Carpenter. The two bartenders testified that they did not know Hughie Weiser and did not remember ever having seen him in the tavern. Barth had served young Satterfy one of two drinks on the night of October 14, he said, and Satterfy had been alone and not intoxicated and had seemed "kind of moody." And in reply to carefully worded questions from Reardon both witnesses swore they had no knowledge that their employer had ever received racing bets or been aware of anyone else's doing it in his tavern. Then Reardon blocked Parker's efforts to question them about their own bookmaking.

Next he called Arline.

Reardon elicited that Arline was the widow of a soldier killed in training during the war, a member of the Ladies' Sodality, and hostess in her father's tavern. Her son usually *was* in the tavern in the early evening, she admitted, but she saw nothing wrong in that. She and his grandparents were always there; besides, he was not allowed on the bar side and all the help knew it. Sometimes he did his lessons with his grandmother at the cashier's counter, and he was usually in bed by nine-thirty. And she testified that she had been on duty on the night of October 14 and did not remember having seen Hughie Weiser there then or at any other time, but that she had talked with Satterfy as he was leaving the tavern that night, and had not thought him drunk.

Reardon asked: "What did he say to you, Mrs. Lucas?"

"Well, one of our waitresses had quit and he asked me where she'd gone."

Sensing a reference to the siren, the townspeople alerted themselves. Parker interposed that the subject of the conversation was irrelevant, but Reardon answered:

"On the contrary, this testimony will bear out that the witness did talk with Mr. Satterfy and that he was in command of his faculties."

Mr. McGann said that he would hold the objection in abeyance.

So there was injected into the record the name of Phyllis Plover. Arline related the conversation, and when asked whether Satterfy's words had made sense replied that they had, and in order to explain them went back, under Reardon's questioning, to the automobile accident and the time in the hospital when the injured girl had told her that Satterfy had left his wife and was going to marry Phyllis, and to the time——

Parker tried to have the testimony stricken on the ground that it was a violation of the privacy of two individuals who were not on trial, one of whom was dead; but Reardon answered:

"I submit that this testimony is relevant because it furnishes a foundation for the establishment of a vital factor which both the police investigation and the inquest overlooked—the motive for suicide!"

A flutter passed over the benches and the newspaper men bent to their note-making; Judge Díaz sat abominating the recitation of this tale into the record in support of an immaterial argument, but bringing down his gavel, Mr. McGann ruled: "On that assurance we will hear the testimony."

—And to the time when Phyllis had said that she was not going to marry Satterfy after all but was going to leave town, perhaps without even telling him; and Arline explained that Phyllis had gone without leaving a forwarding address.

Mr. McGann ruled that the testimony might stand.

Angrily Parker began the cross-examination: "Mrs. Lucas—have you any more waitresses like this Plover woman at the Lost Dutchman?"

"What do you mean?" Arline asked, frowning.

"I'm referring to Reverend Kittridge's testimony about the low moral character of this place. Wouldn't you say this woman's behavior with married customers came under that heading?"

Reardon objected: "Calling for the opinion of the witness."

Parker argued that he was exploring the witness's moral standards, but withdrew the question and put it another way: "Do you approve of your father's employees' having romantic relations with the married customers?"

Red-faced but without hesitation, Arline answered: "No."

"You think it immoral?"

"Yes."

"That's all."

Reardon came back and established that Phyllis's romance with Satterfy had been unknown to the management until after the automobile accident in which the two had been injured, after which she had not returned to work.

Then Reardon called McClatchy.

The tavernkeeper bore witness to his identity and record: owner and operator of the licensed premises known as the Lost Dutchman Tavern, formerly the Traveler's Rest, and holder since 1933 of an on-sale general license for the sale of beer, wine, and distilled spirits for consumption on the premises; never convicted of a felony, never a bookmaker, had no knowledge of any of his employees' having practiced bookmaking and would not have allowed anything like that in the place; never served liquor to an intoxicated person, always careful that his bartenders didn't do it either; and he testified that on the night of October 14 he had seen Mr. Satterfy, Jr., and that the man had not looked to be under the influence at all; and he deposed that so far as he knew he had never seen Hughie Weiser before in his life.

The city attorney confronted the witness with a jovial expression. "I take it you're Irish, Mr. McClatchy."

"Yes, sir!"

"Well, begorra, and what part of Ireland do you claim?"

"Dublin."

"Dublin. And you have your naturalization papers?"

"Who, me?"

"With the Court's indulgence," Reardon put in, rising, "I think the witness means his ancestors came from Dublin."

"Yeah, *that's* what I mean. The both of 'em."

Parker said: "Will the hearing officer kindly instruct counsel not to prompt the witness."

Mr. McGann said: "If there is anything you wish to bring out, Mr. Reardon, you will have the opportunity."

Reardon begged pardon.

Parker resumed: "I didn't ask you about your ancestors, Mr. Mc-Clatchy. What I want to know is if you have ever been naturalized."

"Me? No, I was born here."

"Born here? You're telling us you're a native-born American."

"Sure I am—yes, sir."

"You have a birth certificate to prove it?"

"A—— Well, no. It burned up in the Fire."

"I see. But you could get a copy, I suppose."

"No, I mean the Sampm Cisco Fire."

"Oh! You wish me to believe you were born in San Francisco?"

"Sure I was. Born in the old South of Market and raised in the——"

"But the record of your birth was destroyed in the Fire of nineteensix. Is that your story?"

"*All* the records were destroyed in the Fire. The whole Hall of Records burned down. Everybody knows that."

"Yes, they do, don't they. So almost any immigrant of your age could claim citizenship by saying he was born in San Francisco, couldn't he?"

"*Immigrant?* I'm a natural born citizen of the U.S.A."

"Born in San Francisco, but you can't prove it."

"No, but nobody can prove I wasn't, neither. Nobody can prove I was born at all, but I must have got here some way."

"Before being prompted by your attorney, Mr. McClatchy, you gave us to understand that you were born in Dublin."

"No, I stated—I stated my *folks* come from there."

"No, Mr. McClatchy, that was what your attorney stated."

Reardon got up. "I think the Court will agree it's time an objection was offered to these tactics. The first two questions were so phrased that they might have been misunderstood by anyone with an ancestral claim on Ireland."

"Agreed," Mr. McGann said. "You will refrain from harassing the witness, Mr. Parker."

Parker said: "Under section twelve of the California Alcoholic Beverage Control Act no person who is not a citizen of the United States may be licensed to——"

"I am familiar with the Act, Mr. Parker," the hearing officer said.

Reardon continued: "And I'm sure we all know that San Francisco's vital statistics were destroyed in the Fire of nineteen-six. Counsel can't use that fact to cast suspicion on the witness's citizenship or by the same token the citizenship of anyone born in San Francisco before the Fire would have to be considered doubtful."

"Exactly," Mr. McGann said.

"Then," Parker said, "perhaps the witness can explain where he got his brogue."

The witness looked astonished. "Brogue?"

"Objection!" Reardon said. "Witness has testified he was born and raised in the United States. There is nothing in the record to show he has an Irish accent."

"Out of his own mouth——" Parker began, pointing accusingly at the witness, and he broke off to demand: "*Mr.* McClatchy. Do you or do you not have an Irish accent?"

"Objection! Calling for the opinion of the witness."

"For the record I ask the hearing officer—does the witness speak with an Irish accent?"

"Objection!"

"Oh, yes! I expected that objection, Mr. Reardon."

"I congratulate you, Mr. Parker. Then you do know *some* law."

Mr. McGann rapped once and said: "The hearing officer can give no opinion. I may say, however, that it so happens I too am a San Franciscan, born in the South of Market and raised in the Mission——"

The witness burst into a grin and shook clasped hands overhead at the hearing officer, seeing which, Mr. McGann paused, smiling also, and for an instant seemed about to reach down and shake hands with Mr. McClatchy, but he restrained himself and rapped genially. "I can say," he resumed, "I can say that I have known several men of Irish extraction who, though born in the South of Market and raised in the Mission, did seem to have traces of the brogue—at least to me. But my opinion would not be conclusive."

"In that case," Parker snapped, "I ask that the hearing officer's remarks be stricken."

The hearing officer gave the city attorney a waspish glance, cleared his throat, rapped, and said in a low voice: "Granted."

Reardon said: "The fact that Mr. McClatchy has a liquor license is evidence that the Board presumes him to be an American citizen; and, for the record, the City has not shown the Board to be in error."

"No, and furthermore," Mr. McGann told Parker, "that applies to the whole case. A man is innocent till proved guilty."

"I am aware of that, sir," Parker said acidly.

Parker returned to the cross-examination. He asked the witness if he did not think it his obligation to prevent immoral conduct by his waitresses on the licensed premises, and the witness answered that he did and that if the city attorney was referring to Phyllis Plover he could state that if he had known about that he would never have stood for it. Parker asked about the Traveler's Rest and established that it had been the cheapest kind of combination saloon and eating place. He inquired into the mystery of the Rembrandt. He said he understood that the tavern was in the business of selling pictures, and asked how many had been sold.

"Well, I can't say, exactly," the witness testified. "*We* aint in the business—that's the Organization," and he explained about the Veteran Painters headed by Mr. Kinney, to whom he said he turned over all moneys proceeding from the sale of pictures.

"And you haven't kept any record of the sales?"

"No, sir."

"No record? Don't you know it's a misdemeanor not to keep a record of your sales and that your license can be revoked for a misdemeanor?"

"A misdemeanor! On the pictures? But I never——"

"Haven't you paid the Board of Equalization any sales tax on those pictures?"

"*Sales* tax? Well, I collected that, sure, but I . . . always turned it over to Mr. Kinney."

In the spectators' section Arline looked at her mother in consternation and said: "Turned it over to *Kinney?*" Bessie kept looking straight ahead, the color rising in her face, and said: "*I* don't know."

Mr. McGann said: "Well, this matter concerns the tax division of the Board. It is not in the jurisdiction of the liquor control division."

"I am prepared to demonstrate," Parker said, "that it is! Mr. McClatchy—obviously the Board expects you to know what is going on in your tavern, but you tell us you didn't even know your bartenders were bookmaking——"

Reardon objected that there was no conviction of bookmaking.

"Not yet, no," Parker said. "All right, he didn't know about the conduct of his waitress, either; and by your own admission, Mr. Mc-

Clatchy, you've been selling pictures and keeping no records as the law requires, and all this time you've paid no sales tax. Now let's be honest. Do you think you qualify as a fit and proper person to hold a liquor license?"

The question made Arline's heart ache for her mother as much as for her father. "*His* license, *his* bar, *his* business that he built up from nothing"—her mother had always tried to make him out so smart, and now for her mother to have to sit here and see him publicly exposed as incompetent! Arline remembered hearing somewhere that a man could not be forced to testify against himself, but it was plain that Reardon dared offer no such objection now. Reardon sat leaning forward across the table looking at him, waiting for his answer.

"Well," he fumbled in a weak voice, "I—— It looks like I put my foot in it there, all right. Yeah, but, whereas," bending forward, leaning his elbows on his knees, clasping his hands, and staring at the floor, "the only thing," he explained, "I never made a cent off of those pictures. That was just a service to the Organization for making us the official headquarters. And if I knew I had to keep a record, I would have kep' one. But that aint my business and I never *knew* that. And the reason I never turned the sales tax over to the Board, why, I thought that was up to the Veteran Painters. But I'll pay the fine or anything like that, if they don't put me in jail, and handle the tax myself from now on, if that's the way to do it. Because I know I always tried to run everything on the up-and-up. And I never been in jail in my life. The trouble is they's so much bookkeeping these days." Staring at the floor, he seemed to be talking to himself. "The sales tax and the surtax and the social security withholding tax and the capital gains tax and the—— When I started out they never even had the income tax. I got my start at the old P'trera Saloon; and I worked on the Barbary Coast and at the Techau Tavern and the Palace Hotel. In the old days. Before Prohibition. And when that struck us——" He caught himself, and lifting his head, the bootlegger of a vanished era began to explain to the townspeople. "Then after our boy was killed, when we bought the chicken ranch, why, that wasn't my business, I didn't know that, and the stock market crashed and the Depression hit and we almost lost our shirt, and we bought the old Traveler's because that was the only way I knew to make a living. That's my trade, you know. I don't know nothing else. . . ." He shook his head and stared at the hands clasped between his knees. "But I'm an old-timer. But I'm *only* fifty-eight," he argued with himself. "But the last time I was over to old Forty-one nobody even knew me. It was like old Rip van Winkle—his gun was rusty and he had a long beard and not even the dogs knew him. Now, when you look at it, they's more to that story than you'd think. Twenty years! And the Fire burned up all the records on me and I can't even prove I was born. *I* don't know, maybe I aint fit to have a license with the Board no more; but I had my license a long time, ever since Repeal, so I'm practically a charter member. And I can say I had a lot of experience at the game. And I know I always tried to keep my nose clean and run a decent place. And then, when they found out the picture was a Rembrandt, why, we went in hock to fix the old place up to go with it. Put in a new floor and a brick firewall and got a lot of new equipment and changed the name——" He looked up at the hearing officer. "And the Lost Dutchman's famous, you know. People come to that place all the way from the city. . . . Yeah, well. So anyhow. If the Board'd give me another chance, why . . . I'd be much obliged."

During this rambling apology Arline's soul had been writhing. There was a dead pause. Suddenly the black-haired newspaper woman began to applaud, and the whole San Francisco press corps took it up, and townspeople—towns*women*, Arline saw—were clapping too, solemn-faced. The witness looked as much taken aback as Parker did. He knew what a poor figure he had cut. He lowered his head and looked at his clasped hands again, not knowing where else to look, and Mr. McGann tapped gently.

Parker said: "Well, we all sympathize with you, Mr. McClatchy. But the Board, you understand, is charged with the protection of the public. You admit, then that you have not shown yourself to be a fit and proper——"

Mr. McGann said: "I think the question has been answered, Mr. Parker."

"Very well, I'll *accept* that answer. No more questions," Parker said.

The witness was permitted to step down. Reardon conferred with him for a moment, then rose and said: "May it please the Court, we'll stipulate that these matters will be taken up with the tax division; respondent will plead guilty in good faith and ask the clemency of the Board."

"The record may so note," Mr. McGann said.

Then Reardon called Bessie.

He drew from Bessie that she had first met Dan McClatchy in San Francisco when both were in their teens, that they had been married there thirty-seven years ago, that they had buried a son killed by an automobile at twelve years of age, and that Bessie was cashier in the tavern; all the while standing back to give the courtroom a good view of Bessie, for he felt that she made an excellent exhibit for the defense.

"Now, Mrs. McClatchy," he said, "do you know the penalty for perjury?"

"It's a mortal sin; yes," Bessie said.

"I see. Then can you tell the Court where your husband was born?"

"In San Francisco."

"How do you know that?"

"Well, for one thing, he told me."

Parker objected almost apologetically: "Hearsay."

"If your honor please," said Reardon, "I think such testimony on this point by the woman who has been married to the man for thirty-seven years, knew him from adolescence, and has been not only his wife but the working partner in his business, might be given more weight than hearsay. And I will cite Webster versus Dental Examiners: relevant hearsay admissible if the sort of evidence on which responsible persons accustomed to rely in serious affairs."

Mr. McGann said he would admit the testimony.

"Mrs. McClatchy," Reardon asked, "did you ever hear your husband's birth or citizenship questioned before?"

"Heavens, no."

"Where were you born, Mrs. McClatchy."

"In San Francisco."

"Can you produce a birth certificate?"

"Well, like Danny says, all the records were burned up in the Fire. But I suppose I could get the record of my baptism."

"The record of your baptism; where would you find that?"

"At Mission Dolores."

"At Mission Dolores Church in San Francisco?"

"Yes; I don't think the records there were burned up."

"And the record of your husband's baptism?"

"Well, the South of Market—that was St. Patrick's parish. St. Patrick's was all gutted by the flames."

"I see. Now, Mrs. McClatchy, when it was suggested here that your husband spoke with an Irish accent, were you surprised?"

Bessie laughed: "I certainly was! You know, I never *noticed* it before."

"You mean you noticed it then?"

"Yes!" Bessie said. "When Mr. Parker spoke of it, I did!"

"All right. Now when you and your husband were first married, and when you first knew him, did he talk that way then?"

"No! He never did!" she laughed.

"How do you account for the change?"

"Well, I don't know, but Danny's been telling them Irish stories so long, you know, and talking like that in fun——" She paused, laughing. "I guess he just got into the habit! But he didn't know it neither! Ohhh, dear. He was as surprised as I was when they asked him about his—his *brogue!* And now they don't even think he's an American *citizen!* They may try to—to *deport* him!"

By this time the press and the spectators and the hearing officer too were laughing at the plight of poor McClatchy, who sat sheepishly grinning and wagging his head—acquitted of illegal entry by public acclamation.

"Thank you, Mrs. McClatchy," Reardon said. "That's all."

Even Parker was smiling. "No questions."

Women friends reached into the aisle to seize Bessie's hand and congratulate her as she went waddling back to her seat, still laughing.

As the laughter died Reardon turned to the benches and called:

"Miss Josephine Cantrell!"

Llagas gasped. Faces whirled round. Into Arline's the blood rushed. *Her?* What did *she* have to do with it?

Josephine Cantrell stuffed her knitting into her catchall bag, got up, and rolled like a dockwalloper down the gantlet. Reardon opened the gate for her. On the stand she looked stolidly over the heads of the spectators at the front wall of the Council chamber, a short squat old woman in black woolen coat and black cloche hat, with a square face of wrinkled yellow leather, and on one cheek a mole from which two hairs were growing.

Reardon asked her what her occupation was.

More gasps from the women spectators, broad smiles on the faces of the men. In the front row Link Cotter leaned forward, an elbow on a knee, and cupped a large senile ear.

In a deep voice Josie answered: "Retired."

Titters and chuckles. The hearing officer raised his brows at the spectators inquiringly.

Reardon said: "Now, Miss Cantrell, will you voluntarily tell the Court your former occupation?"

Josie's mouth opened and closed like a steel trap, once, emitting a guttural sound. The stenographer asked her to repeat it. Josie barked: "Madam."

At the back of the room a woman shrieked. Link Cotter slapped his thigh. The benches rocked with delight. The hearing officer was hammering. Josie snorted and kept her eyes on the far wall till order was restored.

Reardon said: "In other words, Miss Cantrell, you once kept a house of prost——"

The witness headed off the ugly word: "A good clean cathouse, yes."

The same woman spectator who had shrieked before shrieked again. Others oh'd and squealed and men cackled, guffawed, and convulsed themselves, but this time amid the merriment could be heard the little suck of disgust. Josie sat apparently unmoved. When order had been restored again she added:

"I kep' one in Denver."

"In Denver, Colorado?"

Another burst of laughter. More bangs of the gavel. The hearing officer threatened to clear the courtroom. Order was restored. Earl Parker rose with a genial face, baring his vest as he swept his coat back to thrust his hands into his pockets.

"Now, Mr. Hearing Officer," Parker said, "this is all very entertaining, I'm sure. But I'd like to know what a house of ill fame in Denver, Colorado, has to do with a disorderly tavern in Llagas, California. Did the good people of Denver get rid of the house of ill fame as the people of Llagas are trying to do with the disorderly tavern?"

Reardon answered: "There is no disorderly tavern—that is only what the city attorney has been trying to prove."

Mr. McGann said: "I urge you to come to the point, Mr. Reardon."

"I'll come to the point immediately, your honor."

"Al-l right," Parker said. "I'll be patient." He flapped his arms and sat down, still smiling. Josie looked at him and sneered.

"Miss Cantrell," Reardon asked, "can you shed any light on the death of Almon Satterfy, Junior?"

The smile vanished from Parker's face; Josie answered: "I can."

"Can you shed any light on what is behind this hearing?"

"I say I can do that, too."

"Were you acquainted with Almon Satterfy, Junior?"

"I knew him," Josie said, "ever since he was a baby. Knew his father and mother before him. She was one of my girls in Denver."

The townspeople caught their breath; Parker was on his feet, but Reardon, turning at the last word, had anticipated him. "You object to something, Mr. Parker?"

"Ob—— Of course I object! This, this witness, a self-confessed keeper, former keeper, of a house of, brought here to——"

The hearing officer was banging again. "Order!"

"—to dishonor the memory of a dead man's mother! And to no purpose! Why, I call this infamous!"

Bang! Bang! "Mr. Reardon, can you show any reason why I should not order the last part of that answer stricken?"

"I can. It is basic to this important testimony. We have now come to the main issue of this case—the point, sir. And the real point, hidden by a smoke screen, is that my client is being held to answer for the death of Almon Satterfy, Junior. That's the whole reason these other charges were trumped up against him——"

"Trumped up?" Parker said. "The record——"

Bang! "Mr. Reardon! Are you suggesting fabrication here?"

"Your honor, I am. And I charge further that the Board of Equalization is being imposed upon here, taken advantage of, used!"

Parker said: "What!"

Reardon said: "I submit that the record already contains ample foundation for these charges. And I respectfully suggest that it will save time if I am permitted to explain myself at once."

Mr. McGann said sternly: "I think you'd better do that, Mr. Reardon."

Silence as the big man turned, walked to the counsel table, and turned back. He growled: "Let's put two and two together. To begin with, the background of this hearing. We heard it suggested by a trained observer, a newspaperman, Mr. Ames, that hostility to the Lost Dutchman Tavern had long existed in Llagas. That suggestion is supported by the resolution adopted by the Ladies' Service Club before the tavern opened, and by the testimony of the past president that she has never changed her mind about the place. It is supported also by the editorials in the *Sentinel*, which the city attorney has told us is owned and edited by Mr. Satterfy's father. It is supported by the mayor's testimony about the popular belief in Llagas that the artists were responsible for the posters. And I submit that it is supported by much of the incompetent evidence given here by the chief of police. Now what brought about the showdown? Why, we have the admission of the chief himself that it was the death of Mr. Satterfy, and that is supported by the admission of the mayor himself that the elder Satterfy did complain to him——"

Parker, still on his feet, broke in: "That is not——"

"Let him finish, Mr. Parker," the hearing officer said. The hearing officer had the feeling that his eyes were about to be opened to some of the things that had puzzled him about this case.

Sam Schuman looked as though he were about to jump up and take back his gavel. Roy Lally was leaning back in his chair with his legs crossed, sneering. Milton Groom had not returned this afternoon.

Reardon went on: "No effort was made in the past to abate this tavern. Why wasn't it? The record will show there was no evidence that could be used against the tavern in a court of law. The mayor

admitted *he* had none. 'No evidence,' he said, 'that would be acceptable in a court of law.' And I cite the testimony of the chief of police
about the drunken drivers and so forth—none of it evidence that would
be adducible against the tavern in a court of law, but all of it now in
the record of this tolerant hearing. I cite the shocking attack made
here on a mother through her child. If Madam Past President had
thought the child's welfare at stake, she should have reported the matter to the proper welfare agency; but the record will show that the
agency would have thrown the matter out. Obviously the object of
that count here is not the welfare of the child but the closing of the
tavern. But if the closing of the tavern is all that is wanted why didn't
the City wait for the outcome of the bookmaking case, hoping to
come here with convictions? Why has it come here with mere *charges*
of bookmaking? Obviously because the closing of the tavern would
not have been enough. Something else is wanted.

"Turning back to the death of Mr. Satterfy, I will cite all that has
been brought out here about the police investigation and the inquest
and the 'common talk' of suicide. I will cite the thinness of the City's
case that Mr. Satterfy was served liquor in the Lost Dutchman while
obviously intoxicated—the testimony of Hughie Weiser, whom no one
remembers having seen in the tavern that night. I ask why the alcoholic content of Mr. Satterfy's blood should be made public here
after having been carefully suppressed at the inquest. I ask why the
death of Mr. Satterfy has been introduced here at all. What was the
object? To establish that he was obviously intoxicated when hit by
the bus? But that would not be to prove anything against the tavern.

"On the record, there is a mystery here, and I don't think I need
go any further into that at this time. But I say the Board is being
taken advantage of here because it is plain that the City has been
counting principally on three things:

"First, paragraph C of section one-one-five-one-three of the Procedure Act." And Reardon quoted from memory: " 'The hearing need
not be conducted according to technical rules relating to evidence and
witnesses. Any relevant evidence shall be admitted if it is the sort of
evidence on which responsible persons are accustomed to rely in the
conduct of serious affairs, *regardless of the existence of any common
law or statutory rule which might make improper the admission of
such evidence over objections in civil actions.*'

"Second, the City has been counting on its own prestige.

"Third, it has been counting on the Board's 'broad powers of discretion.'

"Now I realize that all the incompetent irrelevant immaterial evidence that has got into the record here has got into it because of a very generous interpretation of One-one-five-one-three, and I have no quarrel with that. I merely ask the same generosity toward my client in order that the Board may be supplied with all the facts. And I am counting on the Board's discretion just as heavily as the City is. The City has brought charges against my client; I have just brought countercharges in his defense. As foundation for my charges I have cited a mystery in the record. I submit that the testimony will help to solve the mystery and substantiate my charges to the Board's satisfaction. I contend that it is all bound up with the death of Mr. Satterfy—with the question: Who killed him? I submit that the testimony will place the guilt where it belongs. I ask that the witness be heard."

"*Killed* him?" Parker said. "Are you trying to make a murder mystery out of this?"

"I assure you, Mr. Parker," Reardon said, "I will not try to make anything out of it that is not warranted by the testimony."

The whole courtroom was electrified. The mayor was livid. The chief of police was glowering at Reardon. Mr. McGann turned suspicious eyes on Parker. "You will have your chance, Mr. Parker. Meanwhile we will hear the testimony." Bang!

Bessie whispered to Arline: "He does know law. Did you hear the way he rattled it off there?" Arline, fascinated by the developments, answered with a quick nod. The Offered-up amazed her.

At that moment Hubert Ritter was passing up the aisle on his way to the telephone again.

Reardon turned back to Josie, who had sat rock-like and grim-lipped through it all. "Miss Cantrell, you testified that you knew the mother of Almon Satterfy, Junior."

"His mother," Josie said, "was Babe Fereer."

Arline frowned at the name.

The stenographer asked: "Spelling?"

Josie looked at him. "What?"

"Spell the name, please."

"*Her* name? Her right name was"—Josie munched a moment, then pronounced: "Yvonne Fairyay."

The picture in Arline's mind became a different one. Yvonne Fair-*yay* wore a yellow silken evening dress cut low, with a gossamer-like shawl clinging to her ivory neck and shoulders; she was tall and graceful and gentle and had soft black hair and soft blue eyes and beautiful expressive hands.

"French," Josie explained, "from Detroit."

"And the spelling?" the stenographer asked.

"Yvonne," Josie threw back at him. "That's French for Little Eva. Fair*yay*—I'd have to look at the documents to get that."

"Mm hm. And the alias?" the young man asked.

"What alias?"

"You said——"

"That was in Denver."

"Yes. How do you spell it?"

"Same as you spell it in *De*troit. She didn't use no alias. It was the same name. Yvonne Fair*yay*. But nobody ever ast for her that way in Denver. They ast for Babe Fereer."

The effect of this upon the courtroom was chilling. This terrible old woman was talking, as she alleged, about the mother of A. B. Satterfy's dead son. (And what had she done at one crude stroke to the lovely creature called out of nowhere with the beautiful rune "Yvonne Fair*yay*"!)

Parker objected. The hearing officer sustained him and ordered: "The witness will confine herself to the pertinent facts."

"That's what I'm trying to do," Josie said with a sour glance at the stenographer. He was an earnest-looking youth with shellrimmed glasses.

The hearing officer said: "You referred to documents. What documents?"

"I'm coming to that."

"All right."

Reardon supplied the stenographer with the spelling of the name that he said would be established later: *F-e-r-r-i-e-r.*

The hearing officer said: "Proceed."

"Well," Josie proceeded without further questioning, "like I said, it was in Denver, time of the war, the first one. I had a place there then. Almon Satterfy—the old man, that was; he used to come there regular." She broke off. Earl Parker was objecting again. "Oh, hell," she muttered.

Parker was objecting: "The good name of a highly respected citizen of this community is being ruthlessly dragged through the mire! A man who is not involved, and not even here to defend himself. This"—Parker pointed his arm at Reardon—"shyster——"

"Not involved?" Reardon said. "Mr. Parker is mistaken. The testimony will demonstrate that Mr. Satterfy the elder certainly is involved. And if anyone could persuade him to come here and take the stand in his own defense I'd be delighted."

"*His* defense?" Parker said.

"Wasn't that your suggestion, Mr. Parker?"

"Gentlemen," Mr. McGann said. "I will hear the arguments in chambers."

Josie groaned.

Chambers, Parker thought—Reardon's got him believing he *is* a judge.

With bad grace the mayor got up and showed the Court into his office through a door in George Washington's wall. Standee lawyers and veteran painters withdrew to the corridor to discuss developments while smoking. The witness resumed her knitting.

Arline and Bessie were embarrassed that this ugly scandal about the Satterfys had come out here—out of the closet of Josie Cantrell! And what could "murder mystery" mean? "Gracious!" Bessie said. "It sounds to me like he's only making it worse." People around them were saying it was disgraceful; but the spectators were nervous lest Josie's memoirs be cut off; all except Judge Díaz, who very much feared that they would not be. The mayor returned and went into consultation with the chief of police. Hubert Ritter returned and went into consultation with Alice Fritz. At last the Court returned from chambers. Mr. McGann said that he would hear the testimony.

"Over the City's protest!" Parker insisted above the sounds of satisfaction from the spectators. "For the record!"

"Granted," Mr. McGann said. "Mr. Reardon, proceed with prudence."

"Thank you, Judge, I will."

"And again I will remind you, Mr. Reardon," Mr. McGann said amiably, "that I am not a judge."

Reardon smiled. "Mr. McGann, you should be."

Mr. McGann smiled. "Thank you, Mr. Reardon."

Parker grimaced.

Reardon asked that the last words of the testimony be read back to the witness. The stenographer read: " 'Almon Satterfy—the old man, that was. He used to come there regular.' "

"Yeah," Josie said, "he was working on the *Post* then. And he was crazy about Babe Fereer. They got married. Left town. Went to San Francisco. But it wasn't no time till Almon was back looking for Babe. She'd left him. I aint going to tell why; that was their business. I told him I didn't know where she was, and that was the truth. He left. Then Babe shows up. She's going to have his baby but she won't go back to him. I told her she was crazy, but I helped her out a little, and Bo was born. And that was the time——"

The stenographer interrupted again: "What was the child's name, please?"

Josie looked annoyed. "Almon Satterfy, Junior. Bo, they called him."

"Oh. *B-e-a-u?*"

"What?"

"How do you spell it?"

"What—Bo?" Josie stared at him. "*B-o*—Bo."

"*B-o.* Thank you."

Josie continued to stare at the young man as if she could not conceive of such illiteracy. The spectators began to laugh. The startled court reporter looked up again, saw that the laughter was at him, and turned red.

"All right," Mr. McGann smiled, rapping. "Go on," to Josie.

"Well, I'll talk it," Josie grumbled, "but I aint going to spell it out." Laughter.

"All right," Mr. McGann said.

"Well . . . right after Bo was born the Epidemic come along; the flu. Babe got it. She died. She ast me to take the kid to his father, and I did. Got to Frisco and found out he'd come up here to Llagas and bought into the paper. And I was the one that brung Bo here. Almon didn't want Bo. Said the kid wasn't his. I'd figured maybe he'd say that. I had copies of the marriage certificate and the birth certificate and the death certificate, all three. He took the kid, all right. But after I got back to Denver I got to worrying about it. I was afraid he'd put Babe's kid in an orphan asylum. Was raised in one of them things myself. Well, I was closed up then anyhow, 'count of the flu. Didn't have nothing else to do. So I packed up and come back to Llagas. I told him if he didn't keep that little baby and raise him and treat him right I'd go to the state about it and spread the story all over this town, too. And I planted myself right here, and I been here ever since. . . ."

The only sound in the room was the deep gruff voice of the witness. The people of Llagas were amazed and horrified at this tale linking two of their fellow citizens who stood at opposite poles of repute, old man Satterfy and Josie Cantrell. They were amazed to hear about Satterfy's wife, Bo Satterfy's mother. And suddenly, for the first time in their lives, many of them had a sympathetic feeling toward this corrupt and repulsive old woman who had "got to worrying about it," who had been "raised in one of them things" herself, whose very settling in their midst had been a good deed, hidden.

"The night Bo was killed," Josie said, skipping all the meanwhile, "He come to see me. I answered the door and there he stood. He says: 'Did you know Babe Fereer?'—like that. I didn't know what to say. I told him to come in. 'Now,' I says, 'what's this all about?' He says: 'Did she work for you in Denver?' I says: 'I knew Yvonne, yes, but she never worked for me.' He says: 'Don't lie to me, Josie.' I says: 'Young man, I don't *have* to lie to you. I don't have to talk to you at all.' He says: 'Did you know my father?' I says: 'Did Almon Satterfy tell you he wasn't your father?' He nods his head. I marched upstairs and found the documents. 'Your father's a liar,' I says, and I showed him. He looks at the documents and then he looks at me, and he says: 'Then it's true—you brung me to Llagas, didn't you, Josie?' Well . . . he had me with the goods. I says: 'I brung you to Llagas when your mother died because she ast me to, and I brung the documents with me to make your father take you. He didn't want you; but your mother did. She didn't have to have you, you know. And I'll tell you right now,' I says, 'I tried to talk her out of it. But she was one of the straightest and sweetest kids I ever knew, and if it wasn't for that you'd never been born.' He says he wishes he hadn't, and I see he's crying. I went out and got him a drink. 'Take this,' I says, 'and sit down. Now,' I says, 'you listen to me. I don't know what your father told you, but your mother was good enough for him when she was alive, I remember. It wasn't him that left her, it was her that left him, and he come all the way to Denver looking for her. He wanted her back and she wouldn't go back. And if you want my opinion he wasn't good enough for her, and I don't think you are neither. Who the—— Who are you?' I says. 'You got a wife and a good home and you been playing around with some little hustler—*I* know. And you drink too much.'" Josie gave a little shrug. "Bawled him out," she said. "Then he ast me if I knew what happened to the girl. I says: 'She give you the air, and it serves you right.' Then he told me his father bought her off—offered her five thousand dollars to get out of town, and the little skunk took it. . . ."

Arline and her mother looked at each other. Bessie asked: "Did you know that?" and Arline said: "No!"

"Well," Josie went on, "we talked awhile. He told me his father was trying to make him go back to his wife. Wouldn't have no divorce in the family. They'd had a row and his father'd told him about buying off the girl, and then about Babe. Said: 'You're just like your mother.' Told him he was a—— Said *he* wasn't his father and didn't know who was. . . . I never should have brung him to Almon Satterfy at all. . . . And when I ast him if he was going back to his wife now, he says —he says: 'I'll kill myself first.' I says: 'You talk like you aint dry behind the ears yet.' And he says maybe he aint. I says: 'You're lucky you found out what kind of a little chippy that girl was before you got tied up with her,' and he says he knows it. He says he's a damn fool, and I says—I says: 'Amen.'" She gave the same little shrug that she had given before. "Bawled him out," she said again; and to Arline this time the shrug and the words said plainly that Josie had been trying to help him but hadn't known how; they were her sad confession of failure as a woman, an acknowledgment that she had said all the wrong things. "I says: 'The trouble with you is you got no backbone,' and he says he knows that too. . . . When he left I says: 'Where you going?' And he says he don't know. I says: 'You can stay here tonight if you want.' But he says: . . . 'No thanks.' And then, the next day . . . I heard what he done."

Parker objected to the last statement, and Mr. McGann asked the witness: "You have no positive knowledge that Mr. Satterfy's death was not an accident, have you?"

"I wasn't there, if that's what you mean."

"All right," the hearing officer told the court reporter, "strike it out."

Reardon said: "Miss Cantrell, I want to thank you for coming forward."

Josie mumbled: "That's all right."

"May it please the Court," Reardon said, "I'll offer the documents in evidence at this time."

"I object!" Parker said. "And I ask that the slanderous testimony be stricken in toto! It does *not* prove suicide; it's *entirely* inconclusive. And contrary to Mr. Reardon's assurance that it would support his outrageous 'charges' of fabrication and bad faith, it has no bearing on them at all! It's irrelevant! And where, may I ask, is his 'murder mystery'? This testimony is nothing but scandal-mongering. Mr. Reardon's the one who's guilty of bad faith. He's the one who's been fabricating charges and taking advantage of the Board. And then, if you please, he brazenly thanks this witness for coming here. Why, he ought to be disbarred!"

Reardon was unruffled. He said: "I sympathize with Mr. Parker. He has good reason to be squeamish about this testimony. So have the mayor, the chief of police, and the coroner, not to say Mr. Satterfy, Senior, whom the city attorney has tried so hard to protect. It shows us that Bo Satterfy had suicide in his mind, and it contains the reason why. And the Court will not be blinded by Mr. Parker's statement that the testimony has no bearing on my charges of fabrication and bad faith. Fit it into its place in the record, take it together with the town's hostility to the tavern and with those editorials in the *Sentinel*, take it with the elder Satterfy's complaint to the mayor and with Chief

Lally's admission that the death of young Satterfy brought about the showdown, take it with what we know about the police investigation and the inquest, take it with the introduction of Bo Satterfy's death at this hearing and with all the efforts made here to establish that his death was an accident—then we see another picture. Then we see that what we have here under the guise of a liquor hearing is really an extension of the inquest.

"And now let's look into what Mr. Parker has called a murder mystery.

"I've said that the testimony contains the reason Bo Satterfy was contemplating suicide. What *was* the reason? Was it because his father had told him about his mother and disowned him? Was it because he thought his father had never wanted him? Because his girl had left him? Or because she had left him after being bought off by his father? Or because of the wife that his father was trying to make him go back to? Or because he felt that he was a fool and had no backbone—because he couldn't feel like a man? Or because by that decisive deed he wanted to 'show' his father and punish him? Perhaps it was all those things. But is there any doubt that when he left Miss Cantrell's house that night his spirit was already dead? There is your murder mystery, Mr. Parker. But the mystery I spoke of is a mystery of another kind, and now let's see if this testimony can't provide us with a solution to that one.

"Bo Satterfy's body was killed by the bus, and then what happened? The police investigation. The changed story of Manuel Salazar. The inquest at which the evidence of suicide and even the alcoholic content of the body were suppressed. But it was no good. All that elaborate sham was a failure. There remained the 'common talk'—suicide! Can anyone doubt that there was also conscience? The father 'complained' to the mayor. The police conspired against the bartenders and arrested them with marked money. But the City couldn't wait to proceed against the tavern. Something else had to be proved at once, proved to the whole town—and in particular, perhaps, to one man. So the alcoholic content of Bo Satterfy's blood has been made public here for the first time, and his death has been laid upon a scapegoat. Mr. Parker will remember where the word comes from. Webster tells us"—Reardon read from a slip of paper that he had ready in his hand: "'*Jewish Antiquity.* A goat upon whose head were symbolically placed the sins of the people, after which he was suffered to escape into the wilderness.' I say that Mr. McClatchy is the scapegoat here. Mr. Parker will say that I am theorizing. I am. But I am theorizing with established facts, with an iron chain of circumstantial evidence, and with testimony which, in the language of One-one-five-one-three, is 'the sort of evidence on which responsible persons are accustomed to rely in the conduct of serious affairs,' and which is therefore admissible '*regardless of the existence of any common law or statutory rule which might make improper the admission of such evidence over objections in civil actions.*' I have not proved my charges conclusively, no, but then I only said that I would substantiate them to the satisfaction of the Board; and Mr. Parker has not proved any of the charges in the accusation either. We are both of us counting on the Board's discretion. And I am counting on something else which may not have occurred to Mr. Parker. I am counting on the fact that the Board does not exist for the protection of the public only. It exists also for the protection of its licensees; to protect them against malice, conspiracy, and fabrication; even to protect them, when necessary, *against* the public. Mr. Referee, I stand here on behalf of an old 'charter member.'"

Vigorous applause.

Parker looked flabbergasted. "Fictionizing!" he shouted. "This is not law. Mr. Hearing Officer! The man stands there and tells you to your face that his charges are sheer fiction!"

Rapping, the hearing officer looked at Parker narrowly again. "That is not what he said, Mr. Parker. However, if you wish to present evidence that they are fiction I will give you the opportunity."

"Evidence! The City's not on trial here. Or let *him* present evidence."

"I am going to pass the testimony to review by the Board, Mr. Parker, and receive the exhibits."

Applause; cheers from the veteran painters. Parker shouted: "I protest!"

"Noted," Mr. McGann said.

Reardon thanked the hearing officer and offered the certified copies of the marriage record, birth certificate, and death certificate. Parker demanded to see them and was permitted to do so. He handed them back with another protest. Noted. Mr. McGann asked him if he wished to cross-examine the witness.

Parker was even warier of this human skeleton closet than he had been of the nun, but he asked: "Have you ever been convicted of a felony?"

The witness gave him her sneer. "I never been convicted of nothing."

"Are you a customer of McClatchy's tavern?"

"I never been in the place."

"Are you a friend of his, or of his family?"

"I never met none of 'em."

"What was your motive in coming here—revenge against Mr. Satterfy?"

"Maybe it was. I give him fair warning in 1918. Or maybe it was on account of Babe Fereer—and that little baby. And maybe it was something else."

"What else?"

"That's my business."

"Was it blackmail?"

Another sneer. "I don't take blood money."

Parker spun round to the hearing officer. "Ask that the answer be stricken!"

"So ordered," Mr. McGann said.

Parker eyed the harridan uncertainly for a moment, then turned away. "That's all."

Reardon got up. "I rest my case," he said. "And I move that this matter be dismissed."

"No!" Parker said, turning back. "The City asks a continuance. Mr. Hearing Officer, in view of these unprecedented unseemly tactics which appear to have placed the City on the defensive here, I ask to reopen the City's case. I ask a continuance of—of one week."

"Dismissal denied," Mr. McGann ruled. Hunched forward on his elbows, he bent a dour eye on Parker. "One week, Mr. City Attorney? You were expected to have your case prepared," he said sharply. "We will continue at ten o'clock tomorrow morning."

30

AULD LANG SYNE

The sun came up into a pellucid sky. There was no breeze. At ten o'clock on the streets of the town shirtsleeves were common and summer dresses the rule. But the principal topic of conversation was not the weather.

Llagas was on the front pages of the San Francisco papers. There in print were the words suicide, whitewash, conspiracy, fabrication, scapegoat, and murder mystery, and there was the tale of Josie Cantrell. People were asking what the *Sentinel* would say when it came out, and whether old man Satterfy would take the stand today, and whether he would sue for libel, or what; and some were saying that the chief of police and the coroner had been bought off like the waitress. The mayor too had fallen in public esteem. Then there was "poor Bea Manriquez." And there was the man who had dragged all this into the open.

Walsh Reardon had broken out of his niche with a violence that some people deplored. True, he couldn't have let his client be made a scapegoat, they admitted, but mightn't he have prevented that without telling the whole world about Bo Satterfy's mother? And lawyers criticized him for doing havoc to jurisprudence, and censured Mr. McGann for permitting such license. But they were harder on Earl Parker, and they judged that even with the bartenders convicted of bookmaking the Board of Equalization would do no more than suspend the liquor license for thirty days and might not even do that unless Parker could perform a miracle today; because the Board would not let the public see it taken advantage of and used for persecution, they said. And the bartenders were wondering if they might change lawyers, and they were not the only ones who were thinking of taking their legal business to Mr. Reardon.

For the holder of the on-sale general license for the sale of beer, wine, and distilled spirits, there was sympathy, although many Llagans maintained that the Lost Dutchman Tavern ought to be closed. But in Llagas the tavernkeeper and his license were overshadowed now by other figures and issues in the case about to be continued.

In front of the City Hall, Dan McClatchy and his wife and daughter found the picket line disorganized.

"We're subpoenaed!"—"Subpoenaed!" the pickets shouted to them gaily, waving papers; and "Where's Kinney?" . . . "Do you know if Kinney got one?"

But the McClatchys had not seen Kinney and did not know if he had got one. No one had seen Kinney.

Inside the building they had to push through a crowd. A policeman was at the door of the Council chamber and for the present was admitting only those who were concerned in the case and certain citizens of influence who had secured seats by reservation.

And inside the railing of the chamber this morning the McClatchys saw a great television camera and half a dozen unlighted arc lamps —the hearing was to be recorded on film for telecast in the evening.

Already present within the railing also were the mayor and several councilmen, the chief of police, the city attorney, and the whole press corps. Then a man was shepherding the McClatchys through the gate, they were stepping over heavy cables, the powerful arc lamps were turned on in their faces, and they were being interviewed for the television audience.

"How do you feel about the case, McEndymion?" the interviewer asked. "Do you feel you're being made a scapegoat?" and he held his hand microphone up to the mouth of the tavernkeeper, who cleared his throat and said:

"Well I feel—— Well I don't *know*; that was all news to me, that part of it. But I'm a born and raised citizen of the U.S.A., and I always paid all the taxes they told me, and I was never a bookie, and I never—— But I don't want to be talking out of turn here, neither. So maybe I'd better wait till Mr. Reardon gets here and let him do the talking."

"Mr. Reardon—that's your attorney; uh huh. And Mrs. McEndymion? Do you feel that your husband's being made a scapegoat here?"

"Me? Well, I married a good man, that's all I know, and he's not guilty."

"Not guilty; I see. And your daughter? What do you say, Mrs. Lucas?"

Arline said: "Not guilty."

This ended the enlightening interview. The man said: "Thank you very much and good luck." The lamps were turned off.

The pickets came in and seated themselves in a body outside the railing.

Mr. McGann and the stenographer arrived. The television interviewer went up to the hearing officer, who appeared pleasantly surprised at the presence of the television, and began talking with him. Then the public, admitted by the guardian of the door, swarmed into the benches and standing room. Everyone looked for old man Satterfy. He was not present. Neither was Josie Cantrell. And neither was Salvador Díaz.

The hearing officer ascended the bench. The television interviewer seated Bessie and Arline in two of the chairs ranged along the inside of the railing where they would be handy to his camera. Arline got up and took off the new polo coat that she had foolishly worn on this summer-like morning. McClatchy took his place at the counsel table.

It was at this last minute that Reardon strode down the aisle with a square of gauze bandage taped over his right eye. He came through the gate just as Mr. McGann called the hearing to order, and throwing his briefcase on the table, addressed the hearing officer in a voice that after its exertions of the day before was even hoarser and deeper than usual:

"May it please the Court—I ask permission to explain my embarrassing appearance. Last night in the street outside my home I was waylaid"—the courtroom sat up and stared at him. "I was attacked by two men"—the television lamps flooded the area inside the railing with light, the camera swung round upon the speaker, and the newspaper cameras began to flash at him as he continued: "One man leaped out in front of me; the other pinned my arms from behind while the first one struck me three times with his fist, each time in the right eye. When I freed myself they molested me no further. They ran—both of them. But this morning, sir, I have a black eye."

While the big man had been speaking, Parker, with his hands on the table directly across the U, had slowly pushed himself to his feet. As soon as Reardon had finished, Parker snapped:

"What are you implying, Mr. Reardon?"

"Implying, Mr. Parker?"

Parker said accusingly: "You want the Court to think this is more of that 'conspiracy' you were talking about yesterday. Mr. Hearing Officer! He has clearly implied an attempt to beat him up—to disable or disfigure him. Oh, that sly wording: the man struck him three times, each time in the right eye; his assailants molested him no further; and this morning he has a black eye. And that patch he's put over it, that patch will serve to remind the Court and the public, too, all through the proceedings, of this 'conspiracy' he's invented. Innuendo—the same tactics as yesterday—the cheapest kind of melodrama. And all the while we don't really know if he *has* a black eye."

Reardon said: "Is the city attorney suggesting I'm a liar?" He ripped the patch off and stood exhibiting an eye badly discolored and swollen, and again the newspaper cameras were flashing.

Parker turned and spoke to the chief of police, and Mr. McGann, by addressing Reardon in a tone that disguised his question as a statement, revealed his state of mind at this new complication:

"But you don't know who did this."

"Well, I wouldn't be able to identify the men," Reardon said with irony. "It was dark and one of them was punching me in the eye."

Parker said: "Chief Lally tells me his department received no report of any such attack. Why didn't counsel report it?"

"What good do you think that would have done, Mr. Parker?" Reardon said sarcastically.

"He didn't want an investigation—was that it, Mr. Reardon?" Parker asked.

"An investigation by the Llagas Police Department, Mr. Parker?"

Mr. McGann was looking from one lawyer to the other as if he did not know what to think; and the mayor indignantly announced: "This city has the fourth lowest crime rate in the country."

"How fortunate," Reardon said, sitting down. He began trying to stick the bandage back over his injured eye, McClatchy went to his assistance, and the courtroom chattered.

Arline said to her mother: "Oh, do you suppose somebody really tried to beat him up?"

"Nothing would surprise me this morning," Bessie said grimly.

"But who?"—Arline could not believe what she was thinking.

Bessie shook her head.

Mr. McGann's face showed distaste for the whole affair. He rapped with his gavel and said: "Well, we're here in the matter of the Lost Dutchman Tavern." He rose from his chair. "All those who are here to testify please stand and raise your right hands; I'll swear you in together."

And turning round to see who the witnesses were, Arline got another surprise. She said: "Tom Heath!"

"What?" Bessie said, turning; and she saw him. "Well! I guess they subpoenied him, too."

Heath was standing at the back of the room with his hand raised, taking the oath. He saw them looking at him, and smiled a greeting.

Walsh Reardon also was curious to see who Parker's witnesses were. With his hand shielding his unbandaged eye against the brilliance of the arc lamps he looked across the railing. But his attention was arrested by the sight of someone who was evidently not a witness: a woman in a blue dress, seated in the front row. He would have recognized her at once even if she had not been sitting with her niece, Ruth—she had hardly changed at all! Her face was still young, and the hair under her smart little hat was light yellow. Then Evelyn Traubaugh looked at him and he instantly dropped his hand and turned away.

Mr. McGann, having sworn the witnesses, sat down and asked whether there was such a thing as an eyeshade in the City Hall. A policeman was sent in search of one. Then Mr. McGann said "Proceed, Mr. Parker." And Parker called Tom Heath.

Heath briskly came through the gate and took the stand. Everything about him was brisk: the slight athletic body, the single-breasted gray suit, the tab collar, the narrow brown intelligent face with its unbroken plane of forehead and nose and its startling gray eyes blinking to adjust themselves to the brilliant light, the short tough brown hair, and the voice now giving his name, address, and occupation—teacher.

Parker said: "I understand you're also a painter, Mr. Heath."

"That's a hobby," Heath said.

"A hobby. And you exhibit your paintings at the Lost Dutchman Tavern?"

"No."

"You don't? You—you're a member of this group of artists that makes the place its headquarters, aren't you?"

"No, I'm not."

"You're not a member?"

"No."

"Well, but you're a customer of the place, are you not?"

"I am."

"All right, and you're acquainted with these artists, *aren't* you?"

"I know most of them, yes."

"Yes. And you know something of their bohemian way of life."

"In general."

"And you know, don't you, that free love is generally practiced among them?"

"Objection!" Reardon angrily cut in, rising; and Mr. McGann bristled: "Sustained!"

"Very well," said Parker, unperturbed. "Before proceeding, however, I will recall, if I may, that the Court yesterday denied an objection on the ground that the Board wanted to know something about the character of this tavern. Obviously the character of the tavern is the character of these bohemians who make the place their headquarters and market place. And the City contends that since the respondent is charged with conducting a disorderly house contrary to public welfare and morals, the moral conduct of the bohemian customers is relevant and material here."

"Nonsense!" Reardon said. "You can't put *them* on trial; you can't pry into their personal affairs."

"Oh yes I can, to an extent," Parker said.

"*I* will decide that," Mr. McGann said. Propped on his forearms like a lion, he looked from Parker to Reardon and back again, conscious of the television, the press, and the public. "You will confine yourself in a general way to the moral atmosphere on the licensed premises, Mr. Parker."

"Thank you, I will," Parker said. "Now, Mr. Heath. Isn't it a fact that

the tavern derives from this bohemian band, late at night, an atmosphere of concubinage and sexual perversion?"

"Objection! Calling for the opinion of the witness," Reardon said;
and the townspeople turned to inspect the pickets, among whom were
a girl in shorts, several others in pedal-pushers, and young men in
T-shirts. One of the girls had her hand over her mouth and was laughing in shock and embarrassment; other members of the group were
turning to one another and denouncing these aspersions. Mr. Mc-
Gann restored order. Then, wearing his expression of distaste again,
he said:

"The witness may answer the question."

"The answer," Heath said, "is no."

The policeman who had been sent for an eyeshade had returned
with one; he handed it up to the hearing officer, who thanked him
and put it on while Parker continued the examination of the witness:
"Do you deny that late at night this tavern has a general atmosphere
of immorality?"

"Objection! This witness is not an expert on morality."

"He's a teacher—he ought to be," Parker retorted. "He's a professor; are you not, Mr. Heath?"

"I'm an instructor in physics," Heath said. He was quite calm, giving
the impression that he was amused by all this.

"Well, then. You've studied philosophy, haven't you—ethics?"

"Yes. . . ."

Reardon interrupted: "If the witness is to be examined about his
qualifications as an expert on morality, I'd like to ask some questions
too."

Parker turned, the picture of confidence. "Very well, I will yield to
my learned opponent."

Reardon confronted the witness: "Would you agree that morality is
a relative term?"

"Yes."

"That an illicit love affair is not necessarily evil?"

"Yes. . . ."

"That under certain conditions even stealing and murder might
not be immoral?"

"That's conceivable."

"Is it conceivable to you, then, that under certain conditions perjury might be justified?"

Heath smiled. "Yes. . . ."

"Then what guarantee have I got that in your opinion it wouldn't
be justified now?"

"I see your point," Heath said, crinkling about the eyes.

"That's all," Reardon said, turning to the bench. The effect was that of a clever stroke. But before he could say another word Parker was speaking:

"May it please the Court, I will abandon this line of questioning. The moral standards of the witness are not acceptable to the City of Llagas."

Reardon swung round on Parker, realizing, but without for the moment grasping quite how or to what end, that this time he was the one who had been tricked—the whole courtroom felt it; and Heath said to Parker: "I resent that."

"Oh, nothing personal intended, I assure you," Parker said, strolling up to resume the examination. "Tell me, Mr. Heath, did you take part in the demonstration that this 'gypsy band' put on for Mr. Henry Wallace during the last Presidential election?"

"No, I did not."

"No," Parker repeated soothingly. "You did not support Mr. Wallace."

"I didn't say that. As a matter of fact I voted for him."

"Well! And isn't it a fact that you have refused to take an oath of loyalty to the United States?"

Reardon roared: "The city attorney is attempting to put the *witness* on trial."

"Oh no," Parker returned calmly. "The tavern is on trial. I have attempted to show that it's a nest of immorality as testified by the Reverend Kittridge, and I think, Mr. Hearing Officer, that the Board will be interested in knowing if it isn't also a nest of subversion and therefore contrary to the welfare not only of the community but of the state, the nation, and the whole free world."

"What!" Reardon said. "Now he's hunting witches. The question is irrelevant, immaterial, and contrary to everything in the book."

Suddenly the newspaper photographers were clustered like snipers at Heath's feet in the glare of the television lamps, and the press tables were showing keen interest in him—the reporters had guessed that he might be one of the teachers suspended by Fremont Institute; and Arline sat appalled at what was happening.

Mr. McGann was disturbed for reasons of his own. If the tavern was a nest of subversives the Board would want to know it. Furthermore, if he now blocked an expose of a nest of subversives by imposing the rules of evidence half the public would condemn him; if he did not he would be condemned by the other half. He felt that he had been plunged into the center of the national controversy about witch hunts.

"Mr. Parker," he said with an air of dressing the man down. "The Board wants all the pertinent facts about this tavern that you can present here in a proper way. But, as you are well aware, the witness is not on trial, and I hereby advise him that he has the right to refuse to answer."

"Mr. Referee!" Reardon protested this evasion. "Testimony in this matter could be prejudicial to a court case that the witness has pending at this time."

What was this—a court case involving a question of disloyalty to the United States? Mr. McGann bent his eye on Reardon. "Do you represent him in that matter, Mr. Reardon?"

"No, sir; but I believe the witness will confirm what I say."

Mr. McGann looked irritated. "Well, he can refuse to answer. . . ."

Heath said hotly: "I certainly do refuse to answer. I consider the question prejudicial to the whole case for freedom that's being tried in our time. I refuse to answer because I oppose the forces trying to turn this country into a police state. I refuse to answer because I believe in freedom of conviction everywhere and because I know the danger of surrendering to its enemies on *any* front. Yes—I refuse to answer."

The veteran painters hailed this stand with applause—and all at once found themselves in the glare of the arc lamps and the eye of the television camera; they put more spirit into it. Mr. McGann hammered them into silence, lights and camera swung back again, and he said acidly:

"The television seems to have created an illusion here. You people are warned that this is a hearing before an officer of the State Board of Equalization—it is not a show." He turned to the witness. "As for you, Mr. Heath, no one is forcing you to answer the question; so you see there's still a little freedom left in this country."

"I see there's very little," Heath said, fuming.

Parker asked: "Can you tell us whether these bohemians who make the tavern their hangout are members of the Communist Party or——"

"Objection!" Reardon said. "I request that counsel be instructed to stop this line of questioning."

"The witness may answer the question."

"I——" Heath began.

"Just a moment, Mr. Heath," Parker said, and he put the question complete: "Can you tell us whether these bohemians are members of the Communist Party or of any organization listed by the Attorney General as subversive?"

"I said I believe in freedom of conviction. That means I wouldn't tell you even if I knew."

"You're under oath; are you testifying you don't know?"

"I'm testifying I refuse to answer."

Mr. McGann said: "Witness is excused from answering. . . ."

Parker said: "Pardon me, Mr. Heath, but it struck me that the moral ideas you testified to a few minutes ago bore a curious resemblance to the ones the communists hold. Do you mind saying whether you were aware that the Communist Party sponsored Mr. Wallace?"

"The Progressive Party sponsored Mr. Wallace; the Communist Party merely endorsed him; and the moral ideas I testified to, testified to in answer to purely academic questions, by the way, belong to the philosophy prevailing in American universities today. This is a transparent attempt at character assassination—guilt by association. I refuse to submit to it. I'm not on trial and I'm not represented by counsel."

"All right, all right," Parker said, retiring with a smile. "No more questions at this time."

Reardon began what was technically the cross-examination: "I don't think you're a disloyal citizen of this country, Heath; but after what has occurred I think the question needs clearing up. I ask you to tell the Court whether you are or not."

"Under oath? Oh, no, I'm not going to take a loyalty oath," Heath said. "I protest the raising of the question at this hearing. The issues go far beyond a bar license; and I want to know what the question has to do with a bar license. Does it mean that if a man's ideas don't conform he can be denied the right of free assembly and his drink can be taken away from him? The next step——"

Reardon's angry rasp cut him off: "I ask you if you know Mr. Mc-Clatchy and his family."

Heath flushed. "Yes, I know them very well."

"I ask you to tell the Court whether you know them to be disloyal citizens."

"No, I have every reason to know they're completely loyal citizens."

"Thank you, Mr. Heath. That will be all."

As Heath left the stand he looked at Arline and gave his head a shake, frowning; she replied with a look of sympathetic distress; he passed back through the gate, and she said to her mother: "They had no right to ask him about the loyalty oath."

"Well, it's beyond me," Bessie said.

The next witness was Paul Vogler. His colleagues whispered encouragement and advice to him as he left his seat, and after one look at him coming down the aisle with a long loping step, Parker turned to the Bench and said:

"I beg indulgence for the appearance of these artists. They were served in the picket line outside the building only this morning, since no one seems to know where they live, and they haven't had time to go home and change. The circumstance has, however, the advantage of exhibiting them in their natural state."

"I understand," Mr. McGann said.

Paul Vogler was a lean plow-faced young man whose hairline came close to meeting his eyebrows, and his black hair was cropped so short that the scalp was visible between the shafts, and he had several days' growth of black beard and was wearing G. I. spectacles, a T-shirt which exposed hairy arms, and baggy pale blue denims. The press photographers took his picture on the stand while Parker was establishing that he lived in the hills, that he was one of the artists who exhibited in the tavern, and that he had been picketing the hearing. Then Parker asked him:

"Is painting your only occupation? Is that the way you support yourself?"

"Not entirely; I don't make enough."

"Then what is your occupation, if any?"

Vogler cast a resentful glance at the television camera. He answered: "I get an allowance from home and compensation from the government."

"I see. And you spend your government compensation in this tavern?"

"Objection!" Reardon said. "Where the witness spends his money is his private business."

"Sustained."

"Do you," Parker asked the witness, "pay dues to the Communist Party?"

"Objection! It is obviously the purpose of the city attorney to turn this hearing into a public inquisition."

"The witness is advised that he may refuse to answer. . . ."

Vogler hesitated, glanced at the television camera again, and then said forcefully: "I refuse to answer."

Parker asked: "On what ground—that you might incriminate yourself?"

"No! On the ground that I'm not on trial—and I'm not represented by counsel—and you have no right to question me about my convictions. This is a witch hunt!"

Another burst of applause from the veteran painters, and again they found themselves bathed in television. Mr. McGann beat them quiet again and threatened to clear the courtroom. "Now," he said, still ruffling. "I want it understood that this is *not* a witch hunt. It is the business of the Board to find out something about the character of this tavern; it is not its business to penalize any of the customers for their private convictions. The witness is not on trial and was advised of his right to refuse to answer. Now. Proceed, Mr. Parker."

Parker proceeded: "Will you tell us whether, to your knowledge, your associates in this art group belong to the Communist Party or to any other organization listed by the Attorney General as subversive?"

"May it please——" Reardon quickly began, but the witness was flaring:

"This is the same thing that happened in Germany! No man is an island—now we're the ones the bell is tolling for—I can see the handwriting on the wall—the swastika. Fear——"

Mr. McGann stopped him with a loud bang of the gavel and said: "You are not required to answer the question, Mr. Witness, but I warn you that unless you restrain yourself you may be held in contempt."

Vogler declared: "I refuse to answer on the ground that I'm involved in mankind."

"All right," Parker said, turning to Reardon with a smile. "Your witness."

Reardon's first question was: "You served in the armed forces of the United States during the last war, did you not?"

"Yeah. . . ."

"You were wounded?"

"Yeah."

"And that is the reason for the government compensation you mentioned?"

"Uh huh."

"What did you say?"

"I said yeah."

"That's all."

Parker, resuming, asked: "Did you enlist or were you drafted?"

"Drafted."

"Do you mind telling us whether you would bear arms for this country in a war with Russia?"

"Objection!" Reardon said; but the witness overrode him:

"I refuse to answer."

Vogler was followed to the stand by his friend Sherman Cook, sallow-cheeked, likewise bespectacled, also in need of a shave, and wearing a sweatshirt, and Cook was followed by the girl crapshooter, an ex-Marine, in shorts, and she by little Moe Freed.

All defiantly rejected questions involving political convictions, including whether they belonged to the Communist Party; war veterans all, they refused to say whether they would serve the nation in a war with Russia, but the ex-Marine lashed out that she would fight for peace and world government, and when Parker asked whether she believed in world government strongly enough to advocate the overthrow of the United States Government by force to achieve it, replied:

"I believe in the overthrow of this hearing—it *is* a witch hunt."

Repeatedly but to little effect Walsh Reardon hurled himself at the stampede. There was no law under which McClatchy could be deprived of his license if his tavern were a headquarters of communists, but there were overt reasons enough that could be used for depriving him if in the discretion of the Board the tavern was "contrary to public welfare and morals" for any reason. And now, recalled to mind here by the performance of the veteran painters, the testimony of the mayor and the minister which Reardon had effectively disposed of yesterday was taking on shape, color, and the appearance of substance.

Reardon saw that he was losing his advantage. Losing it because of a lie, because of an incredible foul, because of a hoax that Parker was working with the collusion of McClatchy's own customers. Reardon felt that he was being made a fool of by little Earl Parker, shown up before the eyes of Llagas, before the press and the television, before the woman in the blue dress on the other side of the railing, the yellow-haired girl at the back of his mind—at the back of his mind again after all these years.

He objected, argued, cajoled, lost his temper, roared at Moe Freed and could not frighten him into admitting that he was a loyal American. And the sun had climbed past eleven o'clock, and the television lamps beat down.

As Freed left the stand, Parker said: "I know these bohemians have been trying to the Court's patience, and I must say I'd prefer not to call any more of them. I'd prefer to call Mr. Reardon."

"Mr. Reardon?" the hearing officer asked, looking surprised again, as Reardon, on his feet, glared at Parker across the U. The hearing officer asked: "For what purpose, Mr. Parker?"

"Well," Parker said, "it's irregular, but I think everyone will agree that this is no regular case. Oh, I wouldn't want Mr. Reardon to testify in any legal capacity. I understand he's an old customer of this tavern, one of the oldest customers Mr. McClatchy has; but of course I couldn't

ask him to testify against his client. There's this so-called conspiracy
that he mentioned yesterday; I'd like to question him about that. And
there's this black eye about which there's no police report. I'm afraid
that sensational story he told us has given the City a black eye. I'd
like him to tell us about that mysterious attack under oath. So instead
of calling more bohemians, I would, if permitted, challenge Mr. Reardon to take the stand."

Reardon barked: "Would counsel accept the same challenge from
me?"

"Under the same conditions," Parker said, "gladly."

Under the same conditions meant that it would be difficult if not
impossible to get answers from Parker to the questions that Reardon
would most want to ask. But Reardon's veracity had been challenged,
and he was not the one to refuse a challenge from Earl Parker—not
before the world, not before the town, not before Sis Traubaugh; and
he was spoiling to come to grips with Parker directly. "Mr. Referee!"
he said at once. "If the Court will indulge Mr. Parker, I am quite
willing to take the stand."

At this point in the case Mr. McGann was asking himself which
of these two men it was who was taking advantage of the Board in
front of the town, the press, and the television, and whether indeed
both were not taking advantage of it. That feeling of not knowing
what was going on had been plaguing him all morning. It had occurred to him that the defensive tactic of charging conspiracy and
persecution, which Reardon was using here, was an old communist
one; on the other hand, that patch on Reardon's eye worried him.
The black eye had properly to be considered irrelevant and immaterial here, an incident of which no official notice could be taken, since
there was no proof or even charge that it had come of a conspiracy
connected with the hearing, but it was all so queer, and with the
public looking on Mr. McGann felt that he had better get to the
bottom of it if he could, and Reardon had offered to take the stand.
He said: "If you wish to do so, Mr. Reardon, the Court will permit."

The one-eyed giant took the oath; he stepped up on the platform
and sat down in the brilliance of the witness chair. The powerful lights
made everything beyond the railing hazy to his eye. The television
camera hovered on his left, the microphone hung over his head, and
the press photographers gathered in a quarter circle on their haunches
at his feet.

Approaching him with a smile, Parker said: "Thank you, Mr. Reardon."

Reardon growled: "Don't mention it, Mr. Parker."

Parker looked at the sprinkle of sweat on Reardon's brow and asked fraternally: "Would you like to take your coat off, Mr. Reardon?"

"I don't have to take my coat off for this fight."

The courtroom chuckled.

"Oh, let's not fight," Parker said. "It's just that I don't want you to suffer from the heat."

"Never mind the heat," Reardon said.

"I don't mind it," Parker said, and in fact the wiry city attorney looked quite cool. "Tell me, Mr. Reardon, was I correct in saying that you were an old customer of the Lost Dutchman Tavern?"

"You were."

"You used to frequent the place even before it was the Lost Dutchman, when it was the Traveler's Rest; is that correct?"

Reardon did not like the question. He particularly did not like the verb frequent. Everybody in town knew what a hole the Traveler's Rest had been; even she might know. But many townspeople also knew that he had frequented it; and she might hear. His pride prevented him from challenging the line of questioning and made him answer boldly: "It is."

"It is," Parker repeated. Walking back to his counsel table, he asked: "And the place was located on the same premises—on Hill Street across from the railroad yard, was it not?"

"As already established," Reardon answered impatiently, "yes."

"Yes," Parker said, and there was a moment of silence while he searched his briefcase. He came back with a glossy photograph in his hand. A bead of sweat rolled down Reardon's cheek, and the big man pulled out an already wet handkerchief and wiped it off. "Take mine," Parker said, offering a handkerchief neatly folded. "It's dry."

"I don't need yours," Reardon said irritably, looking at the photograph in Parker's hand. He saw that it was a photograph of McClatchy behind the bar of the Traveler's Rest.

"Perhaps," Parker said, turning, "we can have the windows opened for Mr. Reardon. His shirt is soaking wet."

"It is not soaking wet," Reardon said, glancing down at his shirt.

"I mean under the collar there."

"Your concern for my comfort is touching, Mr. Parker."

"But you seem to feel the heat so much more than other people. I don't want to subject you to an ordeal here."

"*Believe* me, Mr. Parker, that is beyond your power. I ask you to get on with the examination."

"Just as you say," Parker said. Meanwhile a policeman was opening the windows "for Mr. Reardon." And all the time the dry-faced Parker had been standing there with that photograph in his hand. "I show you," he said, "a photograph of the saloon of the Traveler's Rest, and ask you if you recognize it."

The noun saloon, too, affronted Reardon. He took the photograph and immediately turned it over. "I see," he said, "that this photograph is the property of Mr. Satterfy's newspaper, the *Sentinel*."

"Why, yes, it is. Do you recognize the saloon?"

"I recognize a picture that is irrelevant and immaterial, and I hope you're not thinking of offering it in evidence, Mr. Parker. We're concerned here with the Lost Dutchman Tavern, not with a tavern that no longer exists. And I recognize that any further questions about the Traveler's Rest would be irrelevant, immaterial, and a waste of time."

"Sustained," Mr. McGann said.

"Very well," Parker said, walking to his counsel table again, and he placed the picture face up on the table. Coming back, he said: "Now, Mr. Reardon, what is your occupation?"

Reardon gave a contemptuous snort, and the hearing officer said: "The answer to the question is obvious, Mr. Parker."

"Pardon me," Parker said, "we know that Mr. Reardon is appearing for his friend the barkeeper, but it has not been established that he's an attorney."

Mr. McGann raised his brows. He looked at Reardon. "You *are* an attorney, aren't you?"

Reardon shot an insulted glance at the hearing officer, but restrained himself. He answered scornfully: "Why, Parker here went to Stanford Law School the same time I did."

A trace of anger was detectable in Parker's "Yes, but I graduated."

More than a trace in Reardon's retort: "*I* was graduated at Hall Mc-Allister."

Parker's next was barbed with an adverb: "And you're still a member of the Bar in good standing?"

" '*Still*'? You *know* I am."

"Well, if I may remind you, it's many years since anyone's seen you in court."

"Why," Reardon sneered, "I've done *your* legal work for you."

"Oh, those things, yes—clerical work."

"Cler—— Do you think you can put *me* on trial? I didn't take the stand to answer questions about my private affairs."

"Sustained," Mr. McGann said. "Mr. Reardon has testified he's a member of the Bar in good standing." But Mr. McGann had the feeling that there was more to this matter than had come out. Why should Parker have challenged the standing of a fellow townsman and lawyer whom he had gone to college with and probably known all his life? Mr. McGann wanted to know more about Reardon. He wanted to know more about this confusing case which seemed to go back so many years and involve so many people in this unholy little town.

Reardon felt outraged. Earl Parker, after fouling him once and making him look a fool today, had demanded and made him present his credentials, and Parker had committed under the eyes of the hearing officer another foul against him which the hearing officer could not see. Parker had raked up in the minds of the townspeople his reputation as a drunkard and the fact that he had been expelled from Stanford (and in her mind the reason why) and the fact that he had not had a client, a real client, for years, and Parker had revealed to Llagas that Walsh Reardon sometimes worked for him, did clerical work, as it appeared, for little Earl Parker, who was city attorney now. Governor Reardon. And what she might not understand of all this would be explained to her later, perhaps was being explained to her now by the niece with whom she was sitting.

"All right," Parker said. "Are you willing, Mr. Reardon, to answer questions under oath about this attack you say was made on you last night?"

"I'm ready for any questions you can ask me, Mr. Parker."

"Thank you. Now where did you say this attack occurred?"

"I said it occurred in the street outside my home."

"Outside your home; and what is your address?"

Reardon changed his position in the witness chair, and in a low growl meant not to be heard beyond the railing said: "Gore Street."

"What number?"

"Four."

"Number Four, Gore Street," Parker said aloud. "Oh yes, that would be in the dead end of Gore Street down by the slough, wouldn't it?"

Reardon answered with a nod and a grunt that it would be, conscious that she would know the dead end of Gore Street; and the sweat was trickling down his face again, but this time he tried to ignore it.

"Yes," Parker said, running his eyes over Reardon's face, with a faint smile. "Well, the dead end of Gore Street isn't the safest part of town at night, I suppose. And you said it was dark?"

"That's what I said."

"What about the streetlights?"

"There were no streetlights."

"One moment, please," Parker said, turning away.

As Parker turned, Reardon wiped the back of his big right hand across his brow and then with a pinching movement of palm, fingers, and thumb, gathered up as much as he could of the moisture on the lower part of his face.

To Reardon's increased irritation the city attorney was again walking to his counsel table. Then he was opening his briefcase again. Then he was taking out several large folded papers. Then he was unfolding one of them and spreading it on the table, and Reardon saw that it was a map. A map—what did he want with a map!

"The dead end of Gore Street," Parker said again, beginning to prowl over his map; and Reardon objected:

"Counsel is wasting time."

"Excuse me," Parker said, "but I want to check on the streetlights."

"There's a streetlight—it was out."

"What time was it?" Parker asked.

"It was somewhere around eleven o'clock."

Then Parker consulted a booklet. "Number Four, Gore Street— that's the O.K. Machine Shop! Now you don't live in a machine shop, do you, Mr. Reardon?"

"Number Four-B," Reardon barked. "You know where I live."

"Oh, 'B'! Yes, I remember there's a machine shop on the first floor; you live on the second—over the machine shop, over the machine shop. That explains it," Parker said. And he began carefully folding his map.

Of what was being done to Reardon no one in the room except Reardon and Parker was aware, and Parker himself was not aware of all of it and could not have guessed the strength of its effect on this man whose flagrant pride, whose terrible morbid paralyzing vanity, he thought he knew. Parker was recalling to the people of Llagas a Llagas folk tale; he was telling of the dwarfed life of the local giant, with its prodigious feats of weakness and its enormous funk. And sitting just beyond the railing, just beyond where Reardon could see, was the landgrave's daughter, the mistress of the ponycart and the touring car and the red Dusenberg roadster and the great stone house. Whose father had paid his tuition at Stanford. Whose father had told her: "He may be governor of the state someday—mark my words." She was hearing it all, and watching. And now she had heard that after all these years Walsh Reardon lived over a machine shop in the dead end of Gore Street, on the slough.

And Parker was doing something else to Reardon that neither the hearing officer nor the press nor the television could see. Reardon was the town's man who might have been. Approve of him or not, he was the man who could have made a name. Failure or not, he was the man in whose prowess, in whose brilliance, knowledge of the law, cleverness, and eloquence, the town had continued to believe. Yesterday he had seemed to measure up to expectations; in a shocking way, of course, but that was Reardon. Today he was being outmaneuvered, confounded, and pinned down by little Earl Parker. Parker was doing more than retell a folk tale. He was promising to destroy a Llagas legend, perhaps only a myth. He was menacing the one thing that had remained to Reardon in the years of his decline, the thing without which the giant would feel himself a pygmy in the eyes of the town.

Reardon knew what Parker was doing, and knew that he had to keep his temper, had to keep his mind clear. But Parker had roiled the pride in him, and it did not help his temper that the lights hurt his eyes, both his eyes, and his temper was collaborating with the heat to make him suffer the further indignity of oozing sweat from every pore of his great gin-bloated body. He resented the television and the weather also. November, a day like this in November! As he sat illuminated on public view in this leaking condition it seemed that even the weather had fouled him. And this robot Diogenes that peered into people's faces under a battery of hot arc lamps, and caught up speech in a cold electric recording ear, was something new come to judgment. Reardon had never seen a television apparatus before in his life. He was not sure whether it had any right to be here, legally. It had come, he supposed, in the character of an observer, a reporter. But he knew what an effect it was having on the hearing, on the very conduct of the hearing. And he felt as if he were being fed to it, a human sacrifice.

Parker put his map back in his briefcase, and looking up, caught Reardon in the act of wiping his face and neck with the wet handkerchief. Coming back, he said: "Well, I only have a few more questions, Mr. Reardon. But I wish you'd at least loosen your collar; you're making this look like the third degree."

Reardon fixed Parker with a revengeful knowing eye while stuffing the handkerchief into his back pocket. "Isn't that what you had in mind, Mr. Parker?"

"I? Oh, now, Mr. Reardon," Parker said, "none of the other witnesses perspired—this is abnormal! Perhaps," he suggested to the hearing officer, "Mr. Reardon wants a recess."

"Recess nothing!" Reardon said. "Go on—stop wasting time."

"All right, then," Parker said. "I ask you to give us a full account of this attack you say was made on you last night."

Reardon began to rasp out his story in short sentences; and again Parker turned away and receded, leaving him alone in the center of the lighted stage.

The story was quite true. But Reardon was telling it immediately after an introduction that, by calling attention to his "abnormal" sweating, had reminded him afresh of his drunkard's reputation; and, isolated and spotlighted in the witness chair, confronted with the hazy curtain of light that hung between him and the benches, and by the press photographers squatting at his feet, watched by Llagas eyes unseen, watched and listened to by her, scrutinized by the monstrous gray television camera, and eavesdropped on by the microphone suspended over his head like the recording angel, he remembered that black eyes in general were open to sportive suspicion, it struck him that the story he was telling must sound fantastic here, and he feared that no one believed him. It was his opinion, though he could not say so, that his attackers had been set on him by old man Satterfy or even by the chief of police and the mayor himself, and the idea of his being discredited now to the advantage of his enemies, at the climax of the most important case in his life, cheated of victory at the last minute, because of drinking bouts that were altogether irrelevant and immaterial to the story he was telling, incensed him all the more.

There was not much he could tell. The incident, including his brief pursuit of the men, had been over in two minutes, and he had seen very little of it. But all at once it seemed that his whole future depended on his convincing everyone that the story was true, and he told everything he could remember. He jerked out the story in rising anger. It was like talking into a radiant cloud with torches in front of it and a few dim figures in the foreground. The glossy photograph on Parker's table caught his eye: he was seized with the idea that old man Satterfy would publish it: the picture of his crime, of his failure, of his life. And the soft sweat stood on his forehead in globes which dropped of their own weight into his overhanging rusty brows, it stood on his upper lip and in the cleft of his chin, and it came out of his thick hair and ran past the lobes of his ears to his jowls and fell onto his collar; but he would not pull out the handkerchief again for fear of calling attention to it. "None of the other witnesses perspired." He felt that his body was yielding up the truth about him. What were they thinking? He could hear nothing but his own crippled voice, and it came to him that even this was betraying him. Whisky bass! He stopped talking. An interminable instant of utter silence, then the sound of water being poured into a glass from a pitcher held high by Parker at the counsel table—Parker calling attention again to his humiliating sweat.

Parker came back holding the glass of water, but looking abstracted, as if for the moment he had forgotten it. "Now," he said slowly, "as I understand your story, the first man, the man who struck you three times in the eye, as you say, stood in front of you—like this—while the other man held you from behind. Is that correct?"

Reardon growled that it was correct.

"Yes. And yet each of his three blows struck you in the right eye. What I can't understand is, why didn't he hit you in the left eye? That would have been the natural thing, wouldn't it? I mean assuming, of course, that he was right-handed. Or," Parker asked sarcastically, "was this mysterious apparition of the night *left*-handed?"

"How do I know? I hardly saw him, I told you. He was punching me in the eye."

Parker's point was a mere cavil. Grappled from behind by the second man, Reardon might have been turned a little to the left so that the first man was not directly in front of him; but this did not occur to Reardon, and he was stung by the suggestion that he might have been struck by a left-handed man. To Reardon just now the suggestion that the "mysterious apparition of the night" would have had to be left-handed made his story sound even more fantastic.

Parker smiled and said: "I see." And apparently still forgetting the glass of water in his hand, he proceeded with his "few more questions." Had there been any witnesses to this attack? Didn't Reardon know that he should have reported it to the police? Had he called a doctor? Had he been treated at a drugstore, then? But the hospital had been open—had he gone there? No? Then was there no record at all of this black eye? Nothing but his word? Where had he got the bandage he was wearing now? Reardon said he had got it in a drugstore this morning. But only this morning, Parker said—hadn't that been rather late to get the eye attended to? . . .

Pilloried, with the glare in his uncovered eye and the sweat running into both eyes, humiliated and full of wrath, Reardon offered no objections; he forgot the hearing officer, the Code, and the Board of Equalization, forgot that this was a case about a liquor license, forgot the McClatchys. This was something between himself and Earl Parker. *He* was on trial, foully held to answer for his reputation and challenged to prove his ability, challenged by a dwarf, and the jury was out there in that radiant cloud, the judge was out there in a blue dress; and he was acutely conscious of the newspaper photographers, whose flashbulbs exploded at intervals at his feet, of the reporters, and of gray Diogenes, the unexpected supervenient examiner, friend of another court, prying into his face.

And the hearing officer, like every spectator, was absorbed in the spectacle of Reardon. Parker's questions, though put in a slightly quickening tempo, were courteously worded and seemed harmless enough, yet Reardon was obviously in a rage which he was trying to control; and that sweat was amazing.

The revealing agonizing sweat engulfed Reardon, his throat was dry, the sound of his own voice harassed him, his head ached, and at the back of his mind a tune was running—he was remembering something of which he had never had any memory before. He was at bay with a broken leg on the dance floor of the St. Francis Hotel, the spotlight blinding him and the band striking up:

> I'm a ramblin' wreck from Georgia Tech, and a helluva
> gambolier,
> A helluva helluva helluva helluva HELLUVA gambolier. . . .

Parker was asking: "Where had you been? Where were you coming from?"

"Dinner—coming home from dinner."

"At eleven o'clock? Coming from the Lost Dutchman?"

"Yes; what of it? I'd eaten there——"

"With the out-of-town press? With the newspaper people?"

"With the—— You seem to know a lot about my movements last night, Mr. Parker."

"Oh, that was easy to guess. Mr. McClatchy threw a little party, didn't he? You were celebrating, weren't you?"

"No!"

"What? You weren't drinking?"

"You mean was I drunk. No!"

"I asked if you were drinking."

"You're suggesting I was drunk. I was not drunk."

"Yet you didn't have that eye attended to until this morning. Didn't it bother you?"

"Of course it bothered me."

"Had you been drinking?"

"I was not drunk; I don't deny I'd had a drink or two, but I was not drunk."

"You keep insisting on that. Don't I remember a long dark flight of steps leading to your apartment over the machine shop?"

"I was not attacked on the steps."

"I didn't suppose you were attacked on them."

Suddenly the light stabbed into Reardon's wounded eye and his whole body jerked in reaction. Then he saw the sweat-soaked bandage fallen on his knee. Parker smiled and held out the glass of water. Reardon struck it from his hand. It shattered against the mayor's desk. Mr. McGann said: "Mr. Reardon!" and again the cameras flashed at Reardon.

Parker said: "I beg the Court's indulgence for my opponent. Obviously this has been more of an ordeal for him than he was willing to admit."

Mr. McGann continued to look at Reardon threateningly, but said no more. Parker stooped and began to pick up pieces of the broken glass, leaving every eye but his on Reardon. The giant's old brown suit, which yesterday had looked freshly pressed, was all rumpled now, his whole body was awash with his macerating sweat, his shirt was soaked through, his black eye was exposed, and his big face was purple with the fury of his scalded pride. But his burns remained invisible. To the courtroom it was astonishing. It was unreasonable. Then Parker stood up with a handful of glass and said quietly:

"I will spare the witness any further questions"—and retired to drop the glass in the wastebasket under his table.

Mr. McGann said: "Do you wish to offer any testimony on your own, Mr. Reardon? . . . If not, you may step down."

Reardon left the stand with a lunge that scattered the photographers, turned, and made for the television camera. That evening viewers of the film saw his face loom savage and blurring on their screens, and then his body block the lens. But the hearing officer, striking with the gavel again and calling his name, stopped him. Reardon swung round. "You! Why didn't you send for a basin of water and wash your hands?" Then he was charging through the gate and out of the courtroom. McClatchy, on his feet, was looking after him in a frightened way, Parker with vicious triumph in his eyes, and the hearing officer was demanding that he come back, but the standees at the rear of the chamber opened a path to the door and Reardon was gone.

Parker turned back to the hearing officer. "Again I beg the Court's indulgence for a man who seems to be in a fit of hysteria. I submit, however, that his actions speak for themselves—Mr. Reardon is finished. And the City," he said with a little bow, "rests."

Mr. McGann's face was the color of Reardon's. He looked belligerently round the courtroom. "I agree," he said, and cleared his throat, "that Mr. Reardon was in no state to be held accountable for his behavior. In the circumstances I choose to overlook it. The Board will take the case under advisement." And he sounded the gavel for the last time. "This hearing is adjourned."

31

THE SWAN

Arline had never felt so sorry for her father as when, after being surrounded by the press again and then led forth for a last word on television, he stood trying to explain to the camera. Mr. Reardon had not been drunk, he said, Mr. Reardon was a fine man, he was a lawyer, and they had all pledged allegiance, the bartenders and the cooks and the waitresses and everybody, and at the grand opening the orchestra had played patriotic airs, "The Stars and Stripes Forever," and Mr. Reardon had delivered the address, he was a great talker. . . .

"Thank you very much," the television man said, and the lamps went out.

And when at last McClatchy found himself on the sidewalk with his wife and daughter, he stopped and said: "Maybe I better go and see Mr. Reardon." But Bessie advised: "Not now, Danny." He agreed: "No—not now." A few steps later he said: "I don't understand it; I don't understand what happened to Mr. Reardon." "Well," Bessie said, "it's over now."

Yes, it was over. From the day's happenings alone it might have been hard to demonstrate legally that they had lost, but they knew. Reardon's exit after his bewildering breakdown on the stand and his insult to the hearing officer had been like a confession of fraud and defeat. But there were no recriminations upon McClatchy from his women. Over, Arline kept thinking. They would lose the bar license and then the tavern. This season of their life was over.

To escape the reporters Tom Heath had left the City Hall at the adjournment, but he was waiting in his parked car at the corner of Main and Hill streets, and seeing them coming, got out and walked back to meet them. Tom Heath she had forgotten, and now her heart sank a little more as it came to her that she was not going to marry him. Over—this too was over.

Heath said that the hearing had been one of the most frightening things he had ever seen, and she said: "I'm sorry they dragged you into it, Tom," but her father, stopping, asked him: "Are you a member of the Party?"

"What? Of course not," Heath said. "And neither are any of the others. Your tavern's no 'nest of subversion.'"

"It aint?"

"No!"

Walking on, her father grumbled: "Well if it aint, this is a hell of a time to say so."

"The question," Heath said, walking too, "never should have been brought up; it had nothing to do with the case. And I couldn't submit to a loyalty oath at a liquor hearing while I was fighting against being forced to take one at Fremont; you understood that, didn't you?"

"Dad," Arline said, "that's the case he has coming up in court."

"Yes, it's a test case," Heath said, "and I'm not the only one involved. And we're fighting for the whole academic world, for *all* Americans, against all witch hunts and attempts at character assassination."

"But," her father said, "it don't assassinate you to say you're a good citizen."

"That's not the point——"

"And what was the matter with the veteran painters if they aint commies?" her father demanded, stopping again as they came to the corner of Hill Street. "They haven't got no test case."

"They made yours a test case—they were standing up for the same principle, for their own rights and for yours, too. Look at that headline."—Heath pointed to a newspaper in a rack. The headline said: RUSS PILOTS IN KOREA. "What do you think Americans are fighting for in Korea? They're fighting for a free world. Do you want to sell them out at home? That's what's happening. Ask yourself what they'll be coming back to, those who do come back."

McClatchy looked confused. "Well, but," he said, with a shake of the head, "I don't understand what happened to Mr. Reardon."

"Reardon ran out on you," Heath said indignantly.

Arline was no longer following the conversation. Over. Not going to marry him. What now?

Then Heath was speaking to her. "Let me take you to lunch."

"Lunch?" she said dully. Her mother said: "Go on, why don't you? We'll see you later." Her father nodded goodbye to Heath, and Heath said sincerely: "Good luck."

Her parents began to walk down Hill Street and she did not move.

Heath asked her: "Where do you want to go?"

She turned away. "I'm not hungry." She walked a few steps back the way they had come. He followed. She stopped. With face averted she asked in a low voice: "Do you still want me to go to your place?"

"*My* place? . . . Do you want to? Arline—will you?"

She looked at him with pain in her eyes. Then looking away again: "But I don't want any more children, Tom," she said.

"All right," he said softly, smiling. "Don't worry." What a difference it made to her, he thought, that they were going to be married.

She stayed with him almost four hours in his cottage, hidden by trees from the boardinghouse it stood behind; and he knew that he had met his giantess. Afterward he sank into a deep sleep in her arms. Over. And the training, ties, and responsibilities of her life accused her: for Arline, because of them, it was too late. Her heart was leaden. She got up without waking him, and dressed. She left an unsigned note on the pillow: "Goodbye, Tom." And while he slept she walked for blocks, not toward the tavern but away from it, her eyes on the pavement, her bag under her arm, her fists thrust into the pockets of her coat, under the trees. Images raced through her mind: of Billy, of her parents walking down Hill Street alone, of Mrs. Crown saying "People like that have no right to a child," of her dead husband, of Raymond Dirigo and Phyllis Plover, of what had happened in the cottage, of a tree in the jungle, and of a solitary pond hidden from the sky. And having discovered something about herself, she was afraid, afraid for her son. Only half aware that she knew where she was going, she came to St. Peter's. She stopped. Then she slowly climbed the steps and went in.

She knelt at the altar railing for a long time before she raised her head, the only visitor in the church. She was looking at the tabernacle. Her eyes were wet. They moved to the stained-glass Pietà, and her lips moved.

"Mary—take Billy. O Mary . . . at the altar of God I give you my son. I'll help you bring him up to be a priest or whatever you want. He's yours now. Take care of him. He's not mine any more. God has witnessed that I've given him to you."

Heath slept all through the night and till seven in the morning. He remembered and was surprised. He found the note, and smiled. He felt debilitated and realized while dressing that he had not eaten for nearly twenty-four hours. He went into the boardinghouse for breakfast.

That morning he telephoned her at the tavern, but when she came on the wire she said: "I can't talk now. Can you meet me?"

"Now?" he asked, a bit alarmed; but she explained:

"I just want to talk to you."

"What's the matter?"

"Will you meet me?"

"I'll be right down."

"No, I—— Not here. I'll meet you on the bridge."

"The what?"

"The Hill Street bridge."

"What in the world——?"

She insisted: "We can talk there."

"All right," he said. "I'll be there in five minutes."

Today was overcast; as he turned down Hill Street he saw her standing hatless but wrapped in her polo coat, her hands in her pockets, by the railing halfway across the bridge. He parked his car and walked out to her, smiling.

She asked: "Did you get my note?"

"Yes——"

"I meant it, Tom." Her eyes and voice were almost apologetic. "I can't marry you."

"You can't! Why? What's happened?"

"Nothing. I'm sorry, Tom."

"What's the matter?"

She shrugged. "We wouldn't be good for each other."

"Wouldn't be good for each other? Oh, Arline!" he said, and moved to take her by the arms. "Baléte!"

"Don't call me that," she said, turning away. She looked out over the water and he looked at her hair stirred by the breeze.

"Wouldn't be good for each other," he repeated again behind her, mystified. "Can you say that after yesterday? Arline, I love you."

"That wasn't love." She faced him. "I don't ever want to be like that again. That's one reason. And we're not the same kind of people, Tom. It wouldn't work. I knew that before."

"Before? When? At the hearing, wasn't it?"

"Yes. That was when I knew."

"I thought so. You don't understand, do you?"

"I understand. They never should have asked you those questions and you did what you thought was right."

"But *you* don't think it was right."

"I . . . I just think you never grew up, Tom."

"What? Why—because I stood up and said 'No' at a witch hunt? Because I wouldn't let them tear up the Constitution? Because I was consistent? Maybe *you* never grew up. Or you still don't understand the issues."

"Maybe I don't understand the issues," she said, flaring a bit, "but I can't help it. I'm a woman and my father's daughter and I know I'm not going to marry a man who stands arguing about 'the issues' when the house is burning down; and I'm not going to marry a man who thinks about himself all the time."

"Himself?"

She turned away, wishing she had not said that and preferring not to explain it.

"Arline, they can't take your father's license away because of anything *I* said."

"Can't they?"

"Of course not. It had nothing to do with the license."

She did not reply.

He said: "I couldn't have done anything else but what I did. I had to do it. Don't you see?"

"Yes, I see. I know."

"But," he said, "you came with me afterwards. You suggested it yourself. Why?"

"I don't know."

"Arline, you're not being reasonable."

"Yesterday I wasn't. Now I am."

"Remorse?"

She turned back to him. "I'm a grown woman, Tom. There's a child to consider, a little boy. I'm not going to choose you for his father. And I don't love you, Tom. I'm sorry. It's over. Let's say goodbye right here on the bridge." She held out her hand.

Taking it, he said: "You're upset. I'll call you tomorrow——"

"No. I won't answer. And don't come to the tavern any more, will you? Grow up, Tom. This is goodbye and good luck."

He remained on the bridge watching her departing figure, with the physical memory of her hand in his, and anger rising in his heart. He felt humiliated. She never saw him again.

32

END AND BEGINNING

On three successive days the tavernkeeper climbed the stairs to Mr. Reardon's door. No answer; door locked. The third time he inquired of the hammerer below. But Leonard Beiderman said that he had not seen his tenant. The tavernkeeper said that he was worried. The landlord went up with him and unlocked the door. Chaos as usual, but no tenant. He's on a bender somewhere, McClatchy guessed sadly.

Josie Cantrell returned to Denver, leaving her house up for sale. Bea Manriquez, born in Mudtown, went on a cruise to South America. Old man Satterfy stayed, keeping his own counsel. In the *Sentinel*, not a word about anything that had happened. To Arline it seemed eerie and foreboding.

But in the editorial and letter columns of the San Francisco papers the words witch hunt reverberated for a week. Mr. McGann was censured and defended. W. W. Wallace, the district's member of the Board of Equalization, stated to the press that he would take no cognizance of the political convictions or affiliations of the tavern's customers whatever; which seemed to make the censure official. And San Francisco, on the whole, was for McClatchy. Hopeful signs.

Rover Kinney too had disappeared. There was the matter of the tavernkeeper's not having paid to the state the sales tax on the pictures he had sold; and still no Reardon. McClatchy reflected that there was no one in all the world to be concerned about Mr. Reardon but himself and family and Leonard Beiderman and the others of the Old Guard. He reported his lawyer's disappearance to the police. The *Sentinel* noted it in two objective paragraphs on the front page. The San Francisco papers gave it more. And fearing to delay the sales tax matter any longer, McClatchy went to San Francisco and presented himself to an official of the tax division of the Board, alone.

No record of any sales tax paid by an organization called the Veteran Painters could be found. McClatchy estimated that in nearly three years he had sold about two hundred pictures at an average price of thirty or forty dollars; but the official explained that an arbitrary assessment would be levied against him. The amount of the assessment stunned him.

One thousand dollars.

To show good faith he wrote a check for half the amount and promised to pay the balance in five monthly installments.

But it did not save the tavern.

The bartenders were convicted and fined, and a week later the McClatchys received a registered letter from the liquor division of the Board. It was the death blow. License revoked. Violation of Section 58. The bookmaking was cited.

A liquor control officer called to make sure the bar was closing. He ordered that the bar unit be taken out or partitioned off from the restaurant. McClatchy said that he would have a temporary partition built—he would be selling the tavern now, he said, and the new owner would want the bar. Meanwhile, under orders, he removed from the bar its lifeblood, the beer, wine, and distilled spirits, and down the middle of the room stretched a rope, and on a piece of laundry cardboard wrote a sign, Bar Closed, and attached the sign to the rope, and switched off the lights on the bar side. He saved till last the spotlight on the face of the oldest guardsman. "Goodnight, Dutch," he said, and pulled the switch.

The *Sentinel* reported the closure in two paragraphs more, objectively; but the San Francisco papers treated it as a sentimental occasion. Noel Ames telephoned his sympathy and on Sunday gave another column to the tavern and its proprietor. It was an affectionate column. He went so far as to call McEndymion "the last of the old South of Market boys."

Still no Reardon. The idea of foul play was growing on McClatchy. The police could tell him nothing. He offered to pay Mr. Reardon's rent for a month, but Leonard Beiderman would not hear of it.

The restaurant was still in business, of course, but it was doing little. It was a dry restaurant now, and the ugly plywood fence that a carpenter had made to shut off the bar did not help. Even the veteran painters had stopped coming, though their pictures remained and it was presumed that they would come back in force when the place, under new management, had beer. Four waitresses had been let go, but the restaurant was losing money. It was a dismal place to eat now.

And McClatchy's prospects darkened.

Nearly three years after the grand opening his bank balance stood, surprisingly enough, at only about seven thousand dollars, so that, with five hundred owed to the Board and a bit more elsewhere, it was approximately the same as when he had kept the Traveler's Rest, never dreaming who it was on the wall behind his bar. But he had paid his debt to his daughter, and in thirty-eight months paid slightly more than eight thousand dollars on the nineteen thousand he had borrowed from the bank. By some mystery of that ingenious invention called the amortized loan, however, the eight thousand had reduced the principal of the bank loan by only about forty-eight hundred. He still owed the bank just over fourteen thousand, or well over twice his unencumbered balance at the teller's window. But the tavern was for sale, loan, stock, trade, and Dutchman, for fifty thousand, and he reckoned to get out with a capital of almost fifty-six thousand, which, from a materialist point of view, would be consoling. He and his family planned to return to San Francisco, where, he thought, he would buy a partnership with some tavern owner who had a liquor license if the Board would let him. But as yet no shopper for the Lost Dutchman Tavern had appeared, and Mr. Staples, the real estate agent, explained that there were reasons:

First, the tavern's bohemians were generally believed to be communists, and although no one suspected that of the McClatchys it had given the place a bad name. And then, he said, the City wanted the tavern shut, and so apparently did old man Satterfy and the Ladies' Service Club. He doubted whether the Board would approve another license for the premises; but even if the Board should, the threat of another revocation or of abatement proceedings would be hanging over them. In the words of the expert, the tavern that Mr. Reardon had called an enchanted saloon had a curse on it now.

And so, he said, the property might have to be sold for something other than a tavern; in which case, of course, McClatchy would be selling no business with it, and therefore would have to come down considerably in his price.

"How much?" McClatchy asked fearfully.

But the agent only said that they would have to wait and see.

Christmas Eve again. Where was Mr. Reardon tonight? Bessie hoped that he would have a good dinner at least. But whether Mr. Reardon had or not, no one took a Christmas meal at the famous Lost Dutchman—not that day nor that night nor the next day nor that night either. There was no facing the anniversary of the grand opening. It was the end.

In the last week of December the Lost Dutchman Tavern closed its doors.

And just after New Year's Mr. Staples brought more bad news. The neat little, old little tavern, looking so much out of place between the Poultrymen's Cooperative Association warehouse and Jack's Auto Repair, across the street from the railroad yard, down below the slough, was regarded in Llagas, he said, as a white elephant now. For all practical purposes its chief value lay in the space it occupied, and that would be of no practical use till the building had been remodeled or torn down. Mr. Staples had taken the liberty of inquiring whether the Co-op was interested in space for expansion. He had learned that it was interested only in more garage space. It had offered ten thousand dollars, take it or leave it. McClatchy rejected it indignantly. "Those chiselers! Those farmers!"

But he was shaken. He went to the bank for guidance. He came home crushed. The bank had originally appraised his land and remodeled building, apart from equipment and Rembrandt painting, at thirty thousand, but that had been when the place was usable for a tavern. The bare land had been appraised at only seven thousand. Now, he had been told, it would be hard to say what he could get for his property. And he asked himself how long he could afford to hold out. What with payments on his loan and other expenses, waiting six months would cost him half his present savings; he would then owe the bank four times the remainder; and a few months more could wipe him out, property and all—the fruits of a lifetime of labor would be gone.

He calculated that if he took the Co-op's offer now, sold the Rembrandt, too, and the fixtures, and paid off the bank and the Board and his other creditors, he might have nine or ten thousand dollars left before taxes and his next insurance payment; say eight or nine thousand dollars after. Little enough that would be these days for starting life again with a wife, a daughter, and a grandson to secure, when in April he would be fifty-nine years of age. Fifty-nine years of—age! . . . Eight or nine thousand dollars. You couldn't buy much of a partnership in much of a tavern with that. And in his circumstances, at his age, if all you had was eight or nine thousand dollars, you couldn't afford to gamble with much of it. Too late. They would have to conserve.

He began to talk of buying or leasing a lunch counter that Bessie and Arline could conduct while he went back to tending somebody else's bar—it was still his trade.

In bed he said gloomily to his wife in the dark: "It looks like we're going to wind up right back where we started from."

"Well," she sighed, "we still got our health, thank God."

"Soon we'll be old."

"So will everybody else, if they live long enough."

"I give you a hard life, Bessie."

"Me? Why, I've had a good life. So've you, haven't you? We never wanted for anything."

"I remember when I proposed to you I told you I was going into politics. And I was always telling you we were going to be fixed for life, and only a few months ago I thought we would be. Now I only hope I can take care of you, Bess, in our old age."

"Dan McClatchy, you talk like we're going to the poorhouse. We'll make out."

"Sure. I know. We'll make out. But I was thinking——"

"What?"

"With all the work we done in our life we never had a Social Security card."

"No, and with God's help we won't need one. You always provided, Danny."

"But I was thinking—here we done all that bookkeeping on the Social Security and paid over the tax to the government for other people and we never had a card ourself, we never had a number. And it aint even official I was born. I'll have to wait'll I'm dead before I'm certified."

"Well, what does it matter?"

"It gives a man a kind of a funny feeling, that's all."

"Why, look at the success you had. We'd have been pretty well off if they'd left us alone."

"Yeah—if they'd left us alone."

"They had little to do," Bessie said.

"Three years," he remembered sadly, lying there with his hands behind his head on the pillow; and he confessed: "But I never had much of an education; when you come down to it, Bessie, I'm kind of an ignorant man."

"Now what do you mean? You know your business, don't you?"

"Well, but the success we had, it never would have happened if it wasn't for that painting; it was mostly luck if the truth was known."

"*Luck?* Most men would have sold that painting, and then where would they have been? It was because you knew what to do with it, that's what it was. And to think I wanted you to sell it."

"We're going to have to sell it now."

"Lands, Danny, money aint it."

"What about Arline and Bill? They'll be all alone."

"And don't go worrying about *them*. Arline'll manage. She's a good girl and capable; and she's got a little money of her own, remember."

"Maybe she'll get married again."

"Maybe."

"Have some more kids. . . ."

"She might."

"They won't even know us."

"How do you know they won't?"

"Even Bill—he won't remember much. He's too young. She'll keep our picture on the mantel, I suppose, and after a few years it'll get put away in a drawer or a trunk, and someday when he's grown up maybe Bill'll find it, and he'll say: 'Who's that?' "

"Why," Bessie said, "Billy's almost eight years old! And we aint going to die *yet*, are we?"

"Well, but he won't remember this place. 'That was a famous place while it lasted,' she'll tell him. 'People used to come all the way from the city.' But he won't remember. Not much anyhow. He's too young. Like me—when I was a kid my mother used to take me out to Woodward's Gardens that you used to hear about; that's what she told me, but I don't remember Woodward's Gardens at all. The path of glory only leads you to the grave."

"Well, but this side of the grave don't matter. Only, how you live on this side is what counts on the other."

"I know. We always had the faith anyhow. That's the main thing."

"That's the main thing," she repeated for emphasis. "And if we'd got rich, you can't tell, we might have lost our souls. God works in mysterious ways, Danny."

"Yep. Take my old man. Last time we was down at the cemetery I was thinking: He made my mother's life a hell on earth, and there he lies in consecrated ground right beside her; maybe he'll make it yet—even him."

"Why, sure. He had the last sacraments, didn't he? I'll bet she prayed for him."

"She did for a fact." He was silent a moment. "Someday Arline and Bill'll be praying for us. Having Masses said, like we do for our own folks. Like they done for theirs. Time marches on. We come and we go, as Mr. Reardon says—generation after generation. Look at old Dutch. I wonder if anybody ever prayed for him."

"I pray for him all the time," Bessie said.

"You do?"

"Of course."

He was touched. "You're a good woman, Bessie."

"Why, it's the least we can do."

"But how many people would have done it? Maybe nobody ever did. And after all these years! He was the forgotten man. . . . Maybe that was the reason!" he said wonderingly into the darkness. "For the picture, I mean. You know? A sparra never falls—And maybe now he's finally made it."

"God rest the poor soul," Bessie said pityingly.

"The famous Lost Dutchman," he said; and he was suddenly inspired: "If we could just save that picture! If we could leave 'em Dutch! Bill'd always have something to remember it by."

Remember "it" by? Bessie was not confused. He wanted to bequeath to his grandson the proof and memorial of his success, of his best days, of the time when he had made good and the world had beaten a path to his door—"all the way from the city." It was the only way he had of not letting go; the nearest thing to taking it to bed with him forever. Men, she knew, were like that; grown men. "Danny, I think that's a fine idea," she said. "And we'll do it. Of course we will. Now don't worry any more, Danny." She kissed him. "Go to sleep."

After breakfast he heard from Alfred Markham for the first time since the grand opening. He detected no insincerity in the dry and condescending voice expressing sympathy over the long-distance; it hardly ever occurred to him that someone might not wish him well. The art dealer had called to say that he had had inquiries about the Rembrandt and thought that he might get a better price for it now. His blood was boiling when he hung up after hearing the decision. "Family heirloom" indeed—the family of a saloonkeeper!

It was that same morning and McClatchy was poring over his account books in the back parlor when his daughter told him there was a man to see him.

The man was tall, high-shouldered, and buoyant-looking, wearing a trim brown camel's-hair topcoat which protruded slightly over a compact middle-aged belly, and spectacles whose rimless lenses were suspended from arches of gold; he had an astute friendly face with the ineradicable shadow of a strong black beard showing through a light application of after-shaving powder; he was smoking a freshly lighted cigar in a holder and looking at the pictures on the wall. A buyer for the tavern? His eyes, taking McClatchy in, twinkled, and he smiled and warmly extended his hand, identifying himself: "Jim Buchanan," somehow as though people always recognized that name. "I've seen you on television."

"Pleased to meet you, Mr. Buchanan," McClatchy said. "Yeah, that was me."

The visitor said seriously: "I'm sorry the way it came out."

"Well, it's all in the game, I guess. You interested in buying the place, Mr. Buchanan?"

"No—'fraid not."

"Oh"—a stone thudding into the dust.

"I don't suppose you'll be able to get another liquor license?"

"No, not me."

"Too bad," Mr. Buchanan said, with a shake of the head. He motioned toward the wall with his cigar. "Have you sold your Rembrandt?"

"Oh, no, that's behind the bar. They made me put up that partition there. Did you want to see the Rembrandt?" McClatchy led the way around the end of the partition and turned on the spotlight, and they stood looking up at the sneering face of the old Achilles. They were standing in front of the bar, and McClatchy could smell the familiar odor coming through the varnish: the damp sweet odor of wood of the cult of Barleycorn. There was breath in the old bar still, but it smelled of the Traveler's Rest . . . Bob Doughty and Ed Primrose, George Duncan and Mr. Horsfall (the eleven o'clock members), Hump Corkery and Mr. Reardon. For once he did not go into his spiel about the masterpiece.

"Very appropriate," Mr. Buchanan said, with a smile. "What are you asking?"

"Asking? Oh, for the painting? I'm not going to sell it."

"You're not? What are you going to do with it?"

"I'm going to keep it. I'm going to hand that painting down to the daughter and grandson like a kind of souvenir," McClatchy said, looking up at the portrait, and his visitor looked at his eyes and thought: He *is* going to keep it. Mr. Buchanan did not know whether to be disappointed or not. He had no idea what the Old Master was worth but supposed it to be very expensive.

He said: "Then you'd be willing to rent it, wouldn't you?"

"Rent it?" McClatchy said. "Well, I never—— To a museum?"

"No. To the Golden Hind."

"The Golden Hind—oh, that big new hotel they're building in Sampm Cisco!"

"That's right. How would you like to throw in with us?"

"Sir?"

"We've been looking for something distinctive in the way of a cocktail-lounge-buffet; something typically San Francisco. The town's always had a bohemian streak and you've got quite a reputation as a Papa Coppa. I'm sure we can agree on salary and a fair rental for the Rembrandt. The hotel will get the other pictures on loan from the best-known artists in San Francisco, and keep changing them. We'll give you a contract, of course. We want you for the host, the man in charge, nominally the manager—it will be your room with your name on it: McEndymion's Room. So what you'll be doing, in effect, is transferring operations from here to the Golden Hind."

"McEn——"

"That's a wonderful name you've got, by the way. Good enough for the hotel to keep if you put the room over. That's what we want: something to hang a tradition on. Not that you haven't got years ahead of you, of course," Mr. Buchanan laughed. He saw that the man's eyes were swimming; and at that moment the salary and the rent for the Rembrandt went down. "What do you say?"

The voice came out in a tight falsetto, incredulous: "That's—that's on Nob Hill, aint it?"

"Nob Hill."

McClatchy, his throat working with emotion, looked at the floor, unstrung. "Well, I—— It's a great honor; I . . . got to sell the place. . . ."

"You'll have plenty of time," Mr. Buchanan assured him. "We don't open till June." But plainly McClatchy could not speak. Mr. Buchanan smiled. He took out a business card and gave it to him, confident that there would be no difficulty. "You come and see us tomorrow. We'll talk about it then."

McClatchy nodded.

"Tomorrow morning," Mr. Buchanan said.

McClatchy followed his visitor to the door and called after him waveringly, the best he could manage: "Pleased to have met you."

Then he was standing in the back parlor telling his wife and daughter what Mr. Buchanan had said. The flabbergasted Arline could not understand why the Hotel Golden Hind, of which she had read in the newspapers, should want to name its cocktail lounge after her father, or even place him in charge of it. She saw that he was confounded himself. Then she saw what this flattering offer would mean if he accepted it: the loss of his independence and of the prestige of ownership, a curb on his potential earning power, the hotel making capital of his name. He would, in fact, be coming down in the world. And yet he seemed to regard this offer as the most wonderful thing that had ever happened to him. The tears were running down his cheeks. And her mother, head laid over on one shoulder, was smiling on him, glistening-eyed, as she listened, looking as if she too felt that it was. As if this made up for all that they were losing, all that they might have had, and would crown his career with honor beyond their dreams, and they were going to live happily ever after. McEndymion's Room! These innocents, these children, these San Franciscans! For of course she understood their romantic folly, if only a little, and in spite of herself was crying with them. "Oh, Dad, it is wonderful," she said, for in her heart she knew that for them it really was.

And in San Francisco next day her father signed a contract which Mr. Buchanan had all ready for him. The contract was for seven years, but it gave the hotel, at the end of two, an option to dispense with him or not, and another option at the end of four. It gave her father one hundred and fifty dollars a week salary and twenty-five dollars a month rent for the famous Rembrandt. "And besides that," he reminded his family, as long ago he had reminded Bessie Moyles, "the tips!" He would be tipped like a headwaiter now. And Mr. Buchanan had promised to find a job in the hotel for Arline. Not in the cocktail lounge nor in either of the dining rooms (those were to be staffed with men), but possibly as a floor manager or on the transportation desk, Mr. Buchanan had suggested. And her father said that they would rent a flat or an apartment "in the City by the Golden Gate," and that her mother would stay home now—"retire," he called it—and take care of Billy. To hear him tell it with that brief and precarious contract in his hand they were truly "fixed for life"—even Billy. Billy was to study hard in school and get an education and someday follow in his footsteps and be, he playfully told the growing boy, digging him in the ribs, "a big hotel man." At some date in the mined porcelain future Billy might even become "the head of the whole shebang!"

Yet they still had the white elephant on their hands. In its forsaken state it seemed already in the process of decay. How little it took, Arline thought, to start her father going all over again. But she had not the heart to object.

And if it all sounded familiar to Bessie, she did not let on. In bed that night he said to her:

"The Golden Hind—that was the name of the boat some old explorer come over on, in the early days. He was the man they named the Sir Francis Drake Hotel after, Sir Francis Drake, and that was his boat, the S. S. *Golden Hind*. That's like the *Mayflower*. Tradition, that's what they want, Mr. Buchanan told me, a name they can hang a tradition on, he said, a name they can use after we're dead and gone. 'McEndymion's Room.' That's a great honor."

"Indeed it is," Bessie said.

"That name," he dreamt aloud, "might go down in the history of Sampm Cisco, like the Pied Piper Room in the Palace where I used to work. Like Woodward's Gardens. *That'll* give Bill something to remember us by. 'That was my grandfather,' he'll say. 'They named the bar after him.'"

Bessie smiled. "Yes," she said.

And he lay contented, with his hands clasped under his head, blinking, as he envisioned the little sign above the door. Then in the darkness his face became disturbed. "But," he said, "McEndymion, that aint my name, you know. I wonder if they'd change it to the McClatchy Room."

"Oh!" Bessie screamed, laughing. "Would you *listen* to the vain thing! Vanity, vanity, vanity! Heavens, the McClatchy Room! Gracious! Him and Sir Francis Drake!"

He was grinning. "I was only kidding. McEndymion, that's me anyhow, aint it?"

McEndymion—by a queer accident that was he, "the beautiful shepherd," "the last of the old South of Market boys." And under that name, inscribed above a barroom, at the pinnacle of San Francisco, he would at last be certified.

Mr. Reardon lay in the San Francisco County Hospital with a broken leg. The left leg this time. He had broken it in a struggle with a policeman when he slipped off a six-inch curb. He had been drunk, violent but emaciated, trembling, unshaven for a week, his great thatch wild, his clothing ruined. McClatchy heard about the arrest from a newspaper reporter over the telephone, and that same morning crossed the bay to see his friend. But the hospital would let no one see Mr. Reardon yet. It was not till a week later that McClatchy saw him.

The giant lay in a prison ward, wearing a hospital gown, his castbound leg on top of the rumpled bedclothes, a discarded magazine beside him. He was pale and thin after his terrible debauch, and his eyes, overhung by those rusty bushes, seemed to have sunk back in their sockets. Scowling, he watched McClatchy appproach.

"Hello, Mr. Reardon."

"What do *you* want?"

"Me? I . . . just thought I'd come over and see how you was feeling."

Reardon grunted. There was a pause. McClatchy was hurt, but he felt that it was his own fault: he had blundered. Reardon growled: "Did they close you up?"

McClatchy nodded. "Yeah. On account of the bookmaking. I guess I ought to been more careful." No answer. Then he blundered again. "By the way, what do I owe you?"

Reardon's eyes flashed resentment. He said bitterly: "What for?"

"Huh? What do you mean? Hell, *you* couldn't help it they closed me up. That was on account of the bookmaking—the boys got convicted, you know; that was all there was to it—*you* couldn't help it. And besides everybody says that case was a witch hunt; the papers was full of it; they give us a raw deal—that wasn't *your* fault. Oh, and you made me famous! Didn't you hear the news? I'm going in the hotel business now."

"In the what?"

"Sure—at the Golden Hind Hotel on Nob Hill. They're naming the bar after me—'McEndymion's Room.' You give me that name, remember? 'That's a classy name you got,' the man says, 'we want to hang a tradition on it.' You give me that name. And I got a contract—I'm going to be the man in charge. It's all official. And the hotel's renting Dutch. And I'm selling the place. Oh I tellya. I come up sitting on top of the world and smelling like a rose," little Dan McClatchy boasted, grinning, "at the Golden Behind Hotel."

Reardon was staring at him in amazement. "Why, you little son of a bitch!"

"Yes, sir! 'McEndymion's Room.' You give me that name."

"Well! Congratulations!"

"Yep. Oh, it's the luck of the Irish." But then there was something so lost in the big man's eyes that the small one felt guilty being so famous and successful in his presence, and indeed being a witness of his condition. He asked in a voice that begged his pardon: "Can I do anything for you while you're laid up?"

"Send me some clothes. I'll ask for my keys——"

"No, it's all right; the man downstairs will let me in."

"Never mind the man downstairs. I'll get my keys."

"Okay. What'll I get you?"

"My other suit. Shoes. Few changes of underwear. Shirts. Socks. . . ."

"Leave it to me. I'll bring 'em over tomorrow."

McClatchy did not mention the fee again. But when he brought the clothes next day he had pinned in a pocket of the shabby "other suit" an envelope containing one hundred and fifty dollars in cash. Reardon, when he found the money, cursed. But he kept it.

The middle of February. Still not a single offer for the tavern. But the Co-op raised its offer for the property. Eleven thousand dollars. The McClatchys, after a family conference, accepted. They were to be allowed to remain in occupancy for two months while they sold their fixtures and equipment. Then the building was to be demolished. On the site the Co-op was to build a concrete garage.

Fixtures and equipment were sold, and, the bank having been paid, the ex-tavernkeeper was left with not quite six thousand dollars' capital. But he still had the Rembrandt, and his eyes, fixed on the future, brightened again. McEndymion's Room!

Arline knew that the big crowded San Francisco where they were going to live was scarcely the same city that she had known as a girl, and not at all the San Francisco of which her father spoke. And the contract with the hotel was a poor guarantee of security. And her parents were approaching the brink of age. But it was not for her parents that she was fearful. And this time she was not concerned about a new life for herself: that marked the change that had begun in her. When she read in the paper that the governor had denied Raymond Dirigo's plea for clemency she keenly felt the change.

She remembered her child's birth after her husband's death, after her brief broken life with Bill Lucas. She had been twenty-nine then: widowhood and motherhood and waiting on the counter of the Traveler's Rest; the dingy back apartment and the twilit sweet-smelling saloon where the brass rail gleamed and the spittoon and the bottles, and something frying in the kitchen. Twenty-nine then and feeling cheated, sometimes dreaming how it might be if her child had not been born. Childhood, his childhood, cheated too. The discovery of the Rembrandt, and all the plans. Harry Fahs—shot, put to bed, dying of a clot, and buried with a horseshoe on his chest. Nancy Croan found by children in the abandoned boathouse—dead six days. And the kid, condemned to death. Phyllis Plover and Bo Satterfy. Josie Cantrell—"Bawled him out." Mr. Reardon, a burnt offering; Mr. Reardon in the San Francisco County Jail. Heath—the baléte tree. She had seen a good deal since the age of twenty-nine. It made a difference when she thought of the years ahead, of the growing up in the city across the bay, city of strangers, city of paths yet to cross, in a world that appeared to be plunging toward destruction. But her fear was for Billy. She was no longer thinking of herself. That was where the change had begun: she was no longer wanting anything for herself. It was as if, in giving up her motherhood, she had found it.

Having, in her simplicity, given her child to the Blessed Virgin at the foot of the Cross, she had resolved to implant in him the daily practice of the Rosary. At first, she thought, she would make him say but one decade each day, and would finish the chaplet for him. But she wanted to teach him to say it well, meditating on the mysteries; so at his bedside each night, before they began, she would discuss with him the story of the event to be considered. Her efforts to make the stories vivid and meaningful to the boy illuminated her own meditations. She saw things that she had never seen before, about justice and mercy, about love, and often during the day would think about them. "We are better persuaded, ordinarily, by reasons that we ourselves have discovered," says Pascal, "than by those discovered by other spirits," which perhaps is one of the secrets of that simple and profound prayer which has had so much influence over so many lives. And remembering the book that Father Cobb had promised to get for her, she asked him for it. He lent her a volume of Farrell's *Companion to the Summa* of Thomas Aquinas. It opened her mind. But she could have told the date and the hour when peace began.

Did she only imagine that the terrifying words of peace were intended to have a special meaning for Arline McClatchy? But wasn't it true, she asked herself, that the Gospel was addressed to everyone individually, and hadn't Christ said: "He that has ears to hear, let him hear"? And what was it that Father Cobb had said to her? Something about no one ever being converted from a pulpit. But here or there, he had said, might be a pair of ears where something the priest said or didn't say at all would strike home, which was "nothing but the grace of God." And could it all possibly have been nothing but coincidence? Or had there really been a sign, a signature?

Easter, that year, had fallen on the twenty-fifth of March, which was the Feast of the Annunciation, and Father Cobb introduced his text with the words that the angel spoke to St. Joseph in Egypt: *Take the child and his mother, and go into the land of Israel*. To Arline they sounded like a direct answer to her prayer. To her they were like an annunciation in themselves, assurance that the child offered at the altar had been received, word that she was not to be afraid. But they contained a condition, and she *was* afraid. Here was the mark of recognition, the combination of justice with mercy, the same as in the crucifix, the Oneness of infinite majesty and infinite love: she was to "go into the land of Israel." She did not confuse Israel with San Francisco, nor mistake it for a country in the Middle East. Israel, in the language of the Church, was a people. It was the living tree grafted on the root of Juda. It was a country of the heart and spirit, a land of peace but of peace through sacrifice, through death and resurrection, the land where the crosses grew. Here it was again: the merciful call to Calvary. She prayed. The Mass continued. At the elevation she looked at the Host, and moving her lips without a sound, she made her promise—she never knew whether for God's sake or for Billy's:

"I will take the child and his mother, and I will go into the land of Israel."

33

SPRING

Walsh Reardon, wearing his last suit, his gray one, and using a cane, limped into the Seventh Street bus station, San Francisco, and bought the newspapers. He bought the newspapers because he had just been released from jail and he wanted to see whether Llagas would be expecting him, as when years ago he had hobbled into the Ferry Building on crutches and found the headlines running before him with the tale that Stanford had expelled its Goliath.

On the bus he searched the newspapers thoroughly, but he found nothing about himself. They were full of General MacArthur. It was the morning of April 17, eve of the anniversary of the Great Earthquake and Fire, and San Francisco, to Reardon's disgust, was preparing to welcome home from Tokyo the hero of Bataan, whom the President had suddenly relieved of his command and the conduct of the Korean War. Walsh Reardon detested General MacArthur.

Reardon's body had filled out somewhat since McClatchy had seen him, but there was still a gaunt look about it, emphasized by the way his eyes seemed to have sunk inward beneath his overhanging brows. There was pallor in his face. And because of the way the skin hung loose on his neck, one was smitten by the disappearance of the mane. Under his fedora, lined with strips of newspaper to make it fit him now, his gray hair was cropped short. It seemed a terrible thing to have done to him. He was fifty years of age, he looked sixty, and he was going back to Llagas for the last time.

He was going back to Llagas only to leave it forever. His total capital was in his pockets, one hundred thirty-one dollars and a few cents, and he was going to sell his only possession of any value, his library. He had little idea what he might get for his library. Two hundred dollars? One hundred? Seventy-five? After that, he schemed, he would get a job as timekeeper or stakepuncher at some faraway railroad camp, and there save a few hundred dollars more, and then strike out for San Diego to begin his life again. He looked out the window at the passing countryside, green again. He noticed the poppies, the lupines, the young blue sky. The bus raced over the road, and on the slopes of the hills chewing cattle gazed down with indifference on the busy valley.

The outrageous indignity of his imprisonment was over, he was free, and the earth was a child again, but Mr. Reardon felt a deep and bitter resentment, a profound loneliness, and a brazen timidity. Going back to Llagas, he was as sensitive about his changed appearance as he was about his degradation. Six feet five in his brogues, and a public scandal, he hoped that he might slip into Llagas undetected though it was broad daylight, sell his books under cover of darkness, and be gone before anyone knew he had arrived.

But when the bus had pulled up at the Llagas station and he had descended, rather stiffly, with his cane, a familiar voice hailed him joyfully:

"Hello, Mr. Reardon. . . ."

Little Dan McClatchy, in his blue serge suit, stood there with his grandson by the hand; but the grin faded from his face as the shorn giant turned.

Reardon's voice was full of gall. "What's this, a reception committee?"

"A—— No, honest," the blunderer apologized. "We didn't know you was coming. We're just waiting for the bus, Mr. Reardon. We sold the place and we're pulling out for good."

Reardon grunted "Oh" rather foolishly, and then felt the contumely of this coincidence. Pulling out for good. He could not bear to witness this departure of the scapegoat. It was like being confronted with his guilt and his shame. But he could not walk away from it, either. Then he saw Arline standing there in her polo coat, looking at him, and the pity in that look heightened the color that had risen in his face.

"Yes, sir!" McClatchy said with a brave irrelevant grin, looking down at his grandson. "Going home to Sampm Cisco. And going to see General MacArthur. Oh, we wouldn't miss that, would we, Bill. I was telling him," to Reardon, "I seen General Pershing once; and now he's going to see General MacArthur. *In* person. You-u betcha."

With a weak attempt at joviality Reardon looked down at Billy and said: "Well!" But the boy whom the two men thought to use in order to relieve themselves of embarrassment was looking up at the ogre with truthful eyes, and Mr. Reardon saw that the old game would not do. He had never been any good with children anyhow.

McClatchy's chuckle trailed off as he too saw that the game was up. "Yep," he said. And for a moment he could think of nothing else to say. He was grieved at Mr. Reardon's appearance and dared not call attention to it by asking him how he was feeling, and Mr. Reardon would be touchy about his recent experience and about the case and about the closing of the tavern, and McClatchy was suddenly embarrassed about having taken the liberty of pinning money in Mr. Reardon's pocket. So many things had come between McClatchy and his giant that for a moment the old acquaintances who had met across the bar of the Traveler's Rest on Repeal Night found nothing to say to each other. But:

"Wait—here comes the bus now!" McClatchy said, and to Billy: "Run and tell Gramma. Tell her the bus is here. Hurry up! . . . He-e's a dandy. . . . You'll have to come and see us, Mr. Reardon. I'll be looking for you at the hotel. 'McEndymion's Room'—*you* give me that name. The first one'll be on the house. . . ."

He prattled on, but Mr. Reardon was paying no attention. Bessie, accompanied by her grandson, came out of the station building as the bus arrived. She was putting something in her purse. Then she looked up and saw Mr. Reardon, and she stopped. This was an encounter that Reardon would have given anything to avoid. Erect, the sunken-eyed giant stood looking at Bessie, looking as if steeled for a tirade from this woman who, he felt, had never approved of him.

Her husband called: "Come on, Bessie. The bus is here."

Bessie came forward. Her grandson ran ahead of her. McClatchy said: "All-l aboard. Come on, Bill," and boosted the boy into the bus. Arline said goodbye to Mr. Reardon but he seemed not to hear her; she followed the boy into the bus. And to Mr. Reardon came Bessie. Taking him by the sleeve of his coat and lifting a compassionate face to his, "Come here to me," she said, and, astonished, he obeyed, bending down to the dumpy little woman. She kissed him on the cheek and gave him two little pats on the arm. "Now you be a good boy," she said; and it reduced Mr. Reardon to a child. Gratitude, loneliness, and self-pity, mixed with the memory of his mother, who had used to do it in just that way, choked and blinded him.

Then Bessie was climbing into the bus assisted by her husband. McClatchy turned back again and was abashed because of the emotion that he saw in Mr. Reardon's face. "Well," he said, and he awkwardly held out his hand. But Mr. Reardon, struggling with his feelings, turned his back and limped a few steps off. McClatchy called after him sadly: "So long, Mr. Reardon." He boarded the bus. The driver pulled the door shut. The bus pulled out, and Mr. Reardon turned back again to watch it swim out of sight.

As it disappeared he became conscious that someone was standing beside him. A sardonic voice said: "Well, that's over." He turned his head and saw Hubert Ritter of the *Sentinel*. In that instant his emotion changed to rage. His body jerked, his great fist smashed into the face, Hubert Ritter went down. Mr. Reardon stumped away.

Llagas! How he hated it! The scapegoat driven into the wilderness, and Llagas gloating! Full of spite, gossip. Ritter! Wanted an interview, he supposed. And old man Satterfy would be gloating, and little Earl Parker, and the mayor. And *she* would hear. . . . No, there would be no living in Llagas any more for him. He should have left it long ago. He walked on, erect, his rage drowning in his sorrow, in his self-pity, in his homesickness for Llagas, and now and then flaring up again because of someone's stare. But he looked into none of the faces, and no one spoke to him. He turned into the dead end of Gore Street, "down by the slough." He found the corrugated iron door of the O.K. Machine Shop drawn shut, and attached to the handle a hand-lettered sign: GONE TO SEE MACARTHUR. MacArthur! He turned into the narrow opening next door and climbed the dark stairs. On the landing he fumbled for the keyhole, found it, and opened the door.

Dust over everything—cobwebs—the warm lifeless atmosphere of rooms long closed. But as he shut himself in this dreadful loft he had the sense of refuge. He was home.

He went to the window behind his desk and after a struggle opened it, raising before his eyes the back of the peeling sign on the lower pane. The fragrant air rushed in, and he stood looking off at the hills. He turned. Home. He was tired. He lowered himself onto the kitchen chair at the desk and looked round the congested helter-skelter room. His foot kicked something under the desk, and he looked down and saw the half-empty jug of gin, put there on the day of McClatchy's visit. He grimaced in self-disgust. He noticed on the rough wooden table a pile of clean plates. Someone must have washed his dishes—*he* had never washed them till he needed them. And on the wall above the littered cabinet directly across from him he saw the little gilt-framed photograph, blind with dust. He got up, and picking his way round the desk and through the library heaped on the floor, went over to it. He wetted his handkerchief at his mouth and washed off the dust with it, and returning the handkerchief to his back pocket, looked at the picture of his mother and father, his eyes watering again.

He went into the gargantuan bedchamber. Again the green blind was drawn against the morning. Someone had made his bed. He raised the blind and opened that window, too, and looked down at the mechanical bones rusting in the April grass. He took off his coat and dropped it across the bed and went into the bathroom.

The toilet roared.

He came back to the front room shouldering his suspenders and took off his hat. He put it on top of the cabinet and stood, hands on hips, scowling at the library on the floor. He recognized the black volumes of the Encyclopaedia Britannica. He thought: The noble Ninth Edition, knowing that it was infinitely superior to any work of the kind that could be got nowadays, though practically worthless at a bookstore. He got down on one knee to inspect some of his other books with a view to appraising their commercial value——

Penguin Island, Spoon River Anthology, South Wind, The Philosophy of Kant, Don Quixote, The Rise of American Civilization, Replenishing Jessica, Journey to the End of Night. . . . His nonprofessional books were mainly cheap editions, most were in poor condition, and he feared that he would get little for them. The principal value of his library was in his law books, thumbed and battered though they were. But it was a painful task that he had before him, and it seemed a tremendous one. As he knelt there on the verge of leaving Llagas, depression paralyzed him. He prowled over the great dump of books as among the gravestones of his friends. He picked up *The Complete Poems of Keats and Shelley* and turned to *Endymion*, knowing exactly the passage he would seek. . . .

Half an hour later, footsteps on the stairs. Knocking at the door. No answer. Louder knocking. From within, only silence. Then the knob was turning, the unlocked door was swinging inward. And behind the desk, where he had been sitting all the time, the tenant scraped wildly to his feet with a roar of his great broken voice: "What the hell do you mean!"

Through the doorway Chief of Police Lally and Officer Butterson looked at him, struck by his changed appearance, and the chief said: "Hello, Walsh. Mind if we come in?" They moved into the room.

"Wh-what do you want?"

The short burly chief waited while Butterson moved round to the other side of the desk so that the giant was between them. Then he said: "Hubert Ritter's dead."

"Ritter? Dead?" The sunken eyes flashed. "*Dead?*"

Roy Lally nodded. "He hit his head on the concrete. You knocked him down. I don't have to tell you what that means. And you know better than to give us trouble."

"Concrete . . . Dead." The haggard throat worked. "Dead!" Walsh Reardon sank down on the chair.

Then the two policemen saw the dusty jug of gin and the empty tumbler and the open book on the desk in front of him. They looked at each other. The chief's lips twisted in a contemptuous smile.

The prisoner was staring straight ahead of him in amazement. "I hardly knew him," he marveled. "I hardly knew him. . . ."

Up the gracefully curving road roared the bus, and inside there was a sense of imminence, of approaching something big and beautiful. At the crest of the hill the view opened wide into a panorama of water, islands, hills, and sky. Suddenly the bus was plunged into darkness pinpointed with yellow lights, and the tunnel walls hurled back at it the headlong clamor of its wheels. Daylight came up in a burst. Ahead were the overwhelming red towers of the bridge, wheeling gulls, and——

"Look, Bill—over there!" McClatchy said to his excited grandson, leaning forward to point through the windows at the towered hills across the bay. "Sampm Cisco! That's her—the old city and county. Oh I tellya. Yep." There were tears in his eyes. "There she stands."

Far over the Pacific an airplane called *Bataan* was bringing to San Francisco the general, his wife, and their thirteen-year-old son.

In the city, flags and banners were going up.

And the bus was vaulting the Golden Gate, at fifty miles an hour.